THE WANTED
AND THE
UNWANTED

To Jim —
Remember, this is not a "how-to" manual. But it might give you some ideas about your next utopia! I hope you enjoy it. Best wishes,

ROGER HARRISON

authorHOUSE™

1663 LIBERTY DRIVE, SUITE 200
BLOOMINGTON, INDIANA 47403
(800) 839-8640
WWW.AUTHORHOUSE.COM

First published by AuthorHouse 11/01/05

ISBN: 1-4208-7281-8 (sc)

Library of Congress Control Number: 2005907029

Printed in the United States of America
Bloomington, Indiana

This book is printed on acid-free paper.

Acknowledgements

I wrote this book over a period of five months, from November 2001 until March the following year, and then the real work began. I am indebted to my mother, Pauline Gedge, for the editing and writing advice she freely offered through numerous revisions of the manuscript, helping to whittle a 600-plus-page doorstop into the more manageable book you hold now. Rick Kot, Executive Editor at Viking Penguin, spent a weekend of his valuable time reading it and making helpful suggestions, without which I may well have abandoned this project. Thanks to both of you for helping me see the manuscript's potential as well as its flaws.

I had maintained sporadic contact with a few of the people who became characters in this novel since leaving Central America and Mexico, but starting in early 2004, some of the others on whom these characters are based contacted me and offered their insights and personal stories for me to include wherever I saw fit. I am grateful to each and every one of them. Thank you especially to R.R. for the accommodations and for helping me rediscover Vallarta again, for sharing your stories with me, and for trusting me.

Thanks to Eiffel 65 and Claudio at Bliss Records.

And thank you, M.R., for the phone call that started it all.

Lyrics from *Too Much of Heaven* reproduced with permission from Bliss Records and Eiffel 65.

Foreword

The events which truly change the world are usually ones that take place over a short period of time. They burn with a mystical intensity that transforms us forever, and they pass into history as quickly as they come. Something happens – a concatenation of circumstances, a karmic storm of sorts, a drawing together of events and personalities previously unassociated – and from it spring changes that suggest an importance far greater than the sum of the parts would lead us to conclude.

I could cite example after example of this, but consider the following: The cowboy era, which has been burned into the minds of everyone on earth in some form or another, be it through movies, books, et cetera, was a period of only about twenty years, the time between the last Indian surrendering and the fencing of the continent's agricultural areas into 160-acre parcels through which the cowboys could no longer drive herds freely. Only their shadows remain, in rodeos and Stetsons and two-step nightclubs. The Flying Tigers, a band of American mercenary pilots fighting against the Japanese in China, has been immortalized by its shark-mouthed fighter planes and the fact that it lost only four pilots in combat and downed 368 enemy aircraft over the Burmese jungle in six hectic months before being inducted into the regular Army Air Force in 1942. The Sixties, a time which everyone associates with free love, the Vietnam war and its opponents, and the onset of widespread drug use, is often simply a term unknowingly used to describe the summer of 1967, a four-month period with the intersection of San Francisco's Haight and Ashbury at its epicentre. The United States Declaration of Independence, one of the most famous and enduring documents of all time, consists of only 1,458 words and took Thomas Jefferson less than three weeks to compose.

I am not suggesting that the story in these pages is as momentous as the above-cited examples. Indeed, the time leading up to these things and away from them is also peppered with more than its share of poignant and important moments, as any diligent newspaper reader will tell you. And who among us cannot count a magical romantic summer of awakening after which nothing looked the same, or a chance comment by an adult that led our young thoughts down a road we still travel, or any other event our reactions to which became the things our lives are made of? We are all in play, involved however directly or peripherally we choose to be in the way these things will be seen through the lenses we use to view the world, other cultures, ourselves.

This book is based on a true story, the repercussions of which are still being felt. The impact that it had on the lives of those involved is unimaginable to the casual reader, and I suspect that I am not yet a good enough writer to convey it. All I can do is tell my own story as honestly as possible.

It chronicles the last stages of the rise and subsequent fall of the largest internet fraud in history to date; if not in real dollars then at least in scope. I have changed the names of the people involved; other than that it has only minor deviations from the way it was, either to maintain the pace of the book or to illustrate the extent of the deception it describes. Some of the conversations in it are related verbatim from the characters in real life.

It couldn't be more obvious that the protagonist is me, even apart from the similarity between his and mine. The reason why the book is told only from his point of view is because I felt it was inappropriate to assume anyone else's perspective, thereby imbuing other characters with thoughts they may not have thought and words they may not have said. It's bad enough that I'm already reminding them of a time that some of them would rather forget.

Truth is so hard to tell, it sometimes needs fiction to make it plausible.

-Dagobert Runes

In the summer of 1999, Adrian Winter founded the Cyberia Investment Club. Originally headquartered in San Diego, California, it was soon moved to Nassau, Bahamas and eventually Puerto Vallarta, Mexico. It offered returns of 120% per year on investors' money through what it called Prime Bank Investment Securities.

Cyberia became one of the most successful investment clubs of its kind ever recorded, generating over sixty million dollars in revenue by even the most conservative estimate. At its height it boasted almost 20,000 members in over 60 different countries. Its staff lived a privileged existence in some of the best properties in Puerto Vallarta and enjoyed use of the company Learjet, yacht, and chauffered vehicles. From employees to investors, all were told by Winter that Cyberia's affiliate and sole source of income, Panama-based Hammer Investments, made its profits through the trading of assets by bank officials and political figures throughout the world.

It disbanded after a series of events beginning with an incident at Puerto Vallarta's Gustavo Diaz Ordaz International Airport on April 19, 2001.

This is the story of its final days.

Prologue
The Unguarded Moment

April 19, 2001

The red Ford Explorer pulled up to the private terminal gate and stopped at the guardhouse. After exchanging a few words in Spanish, the driver and guard waved briefly to each other as the gate rolled back and the vehicle drove through.

Selecting a parking space near the small terminal building, the driver got out and went inside to pour himself a cup of coffee from the courtesy counter. There was no one in the lounge apart from those in the pictures on the walls. The door was propped open and he leaned against the frame. Sipping the coffee, he checked his watch and looked skyward.

A large passenger jet hung in the distance, its colored marker beacons bright against the rapidly darkening sky. He guessed it to be the last arrival of the day. Soon the main terminal, visible across the parking lot, would close down for cleaning and preparation for another day of rotating tourists in and out. Come to think of it, the private terminal would be closed before too long as well. He looked at his watch again.

The Learjet hurtled toward Puerto Vallarta at just over five hundred miles an hour. As the captain began his descent, the most sober of the passengers grasped his customs card and began to fill it in with an unsteady hand. Name, address, address in Mexico if a resident or citizen, purpose of visit. His companions did the same. One, a small, wiry man in his early fifties, stopped at the question, 'Are you carrying cash, checks, bearer bonds or other financial instruments with you which have an aggregate value of US $10,000 or more?'

One of his companions glanced at him, obviously stuck on the same question. Taller and older, he and his brother handled operations in Belize City, controlling and organizing the deluge of cashiers' checks and money orders the company was now receiving every day. The smaller man took the card from him and made a check mark in the "Yes" box. Under "Amount", he scribbled in a figure and handed it back.

The tall man shook his head and grinned, holding up two fingers and pointing his thumb toward the baggage compartment behind them.

The smaller man swore and crossed off the amount he'd written on his own card. He'd forgotten that he had divided the money into two bags – one to go to Latvia with him tomorrow, and one to be deposited in New York. He had the larger amount in his own baggage.

Impatiently he reached across and grabbed the other man's customs card again. The gesture made him wince in pain. He scribbled out the previous number and wrote "$0" before doing the same on his own.

Holding one hand protectively over his stomach where it hurt the most, he dug into his pants pocket for the ever-present vial of time-release morphine tablets. Screw this, he thought, and screw Customs. They're not the boss of me.

He poured himself another drink.

The customs inspector pulled up at the terminal and got out of his car. Waving his hand at his neck to cool it, he looked around and saw the figure in the doorway.

"*Mucho calor*," he said. "Very hot today. In not so many weeks every day will be like this."

The driver responded in the affirmative and gestured to the sky where he had seen the approaching Learjet a minute before. They watched it touch down and taxi up to the parking ramp, where the pilot turned off the strobes and marker lights and shut off the engines. The inspector strode over to the jet and had opened the door before the freewheeling turbines had even begun to slow down.

The driver heard voices from inside the plane and then he saw the passengers exit one by one, stretching and finishing the last of their drinks. He entered the terminal to throw out his coffee cup. When he reemerged he had begun to walk over to the plane when one of the passengers held his hand up. The man lingered, hesitating, and went over to the Explorer instead. He opened the back cargo door to await the luggage, and sat on the sill.

A porter had emerged from the terminal armed with a large red hand cart and had already loaded the suitcases onto it. The inspector placed his hand on one and said something to one of the passengers. In his other hand he held a sheaf of papers, and on top were the Customs cards. Now the inspector was standing back to allow the porter to open one of the cases.

The driver caught the tall man's eye and mouthed the word "What?", but was met with only a terse shake of the head before he looked away.

Now the inspector was pointing to the aircraft door, and amid protests the passengers slowly filed back into the little jet. The pilots stood apart from the proceedings, obviously a little bewildered, and watched the inspector as he spoke into the microphone clipped to his shirt.

The driver squinted, calculating what might be going on and whether he should wait around, but his question was soon answered. Within seconds, an airport police car emerged from the far side of the main terminal with its flashing lights on but no siren, and another one sped through the entry gate.

He closed the cargo door with a slam. Looking behind him, he could see the customs inspector motioning rapidly in his direction, and the porter took off at a run towards the Explorer. He jumped in and fumbled for the keys.

For some reason he hadn't expected the engine to start, but it turned over and fired immediately. Reversing just enough to turn around, he floored the accelerator and narrowly missed the shouting and gesticulating porter, tires screaming on the hot pavement. The gate, still open from when the police car had come in, grew larger in his windshield, and as he tore past it he swerved to avoid a local news station van and an accompanying sedan that had seemingly materialized out of nowhere.

This, he thought as he blew a stop light and merged with the highway traffic, is going to be a very long night.

1
Secrets Best Kept

…truth is so precious that she should always be attended by a bodyguard of lies.

-Sir Winston Churchill

February 27, 2001

It was evening in Puerto Vallarta, and between the first slackening of the engines' whine and the last piece of luggage Roland Halliwell claimed from the carousel, darkness had descended as though following his aircraft.

He carried his baggage himself, politely refusing the offers of the porters. He could see his old friend Mick waving to him from the other side of the x-ray stations where he sat with another man, both pulling on a beer. Approaching the beautiful uniformed customs girl he breathed deeply, savoring the warm and humid air. He felt instantly at home.

"Press this button, please," she requested in a pleasant but businesslike voice. Her English was good, and she smiled sweetly at him. There were two lights, a green one that said 'Pase' when illuminated and a red one that said 'Alto'. He was rewarded with a green light. "Enjoy your visit," she said as she ushered him through. Her 'j' sounded like a 'y'.

"Hey, buddy! How was the flight?"

Mick embraced him. Tanned and fit, he was several years Roland's junior. His hair was just long enough to be messy on top and displayed the natural bleach of one who spends a fair amount of time in the sun. At six-foot-four Roland was tall, but Mick was slightly taller, and wore a t-shirt that said, '*Welcome to Hell! Get acquainted luau, 7pm*

1

tonight.' His enthusiasm for collecting shirts such as these had earned him the nickname Slogan. His companion, though equally tanned and almost equally tall, sported short hair from a receding hairline which was the only hint that he was older than either of them. He regarded Roland with large, friendly blue eyes. "I'm Mick as well," he said. "Welcome to Vallarta."

Roland stuffed his passport and tourist card into his carry-on bag. "That'll be easy enough to remember."

"He's CIA Mick, or Secret Agent Mick," said Slogan, "because he's always off on some mission for Adrian that nobody else knows about, and nobody calls me Mick at all." He gestured toward the cantina. "Do you want a beer?"

They each picked up a suitcase and Roland followed them back to their little table. CIA Mick waved his empty bottle at the waitress, and she emerged a short time later with three Pacificos – Roland's favorite, when he drank beer at all.

He studied the Secret Agent. "You look like John Malkovich," he observed, evoking a laugh. "What kind of missions for Adrian do you do?"

Mick toyed with his beer bottle. "Oh, mostly just stuff that he doesn't want or need to do himself," he replied airily. "I've been involved with this club almost since the beginning so there's a lot that I know sort of by default, and that puts me in the position of being able to help out with pretty much anything."

Slogan was conspicuously silent.

Roland was curious to know exactly what he'd involved himself with and wanted them to tell him everything right there, but that would have to wait. For now Slogan's description of an investment club in need of more staff had been good enough to bring him here. Not that he had needed much prompting. His life over the last year had become a mess from which he was all too glad to escape.

2

Roland had always loved airports, and as they talked he looked at the Mexican money and the Spanish signs everywhere and listened with half an ear to the sound of people talking in other languages – mostly Spanish, of course, but also English, some French, and something in passing that could have been Dutch.

CIA Mick wanted to hear the story of how Roland and Slogan became friends. "Went to school together," was all Slogan volunteered, and then turned to Roland. "How's your memory?" he asked. "Did you bring the carabiners and the coffee?"

Before leaving home, Roland had stopped by a sporting goods store to pick up two D-rings used for securing ropes when mountain climbing. Slogan had requested them for a friend who wanted to use them for his hammock, in addition to some Tim Horton's coffee for Adrian, his new boss, who apparently never got it himself. Roland produced the carabiners, and as Slogan was playing with them he said idly, "I don't suppose you brought any beef jerky, did you?"

"Aw, hell."

Roland had boarded the plane with a strong feeling that there was something he was missing, and when he had that feeling it was never wrong. But there had been so many things to look after in the process of closing up his little house and organizing what to do with his belongings and all the rest of what went into a move to another country that the beef jerky Slogan had asked him to bring had stayed in the store.

"Sorry, I didn't bring it. I completely forgot." He looked at CIA Mick as he said this, but Slogan said – a little loudly, he thought – "Don't worry about it, it's no big deal."

As they drank their beer, Roland mentioned that he was none too impressed with his stopover in Los Angeles, rainy and gray as it had been.

"Ah, Los Angeles in February," said the Secret Agent. "I'm from the Bay area myself." He left that open to interpretation. Roland decided he had gaffed.

"First I forget your beef jerky and now I'm knocking your home turf. Sorry, but that's what I thought. Besides, it's not like I've really seen any of it. The only Disneyland I've ever been to is in Tokyo."

CIA Mick smiled. "Well, I kind of share that opinion. San Francisco and Los Angeles are about as similar as Vallarta and London, but I haven't been back to the States for years. I left because I didn't like it myself. This is my home now."

Slogan held up his beer bottle. "Speaking of which, this is your home now too, so welcome. Cheers."

"Welcome home," said the Secret Agent.

They gathered up Roland's belongings and wound their way through tour operators holding signs and waiting for their charges; around reuniting families and friends and past uniformed guards who said, "Welcome to Puerto Vallarta" as they exited the terminal. Roland breathed deeply and marveled at the freshness and life in the air as it washed over him. He followed the other two past the line of taxis and across the road through an opening in the chicken-wire fence to the parking lot.

Between the Volkswagens and the old pickups sat a new cream-colored Ford Explorer. Into the back his suitcases went, and they set off with Mick at the wheel and Slogan in the other front seat. Roland stayed in the back, trying to see everything he possibly could all at once. They joined the traffic on a busy road.

"Is this your car, Mick?" he asked. It was quiet, and when he pushed the switch to roll down the window a multitude of sounds – people shouting at each other, buses with no mufflers, cars with windows down and stereos on

– accompanied the perfumed tropical air. He closed the window.

"No, it's Adrian's," Mick replied. "He's got a fleet of them. There's this one, a white one, a red one; Liza's got a Lincoln Navigator; there's also a blue minivan for shopping and courier pickups. I have a little Jeep myself…what else. I think I'm missing a few."

Slogan chimed in. "Tatiana owns a car rental company, so there's always something different parked out front of the Shack."

Roland counted the palm trees, so close to his window that he could almost reach out and touch them, lining the boulevard in front of hotels and timeshare resorts. Sheraton Buganvilias said a backlit sign; here was a gatehouse built to resemble a lighthouse that said Puerto Iguana. BayView Grand, said another. Tall buildings, white ones, shorter ones, illuminated against the black sky by a myriad of colored lights. They passed in front of bars that said "*Chicas, Girls, Table Dancing!*" A bull ring flashed by on their left.

"Who's Tatiana, and what's the Shack?"

Slogan tilted his head so Roland could hear him. "The Shack is what we call Adrian's house," he said. "It's our little joke, like calling your favorite knockout centerfold a mutt. Tatiana's our property manager, and she takes care of all the accommodation for the employees. She's amazing. She knows people that can get things done for you in a day that would take others a month. The first thing you'll learn is that nobody's in a hurry here except us, and she's great because she understands that. Thanks to her we have good staff at the house."

"So what's your story, Roland?" Mick asked. "Why did you slip away to join our band of pirates down here?"

Roland toyed with the window again, closing it before answering. "Probably the best way to explain it would be to say that I am at a crossroads, and I wanted to take the road less traveled."

Mick laughed. "And that will no doubt make all the difference," he said, finishing the allusion to Frost. "Actually that's pretty funny, because it may not remain untraveled for long. We've grown a lot lately. If it keeps up like this…I don't know what will happen, but it's getting pretty crazy."

Slogan was already counting off people on his fingers. "Well, who is there?" he asked no one in particular. "Okay, we've got Adrian, of course. His sister Liza runs the audit department with Roxane. They're great, you'll like them. Liza is about four feet tall and totally tough but she's really neat. Mick knew Roxane from before, so she's been around for a while, she's pretty cool too. There's Amy; she's lived in Vallarta for years but only started with us a couple of months ago. She's marrying Adrian's son Sidney next month. Let's see, who else…" Slogan turned to face Roland.

"Actually, I think you met Sid, didn't you? I used to be friends with him when you and my brother were in school together."

Roland thought about what he had been doing thirteen years previously, but he couldn't remember meeting Sidney and said so.

"No matter. Anyway, there's a whole bunch of people," Slogan finished. "You'll meet them all tomorrow."

They stopped at another traffic light. "You taking the highway?" Slogan inquired.

"I figured we'd go down the Malecon and show him the sights."

"What's the Malecon?" asked Roland.

"It's like a boardwalk," Mick explained. "It borders the shoreline for a half mile or so, and it's where pretty much everybody hangs out. During the day the beaches are full, and at night they have performers and there are lots of bars down there. Fridays and Sundays are generally when the locals swamp the place, the rest of the time it's touristville. But just across the street from the walkway there are lots of neat little cafes and bars, the whole bit."

They started moving again, and the Micks pointed out places of interest. "This here's the Zoo," said Slogan, indicating a nightclub off to his left. "Good place to go if you want to meet girls, if you're into that. Of course, I am not in the slightest bit intrigued by that scene any more."

Roland leaned forward. "Are congratulations due?" He patted his friend's shoulder. "Wedding bells for Slogan. Makes me so proud."

"Married?" asked Mick. "So that's official, then?"

"Not yet," answered Slogan. "At least, not officially, not for a little while. It wouldn't have come up at all yet if *somebody*" – he cast a glance back at Roland – "hadn't said anything."

Roland feigned hurt. "How was I supposed to know you really are getting married? Sorry, but I had no idea."

"We're not engaged yet, but I'm going to ask her this coming month. Couple of weeks now. So keep it under your hat at least that long."

"Done," Roland agreed. Mick said he was offended that Slogan hadn't told him. He looked back at Roland in the rearview mirror. "You're a catalyst, then."

"What do you mean by that?" asked Roland. Then, "Wow, look at her!"

He'd been noticing beautiful girls from the moment he touched down, starting with the officious siren at the airport, but now that he was with friends he had an opportunity to share his enthusiasm. This one was petite, with long, dark hair and expressive brown eyes. Much like many other Mexican girls, but Roland hadn't considered that yet. She waved at him as they passed by, standing with her friend on the ocean side of the Malecon. Roland had just enough time to wave back before they disappeared around a slight curve when he realized that the reason he found her so attractive was because she looked exactly like his beloved Sara, and immediately he felt foolish.

"A catalyst," continued Mick from a hundred miles away. "Someone who acts as an agent of change, who takes preexisting conditions and brings about their natural conclusions sooner than without their presence."

Slogan laughed. "Gosh, that's pretty scientific of you."

"Here?" Mick said, indicating a street to his left.

"Yeah. I'm 584. Big green door." Slogan turned to face Roland. "Mick's going to drop me off at home here. You'll be staying with him for a while, until we find you a place of your own. It shouldn't be too long."

Roland nodded. He was looking out the window intently at how abruptly the scenery had changed. It had gone from jubilant partyers dressed in colorful clothes and sporting the occasional sunburn to a much more local landscape. Carts that would overflow with fruit when their proprietors opened them again tomorrow were drawn up alongside the curb, and Roland could see children running up the sidewalks, chasing each other in the night.

They stopped outside an old brick building. Slogan grabbed his slender backpack and got out of the vehicle, and when Roland got out as well to occupy the front seat he embraced him again.

"Welcome to Vallarta, my friend. It's good to have you here," he said, and turned away.

Mick drove them down more cobblestone streets, narrating all the while. He was not stingy with his knowledge, and it seemed to Roland that he was glad to have someone genuinely interested in what he had to say. Roland knew travellers, and one thing many of them shared was a reluctance to admit that they didn't know the land they were in. Roland did not suffer from that. He listened attentively.

Eventually they turned onto a street that was almost as bustling as the Malecon had been, though in a different way. It was littered with sidewalk cafés under colorful awnings, and had a more intimate feel to it.

"Olas Altas," Mick explained. "Technically that's the name of this street, but it's also the district we're in. It's where all the expatriates end up, and where you'll find the tourists who aren't solely interested in the new resorts. Here, I'll show you what I mean."

He parked the Explorer on an impossibly steep street. When they got out, Roland reached into his suitcase and changed out of his sweater into a t-shirt. It had been bitterly cold that morning when he boarded the plane.

Mick laughed. "Yeah, you don't want to look too much like a tourist."

Roland grinned. "I suppose I'll have plenty of time for that, won't I?"

Mick looked around and dropped his voice as he spoke. "Actually, you're a local now, or at least in a very short time you will be. You will be seeing a side of Vallarta that nobody else ever sees, and you're going to have to remember to keep your head down and keep your secrets."

They started off down towards the main street and Mick's favorite café, soon to become Roland's as well, winding their way through the crowds to discover that all the tables outside were occupied.

"Let's keep walking," Mick said. "There's always someplace else."

Roland had seen the ocean from where they had parked, moonlight glittering on the waves like sequins on a beautiful dress, and now he inhaled the smell of its salt and freshness mingled with the aromas of exotic coffees from the sidewalk cafes and suntan lotion on the people as they passed him on the street. He listened to Mick telling him about where they were in the city (old town, well south of the touristy

9

hotel zone), and about how long he'd been in Mexico (just over three years).

Eventually they found seats outside a coffee bar with internet access rates posted on the door. No sooner had they ordered than a tall, stocky man with a mustache and longish salt-and-pepper hair clapped Mick on the back. In his other hand he held a dark cigar.

"Mick, how are you doing?" he boomed, his voice thickly accented. Mick nodded in greeting and said nothing. The man looked at Roland and sat down at the table.

"How is the Adrian?" he asked, and then immediately changed the subject. "This is perfect weather. I think I stay here longer and not go back home for while yet. But it was nice too, where I was last." Roland listened intently. He loved accents and tried to place where the man was from.

"And where was that?" he inquired. At this the man slowly turned to face him.

"Grecia," he answered. His eyes probed Roland's for a sign of recognition as he took a long draw from the dark cigar.

"And how long were you in Greece?"

Satisfied, the man extended his hand. "My name is Milo. And I was there for two months."

The waiter brought out two coffees and the man called Milo ordered one for himself.

"I'm Roland, and I haven't been there yet. This is my first time in Mexico, too, but I like it already."

Milo regarded him levelly, then smiled a little. "You like it wherever you are, I think." He pointed up the street, to the north. "I'm from Toronto. That's where my wife is too, maybe also that's why I don't want to go, hey?" He laughed.

Mick seemed as though he had slightly withdrawn from the conversation. This became more noticeable with Milo's next question, as he turned to Mick.

"I haven't seen the Adrian for a week now. Everything is okay with him?"

Mick nodded vaguely. "He's fine, as far as I know. Haven't seen him myself much either, actually."

Milo turned to Roland. "What are you doing down here, you are working with these guys?"

This surprised Roland. He was under the impression that no one knew about what he would be doing in Mexico. From the tone of Slogan's phone calls to him before he came down he had assumed the whole operation was a secret, with even its own employees working more or less on a need-to-know basis. He knew that many companies operated in a similar fashion, but that didn't make it any less amusing for him. He'd almost imagined it to be something out of *Reservoir Dogs*, not knowing anyone else's real name and addressing each other as colors instead, which was fine with him as long as he didn't have to be Mr. Pink. To have a virtual stranger interrogate him about it over coffee on his first night there took him aback, and he didn't know exactly what to say. He had been coached a little already and was about to give the story when Mick did it for him.

"He's a friend of a friend of mine who lives here in Vallarta, and we're thinking of doing some web page design together so he can extend his holiday. He's staying with me for a while because this friend of his doesn't have the room. Unexpected company at the last minute."

Milo looked at Mick a little too long, then turned to Roland and grunted. Obviously he wasn't impressed with this answer, but he didn't push for more. In fact, he got up to leave. The waiter brought his coffee and looked at him quizzically.

"You don' wan' this now, sir?"

"No, I don't want. Here, how much? Here is ten."

"Is eight pesos, sir." The waiter reached into his apron for change. Milo waved him away and turned to face the two men at the table.

"Well, I will see you around then, maybe later." He nodded at Roland and continued on up the street.

"Who was that?" asked Roland.

"He's a Croatian guy; one of Adrian's friends who spends his winters down here. There are a few of them. He's a member of the club as well, but that doesn't give him any more rights than anyone else when it comes to knowing what we do."

Mick was a very tactful person, but Roland assumed that everyone in the organization was responsible for showing the same front, and he wanted to know exactly what that should be – or even if there was one. He decided he might as well learn it now.

"If he's Adrian's friend as well as being a member, surely he must know all about this, right?"

Mick toyed with his coffee mug. Roland noticed that the coffee tasted very different than it did at home. Sweeter. Caramelized cane sugar, Mick told him as he stalled for time, instead of beet sugar.

"What he knows is either conjecture or what Adrian has chosen to tell him," Mick said at last. "I don't know exactly what that might be. But there are a couple of guys like him down here. There's an old man named Bill – hang around long enough and you'll run into him too – people who have a membership and who know it's Adrian's project. As far as they're concerned, none of us work here. You don't have to deny knowing Adrian, but don't ever say you work for him. It's not like it's a huge secret, it's just…it would cause more problems than it would solve."

"How so?"

Mick hesitated again. Roland wanted to apologize for pressing him but didn't. He was too used to discovering that secrets covered lies. Upon reminding himself of that, he relaxed a little. Mick wasn't Sara. He didn't need to lie to him.

"There is a lot of interest in us as it is," Mick began, leaning in toward Roland. "Mexico is not the first place in the world that comes to mind when you think of uncorrupted lawmakers, okay? So as long as we don't run around boasting about the fact that we are the kings of this town, nobody pays us any mind. They can be curious all they want. The members of our club want us to respect their privacy. We can't do that by wearing clothes with the Cyberia logo on them, if you get my meaning."

"Kings pay the lawmakers, and the police," Roland pointed out, unsatisfied with Mick's answer.

Mick tried a different tack. "Okay, think about this. There are lots of women down here who are basically just cruising around until they hit upon somebody rich. They want what they have only until something better comes along. If they think you're that somebody, and you tell them how much you make and what you really do, you're never going to be rid of them. Paint yourself a pauper and the government leaves you alone, gold-diggers leave you alone, you can do your own thing. On paper and on the streets you want to be nothing." Mick spread his hands. "It's just so much easier that way."

Roland found it unfortunate that he understood this line of reasoning better than most others that Mick could have provided.

"So when do I learn exactly what I've come all this way to do?" he asked.

Mick stared at the cobbled street and the taxis passing by only a few feet from him.

He was still leaning toward Roland but the look in his eyes made him seem very far away. Quietly he said, "You work for an investment club called Cyberia, which currently has about eight thousand members, give or take a few hundred. They send their money to an address in Belize, and from there it comes by courier here to Vallarta where it's entered into our database and processed through a variety of banks, mostly in Latvia. A monthly transfer is made to a mirror account in New York, and it's from that bank that members receive their dividend checks. Membership is free, but for investors the minimum buy-in is a thousand dollars, and we pay ten percent per month."

"Ten percent per *month*? You're telling me that these people are making *a hundred and twenty percent per year*?"

Mick patted the air slightly in a gesture for Roland to keep his voice down, and nodded. "More than that actually, by the time you figure in bonuses and so on. Also I think Adrian might have some other investment structures in the works as well, but he'll not tell anyone for a few weeks yet. For now, that's what we do and what we offer. Your job will be pretty basic at first, but Adrian needs capable people because we're growing too fast for the staff we have now."

"A hundred and twenty percent," Roland repeated. "This can't be legal. Please tell me we're not dealing drugs or selling kids for adoption, okay?"

Mick laughed. "No, hell, no, nothing like that. No organ harvesting here." He waved a hand. "Look, the truth is that none of us know exactly what Adrian is investing in. Ultimately it's really none of our business. If you need to know, you'll know, and in the meantime it might be best that you don't. We don't work for the investment side of things anyway. What we do is manage the memberships. Have you ever worked for a company that told you every minute detail of its business dealings?"

"Nobody has. It isn't efficient."

"Exactly. And have you ever worked for a company that wanted you to keep its dealings a secret?"

"Naturally. It's called non-disclosure and it's why nobody sees concept cars until they put in an appearance at auto shows." None of these things stop me asking questions though, Roland thought.

"Good," said Mick. "Then you'll fit right in."

Vallarta wasn't where everything happened, Mick continued, but it was where most Cyberians worked, and the club was getting so big so fast that instead of relying on his usual staff, Adrian had to start looking for people with some management and travel experience.

"So when Slogan told us that you'd been involved with business and that you're a smart guy with a lot of jet-setting under your belt, we figured you'd be the one."

"That's flattering. I suppose I owe him a few drinks now. The one to do what exactly?"

Mick's eyes narrowed. "To negotiate the purchase of a nuclear submarine from the Soviets for the Cali cartel."

"No problem," Roland deadpanned. "I've done that hundreds of times."

"Damn," Mick grinned. "Busted." He drained his coffee and licked his lips. "There's a project in the works that will really change things for us for the better and you'll be helping. That's all I can say. It won't be for a while yet, though, so in the meantime just be content to make outrageous money doing things you'd get minimum wage for back home."

Mick had lowered his voice every time someone walked past, and his eyes never stayed fixed on anything for very long. Obviously discussing the subject in public made him nervous, so Roland didn't press him and decided to finish his coffee talking about more superficial matters. He asked about their boss, the owner of Cyberia.

Mick replied that Adrian was originally from the same city as Roland, as were several others he would be working with, and had come to Puerto Vallarta via the

Bahamas almost three years ago. At the time Mick was already in town trying to drum up web page design work and doing respectably well at it. Adrian had been living in a condominium on the beach, now shared by two of Roland's coworkers. He had bought the Shack roughly a year ago, and it was one of the biggest houses in Vallarta. Roland would be working on the bottom floor with everyone else.

"Don't let that turn you off, though," Mick said. "It's no basement, believe me. It has views of the ocean that people would kill for, because the house is high up on the hill."

Breakfast and lunch were provided, as was living accommodation, housekeeping service; everything in fact except dinners. There were staff at the Shack who could shop for things Roland needed, and if anything in his condo or house wasn't exactly as he desired, there were people who could take care of that for him. Adrian employed a former police chief as his director of security, two cooks, a driver, a maintenance man, at least three housekeeping staff; the list went on. Pay was generous, and would be made in US dollars to any account in the world Roland wanted. If that account did not exist, it could be created easily. Figuring in the cost of accommodation, house staff, meals and other perks, Mick informed him that he would be making approximately $8000 per month. A pretty decent setup all around, really, thought Roland, and not the kind of thing that normally drops in people's laps while they're choosing a color to paint the kitchen as he had been doing when the phone call from Slogan came.

"*Listo?*" asked Mick, as he left twenty pesos on the table and got up to leave. "That's your first Spanish lesson. It means 'ready?'"

"*Si,*" answered Roland. "Let's see your space age tropical bachelor pad."

They got back in the Explorer for the drive up to Mick's condo. Roland felt more at home with each passing minute, as though a great weight had been suddenly lifted from his shoulders. Mick related how he used to be a teacher; he used to work in a circus; he used to manage a resort in Tahiti. Roland soaked up the names of the faraway places, some he'd been to, some he hadn't, and leaned close to the open window to breathe deeply the humid and scented air.

The prospect of never again having to drive a vehicle with the window up unless it was raining was tantalizing. The climate he had recently departed from had left no doubt that those thin pieces of glass were lifesavers. If his car died on a lonely highway like the ones around his house in the middle of winter, he might well die with it. In really terrible storms cars went off the road all the time, and if that happened and the occupants were knocked unconscious they might be blanketed with snow and remain undiscovered until spring. Here, the worst that could happen was…what? Lie on the hood and soak up the sun til the tow truck came?

Mick guided the vehicle up a steep cobblestone street after turning off the narrow road he called the highway. They stopped in front of a gargantuan white house directly adjoining a sidewalk. Mick pointed to it with the keys as he said, "This is where we work. This is Adrian's house."

The front entrance was sunken a few steps from the road. Roland noted the front door and laughed. "That gives a new meaning to the phrase 'screen door'!"

"What's that?"

"That door. Back home the outside doors are sealed, weatherproofed, everything. These ones are more my style. Nice wrought iron bars with a big deadbolt, then the inside door with that finely-etched glass on it and probably no lock. What more do you need? I hate doors and walls. I like my space."

"The final frontier." Mick came around to Roland's door and tried the handle to make sure it was locked.

"Is there much crime here?" Roland asked, watching him.

"Not much at all. I've never had a problem with my Jeep, and the only thing really is that sometimes the cops will stop you if they see that you're a gringo in a nice car, and they'll ticket you for some imaginary offense. Not exactly the kind of thing you get a receipt for."

He led Roland down the street by a few car lengths to another tall wrought iron gate and took out a key. "I live practically next door," he explained, "so no matter where I park on this street, I'm always right out front. Very convenient."

They stepped out of the elevator and made their way to Mick's apartment. He had a jacuzzi tub on his downstairs patio, and a simple semicircular built-in sofa in the livingroom. Above a small garden bordered by white brick behind it was what looked like an elevator shaft, partly open to the roof above. "Hey, I didn't design it," Mick said when Roland pointed to the quirky feature and looked puzzled.

Mick helped Roland carry his luggage to his room, and they went out on the terrace adjoining Mick's bedroom overlooking the ocean. His television was on and the volume was turned low.

Roland watched a ship in the bay. It had caught his eye because it looked exactly like a Spanish galleon and was shooting fireworks from its decks.

Mick followed Roland's gaze. "The *Marigalante*. Very good dinner cruise. I went on it once. Every night around this time, they set off fireworks before they dock."

"Who did you go with?" A pirate ship full of revellers sounded intriguing to Roland, the attraction not being strictly the unique look of the vessel but the added potential bonus of female company.

"Oh, just me," said Mick, and Roland thought he detected a tinge of melancholy in his tone.

"Mick, do you have a girlfriend?"

"No." Mick shook his head. "No, I don't. I had one here once, and my advice is that before you decide to become involved with a local girl, keep in mind that you're pretty much dating her family as well as her. It's a Catholic thing, I suppose. Either way, my girlfriend couldn't understand why I didn't always want to spend time with her family and that's what sunk us. I'm too much of a loner for that."

Their conversation drifted over many different subjects until finally one of them yawned, and they decided to call it a night. "I'll wake you up at seven or so," said Mick, and Roland retreated to his room.

He sat on his bed and stared out the window. He thought of Sara and wondered what she was doing now. Probably fast asleep next to her fiancé, her latest Wordsworth Classic by the bed, her clothes dumped on the floor and her dark hair draped across her cheek. Roland remembered it as though it had been yesterday, but he hadn't seen her for almost five months.

Roland Halliwell was thirty years old, a little lost, a little lonely, trying to recover from a broken heart, looking forward to discovering what exactly it was that he came all this way to do, and excited about the change in his life. In fact, he was excited about the very fact that he had something to be excited about in the first place.

After brushing his teeth, scratching a few words in his diary and fumbling with the light switch above him, he listened to the surf on the beach below his window and the fan above his head, and fell into a very deep sleep.

2
Castillo Paraiso

*

Roland was still fast asleep the next morning when Mick tapped at his door. "Can you be ready in half an hour?" he asked through it, and Roland grunted in the affirmative.

After blinking at the ceiling for a couple of minutes, Roland stretched luxuriously and approached the window, pushing back the curtains and yawning as he surveyed his new home town.

Mick's condo, like almost all property in the south half of the bay, was built on steep, low mountains. To the left stood a multistorey building Mick had pointed out the night before. Adrian had told Mick he would buy him a place to live – condo, house, whatever – and this building had a spacious corner unit that he was debating whether to purchase. The one Roland stood in now was a rental, a rather rare thing in the world of Cyberia as most of the employees' properties were owned by Adrian.

Rising from the ocean like the fossilized backbone of some prehistoric monster were three rocks of successive size called Los Arcos. They were hollow, or at least the biggest one was, and one could swim through from one side to the other. These lay to Roland's left as well, though not as far as Mick's potential new home. Further to the right, he could see small boats in the bay already catching fish for the day to be served in the plethora of restaurants in the city, and a larger boat which said *Chico's Dive Shop* on it heading for Los Arcos. He could see Playa Conchas Chinas below him, the beach named after the neighborhood he now lived in ("the Beverly Hills of Puerto Vallarta", Mick had said), and could make out where the bay resumed its curve to present the shiny buildings in the zone of new hotels. They were a stark contrast to the buildings in old town, with their red tiled roofs and curved archways and Mediterranean-looking features.

He padded into his bathroom and pulled back the shower curtain. This was something he hadn't done the night before, but as he did so now he was surprised to find that the wall facing the bay was almost completely glass. This afforded him a panoramic view of the ocean while showering, but it also gave him pause because it meant that anyone happening to look in would have an equally panoramic view of him. Well, he thought, we could each do worse, and was a little disappointed when the window fogged over completely after only a couple of minutes despite the best intentions of the open vents at either side.

Mick was watching television when Roland emerged from his room. They drove down to Olas Altas and claimed a table at the café which the night before had been too crowded to accommodate them. There was a motley handful of expats, English-speaking yet local-looking characters who greeted them. Mick introduced Roland and the two of them approached the counter to order some coffee. As Mick spoke in Spanish Roland hung on every word, and as the girl busied herself pouring two coffees into styrene cups he asked, "Did you ask for these to go? I heard you say '*va*'."

"Yeah," said Mick, "you never know how clean the dishes are. Besides, when you get it to go, the cup is bigger."

They sat down at their table, the morning sun already warm and clear and bright. Roland asked quietly, "Friends of yours?"

Mick made sure that none of them at the other table could hear before he replied.

"This is the same crowd that Milo belongs to. Most of them come down just for the winter. Remember when I told you that as far as they're concerned, we don't work here?

21

What I meant was that as far as *we* are concerned, we don't work here."

He leaned in a little closer. "They all know that there's something they don't know about us, if that makes sense. Some of them are jealous because most of them struggle with money to be down here, so they see my new Jeep and the fact that none of us ever need money and they want a piece of it. It's only going to get worse when they see us stepping out of the Learjet or partying on Adrian's yacht, which will be here in about a month. Vallarta is a small enough city as it is, but when you narrow it down to how many gringos are here long enough to be considered locals it's a very small place indeed. Once they separate you from the beach vegetables and find out you know Adrian it's all going to be uphill from there. And because you're sitting with me, they'll be speculating about you in no time." He sat back and gestured towards the side street that led to the beach. "Here, grab your coffee. Let's take a little walking tour."

No sooner had he said this than they were accosted by a portly young man in baggy shorts and expensive sunglasses. Without waiting for an invitation, he lowered his backpack onto the scuffed terracotta patio and pulled out a chair.

"Morning," he said in a piercing, bratty voice. He began to chew a fingernail.

"Morning," said Mick. "Roland, this is Kevin. Kevin, Roland."

"Yeah, I've heard about you. You're working with us, right? Thank Christ I'm not FNG anymore."

Mick winced. "FNG?"

"Fuckin' New Guy," said Kevin. "I've been here three weeks. Time for somebody else's turn." He assessed his fingernail. "Good coffee here at the Pagina." He said it like 'vagina'.

"Pa*hee*na," Mick intoned in a tired voice.

"These guys kill me," he continued, his freshly-gnawed digit pointing across the street to where a shopkeeper held a hose in one hand and a broom in the other, greeting passersby and cleaning the area in front of his store. "I love how they water the sidewalks every morning. I wonder when they'll notice that concrete just doesn't grow. Maybe they water their money as well. An example of logic applied without the facts." He belched loudly and pushed back his chair. "Well, I suppose the chances are pretty slim that I'll get a ride with you guys, so I'll see you up there." And without waiting for an answer, he continued walking up the street past a large woman pulled out the awning on her taco stand, the tight curls in his red hair visible for what seemed like an eternity. Roland watched him disappear with some amusement before turning to Mick.

"What the hell was that?" he asked.

Mick sighed and motioned for Roland to follow him down the small street he'd indicated earlier. Now that Kevin had pointed it out, Roland noticed several people doing the same thing, watering down the sidewalks in front of their stores. He brought this to Mick's attention.

"I know," Mick replied. "In all the time I've been here, I've yet to meet anyone who fits the stereotype of the lazy Mexican. They're actually very industrious people, but there's no denying that sometimes they do spend their energy on unproductive things. I don't mean washing the sidewalks, though. You'll know what I mean when you see it. Guys shoveling dirt while the backhoe sits idle, that kind of thing."

When they had dodged enough taxis and pedestrians to find themselves more or less alone on the beach, Mick spoke again.

"I get the impression that you came down here thinking we were all more or less professionals in our fields."

Roland paused to compose his answer. "More or less," he admitted. "Truth is, I really didn't know what to expect. One thing I didn't count on was to have to keep what I'm doing such a secret."

A vendor wandered by, laden with beautiful silver jewelry. The man noticed Roland looking at him and Roland averted his gaze immediately, pretending instead to be studying a huge dark bird with sharp boomerang-shaped wings which hovered above the ocean and shrieked before tucking in its wings and diving for its prey. In that instant Roland realized that he wasn't afraid of being approached by a man selling things. He had looked away because he was afraid the man might be a government agent wearing a wire. Already he was becoming exasperated with what he perceived to be more than just an exaggerated discretion on Mick's part. A thought struck him.

"Mick, do you do drugs? Smoke pot or something?"

Mick's eyes, already large and blue, became even more so. He laughed. "No. Why would you ask me that?"

"Because your caution borders on paranoia. If the locals know that we know Adrian, and if there are members of our club right here in Vallarta, and if the house staff sees our faces every day, and if the expats know something's up, what's to be gained by acting like a criminal? Unless it's a natural tendency on your part, which you seem too smart for, or unless we really are selling nuclear subs to the Colombians, which is not without its logistical problems, or unless you're ingesting chemicals that have sideffects like assuming that the world is controlled by a shapeshifting reptilian Illuminati."

"You mean it isn't?"

"Not as far as I can tell, no." Roland sighed heavily. "You know, all this James Bond stuff is starting to rub off on me already."

Mick sat on the beach and grabbed a handful of sand, which he studied intently. Roland sat beside him, watching a parasailer and squinting in the sunlight. Mick opened his fingers and the sand started to fall between them.

"Roland, you're in a foreign country where you don't yet speak the language. If you get thrown in jail here they'll not care whether you live or die, because if something were to go wrong they will give your government all kinds of evidence to prove you were guilty of whatever they chose to charge you with. If you have rich parents who can bail you out, fine. If not, you can either rot in jail or any number of other things can happen to you. Here in Vallarta you are perfectly safe from street crimes, because the police take that very seriously. Not like Acapulco, where it's so far gone that unless you're in your hotel or on the beach right in front of it you are taking a risk. But gringos who think they can come down here and do whatever they want aren't returning the favor, and nobody likes a sore winner. Adrian is probably the richest person here, or close enough anyway, and as such we are all under a microscope. I'll say it again; you don't have to be guilty of anything to be thrown in jail down here."

"Hmm," said Roland, "they don't tell you that in the travel brochures."

Mick didn't laugh. "It's the French legal system."

"The Napoleonic code," said Roland. "No wonder the cops here all look so relaxed."

Finally Mick stopped studying the sand and looked at Roland. "You haven't even seen where you work yet and you already have a better idea of what we're doing than some who've been here for months. And until you find your feet you are going to have to play dumb when it galls you, say nothing when you know you could, and just keep your head down and keep to yourself."

Roland watched the surf rolling in on itself, time and again. Night and day, day and night, it never stopped.

"I ask a lot of questions because I want to know what the extent of my own liability is," he said. "Certainly you can understand that. It's one thing to work here without a permit. I assume that if the Mexicans threw out everybody who was paid under the table there'd be nobody left to sell timeshares or collect tips in the beach bars. But it's another thing entirely to be involved with something that sponsors wars or dumps toxic waste in people's back yards. A hundred and twenty percent return on a purportedly safe investment isn't possible outside the stock or commodity markets because there is no government on earth that wants its citizens to be wealthy, so war or drugs are the only things left that pay that much. You act as if nobody else has ever asked these questions."

He watched the rest of the sand slip through Mick's fingers onto the beach.

"Nobody has." Mick got up and brushed the sand off his shorts.

"You mean everyone I work with thinks this is normal?"

Mick started to answer and then changed his mind, instead abruptly transforming himself back into a tour guide. "This beach is called Playa Olas Altas. That beach there," he said, pointing to the beach on the other side of the pier, "is Playa los Muertos, which means Beach of the Dead. They're trying to rename it Playa del Sol, or Beach of the Sun, but so far it hasn't caught on."

All the way back to the car he kept spouting information. By the end of the previous evening, Roland had felt more familiar with the city than any tourist could have been, but there was always more to know, and by the time they found themselves back at the café he had forgotten all about his misgivings and found it easier to just enjoy being where he was.

They unzipped the canvas windows in the Jeep and set off towards Mick's home and the Shack. Turning off the highway onto the steep cobblestone, they slowed as Mick spotted a thin character with spiky hair and a sparse goatee. He looked to be in his early twenties. "Castanza! *Buenos dias!* Hop in."

Roland got out and moved the seat forward so Castanza could squeeze in behind him. Mick introduced Roland in Spanish, and Castanza said, "Ah, *si.*"

"Castanza is the head maintenance guy, groundskeeper... wait a minute, there aren't any grounds...well, he takes care of everything up at the Shack. Cleans the pool, fixes things, all that stuff. *Es correcto*, Castanza?"

"*Si*," the young man replied.

Mick spoke with Castanza in Spanish. Roland had studied enough of the language before leaving home to pick up most of what they were saying, but the step from understanding the occasional word spoken by others to being able to speak the language himself still seemed a big one.

Mick parked the Jeep in exactly the same place it had been in the night before, and as usual, asked Roland to zip up the window and lock his door. No matter where they went or how long they were planning to be away from the vehicle, even if it was to run in for a beer from the Six, Mick always locked the car. Always.

The garage door was already open when they pulled up. The night before, it had given the impression that the room beyond was able to accommodate only one vehicle, but with it open Roland could see that the garage was rounded inside, allowing just enough room for the two cars now parked in it – Explorers, one the same vehicle in which he'd come from the airport, and a red one beside it. Along the inside wall was a thick rope holding enough lifejackets to have kept the Titanic afloat, and along the other side were colossal stacks of beer and wine bottles. "An army marches on its liver," Mick explained. "Actually while we're here you might as well add that coffee to the collection." Mick pointed to a shelving unit standing beside the lifejackets, groaning with can after can of coffee. Roland had brought his along in the Jeep, and retrieved it now.

"This garage is bigger than it looks," he remarked.

"Every part of the house is."

A tall wrought iron gate of the same type as the one at the front entrance provided access from the garage to the rest of the house, but Mick steered them towards the former. An attractive Mexican woman in an apron stood in front of it, being tolerably rough with a broom on the sidewalk.

"*Buenos dias*," she said to the new arrivals.

"*Buenos dias*," echoed Roland.

"Dive right in! He's speaking Spanish already!" Mick laughed.

The woman smiled. Mick yet again patiently explained who Roland was. "That's Guadalupe," he said to Roland as they entered the house.

Mick closed the door behind them and gestured. "Well, this is it."

Roland smiled. "Nice little Shack."

He was standing on a very large landing. The sound of trickling water from the fountain in a pond in front of him echoed from the domed two-storey ceiling. Black slate underneath the entryway at his feet and the rest of the house's light grey marble tile floors contrasted with the white of the walls and ceiling, and the steps on the huge spiral staircase beside him were a greyish-tan stone. There was a wet bar with glittering crystal glasses in a far corner to the right and two colorful sofas arranged in the huge open space beyond the staircase. The impression was one of freedom and informal elegance.

Roland took the few steps down to the living room. He felt very comfortable in the house and wasn't in the least intimidated by its opulence, but the one thing he did feel humbled by was the view.

What divided the house from the huge outside patio and the curved vanishing-edge swimming pool it embraced was a row of arched columns. The resulting impression was that they were monumental frames, built to display the living and changing scene beyond, and this they did very well. Roland slowly approached the patio.

The white city lay in a graceful, perfect arc, stretching lazily around the bay. The sun's morning angle in the sky made everything it touched glow with a soft orange halo, as though a supernatural energy bestowed upon everything during the night was still visible before wearing off in the heat of the day to come. A long stretch of sandy beach bordered a busy street Roland recognized as the Malecon. Further around the curve were the hotels, low adobe towers housing sleepy couples looking out their windows at the enormous white house he stood in as they waited for room service and marveled at their new wedding rings. The airport was hidden from Roland's view but he knew it was there; he watched a jet rise over the calm blue ocean, expelled from paradise, its nose sniffing for clouds and finding none. The green mountains on which the little city was built were lush and hid unnamed things beyond.

Adrian's house was exactly the sort of place that a pagan would seek out as a base from which to commune with the world.

"This is incredible. This just...at the risk of sounding cliché, it just takes my breath away."

Mick had joined him. He said nothing at first, standing there beside Roland on the patio with his arms folded. Roland noticed that the bottom of the swimming pool had the image of a large white tortoise tiled onto it. The rest of the tiles were blue. He turned his attention back to the scene before him.

"Talk about a million-dollar view."

Finally Mick spoke. "Two point two million, actually."

"That's what he paid for this place?"

"And the rest. You see these windows here, these folding ones that run on tracks between the columns? They go around the other side too, in front of the dining area."

Mick pointed back into the house. Roland could see that if he had turned left when he came in instead of coming straight out to the patio, he would ultimately have found himself in an enormous kitchen after passing a large round glass dining table with eight chairs around it. Behind the table as he looked into the house was a tall marble counter, and behind that he recognized Guadalupe, who had come in after finishing her outdoor duties. She was cutting something at an island counter, the end of which was visible around the side of the other one – at least, that's what it looked as though she was doing, but the house was so big that she was too far away to tell. She smiled at Roland and almost imperceptibly raised her knife to him. Roland smiled back and nodded. All this happened in an instant, and he turned his attention to the windows Mick had pointed out. They were all open, tall ones that rose to a track along the top of the archways, folded back against their respective columns so that the house really ended up being only a palatial shelter from the sun. Mick waited until he saw Roland looking at them before he spoke.

"Adrian had them put in last year. The house used to be open to the outside all year round, but last summer a storm came up and blew the patio furniture away. Some of it ended up in the swimming pool of a house down below, and his living room furniture got blown around too. Glasses smashed, water everywhere, just a mess. So he paid some

German bunch a hundred and fifty thousand bucks to come and install these."

Roland walked around to the side of the house facing the ocean. The wraparound patio, made from the same stone as the steps inside, curved to end where the tall counter in the kitchen met the dining area. Nestled into the corner was a large barbecue. Roland pointed to it.

"You could feed an army with that thing."

"We kind of have to."

Roland peered over the railing. There was a house across the street three storeys below with beautiful stained glass windows and a "Sold" notice across a "For Sale" sign attached to its arched brick entranceway, beside which were three terraced parking spaces, each with its own padlocked gate. The street itself – cobblestone, of course – disappeared as it wandered off to the right, then the left again.

"That's the same street that runs along behind my place," said Mick. "It's a dead end. You should take a walk down there some day. It's not far, and at the end there's a fountain that's unused and overgrown with all sorts of vegetation. It looks kind of out of place, like an abandoned villa around it vanished one night or something."

"Hmm."

"I suppose that's pretty irrelevant. I just think it's neat."

"No, no," said Roland. "Actually I love old buildings. If I had my way I'd live in an abandoned castle."

"Let's go inside," said Mick. "I'll show you where we work." They navigated around patio chairs and waved to Guadalupe in the kitchen, who had been joined by a second lady.

"That's the cook, Ava," Mick explained on their way downstairs. "We have another one but she's on a sort of…temporarily permanent leave. Adrian can't bear to fire anybody but her cooking was awful, plus she was always drunk, so he offered her as much time off as she wanted. Nobody knows when or if she's coming back. Ava does great Mexican stuff but not all of us like that, so we'll see."

By this time they were standing in a large room with the same marble floor found throughout the rest of house. It had been designed as a common living area for the two bedrooms that branched off from either side of it, but now it resembled the control room for a spacecraft launch. There were desks pushed up against every available inch of wall space, and when that had become insufficient, two more had been added side by side between two columns. At each desk sat a computer, their monitors patiently awaiting the day's activity. The electric hum from the machines currently running charged the whole room with the pleasing feeling of progress. Each desk was adorned with its corresponding employee's personality in the form of pictures, stickers, and various other paraphernalia. One in particular, which sat beside an imposing wooden door, was conspicuously messy and arrayed with fantasy action figures.

"That must be Slogan's desk," Roland observed.

"How right you are," said Mick. He indicated one pushed up against the wet bar, beside the stairs. "This one will be yours, for a while at least. You see that monster-sized scanner there? That's for digitizing all our files. There's just too much paper floating around so we're going to hire someone to scan it all in so we can save it to disk. But until we do, this desk is yours."

Roland noted two things; firstly, his back would be to the ocean – that will have to change, he thought – and secondly, that even though he hadn't yet been told what his job would be, it obviously wasn't going to be digitizing files. He wondered what Adrian had in store for him. Mick had been frustratingly vague the night before but he had said that Roland would be starting off doing very basic tasks. He had delivered this news almost apologetically, but Roland knew that rote tasks that would keep him occupied and pass the time might turn out to be just what he needed for the time being.

Empty boxes with styrofoam packing lay strewn about, and on the surface of the desk lay a tangle of unconnected cables. "We honestly haven't got anywhere to put you just yet, and it looks like Garrett is still setting up your system."

An unshaven man sporting an earring had emerged from the doorway beside Slogan's desk and stood there, blinking a pair of deep green eyes. He looked to be in his late twenties and wore standard issue tropical attire – shorts, sandals, and a t-shirt with a short-sleeved, collared shirt over top. He was grinning slightly in a way that seemed almost permanent.

"How right you are. I still have to hook it up to the server and get you a power backup." He extended a hand. "I'm Garrett. You must be Roland. Don't mind the mess, it's always like this. You'll get used to it."

Roland didn't think it was any messier than anywhere else he'd worked, and said so. "Besides, there seem to be compensations."

"Yeah, well, sleep isn't one of them."

"You're obviously the computer guy."

"That's strange," said Garrett. "I'm not wearing my Dilbert tie."

"I used to work for IBM," said Roland. "I recognize that look of frustrated confusion."

Garrett laughed. "That could be any one of us." He looked around the room and yawned. "I'm going upstairs for a coffee. Liza's machine is screwed up again."

"She's here?" asked Mick.

"As always." Garrett pointed to the room he had emerged from as he mounted the stairs.

"And none too happy," added a disembodied voice from within.

"Ah, Liza. The new victim's here." Mick motioned for Roland to follow him. "Hey, you're here too," Roland heard him say.

Two women sat at desks facing each other. There were filing racks on casters everywhere, jammed together against the walls and completely covering the concrete mattress pedestal. Roland had noticed these building features in Mick's condo and had been told that virtually every place down here had them. "It makes it easy to decide where to put the bed," Mick had explained, "but of course nobody makes much money selling boxsprings to Mexicans."

Beyond the bedroom-cum-office lay a marble bathroom with a large tiled whirlpool tub. In front of a small balcony rested a folded blanket and a bowl of dog food. Facing Roland was an attractive, petite woman with dirty blond shoulder-length hair and lively eyes. She looked to Roland to be in her early forties, but he wondered if that was just because she seemed so full of energy and might in fact be a little older. She was wearing a colorful summer dress and expensive earrings, and was examining him over thick-rimmed reading glasses.

"Hello, Roland, nice to meet you," she said, and then swore softly at her computer screen. "It's this goddamn heat and humidity," she explained. "We have to replace the computers every few months because they just get trashed down here."

The woman opposite Liza sighed exaggeratedly. "Through no fault of the user, isn't that right, Liza?"

Liza peered through the stack of files between the two women and then at Roland as he tried to suppress a grin. She lowered her glasses a little and tilted her head. "Yes," she said authoritatively, "it is. Christ, you two are in cahoots already."

"I'm Roxane, and I don't have anywhere near the same kind of problems that Liza does."

"With your computer, anyway," Mick clarified.

"Hello, Roxane and Liza," said Roland. Roxane's eyes became very small when she smiled, which she did a lot, revealing white, even teeth. She looked younger than Liza and had dark hair past her shoulders.

"Are you staring at my tits?" she asked.

"Yes," said Mick.

"What?" exclaimed Liza.

"No," said Mick.

Roxane sighed. "I don't mean you, my friend." She indicated Roland by waving a pen at him. "You there. New guy."

"Not exactly," said Roland, laughing. "I'm staring at what's on them."

"Oh." Roxane feigned disappointment. "Men only want me for my dog. Story of my life."

She had a towel draped over her shoulder. A bleary-eyed little black-and-white creature was struggling up it to sit on her shoulder where it could meet Roland. It made little whimpering noises and bravely offered him a tiny paw. When Roland reached out to it, the dog bit his finger.

"This is Yoda," Roxane explained. "Adrian doesn't like him because he regards the house as his toilet, so you have to keep that door behind me closed. But he's a sweetie, aren't you?" She rested her cheek on Yoda's quivering little body. "He's a rat terrier/chihuahua cross."

"Why is he shaking like that?" Roland asked, withdrawing his finger and checking it for leaks.

Mick said, "He's a chihuahua. They shake."

"Here, hold him." Roxane proffered the diminutive animal. "He won't bite you again." The little dog climbed up Roland's chest and seated himself on his shoulder, where Roland held him with one hand. Yoda began munching nervously on Roland's earlobe.

"Have you met Adrian?" Liza asked.

Mick had been petting Yoda and was now trying to pry the animal's mouth away from Roland's ear. "No. We went down to Olas Altas for a coffee and basically just got here."

"Well, he's in his office. Catch him now, 'cause he's in a good mood."

Roland handed the whimpering Yoda back to Roxane, who was staring at her monitor. Roland noticed that it displayed a spreadsheet program and most of the lines of data were highlighted in red. As if reading his mind, she said, "The red ones are investors still waiting for payment. I have to track down what happened to their money. It's the end of February now and they still haven't got their check for this month. I wish these Norwegians would get off their asses and straighten this out."

"Norwegians? I thought we banked in Latvia," Roland said. Liza and Roxane looked at each other and then at Mick. "Come on, we'd better go," he said as he ushered Roland toward the door.

Roland scratched Yoda behind the ear as he turned away. "Nice meeting you," he said to the women. It had suddenly become uncomfortable in the room. Then Roxane spoke.

"How about now, new guy?" she asked.

"How about now what?"

"You staring at my tits?"

By now Roland was standing in the big common office area and could only see the back of her head over the chair. Yoda was looking at him through her hair. "Maybe next time," he said.

"Men," said Roxane. "They're all the same."

Roland closed the door and followed Mick along the sliding glass windows bordering the balcony to the open door at other side of the large room. Mick knocked on the door frame as they entered.

"Adrian? This is Roland, our new arrival."

To the right of the door was a large mahogany desk. On the side of it facing the room were stacks of papers and a fax machine, on the side against the wall was a hutch with two of its doors open, and in the middle sat a computer monitor. It was towards this that Adrian was facing. He didn't turn around right away, Roland noticed. There were ashtrays all over the desk, and beside one of them two large pill bottles lay on their side.

Adrian Winter was a very small, tired-looking man with disheveled, greying blond hair and flesh pulled so tight across his face that, despite some wrinkles, he bore a not-too-distant resemblance to a walking corpse. He was wearing a blue and green bathrobe and he moved very slowly. Roland found it amusing that Adrian was the brains of the outfit, for his head seemed a little too large for his body, but he cut this thought short after Adrian faced him. In that instant Roland saw that this was a man with a lot on his mind.

"Thanks for coming down here," he said. "Good to have you with us." He was smoking a cigarette and tugging on his earlobe as he spoke. When he smiled his eyes lit up, but during the time Roland would know him that smile seldom appeared unless he'd been drinking. Roland found he had to strain to hear what he was saying. He was to learn that this was Adrian's habitual way of speaking, either a deliberate effort to make sure people paid attention to him or a function of the cancer treatment operations he'd undergone which caused him so much pain that talking loudly was just too difficult.

"Thanks for having me," Roland replied. "Makes a nice change. I brought you some coffee, too," he added.

Adrian nodded his appreciation. "We go through a lot of it. You wouldn't think it, in a warm climate, but I'm up pretty early and by the time these guys get here –" he pointed his cigarette at Mick, "–I've already made two pots of it sometimes."

That figured, Roland thought. Adrian didn't look as though he slept much.

"Besides, it won't take you long to get used to it, and then you'll be reaching for a sweater while the tourists are taking off their shirts."

Mick spoke up. "How you feeling this morning?"

"Not bad," said Adrian. "Not bad at all." He sounded surprised at himself. "Woke up feeling almost normal." He smiled wryly. "But I think I'm going to go upstairs and get changed before the hordes appear." He got up to leave and edged his way past the two men, tugging on an earlobe again. "See you guys after breakfast. Nice to meet you, Roland, and thanks for the coffee." They had heard Liza becoming irritated in the other room. "Mick, I think Liza wants you."

"You sure?" Mick asked. "Normally when she swears it means she wants Garrett."

"She's not swearing, she's complaining. They're different."

He disappeared through the doorway. Roland heard his slippers shuffling on the marble and mounting the steps.

Mick pointed his thumb at Liza's office door. "I'll just be a second. Have a look around." He spun on a spotless white tennis shoe and left the room.

Amiable as Adrian had been, Roland immediately recognized that a man who remained completely calm while meeting someone in his bathrobe with his hair in total disarray was a force to be reckoned with. It was the kind of confidence which separated those who truly were in control from those who only wanted to look that way. Their total disregard for what other people thought of them was their immunity. Roland smiled inwardly and looked around the room.

Adrian's office had originally been designed as a sitting area for the bedroom that lay beyond it, in which two more desks sat shoved against the wall, their backs to the ocean. Generous windows looked out from a monstrous open ensuite and open dressing room sunken from the bedroom. Roland descended the steps.

Heavy wooden closet doors opened to reveal row upon row of expensive women's clothing. A freezer in the corner was crammed full of packages marked "Premium Alaska King Crab Legs", and leaning against that was a stack of cardboard cartons containing cans with Russian writing on which Roland recognized the words 'beluga' and 'caviar'. Piled in the middle of the floor were computers; or their boxes, at least. Spare printers, cables, keyboards and recordable CDs shared shelf space with some very rare movies Roland had heard of but never seen, and hidden in a corner under even more computer paraphernalia was a safe with an electronic lock.

He mounted the steps back up to the bedroom. Unlike the room Liza and Roxane shared, this one actually had a mattress on the pedestal. On it lay a portable CD player and a few colored notebooks, and on the night table beside it was a multi-line telephone. Roland smelled something organic and sickly sweet coming from one of the desks beside it. He continued to look around, and beside an amateurish oil painting of a family of lions under a tree he noted the most interesting feature of the room – a window high up in the wall and only a few feet square. At first Roland didn't recognize what he was looking at through it, but he knew he'd seen those blue tiles before. Just as it dawned on him, he heard footsteps behind him.

"Our little James Bond window into the swimming pool," Mick said in explanation. "We call this the Octopussy room. You'll notice it has a mattress." He was holding out something shiny. "These are keys to the front door of the Shack, and my apartment as well."

"Thanks." Roland took them and put them in his pocket. "Who's the crab meat fan?"

Mick raised an eyebrow. "That's Adrian. He has it flown in pretty regularly. Some of his friends are fans too, and they come over for dinner now and then."

"Same with the caviar?"

Mick nodded.

"Nice work if you can get it. Whose stash of weed do I smell?"

Mick eyed Roland steadily. "Could be Shelly's, could be Kevin's. They both work in this room." He paused, then added, "You snoop quickly. You some kind of ex-field operative?"

Roland smiled. "Are you kidding? I can't even drive a tractor."

"Drive a tractor," Mick repeated.

"I took a private investigator course some years ago but I never did anything with it."

"Oh, I get it. Operating in a field. I can't believe I didn't get it." Mick looked at his watch. "Come on, it's almost time for breakfast. We all seem to be late today."

They slowly made their way upstairs, and as they did so the intercom beeped and a female voice intoned, "*Brehkfazst*, everybody, *brehkfazst.*"

"She means 'breakfast', I suppose," said Roland.

"Yeah, so get out of my way." Roxane pushed past the two men.

"You know, the Chinese love to play tricks with their words," said Mick. "The way that it's a sung language lends itself to some amusing intentional misinterpretation."

"Congratulations for not tripping your tongue over that one," said Roland. They were at the top of the stairs now, looking at the city through the archways and listening to how the voices of those already seated at the table echoed in the huge house with the sound of the fountain as a backdrop.

"I was in China once," said Roland.

"Really? Were you working there?"

"No, I was looking for some old fighter airplanes that crashed in the jungle in World War Two."

Mick stared at Roland. "Do you ever go anywhere and just lie on the beach and then go home?"

Roland thought about this. "No, but one day I will."

"Did you like China?"

"It's filthy," said Roland. "That place is an ecological disaster waiting to happen, but I've never been treated better anywhere in my life. Really friendly, good people. Very different way of doing things, though."

"In that respect, Vallarta isn't the best place to get a feel for how Mexicans are in general," said Mick reflectively. "Here they aren't really jealous of the rich, so there aren't the same kinds of problems you see up north like in Tijuana or someplace – greed-motivated crimes, I mean. They're not unnecessarily suspicious of gringos with money."

Roland wasn't sure if being suspicious of the occasional gringo was an entirely bad idea, but he didn't say so.

Liza dug him in the ribs as she passed and held out a business card. "Here, new guy," she said. "You can use this house to receive your mail until you get your own place, and you can just show this card to a cab driver when you need to until you get the lingo down." She laughed; a loud, two-syllable sound that she choked off as though something had caught in her throat. Roland inspected the card. *Castillo Paraiso*, it said, with the silhouette of a palm tree and the address on Paseo de los Delfines. "Also some get-started money." She tucked a large roll of bills into his shirt pocket and took his arm.

"Come on," she said. "Didn't you guys hear the page? It's time for *brehkfazst*."

3
Digital Pagan

Roland pulled out a chair. The table was crammed with chopped fruit, boxes of cereal, baskets of buns and all kinds of fruit juice, and as he sat down Guadalupe approached with a plate of scrambled eggs and bacon. She patted him on the shoulder as she set it in front of him. Shyly she said, "You need to eat, sir," and then she glided away. As Roland looked at his plate and the table he realized it was true. He hadn't had an appetite for months and suddenly he was ravenous.

Not every seat was taken but there were people he hadn't met yet, nodding at him and waving cutlery in greeting if their mouths were too full to say hello. Except Kevin, of course, who said "Hey, how are ya" through a mouthful of Vector cereal. As Roland reached for some pineapple juice somebody pulled out a chair beside him, and when he looked over, a blond girl with blue eyes was smiling at him. She was dressed very simply – everyone was, he noticed, except Liza.

"Hi," said the girl. "I'm Shelly."

"I'm Roland."

"Have you met everybody?" she asked, buttering a piece of toast. Guadalupe was about to set a plate in front of her but she waved it away, saying something in Spanish. Guadalupe disappeared back into the kitchen to lean over the counter and wait for the next arrival.

"Not everyone, no. I met Kevin this morning, and Adrian as well, and I'm staying at Mick's place so of course I've met him. Liza and Roxane too." He was forgetting somebody. "Oh, and Garrett."

Shelly picked up a knife and pointed it towards a balding man with silver-rimmed glasses and a stout build who had arrived moments ago. Guadalupe was already offering him Shelly's rejected eggs. "That's Ken," she said. "He's not normally here this early. He does the phone contact with the members so sometimes he has to get up really early to talk to people in Europe, and other days he's not here til lunch. The guy with the long hair beside him is Eric. He answers emails, like your buddy Slogan." Eric laughed at a remark Ken made, an innocent, infectious giggle that bubbled up through a small gap between two prominent teeth and a smile that Roland figured probably came in very handy with girls. "Then there's Amy," Shelly continued, "and let's see...I think that's everybody."

Satisfied that she had done her duty, Shelly busied herself with collecting fruits and a bagel, which she slathered with pink cream cheese. Roland noticed as she bent over the table to reach for some orange juice that she was very thin.

Roxane had obviously been watching him. "Settle down, new guy," she said. "I saw you looking."

"I was just thinking that Shelly is very thin to be dumping that much cream cheese on her bagel, that's all," said Roland, trying to conceal his mild embarrassment. Shelly sat back down clutching her bagel and looked back and forth between Roland and Roxane.

Kevin spoke up. "The ankles, not the ass," he said. "You can always tell if a chick's gonna pork out if she's got big ankles."

Roland thought that was a pretty risky thing for Kevin to say, rotund as he was.

"Let's see *your* ankles," Liza said tartly, and when Kevin just stared at her she laughed, *ha HA!*, and said, "I thought so." Kevin gave her the finger and opened his mouth to display the last of his partly-chewed cereal. Liza didn't look away. She just shook her head. "You're a disgrace," she

43

muttered. Kevin picked up his coffee mug with both hands and stared out at the ocean.

Just as everyone was pushing back their plates and the conversation was waning, Slogan bounced in. There was an empty chair next to Roland which he scraped noisily across the marble to sit down in, then scraped noisily forward again. His t-shirt depicted an anonymous person in a suit smashing a vibrant neighborhood with a hammer, while next to it a faceless collection of apartment buildings was being constructed. Underneath that it said, '*Urban Renewal: The Latest And Greatest*'.

"Hullo all," he said, then turned to Roland. "How did you sleep last night?"

Roland was about to give a pat answer but Roxane cut him off. "How did you guys meet?" she asked, sipping her coffee.

Slogan spoke before he tucked into the eggs and bacon that Guadalupe had set in front of him. "Roland's brother was friends with my brother, and we've drifted around each other's lives every few years ever since."

"Scary thought," said Eric.

"Then we were in the CIA together."

"Mm-hmm," said Liza.

Shelly was staring out the window as Roland asked her, "How long have you been down here?"

She drew a breath and let it go slowly. "Five years."

"So you didn't come down here to work for this bunch."

Shelly smiled. "No, no. I just decided one day that I was going to leave. It wasn't til after I met these guys that I realized I'm from the same city as Slogan and pretty much everybody else here."

"Really? Then add one more to the pile."

Shelly's smile stayed the same. "Why, you are too?"

"Close enough," Roland acknowledged.

"Well, so is Ken. That makes me, you, of course Adrian and his wife Maxine, and Slogan. Kevin and Eric are from BC, same as Garrett. Roxane's from Oregon and the Secret Agent's from somewhere in California. It doesn't matter though, because you only think in US dollars anyway."

"What about pesos?" asked Roland. "Ever feel like a Mexican?"

"You pay in pesos, but you think in dollars."

"Of course. Sorry for interrupting you. You were telling me about coming down here."

"Right, yeah." Something in the way she said that made Roland regret he'd come back to it. "Well, I left a message on my boyfriend's answering machine saying goodbye, wrote a note for my roommate that she could keep all the stuff she couldn't sell as long as she sent me some money she owed me, then I went to the airport counter and bought a ticket for the first place they were flying to. Turned out to be here." She bit off a piece of bagel. "With a stopover in Seattle."

"You didn't want to stay in Seattle, I guess."

"Nah. I wanted to keep going 'til I didn't see snow."

Roland wondered if there was less to the snow and more to the boyfriend than she was letting on, but he didn't pursue the matter. It struck him that living in a place like Puerto Vallarta, with a view that seldom changed, could make time do strange things to one's perception of it. Five years could seem like minutes. He was hoping that on him it would have the opposite effect. It was his second day here and already the world he had left seemed so distant as to be nothing more than a mirage.

"Ever get homesick?" he asked.

"No," Shelly said, a little too quickly. "But sometimes you just want something simple that you can't normally get here, like a lemon or something. Plus you obviously can't go skiing. But in general, no, I'd never go back."

Slogan leaned in after Shelly had taken her coffee downstairs to work. "I know you just got here, but I've already heard rumors that we've hired more people. I think there's something fairly big about to happen. Sid tells me a lot, because he's Adrian's son so he's got pretty good firsthand info, but just between you and me I think sometimes he likes to pump it up a bit."

"Why would he do that?"

"I don't really know. Maybe smart people aren't always content with just being smart. The guy's a genius, but sometimes I think that he doesn't believe that's enough to get people to like him or something."

"It isn't."

Slogan ignored him. "If he doesn't know the answer to something he won't admit it. He'd rather make up something that sounds good instead. But he's great and I love him." He looked around the table again. "That's who's missing."

"Sidney works here?" asked Roland.

"No, but his fiancée does. Her name's Amy."

"And she's right behind ya, big boy," said a tall girl as she patted Slogan on the shoulder. She was wearing a denim skirt and a pink halter top, and wore her long strawberry hair in a ponytail. She had a great figure topped with fiery red hair and a large mouth. She looked decidedly Scottish, Roland thought. She pulled out a chair and sat down.

"I just got here and oh my *God*, I've been running around all *over* the place. This morning I went for a fitting for my wedding dress and we're *still* not done. We haven't got all the confirmations back yet but I know some of my friends are coming even though they haven't responded. I wonder why not, though down here at least they can say it got lost in the mail and they aren't necessarily lying." She turned to Roland and gave him a smile – brief, but genuine – and took a breath. "Oh, you're the new guy, hi, I'm Amy." She reached for some juice and picked up three cartons before finding one with any left in it. "Yeah, God, it's just been one thing after another and I am *starving*, thanks Guadalupe, did Maxine leave for San Diego yet or what?"

Slogan looked at Roland knowingly, as if that explained everything. Roland said hello to Amy and took his plate to the ladies in the kitchen. "*Gracias*," he said, but when they responded in Spanish he didn't know what to say. They laughed and said, "*Esta bien*, it's okay," and then as if reading a script and taking his cue, Secret Agent Mick appeared to escort Roland downstairs.

"So that's the crowd," he said. "What do you think?"

Roland wasn't sure yet so that's what he said, and then added, "It'll take some time." He didn't know how to explain to Mick that he really couldn't care less about making friends in Mexico; he was just there to explore something new and figure out what to do next.

Also he was wondering if Amy's demeanor resembled Sara's as she talked with her friends about her impending marriage. For all Roland knew Sara was married already and expecting a baby. How quickly things can turn, he thought. Six months before, she had put her arms around him and looked up at him lovingly and told him that as far as she was concerned their relationship was a marriage and they would work out their problems, not run away from them. He remembered thinking at the time what an easy thing that was for her to say, with another man waiting in the wings to pick up the slack. How noble people are when they have nothing to lose.

"I've been speaking to Liza, and probably the best way to start you out is to get you helping them with a few things," Mick said. Roland barely heard him. He was standing at the bottom of the stairs looking out at the ocean. "Okay," he responded distantly.

He blinked a few times and took a deep breath, then strode into the audit room. "You sent for me, wenches?" he asked in a deep voice.

"Yes, Space Slave," said Liza. She was quick; Roland liked that. "Take these papers and look at the number in the top right corner and then put them in the corresponding folder. Don't drink too much today because the numbers will all start to look the same."

"Fear not," said Roland. "Filing is my *life*."

"Another wild party man," Roxane commented. "Where do we dig up all these crazy ones?"

Roland read each document very quickly as he filed it, so quickly that if either of the women noticed, they didn't say anything. Finally he became curious enough to stop and direct the conversation towards a piece of paper he was holding.

"Okay, girls, what's with this?" he asked. "Apparently I've met everybody who works here now, and I know everyone's names. So why am I seeing file after file with these names on them? Who are these people?"

Liza regarded him over her reading glasses. Roxane didn't look up from her spreadsheet. "Who is James Nicholson?"

"That's Slogan," said Roxane eventually.

"O-kay," said Roland slowly. "So, who's Jonathan Kellerman?"

"That's Adrian," said Liza, returning to her accounting program. "So is Alexander Holt."

"I see," said Roland, as Roxane started to smirk. "And Tony Vanetti would be…"

"That's me," said Roxane. "Obviously."

Roland shook his head and blinked. "Who am I, then?"

Liza laughed. "You're Roland," she said, and mimicked Roxane. "Obviously."

Just then the door opened, and Yoda stirred from his reverie in the little dog bed. Guadalupe entered with another woman in tow, both carrying great lengths of colorful material. Liza immediately took off her glasses and stood up. Roland noticed that she wasn't a great deal taller standing than sitting, much like her brother. She became very businesslike and selected a few colors from the ones Guadalupe was holding, then when her companion stretched to her full height to demonstrate the length of the curtains, Liza said no, they'd have to be a little longer. The two women departed.

"I've bought a new place," Liza explained. "You can see it from here." She took Roland over to the balcony window and pointed out a condominium building across the bay. "Close to the marina, airport, everything. Nice place, called BayView Grand. You'll have to come over and see it sometime." She sat back down and Roland returned to his filing. He learned that both women were single, and while Roxane lived in an apartment under two men she called the Wanderers who gave tours of strip bars and sex clubs in the city, she lamented that no such service existed for women. She alluded to a boyfriend in passing but didn't elaborate.

"Well, what about the guys in the next room?" asked Roland. "Are they all single?"

"By God, I think he's on to something here," said Liza. "Whaddya think, Roxane?"

"I think he just might be."

Roland was mystified. "All this time you've had how many eligible bachelors on the other side of that door and it's never occurred to you to take advantage of the situation? And here you thought they all just wanted to walk by you to get to the washroom."

"Okay, that's it," said Roxane. "From now on, we're in control here. The next guy who walks through that door is going to be Bachelor Number One, and first on my list."

49

Garrett's timing couldn't have been better. Before he could say anything, Liza, who had seen him first, pointed to him and said, "That's it. You're Bachelor Number One, so you'd better shape up if you want to stay that way."

Garrett looked much as Roland had probably done when discovering that Roxane was really Tony. He smiled good-naturedly but had no idea what was going on.

Above the noise of the ensuing conversation Roland could hear Adrian's voice over the intercom on Mick's phone outside the door.

Mick poked his head in. "Roland, Adrian wants to see you upstairs by the pool."

Liza grew suddenly businesslike again. "Hey Roland, before you go, what were your moving expenses? And while you're up there, think about how you want to be paid."

"Moving expenses?" Roland echoed on his way to the door. "A tank of gas and dinner for my cousin and his wife. I stayed at their place the night before I flew down here. Hundred bucks maybe."

Roxane hooted. "That's interesting. Normally people figure it cost them a thousand bucks for a cab ride to the airport."

"And I'd like to be paid in rubles. I'm going to fly to Russia or Ukraine or somewhere and get me a bride. A smart, romantic, pretty girl who is kind and can read Nabakov to me at bedtime in the original Russian."

"With thin ankles," said Kevin as he pushed Roland aside on his way to place some papers on Liza's desk. He didn't say excuse me.

Roland made his way through the main office, and once upstairs he saw Adrian sitting by the pool. He had changed into a bright multicolored shirt and white pants and was adjusting his sunglasses as he smoked a cigarette and looked out over the city. Roland pulled up a cushioned rattan chair and joined him at the little table.

"So, Roland," said Adrian. "Welcome to Vallarta, and our little club."

"Thank you." Roland relaxed into the chair. "You've got a nice place and a very interesting setup here."

Adrian nodded. He stubbed out his cigarette and lit another before he spoke again. "What has everyone told you about Cyberia?" he asked.

Roland thought about this and decided that Mick had probably said too much the night before. Slogan had also mentioned that he had told Roland more than he needed to know when he was offering him this job, so he decided not to give a complete answer. Adrian was tugging at his earlobe and waiting for Roland to speak.

"Well," he said, "Mick told me a few things last night, and I've picked up tidbits here and there. Nobody really seems to know what they can tell me and what they can't. Obviously there's a need for secrecy but I'm not sure that even Mick knows exactly why."

Adrian looked thoughtful, as though filing this comment away for future reference. Then he said, "Slogan tells me that you asked him if what we were doing was legal. You asked him if it was a scam."

"That's right."

"Where we come from, Roland, what's a scam?"

Roland was taken aback by this question. He hadn't considered that there might be more than one kind. "A scam is where somebody hands over money or property expecting something in return, in this case a return on their investment, and doesn't get one," he replied.

"Then our club is not a scam," said Adrian firmly. "Further to that, keep in mind that honesty depends on what your definitions are."

It was all too easy to imagine Sara and her fiancé saying that. "What do you mean?"

"I mean, when I say it's not a scam, when people put money into our club expecting the return that we offer, they get it. There are exceptions, mostly because some of the banks we have to deal with are not exactly professional at the best of times, but we make sure it all gets straightened out."

"How long have you run this club?"

"A couple years," Adrian answered vaguely. "In the Bahamas for a while, then here."

"Why did you leave the Bahamas?"

Adrian was slow to respond. Roland had noticed that he often took time formulating his answers.

"I really liked it, but it was too violent. I just ended up not feeling safe anywhere in the Caribbean at all, actually. Then one night I was out with a friend having dinner and a man walked up to him and shot him right there in the restaurant. Just shot him. Blood everywhere, a real mess. The shooter just walked out and the police never caught him. In the middle of a crowded fucking restaurant and they never found him. Nobody knows who he was."

"That must be very heavy." Roland was surprised that the news hadn't shocked him.

"Well, that's what clinched it. Packed up my wife's bags the next day and put her on a plane. I told her to get a hotel, I'd follow. I put my house up for sale, bundled up everything I could find and got the hell out. If I'd been thinking clearly I would have done things a little differently when I left, but at least I'm here alive."

More than you can say for your friend, thought Roland, wondering what he had been involved in that would have made someone want him dead so publicly. "What would you have done differently?" he asked.

Adrian thought about this. "I suppose... I could have just thought it through a little better. It would have saved me time and money if I had, but I didn't allow myself to think of anything but leaving. I think I got screwed on the sale of my house because of it, and I left some stuff behind that I ended up wanting later on."

Roland mulled this over as Adrian continued distantly, "Also, any time you leave a place abruptly you have to deal with what you feel about it."

"Why here? Why Vallarta?" Roland inquired, leaning back in his chair and noticing how different the city looked now that the sun was strong.

"It's a nice place," Adrian replied agreeably. "We'd been on vacation here before and we liked it. Good people, the city is nice and small; it's an interesting place. It's managed by smart people who think long term. They don't sell out what they want most for what they want now; not like most other places in Mexico in that respect. Hell, not like most places in the *world* in that respect. No matter where you are, there's always something under the surface if you know where to look, but here what you see is what you get, and that's reassuring."

Roland found this curious. Surely Adrian understood that Cyberia was itself the thing in Puerto Vallarta's underneath; the very thing people would find if they came here to scratch the surface. Roland had not even been there for twenty-four hours and already he understood that.

Adrian was looking at him intently. "I could never go back home, if that's what you mean," he said. "They dish it out to the rest of the world but they sure can't take it. The weather up north, the tight-assed people, the laws...fuck, they've got a law for everything. Every single thing that happens has to have a law attached to it or they don't feel safe. They are the least self-reliant people in the world." He stubbed out his cigarette rather violently and lit another. Roland noticed that he always kept a lighter in the same hand as the cigarette he was smoking. "Go back to a country where you need a license to take a piss?" Adrian continued.

"No thanks. I prefer my freedom." He began to alternate his attention between the ocean and his cigarette. "That's something you'll learn about here."

"Freedom?" asked Roland.

"Yeah. And the more you have it, the more you'll realize you didn't before. It's why all these fuckin' guys in Timbuktu or wherever spend all the money they make from herding sheep on AK-47s."

Roland laughed, though he wasn't sure if he was supposed to. "That's not a religious thing?"

"Sure," said Adrian. "And underneath all that is oil, of course. But keep asking yourself, what are they fighting over? In the end, it's about who has control and who doesn't. Believe me, Roland, the only things in this world worth a damn are freedom from others and what you've earned."

Roland had been looking at the beach, but now he turned his attention to Adrian, who waved his cigarette. "Freedom from others is ultimately what freedom is, and by what you've earned, I don't just mean money. I mean there is a price for absolutely everything, and you have to pay it to get what you want. There's no way around that, and that's why back home everybody thinks they have freedom when really it's only license. You can do what the government allows you to do, and no more. But because everybody's so concerned with taking the link away between freedom and responsibility it's easy to make that mistake. The more control you want over your own life the more responsibility you have to accept, but everywhere you go somebody is encouraging you to blame somebody else for your problems. Preferably somebody you can sue. So the less responsibility people acknowledge, the more freedom belongs only to those who are responsible, and to the rest, license looks like freedom. But it isn't."

Roland said nothing. He was thinking of the price he'd paid for his time with Sara.

Adrian absently watched the ash from his cigarette fall onto the stone patio. "Have you ever read the Declaration of Independence?"

Roland nodded. "We did compare and contrast essays between that and Marxist writings at school."

"Those founding fathers were the most loving, honest and strong people this world has ever known, but the country they built has forgotten them. Besides, there are lots of places much more free than the States but a lot less publicized. People think money makes the world go around, but if they stopped to consider what they want that money for..."

"Freedom." Roland said it because it was obvious that Adrian wanted to know if Roland understood him. He watched as a slight breeze picked up the ash from the patio and carried it away.

Adrian was looking at Roland again. "I've said a bit too much for you, haven't I?" he asked. "I'm always like this when I wake up not feeling like I want to die."

Roland nodded. "Mick told me you've had a rough time with cancer lately," he said sympathetically; then, fearing that Adrian might mistake his concern for condescension, he added, "He told me not to bother asking if you want to play beach volleyball for a while yet."

Adrian smiled broadly. Roland liked his smile. It transformed him from a man in almost constant physical pain into a man with playful mischief on his mind. He looked at his watch and Roland caught the unspoken message, but there was something else he wanted to ask.

"So you say this is a club, yes?"

"Uh-huh," said Adrian.

"I understand we have some cease-trading and desist orders against us in various US states."

"Some Canadian provinces too," said Adrian, regarding him coolly, cigarette between his fingers. "But it doesn't amount to much. It means we can't advertise or conduct business in those places, but we don't do that anyway. Our members do a lot of word-of-mouth advertising for us and we have a website, but obviously we can't control which states that website appears in and which it doesn't. Our business is here and in Panama, and that's it. Those are the laws that apply to us."

"The website says we trade a kind of banking debenture," Roland continued. Mick had told him that last night but Roland hadn't seen the website himself yet.

"That's right, yeah," said Adrian. His cigarette hadn't moved.

"So when people invest, are they buying a membership in the club or are they buying these debentures?"

After a pause Adrian asked, "What do you think the difference would be?"

"Well," said Roland carefully, "I'm no lawyer, but if Cyberia is a club, then it can act like any other club, I would say. I mean, if members want to put their money into it and expect some sort of dividend, that's up to them. Show your membership card and get a dividend instead of a discount, that kind of thing. But if we're offering securities, there are a lot of regulations that we are going to have to comply with, right?"

"We're a club," said Adrian simply. "Says right there on the website, 'Cyberia Investment Club'. Our members are each responsible for reporting their own income to their own governments. We don't divulge who these members are or how much they've made from us. That's why the secrecy; it's a privacy privilege. Besides, we're in Mexico. The laws are different here." He waved his cigarette dismissively. "No government on earth is going to make us snitch on our members." He glanced at his watch again.

As principled as his answer seemed to imply he was, Roland found himself more interested in what Adrian hadn't said than what he had. But he also knew that he had pressed enough for one day; especially his first day, and he noticed that behind him, standing between the columns waiting for permission to approach, were two men in dark suits.

He pushed back his chair. "I can see you have an appointment, but can I ask you one more thing?"

"Shoot."

"How do we as employees become members of the club?"

Adrian shook his head. "You are not allowed to invest. You are also not allowed to refer anybody in. No friends, no family members, nothing." Then he gave a smile that looked a little too forced for Roland's comfort. "You're treated well enough and paid well enough without it."

Roland had the feeling that Adrian wanted to say something else, but eventually he just nodded at nothing in particular.

"Good talking to you, Roland," he said. "Now please excuse us." He motioned for the suits to approach. One was Mexican and seemed uncomfortable in his Guccis as he stepped down onto the patio, but the other was relaxed and very European-looking and was about the same height and build as Roland. He smiled at Roland from behind his sunglasses and nodded as they passed.

Roland entered the house but he didn't go downstairs. He still felt a little overwhelmed at how different everything was from things at home...his old home, anyway. He stood beside the bright yellow and blue and green sofa and watched the small boats on the ocean and listened to the happy chatter of the ladies in the kitchen, already making preparations for lunch. He liked the sing-song inflection of their Spanish, finding it comforting in a way he didn't understand and didn't try to. He knew that he liked the complete absence of 'ums', 'ahs', and 'likes' that made some native English speakers sound like schoolchildren still struggling through their third-grade reader, but it was more than that. Maybe he liked it just because it was different, but he hoped not. Novelty had an annoying habit of wearing off like the plating on cheap jewelry.

He thought about what Adrian had said. Apart from revealing a refreshingly simple view of world affairs he had said little about Cyberia and even less about Roland's actual job itself. Obviously he would be expected to find his own niche within the club. Or make one.

Far away on the horizon at the mouth of the bay, visible now that the slight morning haze had lifted, Roland noticed some small islands. Standing on Mick's balcony the night before he had seen lights there, and assumed them to be ships. Guadalupe, passing behind him with a broom, tapped him on the right shoulder. He turned but saw only Adrian on the patio with the two men. He heard her giggling on his left.

"*Hola, señor,*" she said.

"*Hola,* Guadalupe. *Como esta usted?*" he replied, his tongue twisting with the unfamiliar sounds it made. Her jaw dropped and she poked him in the ribs with her free hand.

"Ah, you speak Spanish!" she said, delighted.

"Not really," Roland confessed. "Just enough to get me into trouble."

"*Que?*" said Guadalupe. Apparently her English was about as good as Roland's Spanish.

"*Un poquito,*" said Roland. "A little bit."

"Aaah." She drew out the word like chewing gum. Then she patted herself just below the neck. "*Su maestra d'español,*" she said. "I teach you Spanish, you teach me English. Ask is okay with Adrian, I teach you."

"*Si,*" said Roland. "*Esta bien.*" He was wondering how to tell her to give him some time to settle in, but on reflection he knew that he disliked easing into things. He preferred to jump in headfirst or not bother at all. Sometimes that got him into a lot of trouble. She sensed his hesitation and said, "*Una semana*, one week, then we start."

Roland nodded and was about to speak but she tapped his shoulder with the broom handle. "*Bien*," she said, satisfied. "*Hasta luego*. That is 'see you later'." She clutched her broom and immediately started talking loudly to Ava the cook and another woman, who had been watching the two from behind the large kitchen counter. Roland made his way to the stairs, and as he disappeared down them he caught sight of Guadalupe as she waved. "*Hasta la vista*," she called out, and the other two ladies joined in with, "Baby!", and dissolved into fits of laughter. This, Roland thought, must be how cats feel when they fall off the television in a room full of people watching.

Before long it was time to take a break. There weren't any formal times for anything, much to Roland's delight; not for beginning work, and certainly not any official say on when one should go home, as he was to learn very soon, but everyone sensed when they'd been working long enough to warrant a few minutes on the balcony to soak up the sun and watch the occasional school of dolphins as they leaped about in the bay. Roland noticed that Liza was still glued to her computer but everyone else downstairs had migrated outside and was talking and smoking; either cheap Mexican cigarettes or hastily-rolled joints. Eric passed Roland on his way to the stairs. "Hey FNG, you want a beer?"

"Sure," said Roland.

"Well, come on. Everybody else wants one too and I can't carry them all myself."

He led Roland upstairs to a room behind the kitchen where a huge refrigerator, even bigger than the one in the kitchen, proved full of different kinds of beer and soft drinks. Beside it were a washer and dryer and an ironing table, and above those were shelves of very expensive wines of all description. Reds, whites, champagnes, everything.

"Nice," Roland observed as he studied the labels. "This stuff's worth a lot of money."

"Is it? I just like my beer." Eric was still raiding the refrigerator. "Here, carry these." He held out four bottles and closed the fridge with his foot. One of the maids walked past and, upon noticing their cargo, waved a finger at them. "I'm very thirsty," Eric explained. She laughed.

Back downstairs on the balcony, Roland listened to the conversation between his coworkers. Amy was gracious enough to try to include him, but Kevin talked incessantly and Roland didn't feel like talking anyway. Kevin either rattled on about his sunburn, which for someone with his red hair and fair complexion wouldn't have been difficult to get, or the fact that he was playing at a bar that weekend.

"Playing what?" asked Roland. It could have been anything, from guitar to drinking games.

"I deejay sometimes," Kevin explained. "I brought down all my stuff from home and I'm going to spin this weekend. You should come."

Roland could tell that he didn't mean it, but he appreciated the obvious effort Kevin had to expend in order to be nice to anyone so he just said thank you.

"On that note," said Amy, "you have to come to my wedding as well. It's going to be just awesome, a sunset wedding at a friend's house right on the beach. Friday the twenty-third." She smiled at him. "If you work fast, you can get yourself a date by then."

Roland didn't know what to say. Amy was sociable but that didn't mean she was genuine, and it would have been a stretch to invite a complete stranger to her wedding just out of obligation. He had heard her swearing at her computer and insulting the members who wrote her asking even the most obvious of questions. He didn't like anyone who slighted people who weren't there to defend themselves, but on this subject he knew he was still touchy because of things he knew Sara had said about him. He just thanked her for the invitation and left it at that.

One by one people trickled back to their desks. Roland was about to do the same, because Garrett had finished setting up his system while he had been upstairs with Adrian, but Slogan motioned him to stay as he brought a cigarette out from a fresh pack. They leaned on the balcony railing together. There was a sailing yacht looking perfectly at home on the ocean.

Behind them they heard Eric's voice, and Roland turned to see his face sandwiched between two sliding doors. "Hey, um, just so FNG knows, please keep these closed, okay? 'Cause even the slightest breeze is enough to make a mess of paper everywhere."

"Sorry," said Roland. Eric withdrew. The doors closed behind him with a dull thud.

Slogan gestured at the house across the street.

"Adrian bought that place," he said. "A million bucks, give or take."

"Really."

"Roxane's going to live on the bottom floor. It's beautiful; huge patio out front with a nice pool. Upstairs has its own separate entrance and there are two bedrooms with ensuites." Slogan tapped his cigarette and the ash fell onto the street to join hundreds of discarded butts lying between the cobblestones.

"Who's going to live upstairs?" Roland asked.

"Don't know yet," said Slogan. "I think Eric might want to; him and Kevin. They share an apartment at the end of Olas Altas at Vista del Sol, same building I used to live in. Not the same condo though; Garrett and Ken live in that one now."

"Do you miss it?" Roland asked. "I mean, you have to pay your own rent now that you're living with the wife."

"Yeah, nine hundred bucks' worth, but I don't miss it. I have my dogs and a swimming pool on the roof," Slogan replied. "And it's not like I can't afford it."

Roland was surprised. "There's a pool on your place? It looked a little too…"

"Old?" Slogan suggested.

"Yeah."

"Mexico surprises you."

They heard Yoda whimpering and whining and looked over to where the little dog stood on the balcony that adjoined Liza and Roxane's office. He was leaning up against the glass as he watched the two men. "Here, boy," said Slogan, and Yoda started running in circles.

After a time Slogan asked, "So what do you think of everything?"

Roland considered how best to tell him. He said that so far he loved Vallarta and already it was hard to imagine going home, but when Mick had offered his impression of Roland's expectations that morning he hadn't been far wrong. "I don't really understand everything yet, or everybody."

"I know." Roland didn't expect him to say that, but he let him continue. "If Kevin was any less amusing than he is annoying, we would have hurled him off this balcony the day he got here. Conversations with him are impossible because he sees everything as a personal attack. As for anyone else; well, I used to go to college with Garrett and that's why he's here, he's a good person and a good friend. Mick and Roxane knew each other before they started here, and nobody's sure if Shelly is Adrian's girlfriend or not. Probably not, but keep in mind that just because you might see them in a certain way doesn't mean that that's how they really are."

Roland was sorely tempted to say 'I think it is' but his friend did have a point. Besides, Roland wasn't himself after the strain of his past year anyway. He knew that people were perceiving him differently from how he really was, so he didn't feel that he had a right to judge. His own clouded perception of himself meant that his perception of others was equally vague, and he would have to live with that until he could trust his intuition again.

Most importantly, though, he knew that this was what he needed. There was no doubt that getting away from the house he'd shared with Sara and all the memories it contained was a good idea. He knew there had been enough holes punched in him that any experience which made him think on his feet and discover his wholeness and self-reliance again would be invaluable.

Secondly, the people he worked with seemed competent enough but not very motivated, and daunted by Adrian. Living with the constant pain of cancer and the effects of its surgery gave him a lot of leeway with his temper, which Roland respected, but in all the time he knew him he never so much as raised his voice to Roland. His coworkers also seemed disappointed that Roland hadn't been awestruck or intimidated by the amount of money floating around Cyberia and because he didn't seem interested in joining them in the bars every night, but he was there to make as much money as he could and reclaim himself during the process. In that respect Puerto Vallarta was going to be the same to him as if he'd landed in Melbourne or Zurich. Roland knew it would be hard to avoid alienating these people, but he didn't care.

In addition to this, whatever Adrian was up to probably fell into the category marked 'questionable', but Adrian had been adamant that the investors got paid, and in Roland's eyes – for now at least – that was enough to keep him around.

And lastly, the conversations in which the Secret Agent and Slogan had mentioned Adrian's new yacht and the purchase of real estate such as the beautiful house across the street made something else obvious. Roland had arrived just when Cyberia was reaching critical mass, the point at which the speed and momentum that everyone had worked so hard to achieve had finally arrived. Now the only questions were where to direct it; and more important, how carefully.

"Well, I should go inside and look busy for a while," said Slogan. "You're fairly well oriented now, right?"

"I think so," said Roland. "Thanks for bringing me down here. I owe you."

"Well, you'll have to come visit us one night. Come over for dinner this weekend."

"Sure," said Roland. "Thanks."

Slogan looked at Roland for a while. "Give everyone a chance," he said. "You'll never regret that. And don't worry too much about what anyone thinks of you or how you do your job. If Adrian's happy with you, that's really all that matters."

Well, thought Roland, if anyone would know, it would be Slogan. He had known Adrian long enough.

Roland went to his desk, and under Shelly's instruction he learned how to enter information into the database. She left him with a stack of membership application faxes to input and said, "If you need me, just give me a shout."

Roland played around with the program. There were so many things it could tell about the members – basic information such as name and address, of course, but also how much money they had invested and how much return they had made so far. He probably wasn't supposed to be snooping, but he couldn't help it. Eventually that's what he had to tell Liza when he noticed she'd been standing over his shoulder watching him for some time.

"It's why I got my pilot's license," he told her. "All those buttons and switches, it's just too much fun. Same thing here."

"I'd just stick to the job, new guy," she said.

"Well, what's all this stuff there for then?" Roland asked defensively.

Liza chewed on the end of the arm of her glasses and looked at Roland. Finally she put them on.

"Well, if you have to rummage through the files, it's best that you at least know what you're doing." She leaned over his shoulder and clicked the mouse around. "This here," she said, pulling up a screen Roland hadn't seen before, "is where you enter members' payments. You input how much they sent in and it calculates how much return they get and when. Now this," – she closed that screen and opened another – "is where you go to make adjustments and enter things like debt recovery. You'd do that if a member owed us money for something."

"Like what?"

Liza straightened up. "Like if they say they sent in money and we say they didn't."

Roland said, "I imagine that happens all the time."

"Less than you think," Liza replied. "Most of the problems we have aren't with the members, they're with the banks. Every possible thing they can screw up, they do. We're here all the time, or at least I am, because every day there's a hundred messages saying 'did you get my money?' and we have to look for it in every wire transfer we've got that month. It's infuriating."

"So when a member says they sent money but it doesn't show up in the system, the first thing you assume is that a bank screwed up somewhere?"

"If they say they wired it, yes. If it's a check it's not so easy. But as soon as they say they've wired us, we go to that first screen I showed you and enter it as an investment pending. Then when we get the wire we go in and mark it as a paid investment."

"Whereas with a check, you just go in and mark it paid when you receive it."

"Right." Then Liza laughed; just that brief, short, unmistakable laugh. "Now you know what you can do, new guy, and you also know what you can't." She took off her glasses and pointed them at him. "*Lemme 'splain jhou someting*," she said playfully in her best Mexican accent. "You stay the hell out of those screens. Accounting is my job; mine and Roxane's."

Roland nodded. "I need a glass of wine," Liza announced, and disappeared up the stairs.

Roland continued staring at the screen. He understood; not only Liza, but how unbelievably simple the whole thing was.

Yoda escaped from the accounting office and rocketed across the marble, his tags jangling like spare change as he furiously mounted the stairs and disappeared as fast as his short little legs could carry him. There was a pause during which no one said anything. Then the intercom beeped. "Lonch, everybody, lonch," said the incorporeal voice.

"*Lonch*," said Eric, imitating it.

"They sure cooked him quick," said Kevin, who had watched Yoda's progress from his office door.

Roland joined the others on the steps, his mind miles away from where he saw his feet beneath him.

4

The Wanted and the Unwanted

The easiest person to deceive is one's self.
> -Edward George Bulwer-Lytton,
> "The Disowned"

CIA Mick often worked late. In fact, he was at work until sundown more often than not, and Roland usually stayed and worked with him.

On some evenings, Roland stuck around just because the sunsets were so breathtaking that he didn't want to miss them. Something magical replaced the workday hum at that gentle time, something in the colossal house after everyone had gone, and the white walls became soft and subtle diffusers of the glorious oranges and reds that burst through the huge windows and raced up the stairs.

The work itself wasn't fascinating to him. Roland had held many more interesting jobs than filing documents and entering data, but he was mesmerized by the ethos of this new experience. Apart from tuning up the website now and then he still wasn't exactly sure what Mick did. Nobody was, and because their desks were across the big room from each other Roland didn't have a chance to see his computer. But they talked and joked as they worked, Roland entering data from membership applications faxed in from Kenya, England, the United States, New Zealand, everywhere. He studied the names and the handwriting on the faxes and tried to imagine what kind of people these were and what their home towns looked like.

One night very soon after his arrival he joined Mick and Roxane for dinner at a little place on Olas Altas. Afterwards they wandered up to the Pagina en el Sol, the corner café/

bookstore where Roland and Mick went every morning with the strange crowd of stragglers they belonged to and didn't know it. Roxane sat down and took Yoda out of her purse. She tied his leash to the railing beside them and he jumped around, straining to sniff every ankle he could. Mick and Roland brought coffee and coconut cake for themselves and Roxane. Suddenly Yoda wasn't so interested in people's ankles. From behind them a voice called, "Mick!"

For an instant Roland was sure both Mick and Roxane braced themselves for something, but when Mick turned around he said, "Hey, how are you?" Then to the other two he explained, "I know this guy. I designed a web site for him and I want to chat for a while. I'll be back." He bent down to scratch Yoda behind the ear. "You leave my cake alone, okay, little guy?" Yoda didn't respond, but as soon as Mick left he usurped his chair. Roxane moved the cake to the other side of the table. Yoda licked his lips and whined.

Roxane stirred her coffee thoughtfully. Without looking up she asked, "So what's your story? What brings you to sunny Puerto Vallarta?"

Roland was about to make a smartass comment about playing piano in a whorehouse to pay off his tab until they discovered he had no talent, but decided against it. He could sense that she was more interested in his response than Mick had been when asking the same question, and that she wasn't just making conversation.

Yoda jumped off Mick's chair and went back to scrutinizing ankles.

"It's kind of a long story." Roland didn't know where to begin, and he was uncomfortable. He barely talked at all anymore.

"Well, obviously there's a woman involved." Roxane produced and lit a cigarette. Roland didn't know she smoked.

"What makes you say that?"

"Because you avoid talking about yourself when it comes to women in your life."

"Maybe they're too boring to warrant talking about. Or maybe I am."

Roxane blew smoke out her nose. "I'd hardly call you boring. I heard you tell Mick you went traipsing around in the Chinese jungle looking for some old airplanes. You also told Liza and me that you spent your first year of school in Australia and sang in a rock band and all sorts of other stuff."

"I was just making conversation. Besides, you just finished saying I don't talk about myself." He took a forkful of cake and tried to taste it. He was pretty sure it was delicious but suddenly he was too nervous to notice.

Roxane waved her cigarette around and slapped her lighter down on the table. "When people make conversation they talk about their gall bladders and the price of gas. I said you don't talk about women."

Roland swallowed his cake and reached for his coffee. He thought it was a very good policy not to discuss women with any woman. "Okay, so what brings *you* here?"

"Don't change the subject." Roxane wagged a finger at him. "Plenty of time for that. I'm trying to find something out here."

"Find out what exactly? About my love life?"

She frowned impatiently and sighed. When she spoke again the levity in her voice was gone. "Roland, there are only two kinds of people who come to live here in Puerto Vallarta." She brought the cigarette between her lips and inhaled, then blew the smoke up towards the blue awning where green vines strangled the decorative iron supports. She didn't take her eyes off Roland. "The wanted, and the unwanted. I want to know which one you are. You're here with us away from the travel brochures in the underneath of this town; a strange underneath because really, we're on top.

Not much can touch us. Creditors chasing you? Jealous husband? Give it up, mister."

Roland was about to say, 'or what?' but decided against it. He could see that she was sincere.

"Yes, there's a woman involved."

"Ah *ha*! I knew it."

"What about you? A man in your past?"

"I already told you, plenty of time for that later."

"Is this my security hearing? Am I being vetted?"

"Hardly," she replied. "The only credentials you need to work here are an ability to swear and drink a lot. *A propos* of that, actually, you seem a little underqualified. But no matter. Pray continue, but keep your voice down. This is a very small town."

Roland was already almost halfway through his cake. He had idly pulled a small piece from it and when Roxane was aiming her cigarette at the ashtray again he held it under the table. Presently he felt tiny teeth snatch it from him.

"Don't do that," said Roxane, still tapping her cigarette. "He'll get fat."

"He can't get fat," Roland objected. "He uses too much energy shaking."

Roxane stared at him, impassive. Roland had been secretly waiting for Mick to come back to the table so they could talk about something else but there he sat, chatting away with a short man sporting stringy grey hair and bulky sandals. Roland suddenly wanted a stiff drink. He looked back at Roxane.

"Okay," he said, sipping his coffee. "Yes, there *was* a woman involved but that was some time ago now."

Roxane gazed at him and exhaled that grey smoke. Roland watched it curling away. Sara had smoked.

"She ended it with me because she was seeing somebody else, took me back when I asked her to, then lied several times about breaking it off with him. Finally I couldn't take it anymore and asked her to leave. Three weeks later they got engaged."

"What kind of relationship was it?"

Roland thought about this. "When we first started seeing each other, lots of time in the bedroom. That's pretty standard, I guess, but all Sara talked about was her past boyfriends and how many men she'd slept with. That's the only language she spoke, so that's how I talked to her. Anyway, after we'd been together about eight or nine months we bought a house in a small town that belonged to my grandparents, just in time to endure a pretty terrible winter. Sponge-bathing at the kitchen sink because we weren't finished renovating the bathroom yet, up at four-thirty in the morning to get to work in the city on time, tough stuff. To top it off, our dog froze to death in a violent blizzard. We went through a lot together."

"I'm waiting for the part when things get better," Roxane said. She was watching Yoda, who was deciding whether or not to chase his tail.

"Summer came. Sara quit her job in the city and got one in a town closer to us, which is mostly what inspired me to quit mine. The job I replaced it with was in another city, mind you, but most of my work I could do from home so that's why I took it. I wanted to spend every waking second with her. We explored every little back road we could find, stopped in at little teahouses tucked away everywhere, shared some dreams and made some friends in town."

"Excuse me while I stick my finger down my throat. Haven't I seen this on an old TV show?"

Roland sniffed. "Joke if you want to, but in all this the most incredible thing happened."

"The town drunk cleaned up his act."

Roland shook his head. "Better. When I met Sara she was a hurt and angry girl. Very angry. And I don't know what it was – I'd like to think it was my love, but the way things worked out she might debate that – anyway, she just absolutely came alive. All that armor plating dropped off and I got to see what she was really like. I'd known it would happen all along but it amazed me anyway. She was loving, she took pleasure in the tiniest little things and she would talk with me at night for hours. The garden was in full bloom and she was in her element there. I learned a lot from her, and I envied how free she had become. In fact, the more of her friends I talk to, the more I realize that not one of them knew her the way I did."

Yoda decided to chase his tail after all, and within seconds he had his leash wrapped around Roxane's chair and bumped his head on her leg. He barked once at the offending obstruction and pulled at his leash. Roxane bent down to untangle it. As she held the little dog steady she asked, "Was it during this particular wonderful, romantic summer that she screwed around on you with this guy?"

"Thanks," Roland muttered. "I needed the reminder."

"Just getting my chronology right." Finished with Yoda, she reattached the leash to the wrought iron railing.

"I think it only happened the one time that summer, and then not again until last year. I had gone to visit a friend down south. Sara was eternally suspicious–"

"–Like all promiscuous women," Roxane interrupted, an edge to her voice.

"Okay," Roland conceded slowly. His coffee finished, he looked around as if expecting someone at the next table to offer him theirs. "Suspicious, yes, so I think she slept with him to get the jump on me, so to speak."

"So that if you came back and had screwed around on her, she wouldn't feel like such a fool."

"I think so, but I wasn't there. I don't have proof of that."

Roxane snorted. "She married him, didn't she? I'd say that's enough proof."

"I guess."

"Don't guess. Either she married somebody that she'd only had a romantic relationship with for however long it took you to make up her mind for her plus the three weeks after you showed her the door, or you were taken for a longer ride than you know."

Roland pondered this. "Let's put it this way," he said at last. "In the grand scheme of things it's irrelevant whether they actually slept together, but something happened between them that weekend which made it inevitable that we would end the way we did." He was about to add that he'd known it at the time, had known it so surely that he'd felt sick while at a restaurant the night it happened and had to pull the truck over to the side of the road on the way home the next day long enough to figure out why he was nervous and shaking and crying, because he had picked up on the signals Sara hadn't known she was sending about how guilty and upset she was, but he doubted Roxane would understand this and he didn't feel like trying to explain it.

Roxane sipped her coffee. "Why didn't you do anything about it that first time?"

Roland forced a smile. "I knew it would happen again. In the meantime that obviously was the biggest reason why I didn't ask her to marry me, and I just wanted to enjoy being with her for as long as it lasted."

Roxane shook her head. "Love really is blind." She had barely touched her cake. Roland's was gone and he was wiping the plate with his fork. "So what happened? In the end, I mean."

Roland took a deep breath. "On top of all this I spent too much time wondering whether she would be as faithful to me as I would be to her, and that interfered with building up the confidence to ask her to marry me. Ultimately she just didn't want to wait anymore. Besides, I knew I wasn't mature enough to be a husband yet anyway. Not the kind of husband and father I want to be."

Roxane snorted. "You don't have to be mature to marry somebody, Roland. Or to have kids, for that matter. There's no lifeguard at the gene pool."

"I know, but it's whether or not you're ready and mean it that decides which half of the divorce statistics you end up in."

Roxane blew smoke out her nose again. "I suppose the road to hell really is paved with good intentions."

"So is the road to heaven if things work out in your favor." Roland toyed with his mug. "After a while I got a different job that took me away a lot. I got an apartment in the city because I had to work all kinds of stupid hours, but I came home as often as I could. I quit the job and came home for good when I realized what it was costing me, but by then the damage was done. Sara needed someone and didn't tell me how badly."

"'Someone'? Not you in particular, then."

Roland stared at the table. "Apparently not."

Quietly Roxane said, "It wasn't up to you whether or not she kept seeing this guy, Roland. She made her choice. Besides, if it was you she wanted, coming home for good would have been the end of it." She sipped her coffee. "Still, that doesn't completely explain why you're here."

"I'd wake up in our bed, get my clothes from our closet, make meals in our kitchen, but she wouldn't come home after work and she wasn't there when I went to bed at night. It was hard to accept that she had really left."

"But you're the one who showed her the door."

"I could see where things were headed. That doesn't mean it was easy."

"Probably a different story for her, I'm sure," Roxane observed. "New guy, new house, wedding ring, Roland who?"

Roland watched in silent protest as she pinched a piece from Mick's cake and offered it to Yoda. "I'm not kicking you when you're down, you know," she said, smiling kindly.

"I needed some perspective," Roland continued. "I don't know what the clinical definition of a nervous breakdown is but I'm pretty sure I had one, in spades. Everyone I know, including myself for a while, assumed it was brought about by my breakup with Sara, but there was so much more to it than that. Layers and layers of problems and issues and things left emotionally incomplete. I knew I needed to get my confidence back. The best way to do that is to tackle something I've never done and have a rule set up so I can't lose, no matter the outcome."

Roxane was intrigued. "What's your rule, then?"

"In this situation? If I do my best, learn some things, see some places I've never been to and stand up for myself if and when it's needed I'll think that's an acceptable success. More than anything I want a new direction for myself. Even just a foothold would be enough for now."

"I like that."

"The only rules about success and failure are the ones we make for ourselves. Might as well make ones that help you win."

Roland was pleased that those words didn't sound hollow to him. For all the times he had been thanked for his good advice and counsel, he couldn't remember the last time he had followed any of it himself.

He drew patterns on the plate with his fork and drew Yoda up onto his lap. Roxane drained her mug.

"What else?" She looked very thoughtful. "What else is there?"

She seemed to be growing irritated, almost angry. Roland wondered if he had upset her with something he said. He was always second-guessing himself around women now.

He never knew if what he was going to say would scare or insult or provoke them in some way.

"What happened between when you left the apartment to come home for good and when you told her to leave the house?"

Yoda was trying to get some sleep but the empty cake plate was still too tempting. He stuck his tongue out and licked the air. Roland scratched the dog's furry cheek. Yoda closed his eyes and yawned widely.

"Just a lot of back and forth, I guess. I think Sara felt obligated to us both and didn't really know what to do. I didn't make it any easier for her, either, because I was so hurt I couldn't see straight most of the time. I sent them both emails telling them what I thought of them when I found out that they were still screwing around. Pretty double-barreled stuff, for which I make no apologies, but in the process I destroyed any last hope of communicating with her in a civil fashion."

"I wouldn't worry about that," Roxane said. "It was her responsibility to tell you how much she needed you and she didn't. She took a cowardly way out, one that required no communication at all."

"But as you pointed out, maybe it wasn't me she needed. So what would she have cared how I felt either way?"

Roxane nodded thoughtfully.

Roland continued talking. It made him feel strange, as though he was being let out of a cage. "My communication was awful. I was accusatory, spiteful, angry, childish – things people become when all they really are is hurt. We scared each other with how unstable we were and did stupid things, and if we'd been even halfway using our heads we would have been able to bring some dignity to the mess."

"And let me guess…her other man was kind, understanding and gentle towards her. A sheltered port in the storm that was Roland."

Roland searched Roxane's face for something, anything, that would give away what she was thinking, but found nothing. "I suppose so," he said guardedly. "I don't know, but I would assume so, yes."

"Because he wasn't fighting for his life like you were."

Yoda rested a paw on Roland's forearm.

"What would you say if she called you tomorrow wanting to come down here and join you?"

Roland shrugged and avoided the question. "I want to believe that she loved me."

"In spite of one hell of a lot of evidence to the contrary."

"I don't know about that," Roland said slowly. "Who knows how long it would have continued if I hadn't done something about it? I have no idea how much longer she would have stayed living with me and continuing on with him for whatever reason. But for every time she left me for him, she left him for me. At least, I suppose that's what his perspective would be."

"I'm surprised you even noticed what his housewrecking little perspective might be."

Roland said, barely audibly, "You can't just push over a solid house, Roxane."

"True," she conceded, and studied the end of her cigarette.

Yoda had decided that he wasn't going to get any sleep and had jumped off Roland's lap to greet two girls who sat down next to their table. One of them scratched him behind the ear as the other offered him a little piece of her pastry.

Roxane flicked her ash over the railing where it fell onto the bumper of a blue Volkswagen convertible. Roland was close enough to wipe it off with his sandal. He reached his foot out and caught it between two wrought iron leaves.

"Anyway, it all worked out for the best," he continued, extricating his sandal. "She had always wanted to be married and now she is, or will be soon at least, and I'm wiser for the experience."

Roxane rested her chin on her hands. Roland thought he could see tan lines from an old wedding band but she noticed his gaze and covered her hand. "What's he got that you don't?" she asked.

"According to her, lots. You mean, why did she choose him?"

Roxane nodded.

"They're both in the same company and had been friends for some time. One night after we'd started dating he came to her apartment and offered her a promotion if she slept with him. She declined, but she told me she knew he'd never say no to her. Later on when things got rocky I suppose it was obvious who she would call."

"Simple as that?"

Roland took a while to respond. "No, probably not."

Mick and his friend had been joined by a woman in her mid-thirties. She was very beautiful and wore a long, elegant sequined yellow dress. She was cradling a glass of wine and threw her head back to laugh as Roland watched. He guessed that she had seen them talking from the restaurant across the street and decided to join them. Puerto Vallarta was a very small town indeed. Roxane lifted Yoda onto her shoulder where he nibbled on her ear and played with her hair.

From his perch on her shoulder, the little dog looked at Roland. Roland looked back at Yoda. He bore no resemblance to the fictional wise alien he'd been named after, but nonetheless Roland could imagine him saying something astute and dangerous. Roland wondered what his advice about women would be.

He watched the beautiful woman standing with Mick and his friend. She glanced at Roland and smiled. She had a beautiful smile. Roland tried to return it. The woman turned back to Mick.

"It's obvious that you loved her very much," Roxane was saying. "I think she loved you very much as well. Nobody rebounds that hard unless it comes from deep within them."

"It wasn't a rebound. I told you they'd been friends for a long time. Besides, she said she didn't love me."

"Sounds to me like Sara said a lot of things." Roxane stubbed out her cigarette deliberately, having returned from wherever her thoughts had taken her.

Roland found it strange to hear another woman saying Sara's name. He decided that he didn't like it. "But nowhere in there is there room for somebody who lies to you," he pointed out.

"No, I'm not saying there is, but what else was she going to do?" Roxane put her elbows on the table and folded her arms. Yoda was still glaring at Roland through her hair.

"What's that supposed to mean?"

Roxane spoke slowly and patiently, as though explaining to a toddler how to make the colored blocks fit together.

"Look, Roland, I'm not her, but I think that if I was, I'd feel pretty silly ending an affair only *after* you kicked me out because of it. If it was a choice between that and looking silly for agreeing to marry someone when I was three weeks fresh out of my last relationship I'd choose the latter. At least that way it wouldn't look like it was all for nothing. Your problem is you take women at face value."

"Of course I do," Roland snapped. "I'm going to marry the first woman I meet who says what she means and means what she says and doesn't force me to guess what she's feeling."

Roxane laughed. "I hope you don't mind dying a bachelor."

"Suits me just fine."

Roland knew that the two girls next to them were listening, because they had become very silent. He chewed his lip.

Roxane looked at him. "She must really have been something wonderful, to hit you this hard."

Roland returned her gaze. "I thought she was."

"Don't worry. Stay here and worship the sun in your mansion and be a tropical Gatsby, and eventually the right woman will step through the door."

"I'm not worried, and I think Gatsby was wasting his time."

Yoda's tail began wagging furiously. Mick approached the table and pulled his chair out.

"Mm, cold coffee. My favorite. Hey, where did that big chunk of my cake go?"

"You're the Secret Agent," said Roxane. "You figure it out."

"So who was that gorgeous thing I saw you talking with?" Roland asked.

"The one in the yellow? That's Glenda. She's always complaining about how little money she has, especially to guys who have a lot of it." Mick sipped his coffee and made a face. His cell phone rang. "She's having dinner with a guy who works for a cruise line. I think she's a kept woman. Kept by several different men, that is." He answered his phone. "Hello? Adrian, how are you?…just here having coffee with Roland and Roxane…Olas Altas…when?… sure, that's no problem…okay…no, tomorrow's fine, I'll take Roland…when are you leaving?…yeah, give me a call when you get back and I'll pick you up…see you then." He hung up.

Roland picked up the phone. "This thing's tiny," he said, examining it. He was glad to have something else to talk about. "Where are you taking me tomorrow?"

Mick hunched over the table and lowered his voice. "Oh, a couple of Adrian's thrice-removed cousins or something are coming to visit. He's leaving for Costa Rica tomorrow but he wants his driver to take him somewhere before he goes to the airport, so he can't get him to pick them up. I'll take you away from your exciting desk job so we can do it for him, and tour around the city."

"What's in Costa Rica?"

"Pleasurable business trip," said Mick.

Roland looked back at Mick's phone. "Why does your phone say 'No Service' but the signal strength meter is full?"

"Because," Mick replied, wolfing down his cake and cold coffee, "that way if somebody wants to borrow it I can flash it at them just long enough to show that it isn't working. Airtime is expensive down here. Maxine puts a few hundred bucks on them for us every now and then, but it goes pretty quickly."

"Maxine's in San Diego picking up the yacht, right?" Roland asked. On his first day at work he had seen Adrian's wife on the stairs at lunchtime and had overheard her chatting with Amy about it, but he hadn't been introduced.

"Something like that," said Mick, looking around dutifully. "Ixnay on the estionsquay."

"That's rich," said Roland. "I just got interrogated by this one here." He pointed to Roxane.

Mick looked back and forth between the two. Then he said, "Roxane, were you feeding Roland your stories again?"

Roxane glared at him. She raised a finger in warning but Mick ignored it. He turned to Roland.

"Roxane's husband left her for some bimbo he met at a bar. One day a couple of months later the bimbo came in to the bank where Roxane worked to apply for a loan. Roxane pushed her personal feelings aside and made the loan because everything looked kosher. They missed a couple of payments and when she went around to see them she found the house empty. No note, nothing. They just took off together. When she tried to foreclose on the house she discovered that the sale documents to transfer the title had been falsified, so the bank had to eat the loan and they fired her."

Roland stared at Roxane. "Why did he have it in for you so bad?"

Roxane shrugged. "It happens to the best of us," was all she said, but she had become very reserved.

"I need more coffee," said Mick. "I'm shooting for a shake like Yoda's." He got up and took his mug to the counter.

"Is that why you kept grilling me?" asked Roland. "To make yourself feel better?"

Roxane scratched at an imaginary stain on the table.

"That's pretty harsh of him," Roland continued. "Of them. That's awful."

"There must be a reason somewhere," she said. "I just haven't found it. I can't talk to him to ask why he did it. I don't know where he is."

"He can't give you closure, if that's what you mean," said Roland. "Even if you did ask him, what would he say? He'd probably lie to avoid hurting your feelings, not understanding that the lie hurts more than what it covers up." He nodded. "Trust me, his reasons for doing this aren't anywhere near as important as you facing the fact that he did. At least that's something you can control."

"I guess you're right." Roxane sounded unconvinced but Roland didn't care. At least she'd heard him.

"He *is* right." Mick poked her. "I wish I'd said that to you ages ago."

Roxane looked at Roland. Mick looked at Yoda. Yoda sat there quivering and looking up at Roxane.

"Yeah," she said. Then, "I'm ready to go when you are."

Mick looked at his coffee. "I put too much sugar in it anyway, plus I forgot to get it in a to-go cup," he said, and pushed back his chair. "Shall we?"

"Sure." Roxane got up and untied Yoda from the fencing.

"Guys, I'm going to walk home," said Roland.

"Walk? Are you sure?"

"Yes," said Roland. "I know where to go." He'd kept careful track of the few turns necessary to get back and forth between Olas Altas and the condo in Conchas Chinas.

"I don't advise it," Mick cautioned him. "We've only ever taken the highway, and these drivers are pretty nutty at the best of times." Mick didn't include himself in their group, apparently. Roland showed no signs of changing his mind, so Mick relented. "Take this street instead," he instructed, pointing at some nebulous destination over his shoulder. "Take the road up in front of the Tropicana – you'll know it when you see it – and keep going past the houses. You're on the right track when you see one with a plaque about Richard Nixon peeing there once a long time ago or something. Anyway, it spits you out right at our turnoff so you just have to cross the highway and come on up."

"Okay," said Roland. "I'll be careful. I just want to poke around for a while, that's all."

Mick looked at his watch. "It's a long walk," he said. "Twenty-five minutes or so, and it's already late." But Roland hadn't moved to get up. "Okay, see ya," he said.

"Goodnight, you two." Roland looked at Roxane as she coiled up Yoda's leash and stuffed him into her purse, looking as though he were being carried off to the gallows.

Roland watched them get into Mick's jeep and wave as they turned on to Olas Altas and disappeared.

So that was it, he thought. Roxane had never recovered from her husband's betrayal. Well, that was understandable to a point. Roland hadn't slain his dragons yet either, but he was certainly sharpening his sword. Roxane, for all her apparent strength and selective humor, seemed as though she was still waiting for a reason to start. Roland made a silent wish for her that she would find one.

Tired from the walk, which was every bit as long as Mick had said it would be, Roland recognized the sign saying "Ocho Cascadas" and turned up Paseo de los Delfines to his home.

Outside the Meza del Mar hotel three huge parrots preened themselves and cooed softly in a two-storey outdoor cage, and it wasn't long after that when he spotted a small metal plaque saying that Richard Nixon had stayed there a long time ago. He crossed the highway and became disoriented for a moment because it deposited him at a residential intersection, but he knew that if he just kept going up the hill he would be home soon. And sure enough, it didn't take long for him to recognize the imposing silhouette of Adrian's house and the real reason he'd wanted to walk home.

Below the Shack, down the hill with its gate facing the same street, was a house that had caught Roland's eye. It was named, like all the houses there. This one was called *Casa que Canta*, 'House that Sings'. It had a long, low brick wall that reached almost up to Roland's knees, on top of which was a tall iron fence joining sparsely-placed brick pillars.

Between the railings grew lush, healthy copa de oro, so intensely red and orange that it seemed as though there was a fire in the roots, spreading to a glow at the petals. Even in the yellowish light cast by the streetlamp the blooms were defiantly bright, and they had held on to the railings as they grew so thick that nothing could be seen beyond. That was fine with Roland. He didn't want to see beyond them. He looked around. It was important to him that no one was watching.

He placed his hands on the fence and closed his eyes. In the faint breeze the scent of the flowers surrounded him, enveloping him in an invisible shroud of fragrant air so delicate that it was all too easy to imagine he had left the ground. He let his thoughts drift to where he knew they would; to Sara. When they wandered, that was where they went. He still had to herd them away from the big attraction sometimes like children mesmerized at a magic show; she was colored lights and sleight of hand.

He was standing in front of their little house on a late spring evening marveling at the perfume of the lilacs; she was beside him holding his hand and drinking it all in with him. She loved the gardens, and when they bought the house she had taken him by the hand and led him to each one, telling him the name of every flower, but he had been too distracted by her beauty to remember any of them.

Roland longed to have her with him now. She would love it here; every tropical flower she could name, all decorating the air with their exotic aromas and reflecting the sun in their shamelessly brilliant colors.

She was holding his hand and then pulling herself towards him as she always did, she was telling him how much she loved him, murmuring softly.

Roland opened his eyes. She wasn't there. The breeze had taken something from where he'd imagined she was standing and tugged gently on his sleeve in passing.

He was saddened, but only for a minute. It was just that Sara would love this. She should be here.

Or maybe not, Roland thought as he passed in front of Adrian's house where the radiator in Mick's jeep was still ticking. She would read too much into his friendliness with the house staff and decide he was having an affair with one of them, then she'd go off and have one of her own. The conclusion was inescapable no matter where he looked. In some ways he couldn't blame her. He would have done anything to avoid being the last to know. It was degrading and humiliating.

He let himself in to the apartment and opened the fridge. Mick had nothing in there but a half-full bottle of water and an unopened bag of pretzels. His cleaning lady had a very easy job.

Roland went into his room and closed the door and kicked off his sandals. He did not wash or even get undressed. He just lay there on the bed watching the ceiling fan going around and around and around. When Mick knocked on the door at seven-thirty the next morning he still hadn't moved.

The days passed.

5
Kings of Sunset Town

When the work day was over, Liza would often appear from the office on her way to the safe and ask, "Who's got plans for dinner?" Whoever didn't put up their hand was invited out, and Roland always went. "Hmm," she'd say, surveying the crowd. "We'll need about this much." She would part her finger and thumb by about half an inch, and take a stack of cash that high from the safe.

One night Roland accompanied Liza, Roxane, Eric and the Secret Agent to the Camino Real, a prestigious hotel on the south side. Liza drove them in her Lincoln Navigator, always a fascinating sight for everyone because she was so small and her vehicle so large. They had dinner and decided that a different restaurant in the same hotel would be a good choice for dessert.

By this time they had already shared six bottles of wine, and as Eric stood waiting to be seated he started laughing that infectious laugh of his. "I'm so self-conscious in nice places," he said. "Especially dressed like this." He was wearing his usual uniform of a t-shirt and the quick-drying baggy shorts he used for his swim in the pool after lunch at the Shack, in noticeable contrast to the lavish décor. He was clutching a styrofoam container with the remains of his pasta from the other restaurant. The hostess approached. Eric turned to Roland and said, "I just need a glass of water, thanks. I brought my own dinner."

They staggered across the floor to the table the hostess had chosen – as far away from the rest of the patrons as possible, Roland noticed with some amusement – and ordered whichever coffees and desserts needed the most ostentatious presentation. A waiter wheeled a cart up to the table and began flambéeing something Liza had ordered.

Even though he was truly enjoying himself, this wasn't the way Roland anticipated spending most of his evenings. It was good to see Mick letting off some steam, as he always seemed to be wound a little tight, and Liza was even more entertaining to be around than usual, but the main reason Roland was having fun was because for the very first time he was doing so without longing to be able to share it with Sara.

Eric sat cross-legged in the archway beside their table, drinking wine from the bottle when nobody was looking. The waiter presented their bill; two hundred dollars. Liza scoffed, "Is that all?" and a flutter of bills descended on the table.

Roxane closed her eyes to listen to the surf and a steel drum band some distance down the beach. "Another day exiled in Cyberia," she said softly. Roland watched her as she opened her eyes. Catching his gaze, she said, "Soon you will learn not to see anything as strange." She ran her fingers through her hair and drained the last bottle of Veuve Clicquot, then tilted the neck towards Roland.

"We do not live in the real world."

On the way home that night and right up until he left Vallarta for good, Roland thought about those words. Roxane had said as much before on the first morning he had spent in her and Liza's office, but he was only now beginning to understand what she had meant, and the implications were staggering. No matter what happened or what they did, their money granted them absolute immunity.

It was also what Roland thought about one night when he was sitting by himself at a sidewalk café and a grubby Indian girl selling Chiclets came up to him. He waved her away with a '*no, gracias*', and she looked around and pulled up her shirt to expose a small breast and a brown nipple as she licked her lips. It happened so fast that she was two tables away before Roland realized what she had offered him. It had taken him that long because she couldn't have been older than nine, ten maybe, and it was the last thing he had expected. It wasn't until she kept looking back at him periodically as she made her way down the sidewalk that he had understood. He had watched her disappear and heard Roxane in his mind, telling him that he no longer lived in the real world.

Those, he thought, were famous last words, and if they weren't, they soon would be.

Roland's first hint of what Adrian had in mind for him came after barely a week. By this time they had been joined by a man in his mid forties, a pilot whose name was Grant. Grant wore glasses and had a large belly. He had known Adrian for many years, and like Adrian he swore a lot. He thought it was funny that some of the people at Cyberia smoked pot because, as he told Roland on several occasions, he'd rather make money flying the stuff around than lighting it up and burning it. He and Roland got along fairly well, and one night after work – that is, after everyone but Roland, Mick and Liza had gone home – Roland found Grant and Adrian on the office balcony together, smoking and drinking as they watched the sun set.

"Pull up a chair, Roland," said Adrian, adjusting sunglasses that were too large for his face. "It's time to talk about your future, son." Then he laughed. "Actually, not so much your future exactly as just where you're going to live." Roland sat down. Adrian was smoking, of course, the ubiquitous pack of Derbys at the ready, but he wasn't tugging on his earlobe. "I bought this house here." He indicated the one below them, across the street and closer to the ocean, the one Slogan had pointed out on Roland's first day of work. On such a steep hill, even while sitting on the basement balcony Roland could still only see its roof. "Roxane's going to live on the main floor," Adrian went on, "but the top is up for grabs." He looked at Roland. "You can either wait for your own apartment down at Vista del Sol, those condos on the square at the end of Olas Altas, or you can share with Grant here and live in a bigger, nicer place with your own pool."

Grant said, "I've already claimed the room at the south end. The other one's yours if you want it." He pointed to a series of stained glass windows with arched wooden frames.

"I wasn't too keen on sharing, to be honest," said Roland. "How long will it be before this other place comes available?"

Adrian cleared his throat. "There's a totally self-contained maid's suite beneath the house if you want it, but there's no pool and no view. I don't think your maid's going to move into it because she lives close enough as it is, so I suppose you could live down there. It'll be about a month, give or take, til you can move into the apartment if you wanted that. Keep in mind, though, that Grant'll hardly be here anyway."

"Oh?" Roland raised an eyebrow. "Why's that?"

Grant said, "I'm a pilot. So that means I'll be flying around a lot."

Roland nodded. "You've mentioned that before, but darn it all, there's no airplane around."

"Ah." Adrian smiled. "But there will be. A helicopter too. We're going to need them both."

Roland looked at Grant. "You have your chopper ticket too? I thought you were a fixed-wing guy."

"I am," said Grant. "But to hire somebody to fly our helicopter in Costa Rica there are some convoluted rules we have to follow, so I'll probably just end up taking the course and flying it myself because hiring somebody who already has all the fuckin' papers they want will be too difficult."

Now when Roland nodded he really did understand. "So we're getting a plane to ferry us between here and a main airport in Costa Rica, and from there we take a helicopter to someplace where the big plane can't land."

Adrian nodded and was about to say something but was taken with a violent fit of coughing. "Jesus, that hurt," he panted as he recovered, holding his stomach.

Roland noted real concern on Grant's face as he looked at Adrian and asked, "You okay?" He could almost feel Grant wanting to put a hand on Adrian's shoulder but Adrian straightened up and said, "There's only one main airport in Costa Rica anyway. In the capital, San Jose."

Grant said, "And don't ask me if I know the way to San Jose, where all the stars that never were…"

"…'are parking cars and pumping gas'," sang Adrian and Roland. Adrian started coughing again but he was smiling. He patted his stomach. "Fuck, y'know, you'd think when they take half your guts out, you'd hurt half as much as when you had them all in there, not twice as much." Recovered, he pointed his cigarette at the house again. "Everything's there. Satellite TV, you guys have no expenses, everything's covered, even your phone bill to your wives and mistresses and bookies back home. So are you moving in or what?"

Roland looked at the graceful archways and brickwork over the iron gates. The house even had a little lawn, and bordering the parking pads were planters with all kinds of beautiful flowers in them. Whatever Slogan had said about Eric and Kevin moving in to it had obviously been rendered null and void since that conversation. For a fraction of a second, quicker than if he had blinked, Roland had a picture of his little house back home after a summer of neglect. The gardens would become overgrown and the flowers would die, losing their battle to the omnipresent weeds, and it would go from being one of the prettiest houses in town to one of the most forlorn-looking. The thought of it made him a little ill.

"Okay," he said finally. "I'll take it."

"Thought you might." Adrian held out a plastic bag he had pulled out from under his lounge chair. "Here are the keys." There must have been twenty of them clinking around. Adrian noticed Roland's surprise. "It has ten front doors, and there's a key in there for a chastity belt too." He blew smoke out as he coughed and laughed. Roland examined the keys. "Actually there were a whole bunch of copies made but they don't all work. Mexican locksmiths don't seem to be too concerned with getting it right the first time. Whichever ones work, keep 'em, then throw the rest away."

"Thanks," said Roland. "I'll do that."

They were running low on drinks and Roland showed Grant where the beer fridge was. When they returned, Adrian had taken his sunglasses off and was staring pensively at the *Marigalante* as it put out to sea.

"We're all going to Guadalajara this weekend," he said faintly.

"Bossman and I are going in the Learjet," added Grant. Adrian's face went stony. Roland ignored his expression. "Mind if I fly with you?" he asked. "I love planes."

"Fine," said Adrian in a voice that made it clear that it was okay, but not exactly fine. Roland didn't care. He was beginning to understand Adrian better but it was hard work. The man was cheerful and friendly enough yet somehow still maintained a distance, but then his countenance changed. "Yeah, in fact, that's just fine," he continued as he thoughtfully nodded to himself. "Leave your passport on my desk tonight, Roland. I'll need to make a copy of it for the passenger manifest on the Learjet."

Roland saw Grant turn his head imperceptibly towards Adrian and then back out to the ocean.

"Sure thing," he replied.

Their conversation turned briefly from the Learjet – an older one, apparently, but a fast one and captained by a man chosen by Grant to have a fanatical attention to detail (Grant didn't have a Learjet ticket either, evidently) – to women, then back and forth between that and life in general.

Their mood was lifted by the cloudless sunset and the tranquil ocean scene before them. The sea air was sweet, scented almost imperceptibly by legions of flowers hiding just out of sight – perhaps in the gardens of the house adjacent to Roland's new one, which afforded a decent view of the balcony they were now on. Sunsets happened quickly there, and as the short palm tree beside him on the balcony rustled in the faint breeze Roland realized how lucky he was to be there to enjoy it. He said, "It's moments like this that remind you that life's worth living."

Adrian touched his stomach and said, "You couldn't have convinced me of that three months ago."

No one said anything. Perhaps Roland and Grant were thinking along the same lines, that if Adrian's generosity was what kept him going he had a lot to teach, and perhaps Adrian was thinking that he'd said too much. Either way, he got up and put his cigarettes in his shirt pocket.

"You guys can move in next week," he said. "Maxine gets back from San Diego on Friday and she'll go shopping for you and set you up with whatever you need." Today was Wednesday. Roland had been in Puerto Vallarta for eight days.

"You turning in?" Grant asked.

"Yeah." Adrian fidgeted with his sunglasses. "I'll watch some Mexican soap opera or something and call it a night. The ladies on TV down here are definitely worth looking at." Roland thought that was funny. As much as Adrian usually liked swearing, he never called women 'broads' or 'chicks'; in fact, he seldom used slang at all. He talked quite properly most of the time, but just to keep you awake he'd throw in an f-word here and there.

Roland watched him disappear through the slider. Before it closed behind him he said, "Adrian."

Adrian turned to face him.

"Thanks." He gestured around him. "For everything."

Adrian smiled that genuine and complete smile. "I like to make my people happy." He closed the door and shuffled slowly between the desks to those huge stone spiral stairs. Roland watched him wave to Mick and heard Liza say something, then he was gone.

"Our new house," Grant said, pointing the neck of his beer bottle towards the ocean.

"Our new house," Roland said, returning the cheer. "Just don't expect me to carry you over the threshold."

From behind them they could hear Liza's voice as she approached. Then the sliding doors opened and she stepped out onto the balcony. Her eyes were a little red but she wasn't swaying. Roland thought it was amazing how someone so small could drink so much. She dropped into a lounge chair and said, "Phew!" very loudly. Mick appeared behind her.

Despite the fact that the sun had set, the sky was still light. Against the backdrop of a tiny bluish-grey cloud appeared a small black jet. It wasn't a fighter, it was a Lear, and it was very, very low and slow above the beach, heading south but too far inland to have come directly from the airport. As they watched it made one pass over the city, turned around and went almost as far as the hotel zone again, then came around once more. A little higher this time it made another trip over the beach, but as it got closer to the south side it banked further inland, close to Adrian's house. Mick turned his face away slightly. The jet headed towards the ocean and then banked to finally disappear over the mountains on the south side of the bay.

"What the hell was that all about?" asked Roland.

"I don't know," Liza replied momentarily, still gazing to where the aircraft had gone. "I've never seen that before." Mick didn't say anything and neither did Grant.

They resumed chatting for a little while longer until Mick, Roland and Grant decided to go for dinner at the marina. When Roland returned to his room he found microscopic brown ants in one of his suitcases.

The next day found everyone in high spirits. By now they all knew that they were going on a trip, and the Shack was full of excited chatter.

Mick and Roland were sitting on either side of Eric at lunch. Adrian wanted them all to stick around afterwards for an announcement. Eric said to Roland, "I had an alien in my bedroom last night."

"Was she a hottie?" Roland asked. "I hear ghosts and aliens are the best. Illegal aliens notwithstanding, of course."

"No, I mean a little grey guy with big eyes." Eric smiled, and for the first time Roland noticed that Eric was self-conscious. "I woke up and there he was, staring at me."

"Was he consulting a clipboard and requesting a urine sample?"

Eric persisted. "No, I'm serious. I must have blinked a hundred times and he was still there. Then he just disappeared."

Roland was quiet for a second. Then he asked, "About what time was this?" He was thinking about the black jet. He watched Slogan as he played hackysack beside the pool with a thin blond man. Amy lounged on a chair nearby, reading a book and chatting about something with Kevin.

"I dunno," said Eric. "I think it was still light out, but not by much. We rolled a big fattie at sundown and I went to bed early." Eric was looking at Kevin, who was motioning him to come over to the pool, and as Eric got up to leave Ken said, "Don't go too far; there's a meeting." Eric nodded as he went through the living room and out to the patio.

Roland didn't need to ask who the fourth man by the pool was. From the facial resemblance alone he couldn't have missed that this was Sidney, Adrian's son. He had the same ectomorphic frame and prominent cheekbones, and although he was wearing sunglasses against the glare of the tropical light Roland guessed he had the same blue eyes.

Mick looked at Roland over Eric's empty chair. He put his thumb and finger together and brought them to his mouth, inhaled through almost-closed lips, then rolled his eyes upwards and said, "Aaaah, yeah, man."

"Obviously you aren't too impressed by his close encounter," said Roland. "Do you suspect a hallucinogen at work here?"

"Perspective," said Mick, and now he brought his thumbs together, fingers straight, as a photographer might frame a scene before shooting. "This from the guy who lost an hour."

"Lost an hour?" echoed Roland. "What, behind the sofa?"

"No, on it actually. Eric made a big deal one day about the fact that he lost an hour. He was sitting on his couch staring out the window and looked at his watch, then he looked at it immediately afterwards and it was exactly an hour later."

"I see," said Roland.

Adrian had appeared, carrying a plastic bag. He climbed up onto one of the stools in front of the counter, where he surveyed his employees and opened the bag. Not everyone was seated at the table yet. He looked at Mick. "Somebody's watch broken?" he asked.

"Not exactly," Mick replied. "We're talking about Eric's experiences with time wrinkles and aliens."

Adrian made a face and Roland pointed out the window behind him. "Speaking of aliens, just after you went upstairs last night there was somebody fooling around in a black Learjet out here."

"You saw that too, eh?" Adrian asked thoughtfully, lighting a cigarette. "I wonder what that was. I've never seen that before." He exhaled a cloud of smoke. "I've heard of it though. I ran into a guy on the Malecon once who told me that Vallarta is some big planetary energy center. There's always something like that going on." Sarcastically he added, "Apparently I've just never noticed."

"What, lots of psychics or something?" Roland asked.

"No, aliens and men in black, that kind of thing. It's supposed to be one of the places on earth that's some big spiritual crossroads or some fuckin' thing. This city seemingly attracts all kinds of weird shit."

"You don't say," Roland observed, looking at his coworkers. They had materialized back in their chairs after returning their plates to the kitchen and retrieving beer and wine and whatever else they wanted. Sidney lay on a floating chair in the pool and stretched his arms toward the sun.

Roland noticed a very tall Mexican man with big ears who stood by the liquor room. He wore a blue shirt and jeans, and was obviously one of those people who had a permanent jovial smile.

Everyone quietened and looked at Adrian expectantly. Out of the bag he'd been holding he pulled several envelopes which he handed to Mick, who was sitting closest to him. "Take the one with your name on it and pass the rest around," he instructed. He produced a gold Visa card from his shirt pocket.

"This is what's inside," he said. "It's a Visa, obviously, but it's a debit card, not a credit card. So unlike your bank debit card, you can use this to buy blowup dolls over the internet or whatever. Take out your card, put it somewhere safe, memorize the PIN number that's printed on the accompanying paper, then throw the paper away." There was loud rustling as everyone opened their envelopes. It sounded like Christmas. If it weren't for the midday heat and the marble under Roland's bare feet he would have been more convinced. Adrian was still talking.

"There's a two-hundred-dollar setup fee plus a hundred-dollar yearly fee, which I've paid for each of you, plus there's a thousand bucks on each card for working so hard." Roland wondered what that was supposed to mean, what with all the beer bottles around the swimming pool after lunchtime every day, but they were all having fun, including him. Hard work was beginning to sound like a very relative term.

"Also we're going to Guadalajara this weekend for a shopping trip, so whatever plans you have, cancel them. Except for Slogan, who's not coming. Instead, he will emerge on the other side of this weekend an almost-married man, God rest his soul."

Slogan put a hand up to stop the round of questioning and congratulations. "It's true," he said. "We're going to a great little place south of here. Very private, pelapas on the beach, that kind of thing. It'll be very romantic." His t-shirt said '*Currently Unsupervised*'.

Kevin said, "I hope you've polished your sales skills, because she'll need some convincing."

"Bring lots of booze," Liza advised. "That always works." Everyone was nodding and offering suggestions.

"Thank you very much. Thank you all for your confidence in me." Slogan was beaming like a lighthouse. "I know these are all great ideas from people who love me and I will offer my new Visa balance to whomever's idea works the best, seeing as how just asking her to marry me apparently isn't going to work."

"Okay, okay," said Adrian, "it's clear there's another one who's chosen the path of evil. Let's not stand in his way." He stopped smiling and became thoughtful, and everyone quietened down and looked at him again.

"I need names for people who want to drive to Guadalajara. Tell Liza if you want to volunteer. We'll leave tomorrow and come back Monday. I've rented three Suburbans with drivers to take you around the city anywhere you want to go. It'll be a nice long weekend for you, and of course your expenses are all taken care of."

"Aren't we flying there?" Shelly asked. Word had got around that Roland was tagging along in the jet.

Adrian tried not to look exasperated, and Roland regretted having asked if he could go with him in the first place. Liza looked at Roland and said, "Roland and Grant are flying because Grant is our company pilot and Roland has his pilot's license as well, and he might be our copilot when we get a plane." Now people were looking at Roland, but Roland was looking at Adrian, and Adrian looked surprised. The situation needed defusing and Liza had planted a great seed, so Roland cultivated it by saying, "I don't know how many this one seats, but I'd be willing to fly only one way if everyone else did the same." So it was agreed that half the expedition would fly there, and half would fly back.

After the meeting Roland hung around with Adrian and Grant for a while. Grant was wearing a very colorful polo shirt and Adrian had on the only kind of shirt he ever wore – a bright one with a dress collar and a button front and short sleeves. "Is that what you've got in store for me, chief?" Roland asked. "Am I our new copilot?"

"No," Adrian replied, "that was some fancy footwork from Liza to ward off jealousy and office politics which, if you haven't noticed already, are just as rampant here as if we were fuckin' General Motors or whatever."

"Of course, it couldn't hurt to knock the rust off that license," offered Grant, his polarized prescription glasses darkened in the afternoon sun. "You never know."

"That's right," agreed Adrian. "Though make sure you study the documents with that Visa very carefully, and then sit down with Mick and go through it until you understand it completely. It's important that you do that."

By now Roland was used to making an effort to hear what Adrian was saying, so his words had taken on a reality that other people's communication didn't because of the concentration required to focus on them. It was rather unsettling at times, and in Adrian's instructions obviously lay the clue as to what was in store for him – his niche at Cyberia. And it didn't have to do with flying, but he might sit in on that job as well.

Roland was silent for a time. The only thing he could remember ever really wanting to do with his life was to fly airplanes in the tropics, but that was a long time ago. He allowed himself the luxury of imagining what it would be like if this really happened, and it felt wonderful. Even the growing distance he could already feel between himself and his coworkers couldn't dampen it.

He stood there listening to Grant and Adrian talking with one of the housekeepers who had stopped by to say hello. He heard the splashing and laughing of people in the pool reflected off the distant cathedral ceiling. He saw women in bikinis on the beach up around the curve of the bay, so far away that he felt he could be admiring them through the wrong end of a telescope. He saw boats on the ocean, little folded paper hats in a blue sink, and he smelled that incredible air, and suddenly he felt very much awake. Awake and alive.

For the first time since landing in Vallarta, Roland started to feel invincible – his old self – again.

Mick, Kevin and Roland drove to Guadalajara in the blue van Tatiana used when running errands and picking up the daily courier envelopes that were forwarded from Cyberia's address in Belize. Kevin put in a CD of music he liked and it bored Roland to tears. It was the same drum beat, over and over and over. It reminded Roland of a conveyor belt. It would have been ideal if he was on drugs.

Guadalajara was only a couple of hundred miles from Puerto Vallarta, but even on the new highway through the mountains the trip took several hours. When they reached the hotel they all fooled around like schoolchildren in the lobby while Adrian checked them in. Shelly had her own room because it was her birthday that weekend, and Roland shared with Mick. When everyone had taken their bags up to their assigned rooms, they met at Adrian's suite.

Roland was no sooner in the doorway than Adrian beckoned him over to a sitting room with a view of a building flying the Mexican flag from its rooftop.

"I know you haven't been paid yet," he said, tugging on his earlobe, "so if you see anything you want just let me know and I'll take care of it."

"Thanks, Adrian," said Roland. Adrian nodded and held out a wad of bills held together with a gold money clip bearing Aztec symbols. "In the meantime, here's something to play with. Keep the clip." He smiled. "You'll need it."

Adrian's suite was at the top of the hotel and had a rooftop patio, where everyone gathered to admire the view.

The city stretched in every direction for as far as they could see.

The tall man with the big ears whom Roland had noticed at lunch the day before approached him. He was holding up two fingers. "Guadalajara is the second-biggest city in Mexico," he said in Spanish, which Roxane translated for Roland. "Carlos Santana is from near here."

Roland tried to say that he must be very proud but even with Roxane's help he was forced to give up. He did learn, however, that this was Guillermo the security man. He had been hired some time before but hadn't put in an appearance to the staff until the meeting.

They all drank champagne and decided what to do with the rest of the day. The only thing none of them was allowed to miss was Shelly's birthday dinner that night, a lavish affair catered in a private dining room in the hotel and serenaded by a mariachi band – a brave thing for Adrian, who hated them.

Back in his room after the party, Roland was suddenly tired. He climbed into bed and turned away from the television show Mick was watching with the sound way down. He had left the curtains open because he liked to look out the window and far away he saw the lights of an airplane suspended in the sky. He fell into a deep sleep and he dreamed.

He was a hawk, hovering far above a deserted country road with an abandoned pioneer house at the edge of a boundless prairie field. There were two ghostly figures beside an old silver sports car whose doors were open. Its radio was playing an old song and the phantoms of Roland and Sara were dancing to it, slowly swaying and turning.

He felt the air on his wings as he looked at himself dancing there below. Sara had her eyes closed, and her skirt flared with her soft dark hair as she moved. She was graceful and every bit as beautiful as Roland remembered. He tucked in his wings and tried to dive but he couldn't, so he just stayed there, riding on the wind, watching the simple scene beneath him while the sun gradually set. Even when the moon rose full in his dream he still hung there and he knew that these two would be here for eternity, cherishing the same music and delighting in the way they flowed so beautifully together. He could still see them clearly in the night, reflecting more than the available light, imbued with the glow of the apparitions they were.

He felt himself leave the hawk. It ignored him as he floated away, staying there riveted to the scene beneath it. As Roland withdrew he noticed that the land underneath him was that of pure fantasy, with magnificent castles made of ice on the summits of majestic mountains, vast desert palaces on lowlands, and inside them he felt the voices of dreamers vibrating within him as though he had found and grasped the single sound of the universe with both of his eager hands.

When he awoke, he felt warm sun on his face and listened to the steady hum of the air conditioner. He remembered the dream vividly and knew he had in some way crossed a bridge when it came to Sara, and when he showered and Mick said, "Time for *brehkfazst*," Roland agreed wholeheartedly.

The day found various Cyberians scattered around the city as seeds thrown to the wind. Roland ended up at a large shopping mall with Liza and Tatiana, and while there they met up with Garrett and Mick and Roxane.

Mick and Garrett were interested in computers and technical gadgets, so those were the stores they visited. Roxane had left her life back home to come to Vallarta and start a gift shop, so she spent time poking around handicraft stores and artisan's booths, and finally there was Liza, who brought Tatiana along more as a pack horse than anything else as she exuberantly purchased everything she could get her hands on. And no doubt Kevin and Eric had joined up with Amy and Sidney and were poking around some forgotten corner of the city getting into who knew what sort of trouble. Roland wished he could be with all of them but he ended up wandering off on his own. He still needed solitude more often than not.

He caught sight of Liza and Tatiana coming out of a clothing store, Tatiana laden with bags and smiling good-naturedly as Liza admired something in the window.

"Is that what you just bought?" he asked as he drew near, pointing to a beautiful dress loaded with sequins draped over a seductively-posed mannequin.

"No, but I'm thinking I should have," said Liza, and then she laughed that brief laugh. "I've spent enough in this store. I was thinking I need some furniture for that whizzy new place of mine, so we're going to Tlaquepaque."

"Lucky Paki?" Roland echoed.

"Tlaquepaque," Liza repeated patiently as she took some of the bags Tatiana was carrying and handed them to Roland. "It's a shopping district full of all kinds of great stuff. Come with us. Tatiana's originally from Guadalajara and she knows all the best places." She took his arm and said, "You'll have to walk slowly, Bachelor."

She chattered away happily as they wandered by the store windows. Roland had found out only recently that she had been in a relationship with Ken a long time ago which had lasted for four years. They had apparently talked about marriage until one of them, Liza didn't elaborate which, had decided that it wouldn't be such a great idea, but they had kept in touch. That was how Ken came to be in Mexico. So her life had taken her who knew where else for years until one day she found herself in a shopping mall in Guadalajara with somebody named Roland on one arm.

Tatiana drove Liza's Navigator as Roland sat in the back and played with the rear air conditioner controls. Guadalajara had some beautiful architecture and Tatiana knew all about the statues and buildings they passed. Finally she parked outside a ratty-looking building with a fat Indian woman sitting out front. Roland said, "I've seen this before, in National Geographic."

"Me too," said Liza. "Every month. Do you have change for the meter?" but Tatiana was already feeding the contraption, twisting its handle nose and making it squawk like a crotchety crow. "There's lots more up this street too," she said. There was nothing but an empty adobe building where her finger was pointing but Roland could see where a street began next to it. Even so, he looked blankly at the building until he knew Liza was watching him. "Not there, dummy," she said. "*Over* it." She jumped a little to emphasize her point.

"Ah," said Roland.

They entered the little shop and the Indian spat on the sidewalk as they did so. "*Hola* to you too," Liza said when they were safely in the store.

She saw Roland admiring some candle holders and said, "Buy them. That's my rule." She nodded her head emphatically. "If I see something and I like it, I buy it. You might never pass this way again, and then what?"

"I've got too many debts to pay first," Roland replied. "Liza, do you remember that money you gave me at breakfast last week?" When Roland had returned to his room that evening and counted it, the roll of bills had amounted to almost two thousand dollars. The clip Adrian had given him held another two.

"Yeah." She had picked up a beautiful candle sconce and was peering at the price tag stuck to the back of it.

"I didn't spend all of it." In fact, he'd spent hardly any.

"Mm-hmm," she said. "You'd better start, then. Inflation means the longer you wait to use it, the less it's worth."

This made Roland laugh. He'd never quite thought of money in those terms before.

Guadalupe had told him she had children and he thought it would be nice to bring something back for them. He started with something for her, a tall, elegant glass candleholder, but when he paid for it he felt as though he'd just bought a mansion. For Roland, money was still hard to part with. He couldn't wait to be like Liza, who liked spending it instead of viewing it as a leak in a ship every time she flashed her Visa.

And flash her Visa she did. The street she had pointed to earlier was indeed everything she had promised and more besides. Even apart from the beautiful things offered for sale there – towering two-storey mirrors, with frames carved so intricately it was impossible to guess how long it must have taken to complete them; paintings of nameless colonial streets in eternal sunshine; furniture in antique stores that dated back hundreds of years, the list went on and on with each new shop they visited – the shops themselves were beautiful. They all opened directly onto the street, but inside they were huge, some with gardens and fountains, one with a restaurant, and one with a parrot that waited until Roland was almost right on top of it before it said "*Hola*" and Roland nearly had a heart attack.

"*Hola*," he responded, and the bird bobbed its head and ruffled its feathers. "*No yo hablar mucho español*," Roland said gently, and the bird said, "*Hola*," again.

"You don't speak much Spanish either, apparently," he said to it, and it squawked loudly and bobbed its head again and shifted from one foot to the other on its perch.

By the time they made their way back to the hotel it was dark. They stuffed Liza's vehicle full of everything they could carry – that is, everything that wasn't being shipped out to Vallarta later on – and drove through the sunset back to the hotel.

Roland bade goodnight to Liza and Tatiana and found Mick in the hotel gift shop looking at a watch. "Buy it," said Roland. "You might never pass this way again."

"You must have spent the day with Liza," Mick observed, and brandished the timepiece. "It is nice, isn't it? I don't know. Do I want it just because it's expensive? I mean, you can buy a waterproof digital at the Pemex for a hundred pesos. That's ten bucks."

Roland said, "True, but you can't use a digital as a compass if you ever need to."

"Mm-hmm." Mick stared at him and noticed his lack of cargo. "If you spent the day with Liza, why are you empty-handed?"

"I'm not," Roland replied. "There was too much stuff to lug up to the rooms so we left it in the Lincoln."

"Oh, right."

"The furniture will be shipped out in a couple of weeks."

Mick laughed. "Why did I even ask? Nobody can outshop that woman. Except maybe Maxine." He put the watch down. "I'm hungry, how about you?"

Roland was starving. They found Garrett sitting by himself in one of the hotel restaurants reading a newspaper, and compared notes on their day over delicious dishes with long Spanish names.

There was a standing invitation to go up to Adrian's suite for a nightcap and social, but upon learning that everyone

107

else was still out in the city Roland changed his mind. He wandered around the hotel for a while and was on his way back to his room when he caught sight of Shelly in a red lace teddy closing the door behind her, the sound of a man's voice becoming muffled behind it.

The last day there found the Cyberians in a distinctly shabbier but very lively district where Adrian bought them all drinks before they headed for the airport. On the flight home was Adrian, naturally; also Guillermo, Roxane, Mick, Kevin, and Grant. Grant sat near the pilot, a man named Heinz, and kept watching the instruments and talking to him. At first Roland sat at the very back, separated from Adrian by the aisle; but Roxane, who took the club-style seat facing Roland, was obviously anxious.

"Here, let's trade seats," Roland offered. "You'll be a lot less nervous if you can see where we're going."

Roxane accepted his offer, and once settled she stared intently out the window as they taxied out to the runway. "You've been in one of these before?"

"A few times," said Roland. "I used to go to boarding school with a guy whose dad owned an oil company that had a really nice one. Flew back and forth to school in it a couple of times. Then I got a job working for a gold mining company and one day they announced they'd bought a Learjet. Guess which one it was?"

"Same kind?" Roxane asked absently, her hands grasping the edge of the seat.

"Same *airplane*. The very same one. They let me go up in it while they flight-tested a pilot they wanted to hire. I'd never been in a Lear that was upside down with one engine out before."

Roxane shuddered and closed her eyes. The plane picked up speed. Adrian didn't even look out the window, his attention fixed on the paper he was reading, rum and Coke already in hand. The little jet strained to overcome the heat and heavy load, and finally the ground released it into its invisible home. Roxane stared out the window, her eyes wide.

The wing pointed at a volcano in the distance, gently pushing ash and smoke into the air. A subtle ring of cloud radiated around it while the sun, beginning to set, cast its deepening glow onto little lakes up in the mountains.

"Beautiful," Roxane remarked. "This is the only way to fly." She had calmed down and was enjoying herself.

"I agree," said Adrian, his feet up on the seat in front of him.

Everyone had too much to drink, which made the waning afternoon sun they were chasing seem that much more beautiful. Even Kevin, who was holding his stomach and moaning after downing two screwdrivers on top of his tequila, managed to put in his two cents' worth.

"Looksh like a tequila sunseh, all kindsa colorsh," he mumbled. Adrian looked across at Roland and raised an eyebrow. "Does he know where the barf bags are?" he asked.

They pulled in to the private terminal and shut down beside a Canadian-registered Gulfstream IV. Across from them sat a Sabreliner with markings that Roland didn't recognize and two American Learjet 55s.

"Nice hardware," said Roland.

Adrian craned his neck to look out Roland's window. "You got that right," he said, his gaze lingering on the G-IV.

The sun was gracefully beginning its descent into the ocean. Roland noticed how much more humid the air was here than in Guadalajara, and decided that he liked the humidity better. He also contemplated how glad he was to be home, a thought that caught him off guard at first. It wasn't too surprising, though. Puerto Vallarta had felt like home to him the minute he had stepped off the plane and the beautiful uniformed lady in the airport had smiled at him, but it was the first opportunity he'd had to say it to himself and he felt a tinge of nostalgia for his little house in the country. How completely, utterly different his life was now from how it had been then, with Sara beside him at night and the spaces on the walls he had left empty on purpose to hold pictures of the children they never had.

As a porter approached with a baggage dolly and Adrian handed the pilots a thousand-dollar tip, the only sounds around them were traffic from the airport buses at the main terminal along the access road and Kevin being violently ill on the tarmac.

On the way up the narrow, busy street they passed in front of the Pagina en el Sol. Roland noticed two men sitting at a table outside, watching them approach in the Suburban. One was Milo, the tall Croatian who had introduced himself to Roland on his first night in Mexico. The other was "Duck" Bill, a squat man in his seventies who always wore a baseball cap. Mick had mentioned him on Roland's first night in Vallarta. He was a Southerner who talked with a slight twang and the sound of gravel stuck in his throat. Since Roland's arrival in Mexico he had briefly chatted with both of them at Adrian's house now and then in the late afternoons as they sat around the pool or had a cigar and a glass of port.

As they drew closer Roland waved and called hello out the window. Milo raised his bottle of Sol in greeting. Then they were gone, replaced by other scenery.

6
Charlatan's Alchemy

Sunday, March 11

Roxane had moved into her house the previous week, taking things in piecemeal during lunch breaks until the rest of the crowd on the balcony got bored with shouting things like, 'Hey, isn't that *my* underwear?', and now Roland and Grant wanted to make their place upstairs ready to move into as well. Mick wanted to go home to pack, as he was leaving for Costa Rica the next day with Adrian, so they all piled out of the taxi at the Shack. He and Roxane bade them farewell and walked down the street to their respective homes. Roland let himself into Adrian's house.

Adrian and Grant had arrived before him, and Adrian was on the phone when Roland entered. He raised a highball glass and pointed to the oak and marble sideboard in the kitchen, where an open bottle of Amaretto beckoned. Grant was pouring himself some but Roland decided that he had started drinking too much lately and gave it a miss. Besides, he had developed heartburn which had started bothering him earlier that day and he didn't want to aggravate it.

"That was Sidney," Adrian said as he returned the phone to its cradle. "Those who drove back are all in Bucerias, so they're just under an hour away." Grant held his glass under the fridge's ice dispenser for a second and the three of them settled at the patio dining table.

"So what did you think of Guadalajara?" Adrian asked Roland.

"The women are absolutely gorgeous," Roland admitted. Adrian laughed.

"Wait'll you see the ones in Costa Rica," he said. "Holy shit, they're amazing. Smart, too. I get the feeling there's not much else to do down there except go to university."

He stared out at the orange sky. "You know, I've been watching the sun set from here for almost three years, and it's still as beautiful as the first time I saw it."

Roland excused himself to go downstairs and check his e-mail. On his desk he found three tiny new cell phones. He knew that two of them were for Grant and himself, and he stowed the third in the trophy alcove beside his desk after discarding the packaging around his. There was no English manual with them so he downloaded one from the internet and printed three copies before returning upstairs. He handed a box to Grant, into which he'd tucked a copy of the manual, and thanked Adrian for the phones.

"Thank Maxine, not me," Adrian replied. "She got back from San Diego on Friday. That reminds me, there's some stuff for your house in the garage, too."

"Show's over, I guess," he said as the tip of the sun slid beneath the horizon. He carried his ashtray into the kitchen and then led the two men into the garage, where he pointed to several plastic bags with utensils and frying pan handles sticking out of them. "There's probably more but I don't know where it is."

Grant and Roland gathered everything up and found they could take it in one trip, so they said goodnight to Adrian and made their way around the corner from the Shack and down the steep street to their new home. Grant was panting in the still-warm humidity, and when they reached their door he put everything down on the tiled entranceway. "I could use a run on the beach now and then," he said.

"Just get yourself an insatiable girlfriend," Roland suggested, finessing his key into the stiff lock. "That'll be exercise enough. Besides, you might step on something sharp while you're jogging, and the risk just isn't worth it. Don't take chances with your health." He turned the key and they entered the living room.

"Whoah," said Roland.

"Fuck me gently," said Grant.

Maxine had been shopping all right. The things they had brought from Adrian's garage had given them both the impression that their basic needs would be met and everything else was up to them. Which was fine, Roland thought. Nobody ever promised him a rose garden. But now, standing next to a pile of empty boxes and surveying their home, it was clear that Maxine was indeed a woman who could put even the indomitable Liza to shame when it came to shopping.

Roland had been in the place before several times. He and Castanza had brought up a king-sized bed for his room, and he had gone in with Tatiana to describe the kind of curtains he wanted. Although it was a beautiful place, made even more so by the intricate stained glass on the windows and the great cherrywood front door with tropical flowers stained and etched into its glass, he had thought it a little bare. It had a couch and loveseat and some beautiful Santa Fe-style wooden tables but not much else. Now, though, those tables were barely visible underneath towels, kitchen appliances, DVDs and a stereo. A huge TV occupied one wall in the living room and colorful artwork hung on either side, and a check of their bedrooms revealed just as many new things there.

"I have to meet this woman," said Roland, once he and Grant had recovered.

"I'd forgotten she was like this," Grant admitted. They stood on the main balcony together, watching Yoda running around on Roxane's patio beneath them.

"How long have you known these guys?" Roland asked. "Adrian and Maxine, I mean."

113

"A long time," Grant answered. "Never knew Sidney though. I met them when we lived in the Bahamas."

"You were there?"

"Yeah." Grant adjusted his glasses. "We owned condos in the same complex in Nassau. We grew pretty close in that time; lots of adventures. Ask Adrian about the eighteen fuckin' months it took those clowns to build him a pool."

For the next half an hour, as the ambient sunlight faded and the stars came out, Grant regaled Roland with stories of life in the Bahamas. He had known a man who owned a Cigarette boat but for some reason was never around, and had given Grant the keys. "'Take her out whenever you want,' he told us," Grant said. "'Beats sitting in the slip all the time, rusting', so we did. Man, we had a great time."

"Sounds like it," Roland agreed. He liked listening to people's stories, and Grant was good at telling them. Not that Roland believed everything he said, for he had already made Grant out to be in some ways a bit of a fish flyer – that is, someone who tells fish stories when it comes to flying, ones that get bigger and less believable but more interesting each time they're told. For this reason Liza had already expressed some disapproval when it came to Grant. Once she had asked Roland, "What the hell does he *do*, anyway?", because so far as anyone could tell he spent the majority of his time playing around on the internet. Liza obviously didn't always appreciate the decisions her brother made. But Grant was entertaining if nothing else, and there was an air about him that Roland liked. Something about him said he was game for anything and that he was used to strange situations like Cyberia. It was also obvious that he thought a great deal of Adrian and probably knew him fairly well.

"I'm just here to fly, though," Grant said. "I don't know what you guys do and I don't want to know," he added in a way that made it very clear that he did indeed want to know. Grant seemed to have the notion that Roland held some kind of senior position in Cyberia, probably because he had clearly set himself apart from the other employees, and in this Roland saw an opening.

"So, Adrian said we're getting a helicopter."

"That's right," said Grant. "Shelly gets to pick the color scheme."

"So what are we getting?"

Grant was silent for a little while. Then he said, "Don't know yet. Probably a Bell JetRanger; LongRanger maybe. There's a nice one at the factory, and the customer who ordered it changed his mind in mid-build. So if we want it, it'll be ready a lot sooner than ordering one from scratch. But it's stupid what they charge for basic instruments. If we want floats on it, that's a less expensive hit than a cheap little extra fuckin' ADF. That's practically standard equipment on ultralights, for Christ's sake."

"They're that chintzy?" Roland remarked. He was familiar with inexpensive ADF radios, navigational aids using the AM band being rendered obsolete by global positioning satellites.

"Well, I'm exaggerating a bit," Grant conceded. "But all told, with the leather interior and the CD stereo and headphones for everybody, we're looking at around a million and a half."

"I see," said Roland, starting to calculate. "And what kind of airplane is Adrian looking at?"

"Probably a King Air. Nice one, though, 500 model or something, brand new."

King Airs were turboprops, and Roland was expecting to hear that they were getting a jet. "I understand we're chartering Heinz's Learjet exclusively until we get a plane of our own. Why don't we just buy it, or something like it?" he asked.

"Frankly, I don't know," Grant replied. "Costa Rica is around fourteen hundred miles away, just over three hours in the Learjet, and a turboprop will tack another couple of hours onto that easily. But Adrian wants a new plane. He'd rather have a new turboprop than a used jet. Besides, the Lear's useful load is hardly that airplane's main attraction."

Roland noticed the *Marigalante* cruising near the shoreline. "How much does Adrian want to spend?" he continued. "I mean, why don't we just go all out and get a Gulfstream Five?"

Grant looked sideways at Roland. "Have you been listening to my phone calls?"

Roland shook his head. "What phone calls?"

"I've got a friend who runs a charter brokerage. One of the biggest in the world. If anybody needs anything they can't organize themselves, they take care of it. These guys don't just set you up with the plane and crew, they plan the whole flight, take care of the payments, passports and visas, all that shit."

"And?"

"And Adrian needs to fly to Latvia to meet with some bank we deal with over there, but he can't go to the States or Canada." He shuffled uncomfortably. "You knew that, hey?"

Roland didn't know that, but it explained why Adrian never got his own coffee. He played along.

"I've heard as much. So what are his options?"

"Well, there aren't a hell of a lot of smaller business jets that can fly from Mexico direct to Latvia. None, actually. But the Gulfstream Five can go direct from Mexico City to London, no stop required in Miami or JFK or anywhere."

"I assume it could go the few extra miles to Riga then." Roland retrieved two glasses of Coke, the only thing in the fridge, to which he added ice, the only thing in the freezer. He wondered if this was what Mick had first done at his condo and then only ever added that one bag of pretzels, keeping them in the fridge to prevent them getting stale.

116

Back home, stale bread meant it was crusty and dry. Here, it meant that the humidity made it overly moist to the point of being floppy. He handed a glass to Grant.

Roxane appeared below them, accompanied by Kevin and Eric, who pulled out chairs and sat down at the patio table. Roxane lit a tealight candle which flickered in the darkness. The sweet smell of their cigarettes was unmistakable. Grant and Roland looked at each other and wordlessly moved inside.

Seated on the couch, Roland continued his train of thought. "G-Five, then? Bingo," he said. "Let's get one." He knew that the jets were outrageously expensive but this was a good chance to find out how much money Adrian was playing with.

Grant laughed and loudly crunched a piece of ice. "Yeah, wouldn't that be great. But do you know what they want for those things? Forty, fifty million or something. Eighty, for all I know. One charter alone between Mexico and Latvia is going to cost around three hundred grand."

"I bet they don't charge extra for dual ADFs."

Grant laughed again. Roland asked, "Why not a cheaper jet that can go from here to, say, the Bahamas, then to the Azores, then to Europe?"

"Too many fuckin' stops. He's got his health to think about. Besides, it's not like he'll be making this trip all the time."

"Good," said Roland, before he understood why. Grant raised his eyebrows in silent question. Roland didn't know what to say exactly so he just told the truth. "Call me crazy, but I think it's a bad idea for Adrian to go there at all."

"Why?" Grant adjusted his glasses again.

"Just a feeling," said Roland rather feebly, but when he imagined Adrian making that trip, he couldn't do it without a black filter clamped over it. "It just doesn't seem like a good idea."

"Tell him," Grant said. "He listens to that kind of thing. He's big on instinct. You wouldn't think it but he is."

Roland decided right then and there not to. He had run into trouble before trying to understand and use his intuition, and if something did go wrong in Latvia he didn't want to make it look as though he had any advance knowledge. It would have to be enough that he had mentioned it to Grant. He asked, "Why is he going at all?"

"Bail the bank out," Grant replied frankly. "They've been fucking up all over the place and some members are getting pissed off 'cause they aren't getting their payments. Adrian called them up and said what the fuck's going on, and they said we're their biggest customer and what we do affects them too much. If we write one check too many it can throw them off 'cause they may not have enough other reserves to cover it. So we're going to buy the bank."

So that's where we are, thought Roland. Cyberia – or Adrian, at least, if he had other sources of income – had enough money to buy an overseas bank but not enough money for the jet to get him there. At first that sounded ludicrous, but when Roland thought about what Adrian's priorities were it made more sense. Owning a bank was an obvious answer to the trouble he knew Liza and Roxane had to deal with every day, and if Adrian could set the deal up with even three trips over there, he had only spent a fraction of what it would cost to own the jet he needed.

"Why can't he go to the States or Canada?" Roland asked, then added quickly, "I'd heard he can't go but nobody said why."

Grant stiffened. "Some tax thing. On principle he refused to pay some stupid tax bill and left the States. I don't know what Canada is all about."

This was vague enough to sound as though it had a basis in truth somewhere, and Roland left the conversation at that. Maybe Grant honestly didn't know. The only one who knew how Adrian invested the members' money, and probably the only one who even knew exactly how much they had, was Adrian himself. Of that, at least, Roland was sure. Not even Liza knew, as far as Roland could make out.

He closed his eyes for a moment. Four days away from work would mean literally hundreds of faxes to be taken care of. Also he was starting his Spanish lessons with Guadalupe tomorrow. He explained this to Grant and took his leave.

"Besides, I told Roxane I'd drop in," he said. "I'll see you tomorrow."

"Same time, same channel," said Grant.

Roland descended the stairs, wincing as he did so as the heartburn came and went. Lights hidden behind shades of all colors in the open stairwell made him feel as though he was on the set of a surreal movie. He knocked on the door, listening to Caetana Velosso wafting through the doorway.

Roxane's home had a beautiful open design. It was like Roland's but bigger, with built-in shelving for the television and stereo and a blue-tiled kitchen with a large island. Roxane had made it into a home very quickly. She had amassed an impressive array of artwork and various other nicknacks now decorating the light yellow walls. "My boyfriend made these," she explained, pointing to some beautiful objets d'art. While she was giving Roland a quick tour of the place, Mick stopped in to say hello. "Come out and have a beer with us," she said to the two.

Roland's heartburn was worsening by the minute so he opted for water as they joined the little group on the patio.

The conversation was somewhat forced. Eric and Kevin in particular had decided that because Roland objected to their use of drugs, he also objected to them as people – which wasn't true, but Roland did nothing to dissuade them from believing it – and they were suspicious of how close Roland had become to Adrian. Or rather, not how close, but how trusted. Nor did they like Roland working harder than they did.

Mick had explained to Roland that no matter what Kevin's other talents were, he would only ever do data entry at Cyberia. This was for two reasons – one, because Kevin had apparently told him that he was the fastest typist Mick would ever see, so Mick was relieved of the burden of wondering how to promote him when nobody wanted him to; and two, because Mick wanted to keep him beside Shelly in the room off the main office and away from the rest of the employees. Grant now had a desk in that office also, looking out over the ocean. Roland had moved his own desk so that now when he worked all he had to do was lift his gaze and he could see straight out to those islands at the mouth of the bay – the Marieta Islands, a bird sanctuary, Guadalupe had told him – and he wondered if its new position made his coworkers nervous. Having his desk there gave him a vantage point from which he could always see what they were doing. Everyone but Mick, anyway.

Inevitably the topic of their drug use came up. Roland tried to explain his opinion on it but he didn't get very far.

"I couldn't care less about it," he said truthfully. "One of the things I hate the most is people telling other people what they can do and what they can't. It's just that if what we're doing here is supposed to be such a secret it definitely doesn't help things to be a heat magnet."

He was going to continue but Eric cut him off. He held his hands out placatingly and said, "Roland, don't worry. It's…it's taken care of. Trust me."

If there was any phrase gauged to make Roland even more uneasy about this subject, it was 'it's taken care of'. At this he balked. "Taken care of how?" he asked.

Kevin piped up in his nasal voice and said, "It's not your business. Just don't worry about it."

He reminded Roland very much of those smarmy sidekicks that Disney characters always have. He was never the first to say anything but he would emphasize the point of anyone he was trying to ingratiate himself with, and this was no exception. He was like a yappy terrier hiding behind a bulldog.

"You're putting me at risk of prosecution because of your habit, and you think it's none of my business?" Roland retorted. "If you mean that somewhere somebody has been bribed, that only works once. After that, people get greedy, and when they get greedy they get unpredictable and all sorts of stupid things happen. So don't tell me how it's taken care of if you don't want to," – if you even know, he thought – "just tell me it's not bribery somewhere."

"It's taken care of," Eric repeated.

Roland could have been wrong, but he figured that it was Sidney who bought the drugs for everybody with his dad's money as insurance. He knew that the police in Mexico were famous for their corruption, and normally it wouldn't have worried him at all that people he knew there were smoking anything illegal, but he couldn't understand their hypocrisy. Either Cyberia was a secret that each employee had to be trusted in guarding, which obviously included not attracting unwanted attention, or it wasn't.

"So what do you guys say when people ask what you do here?" Roland pressed them.

Eric said, "I just tell them I come up here to use the pool and get on the internet for a while."

"That doesn't strike you as stupid?"

"Why would it?" Kevin asked defensively.

"Because I wasn't even here a week before Mick told me that already people were asking who I was down on Olas Altas. So obviously we're noticed. Do you really think anyone is going to believe that we all come up here to use Adrian's pool and play on his computer?"

Roxane said, "Well, it's got truth in it. We do use his pool and we do use his computer – all fifteen or twenty of them."

"All anyone has to do is sit outside Adrian's house and count the people who come in, and see when they leave. It even *looks* like a regular workday. Plus any of the house staff could probably be bribed. They all know what's downstairs and I don't even know if they've been told it's a secret. It's as though we're supposed to stand in front of an erupting volcano and say we don't feel any heat, we don't see any ash."

"Well, so what do you do?" Eric asked.

"I don't tell the truth, but I don't tell obvious lies either," Roland answered. "I say I come to the house to design web pages and use Adrian's computer to maintain investments I have back home that allow me to live down here."

"You shouldn't even mention investments," said Kevin. "You could probably be fired for telling us this."

All you need is a sandbox, Roland thought. "You're telling me that my explanation isn't sufficient? Why not? It answers how I'm financially able to stay here and why I go to Adrian's all at the same time."

Mick spoke up. He had been very uncomfortable with the conversation and had hardly said anything all night.

"Actually, it is a pretty good one. Adrian himself hears all kinds of rumors as to what we're doing. He says if you haven't heard a new rumor by noon, start one of your own." He looked around the table. "He finds it entertaining. And face it, it's not like no one talks about us."

If this was intended to defuse the situation it worked tolerably well, and the conversation shifted to other territory. Eventually Eric said, "I can't wait til we have our places in Costa Rica. That'll be awesome."

Mick studied Eric closely and then looked at Kevin. "What have you guys heard about it so far?" he asked.

"Not much," Kevin replied. "Just that we'll be living in a gated compound with armed guards somewhere up in the mountains in Costa Rica and if we want to work there, we can, and if we want to stay and work here in Vallarta we can do that too."

Roland wasn't exactly stunned at this news, but it was something major. He tried not to show his surprise and was glad he'd done so when Roxane looked back and forth between Mick and Roland and said, "That's just what we've gathered, unless you guys know something we don't."

Mick didn't respond. The *Marigalante* was setting off its nightly fireworks. No one else mentioned drugs or Costa Rica, and after some desultory conversation about the preceding weekend, Eric and Kevin left for the night and Mick soon followed. "I have to leave at five-thirty in the morning," he explained, "and I still haven't found the power cord for my laptop."

Roxane and Roland followed him inside, bringing ashtrays and empty bottles. Roland was about to leave as well but Roxane said, "Stay a while."

She stretched out on the couch and Roland sat in the big papasan chair across from her. Yoda tried to jump into his lap. Roland picked him up.

"So what's your story?" she asked. Her eyes were very red.

"I already told you last week," Roland said. "Remember?"

"No, not that," Roxane said. "I mean, who are you really?"

"What's that supposed to mean?"

"Are you a plant?"

Roland didn't know whether to be offended or amused. "What, like a fern or something?"

"Huh?" Roxane rubbed her eyes. "No, not like a house plant, I mean…"

"I know," Roland said. "You mean, am I planted here by the shapeshifting reptilian Illuminati."

"What the hell? No, I just mean, are you some customs guy or something."

"Customs guy?"

"Don't be difficult. You know damn well what I mean. I mean, are you planted here by DEA or the securities commission or something."

Roland was curious. "Why? Are you expecting one?"

"I don't know. You tell me." Roxane grew defensive. "You're in close with Adrian and his buddies."

"I understand him," said Roland. "Sort of, anyway. But that doesn't mean I know something you don't. You're the one in the audit department, remember? If anyone would know the books, it would be you and Liza."

"It's just...I don't know." Roxane was obviously not pleased with how the conversation had gone. "It just seems..." Roland felt for her. He hated searching for the right words and not finding them. "...too good to be true," she finished. "Not in *that* way, just...I don't know."

"How?" Roland asked. This was interesting.

"Okay, here it is. You have your shit together, you're nice, you know a thing or two about a thing or two. You spend time talking with Adrian's friends, those two weirdos at the café that you waved at today. You work a little too hard. I mean, this is Puerto Vallarta, for Christ's sake. Shouldn't you be out at the bars, bringing home beautiful girls every night?"

"Who says I'm not?" Roland asked, though he wasn't. "Besides, making life look easy takes a lot of hard work."

"Basically, you're just a little too comfortable with all of this."

"All of *what*? What are you talking about?" He still didn't understand. "I'm confused as to why I *shouldn't* be comfortable with this. Maybe it's me who should be asking if *you* know something *I* don't."

Roxane fixed him with her red gaze as steadily as she could.

"No," she said. "It's just, this is a secret."

"I think, if I may be so bold as to say so, that I understand that fact a little better than you do," Roland said.

"How's that?"

"Look, I know it's popular not to sweat the small stuff, but the devil is in the details. I wasn't kidding, what I said about being a heat magnet. You and Mick especially, you make me nervous just being around you." Roland could feel their constant unspoken apprehension through a sense that had become all too tuned from overuse with Sara, from knowing when she had been lying to him. Well, he reflected, nobody calls disasters 'learning experiences' for nothing.

"Do you know if Cyberia is a scam?" Roxane asked.

"A scam?" Roland echoed, surprised. "I thought you and Liza swore so much because you're having trouble with banks not paying dividends to members on time."

"We are." She went to the kitchen and brought back a very large glass of water. She drank over half of it before she put it on the table and sat down again. Yoda left Roland's knee to clamber onto the couch and curl up beside her.

"Well if you're trying to move heaven and earth to get people their money, why would you ask if it's a scam?"

"I don't mean a scam that way," she said. "I mean, a scam like if it's illegal."

Roland had thought about this a lot. Almost since the day he landed he'd been at one of those crossroads where his head was telling him one thing but inside there was someone knocking with a different message.

"For now at least, I don't see how it can be."

"Why not?" Roxane asked, finishing the rest of her water. In the kitchen again she held up a glass inquiringly and Roland nodded.

"Two reasons." He spoke up so she could hear him over the crackling ice as she poured. She held up a lime wedge and wiggled it around as she looked at him. Roland nodded at that too. Everything in Mexico had limes in it because they were such a good disinfectant, and he was developing a taste for them.

"And they would be?" Roxane set the glass in front of him.

"Thanks," he said as he drank deeply and wondered how best to continue. Finally he said, "The first reason is because we're just too big. I mean, what kind of scam could get this big and not be taken down? We're not talking about charging old ladies for roofing work that doesn't get done, or pulling quick-change stunts on beer tub girls. Let's face it, we were just talking earlier about how we attract so much attention that we have to make up a cover story for why we're here. We work in one of the biggest houses in the city. For all his talk about secrets, Mick brings his cell phone and laptop when we go for coffee every morning. Tell me that doesn't attract attention. We just took a Learjet to Guadalajara for the weekend – one that wasn't our own, with pilots not sworn to secrecy who right this very minute might be in a bar in town talking about it. They're staying overnight to take Adrian and Mick down to Costa Rica tomorrow, which will be more fuel for the fire."

"That's all true," Roxane agreed, "but people don't know what they don't know, if that makes sense. I mean, it's really nobody's business where Adrian gets the money from or why we go up to his house."

"You're right, exactly. It is nobody's business but ours and his. So then why do we have to make up a story about it?" Roland asked. "Simply because we promise our members that we will keep their identity private. But Milo and Duck Bill are both members. Do you wonder what *they* tell people? And you have no control over that."

"Okay, but they don't *know* they're members. They were just put into the computer when Adrian was getting the database going because he needed to make it look like he had more members than he did."

Roland was taken aback at this. He knew from talking to Milo that at least Milo was very aware that he was a member, and had assumed the same of Duck Bill. Not that he'd spent much time talking with them about Cyberia, just the occasional few words in passing, but he had learned at least that.

"Okay, so let's say that doesn't convince you. Fair enough. But consider the second reason, the best reason I don't think it's a scam." He drank the rest of his water. Roxane was watching him intently. He put his glass back on the table. "Simply put, we're too easy to find."

"*Easy to find?*" Roxane was incredulous. "In case you haven't noticed, we're in a tiny little vacation port halfway down Mexico's Pacific coast. Even if you figure that the best place to hide something is right under people's noses, this is a pretty good compromise between literally hidden and hidden out in the open, so to speak."

"Maybe," said Roland, "but there's a pretty obvious trail, isn't there?"

He leaned forward in his chair. "Let's say you want to investigate Cyberia because you suspect it's illegal. So you check out the website, which says that members' checks should be sent to Belize. You fly to Belize to see that the address is actually the headquarters of a shipping company. You corner one of the employees with a few bucks in your hand and ask where the Cyberia envelopes get sent to, and who sends them. You learn that they go to Puerto Vallarta, Mexico by courier. So you hop a flight to PV and hang out in the lobby of the courier's office until somebody comes in and says, 'Hey, I'm here to pick up Cyberia's stuff', at which point you follow the guy – actually it wouldn't be a guy, it would be Tatiana in one of her big floppy hats but you get the point – and end up being led straight to the Shack. Even if you had to repeat that process ten times to get to us, it would be worth it. Total cost of the investigation, what, ten grand? Twenty? That's nothing to shut down the millions we're making." At least twenty thus far, in fact, Roland had estimated. With the value of real estate alone there was easily ten million floating around, plus a King Air for another five, a million-dollar yacht and sufficient reserves to pay salaries and all the associated expenses with no apparent strain at all. If there was even a hint of truth in the Costa Rica story it would easily be even higher than that. "So if it's illegal, if it is a scam, I'd say that the governments of the world care about as much as they have to and no more. And they won't care until somebody or something forces them to. Remember, that's *if* it's even a so-called scam in the first place."

This seemed to put Roxane at ease. She relaxed visibly and said, "Is it really a shipping company?"

Roland was sucking on his lime. "Mm-hmm," he said. "Old friend of Adrian's." He dropped the lime back into the glass. "One more thing," he said.

"And that would be?"

Roland carried his empty glass into the kitchen and set it by the sink as he spoke.

"Adrian obviously isn't trying to bribe us into being quiet. That is to say, if he knows something we don't, he isn't telling us what it is and then treating us like kings to keep our mouths shut. We aren't co-conspirators in anything."

"True," Roxane mumbled, rubbing her eyes.

Roland tapped a finger on the countertop as he looked out the window at the night. Finally he said, "And with that, good lady, I take my leave."

Back at Mick's condo, Roland felt his heart pounding as it tried to keep him from fainting on the way up the stairs. Even letting himself in through the back door of the building, which adjoined the street his new house faced, he wasn't spared the pain in his chest he had hoped to avoid by not climbing up the hill and going around Adrian's house. He'd never had heartburn this bad. He found Mick still awake, watching television.

"You're still up?" Roland asked. "I thought you had to leave really early. Didn't you find that cord?"

"I do and I did," Mick answered. "I'm just not tired, that's all."

"Roxane thinks I'm a government agent or something," Roland said, trying to sound nonchalant. "And what the hell's this about a gated compound in Costa Rica?" As he spoke, Roland realized that he was angry. He hadn't felt it at the time because he was very slow to realize when he was hurt, but his conversations with the other three that night had annoyed and offended him.

Mick laughed. "When will you learn that you can't take those guys seriously? It sounds to me like some information trickled down through Sidney, and something got embellished in the translation. Adrian *is* buying property in Costa Rica, and I'm going down there to look for an office and see about a couple of things to do with our website. But as for the rest, don't even worry about it."

This didn't do much to assure Roland. "It's just stupid that that they think even mentioning investments is enough to get me fired, when any minute some cop could bust down the door looking for drugs." Roland had to sit on the floor because standing was too difficult; his breathing was too labored. "I mean, the cops can't *all* be on the take."

"They aren't, and you're right," said Mick. "But obviously it's a risk Adrian's willing to take. We just have to live with it."

Roland listened to the Spanish voices on the TV. The sound was like music to him.

"You know, I think Adrian cares less about keeping this thing a secret than anybody," he said.

Mick set a small suitcase by the door. "Especially when he drinks," he said severely. "You get him going down there at the dot-com café on Olas Altas after he's had a few, and he might as well just call the newspapers himself."

Roland remembered the bottles behind Adrian's desk. He couldn't read one of them, but he was sure the other was labeled 'Halcion'. "Mick, what kind of medication is Adrian on?"

"Time-release painkillers. Morphine, basically," Mick answered. "Oxycontin and something else, I don't remember what. Why do you want to know that?"

"Just curious," Roland replied. "About everything."

Roland wanted to pack up his suitcases and take them up the street to his new home, but he was in too much pain. Besides, the maid had taken his laundry to be cleaned but hadn't returned it yet, so he decided to stay another night. He said goodnight to Mick and had risen to leave when he noticed the light playing off Mick's wrist.

"Nice watch."

Mick smiled. "Patek Philippe. Tells the time and everything."

7

Lonesome Revolution

Slogan's arrival at breakfast the next morning was greeted with a round of applause. There had been no question that Amy would agree to marry him, but it was nice to hear it confirmed. He came in late as usual, (on today's t-shirt, *"You must be this tall to ride"* and a dotted line halfway up), and waved to everyone as he dumped his knapsack on the floor to receive hugs from Guadalupe and Anita. Castanza, casual as ever, gave him a high-five and patted him on the back as he passed by with an oily rag in his hand.

"Congratulations, my friend," said Roland, returning from the kitchen with a cup of coffee to take downstairs.

"Thanks." Slogan eschewed Roland's proffered hand for a big hug instead. Roland winced. His heart still hurt.

"I'd rather be disemboweled with a rusty fork and strangled with my lower intestine," Kevin said as he pushed back his chair and carried his dishes in to the kitchen. "But it's nice to see you happy."

"Great. Thanks." Slogan sat down in Kevin's vacant chair and Roland pulled one out beside him. The multitude of faxes from the weekend could wait a little while longer. Besides, he'd come in early, and walking just the few short yards up the street between the condo and Adrian's house had been enough exertion for his heart.

"You know, it was all I could do to keep my mouth shut about your imminent proposal when I was over for dinner last week," Roland said. In fact, now that he thought about it, he had been more excited about it than he'd let on, and if it weren't for the fact that Slogan and his fiancée had two dogs whom Roland had used as conversation pieces he would have blurted it out. Roland loved animals and it was nice

131

to see that Slogan's girlfriend did too. Roland thoroughly approved of her. She was tall, with long, dark blonde hair, a genuine laugh and an active mind. She would be good for Slogan, who said, "It's great that she said yes."

Roland laughed. "What else would she say? She's obviously a smart woman."

"I don't know," Slogan replied. "It's a pretty important question. I mean, you don't treat that one lightly, do you?" He said it more like a statement than a question.

"No, you don't," said Roland reflectively. "But you don't let that fact paralyze you, either."

Slogan didn't respond at first. He was still staring at the table, still happy, when finally he said, "I'd hate for her to have said yes if she didn't mean it."

"I can't imagine her ever doing that," Roland reassured him. "She seems like the kind of person whose yes is yes and whose no is no."

"That's true." Slogan smiled. "Yeah, that's her." He lifted his gaze from the table in front of him and looked at Roland. "I took some great pictures over the weekend. I'll download them onto the computer after lunch and you can see them." He took a long drink of mango juice. "How was Guadalajara?" he asked.

Roland could tell that Eric had been waiting to join the conversation, so he just said, "Good," and nodded at Eric, who took up the cause.

As he sipped his coffee and chatted with those still seated at the table, Roland found it reassuring that he felt no envy at his friend's happiness. Slogan and his fiancée loved each other and they were getting married, just as Sara was going to – or had already done, as far as Roland knew. Well, the world could always use a few more weddings and happy couples. Roland smiled a little as he looked out at the dolphins playing together in the ocean.

Guadalupe had to stay until five o'clock but she was usually finished her work by four, so that was the time Roland had his lessons. Mick had lent him his well-worn copy of Margarita Madrigal's *Magic Key to Spanish*, and armed with this and a blank notebook he went upstairs and joined Guadalupe where she already sat by the pool. She was squinting into the sunlight and smiled when Roland approached.

Over the next hour they talked in whichever language was easiest for them to use. Although Roland's pronunciation was excellent his vocabulary was still very limited. They talked about the weather, Mexico, all sorts of things, touching on each subject like a flat rock skipping across a lake. Eventually they talked about themselves.

Guadalupe was the same age as Roland, though he had judged her to be younger. She had married young and had children but was now divorced. Her husband had been cheating on her. "*No mas,*" she said, making a cutting motion with her brown hand. "*No mas.*" No more. Roland agreed. She told him how much money she made. Roland made almost ten times that just in his salary alone, not including what it would cost for his paid expenses. She told him how she had been hired on by Adrian and was now *jefa* of the house staff. She had been recommended by not only Amy and Sidney, who occupied the penthouse in the building she manned the front desk in, but by Shelly as well, who lived two floors below them. It took her almost an hour on the bus to get to Conchas Chinas from La Aurora, the district where she lived. She and another of the housekeepers were friends and lived near to each other and often rode together.

Many of the locals weren't really from Puerto Vallarta at all, she said, having come from cities all over Mexico including large numbers from the country's capital. When tourists said they were going to Mexico, they meant the country, but when a Mexican said the same thing it meant the city. "*Distrito Federale*, or *El Deffe*," meaning 'The D.F.', Guadalupe said. "*Ciudad Mexico*." She was originally from Mexico City herself.

She wanted to know about snow, but Roland's Spanish didn't yet extend to the complexity required to satisfy her curiosity. Snow was like sand but not sandy; it was heavy but a snowflake was light; it was water but it wasn't always wet; it was white but a full moon on a field at night made it glow a brilliant blue. Roland told her it was fun to play in and left it at that.

The time flew by and eventually they noticed her friend leaning against one of the columns, divested of her apron and watching them in silent signal that it was time to go. Before they broke for the day, Guadalupe opened a notebook that had been sitting untouched in front of her. This was one that she had used to teach Spanish to an American woman who had befriended her when she came to stay for the winter at the condo building where Guadalupe had worked.

Every single page was filled with Guadalupe's neat handwriting. She had painstakingly copied the singular, plural, transitive and intransitive forms of hundreds of Spanish verbs, as well as basic vocabulary words and their corresponding English meaning. Roland couldn't even begin to guess how long it had taken her, and he was awed and humbled that she would have even thought of it in the first place. He stared at the pages, and the one question running through his mind was whether he would have done this for somebody he'd only just met, as Guadalupe had done, or simply have referred them to a textbook. To see evidence of what had obviously taken hours for her to do, and to take hard-earned pesos away from other things she needed in order to buy the notebook in the first place, was something Roland would never forget.

They ended the lesson with Roland presenting Guadalupe with the small candelabra he'd bought her in Guadalajara. She wouldn't accept money for the lessons; in fact, when Roland had approached Tatiana – who, as property manager, also was in charge of paying the staff – with the intention of adding some money to Guadalupe's paycheck he discovered that Guadalupe had already instructed her not to take any money from Roland. He'd had to think of something else.

It had taken Roland until just after lunchtime to clear away the weekend's accumulated work, and even as he did so a backlog was already building up. Tatiana had brought him some mysterious pills from the pharmacy on a suggestion from Ken, who said that back in the States the medication was by prescription only but was available here over the counter. Roland had taken four times the dosage indicated on the bottle and felt no better. He was getting worried. Maybe Adrian would part with some of his morphine. At five-thirty when Roxane passed by his desk with Yoda in tow she stopped and said, "Were you having kinky sex up there by the pool with Guadalupe or something?"

"No," Roland answered. "Why do you ask?"

"Because your breathing is shallow and you're sweating like crazy." She studied him more closely and added, "Actually you look like hell. You sure you're all right?"

"No, not really. I've never had heartburn this bad before. I'm not even sure if that's what it is."

"Huh," said Roxane. "Well, if you need somebody to take you to a doctor, you just let me know. I'm going home and I'll be in all evening."

"Thanks," Roland said. Yoda licked his hand in passing on his way up the stairs.

Eric was still at work. Because CIA Mick was gone, the only people working late were Roland and Liza, as usual, but Eric sat there too, tapping away at his computer. Over the weekend Adrian had instructed him to start helping out with the audit department, which meant that he was not only answering emails during the day but learning the ropes vis-à-vis checks and balances as well. Roland watched him looking back and forth between a pile of certified checks to his right and the accounting software in front of him.

Roland didn't feel like working anymore. He had stayed late almost every night since he was hired and he was sick of it. Also he was in a lot of pain. He shut down his computer and was halfway up the stairs when Eric called to him.

"Hey, where are you going?"

"Home."

Eric climbed a few steps so he could look up at Roland around the curve of the massive staircase. "You know, there's about a hundred new faxes sitting here."

He stood there looking indignant. Obviously working late was going to take him some getting used to. Roland felt like swatting him. It was none of Eric's business how Roland did his job and besides, it had taken him hours to wade through the paper he'd found on his desk that morning alone. Not only that, but when he'd wandered in to chat with Grant before work started he'd noticed that the pile that had been dropped on Kevin's desk wasn't nearly as big as the one on Roland's.

"I'll take care of it," Roland said, though he didn't say when. He turned and left without waiting for an answer.

He hadn't slept very well the previous night. Every time he chose a new position it wasn't long before the pain in his chest became unbearable and he had to move. Eventually he found that lying on his back provided enough relief to spend the night in that shallow and mysterious zone between sleep and wake, but now as he let himself in to Mick's apartment and packed his suitcases he wished he had some sleeping pills because tonight didn't look as though it would be much better. Well, if he was still sick tomorrow he'd take Roxane up on her offer of a ride to the doctor. For now, though, the prospect of sleeping in his new place, his own place, was exciting enough to push the pain aside.

He brought his bags down to the door and returned upstairs for a last look around. He had been at Mick's for only two weeks, but his first night there already seemed a lifetime ago. He gazed out at Los Arcos and the bay through the huge window beside the shower and smiled. A different view awaited him from a place he could call his own.

He let himself out the back door and started up the narrow street that ran parallel to the ocean, dividing his new house from Mick's condo building, and Adrian's beside it. One more good thing about staying in Conchas Chinas instead of moving down to Olas Altas was that Tatiana had an office in a condo two floors below Mick, so if Roland needed anything she was likely to attend to it more quickly than if he lived across town – near Liza, say, at the BayView Grand.

He felt laden with what seemed like twice the amount of baggage he'd arrived with in Mexico only two weeks before, mostly due to the fact that every time he tried to take a deep breath an unseen hand drove a knife into his heart. He stopped for a break as he struggled up the street and noticed Guillermo the security man standing on a balcony at the Shack, watching his progress. Roland pulled out his video camera and recorded him waving, that big genial smile on his face. He stopped the camera and stood there for a few moments, his eyes closed in the warm sunshine.

At the top of the stairs outside his doorway he paused for breath again. Seeing a figure through the stained glass, Grant got up and let him in.

"You get hit by a truck or something?" he asked.

"Feels like it, but no such luck," Roland answered, and explained his condition. "I think if it doesn't let up I'll go see a doctor tomorrow."

"Coroner, you mean. You could be dead by tomorrow. You really look awful." Grant was toying with his new cell phone. He continued, "One thing Maxine forgot to get was alarm clocks, so if you don't have one, use the one that came with this."

"Thanks for the tip." Roland dumped the suitcases on the floor of his huge bedroom. "For now, I just want to rest awhile."

Grant had followed him in. "Hope you don't mind sharing space," he said, nodding at the window where a small, quick movement to the left of it caught Roland's eye.

A little gecko, its feet allowing it to stick to virtually anything, had attached itself onto Roland's wall and sat there studying the two men. As they watched, it crept closer and eventually stopped just over Roland's night table.

"He came in off the balcony," Grant explained. "Sat there on the floor soaking up the sun for a while, then buggered off into your room."

"We'll be fine," Roland said. Grant withdrew, but before he closed the door he said, "I'm going to go down to Olas Altas for a late dinner. Want me to wake you?"

"Sure," said Roland. "I've started to like that veggie restaurant."

"Fuck that," Grant rejoined. "I didn't fight my way to the top of the food chain just to eat plants."

Roland barely had enough energy to grunt at this. Most Mexican food was very high in carbohydrates, and that plus all the alcohol he'd started to drink meant that he was putting on weight. His breathlessness on the short walk up the hill couldn't all be attributed to heartburn, or whatever this was. And as used to the heat as he had become, he still found the restaurant's salads and fruit drinks refreshing.

Grant closed the door. "About an hour or so, then," he said. "Get some rest."

Roland collapsed onto the bed. He programmed his cell phone to wake him up in time to shower, walk down to Olas Altas for coffee, walk back, and still get to work early. There were a multitude of tones he could use and he eventually chose a tinny version of an old but enduring Fifties hit. Then he rolled over and squinted at the gecko through the slanting sunlight.

"Do you live here, little guy?" he murmured. The gecko said nothing.

"I'm going to call you Dave," Roland continued. "You have some qualities of Daveness about you, reminding me of Daves I Have Known. Enigmatic. I suspect you're entertaining and somewhat devious, and perhaps your family ties could use a little strengthening. Is this true?"

Dave moved his head a little. Struck a nerve, Roland thought. "A good friend too, probably."

Roland's heart had chosen a steady level of pain which wasn't intensifying, thankfully. He noticed a switch on the wall above the bed and absently reached up and flipped it. Nothing happened. A thought occurred to him.

"Dave, have you ever seen snow?"

Dave blinked and stuck his tongue out.

"Exactly," Roland said. "Catch it on your tongue if you can. Of course, by the time it gets down to Mexico, it's just rain."

Dave retracted his tongue. Roland closed his eyes. As the sun moved across the floor and up the walls and deepened its redness Roland dreamed of a forgotten race of snow lizards.

It was dark. At least, it was dark outside, but above Roland's head a light bulb in a multicolored jeweled shade cast a soft glow into the room. The switch he'd played with before falling asleep had some purpose after all.

Dave was closer than he'd been when Roland fell asleep. He was pounding on the wall with one of his feet.

"Hey, you wanna go for a beer?" he asked.

Roland blinked and groaned loudly. "Eh?"

"Are you alive?" Dave said. "I want to go for dinner."

"Bite me," said Roland, pulling a pillow over his head. Then he remembered that Grant had wanted to go out, and he woke up fully.

"Sorry, Dave," he said. "I'm going for dinner with Grant." He pushed back the covers.

The little lizard shot up the wall and disappeared behind the air conditioner, the remote control for which hung on a cradle by the bed. Roland had never turned it on, though. He wasn't afraid of the heat. As he slipped into his sandals he was relieved that he didn't want to yawn. That would have hurt.

Grant poked his head around the door. "You look a little better," he observed. "All the same, let's take a taxi down instead of walking."

At Señor Book's they found Duck Bill sitting with a man Roland didn't know and Glenda, the gorgeous woman who had been talking to Mick on one of Roland's first nights there. By now Roland knew that she worked at a shop across the street from where they sat. He had seen her there as he passed by a couple of times.

"I'm Glenda," she said. She was even more beautiful up close. She was sitting with one leg crossed over the other, exposed by a seam in her thin, shiny dress. Her green eyes sparkled at him, topped with a pair of eyebrows so fine they looked as though they'd been meticulously applied by a forties movie star. Roland became instantly self-conscious.

He introduced himself and Grant and she produced a cigarette. The other man got up to leave, noticing his girlfriend waving to him from across the street. Roland found it strange that he wasn't relieved to learn that the man wasn't Glenda's boyfriend.

He drank two bottles of water before his dinner arrived. Bill was talking about his flying days. He was an expatriate American who had been a pilot in the war and afterwards had made good money flying for the airlines. In between he had bought a crop duster and used it to pay his way as he flew around the States. "Bit of a gypsy, I am," he said in that gravelly voice.

"Damned if one day somebody didn't steal my airplane," he continued. "Waited around for word on it, but the cops never found it. If they even looked. Had to take a bus back home halfway across the fuckin' country." He adjusted his baseball cap and coughed. "One day six years later, I'm on a train going through Kansas, and we passed right by an airfield. Right by it. There was this nice old Stearman biplane cropduster sitting there with no engine and the same red upper wing mine had. We get closer and I said, 'God damn, that's my airplane!'. If it had had an engine I woulda stole it back again."

Glenda wasn't paying much attention to Roland, which was fine with him because that meant he didn't have to explain his appearance. He knew he must look awful; not just unkempt but sickly too, and his appetite had waned. He pushed his plate away and ordered coffee. Grant switched plates with him and continued eating as though nothing had happened.

"Time for my beauty sleep," said Glenda as she got up to leave. "Besides, when it comes to flying I just can't relate. An airplane is something you get served cocktails in, and that's all I need to know." As she withdrew Roland couldn't take his eyes off her.

141

"Bill, you are my hero," he said. "How do you know her?"

Bill laughed. "Like you said, it's a small town. She's more or less single, by the way." He watched her as she disappeared down the street. "Phenomenal ass." He waved a freshly-lit cigar at Roland. "She's perfect for you, you know."

"Maybe," Roland said, although he felt like saying something more definitely in the negative. "But am I perfect for her?"

Grant laughed. "You'd have fun finding out."

Roland watched the end of Bill's cigar as it glowed red and then bright white. Glad to have a new subject to switch to, he said, "The soil where that tobacco was grown is high in magnesium. That's why the end is white like that."

"Really?" Grant piped up. "I thought it meant the cigar was good."

"It might be good, but not because of that."

"Bummer," said Bill.

"The criteria that people use to decide quality is all too often irrelevant." Roland said this faintly, thinking of how women were too often judged solely by their appearance. There weren't many women as beautiful as Glenda, but he didn't feel any urgency to talk with her.

He'd found Sara that beautiful too, even before he really knew her.

If Dave was startled at Roland's arrival, he didn't show it. He was stretched out luxuriously at the foot of Roland's bed, all seven inches of him. Even after Roland had brushed his teeth and washed his face and stared at himself in the mirror awhile, he showed no sign of stirring.

"I bet you think you're the first cold-blooded creature I've shared a bed with," Roland said. "You're not."

Dave disappeared over the edge of the bed. As Roland drifted away to sleep he heard an intermittent rustling in one of the tall tropical plants in the corner by the balcony door.

She was in the kitchen making jams when he came home late that afternoon. Her dark brown hair looked red in the light from the dying sun through the stained glass windows of the church next door and then through the windows of their little old house. She shrieked with glee and giggled self-consciously, casting her dish towel aside to throw her arms around him and hold him tightly. He had picked beautiful wildflowers on the way home, stopping first at a small overgrown cemetery at the edge of a ghost town and later, as a river wandered lazily through a valley and the sun warned him that it was setting by throwing his shadow into the ditch, he had followed it to where wild roses and bluebells stirred in the late summer breeze, arranged in an irresistible symphony of pastel wonder.

"My love," she murmured into his shirt where her lips pressed against his heart.

"My love," he whispered into the sweet air above her; air she carried with her everywhere; scented soaps and the store where she worked and the way she was.

Their little dog danced around them but they didn't move, they didn't stir, drinking in the joy of being able to hold what was in their hearts; to feel what they had waited their whole lives to feel, savoring the closeness and reality of love like cool wine settling on dry and waiting lips.

"There's enough light left in the day to pick berries for a pie. Would you come with me?" She looked up at him excitedly, expectantly. She was the most beautiful thing Roland had ever seen.

He kissed her cheek softly, barely brushing her immaculate skin with his lips. Her brown eyes were magnetic, loving; they enveloped him in a swirl of home and life and hands held loosely together even in their sleep. He closed his eyes and suddenly he was in bed with her at the beginning of the night, and through the open window he could hear the fountain in their little pond, and a train's sad whistle through the lonely darkness, and coyotes calling to each other across golden fields and bales of hay; bales made for just the two of them so that they could have something from which to command the sun's performance as they watched it gracefully say goodbye and slip beneath the prairie horizon. Her eyes told him of life and dreams together and hope, once lost, held shining once again.

She took the flowers and put them in a vase while he put the little dog on a leash, and then they walked hand in hand to a little trail through the bush at the edge of the field. They released the dog and watched it chasing everything that moved.

They filled a pail with sweet ripe berries and talked and laughed until finally, too dark to do anything other than kiss each other and taste the sweetness on the other's lips, they coaxed their dog back onto its leash and retraced their steps to the house. Along the way she spied wild strawberries as a telescope does a glowing and distant star and mixed them with the dark ones she already held.

Candle lit, house safe, they held each other and whispered to each other until finally she summoned the strength to lean over and kiss him goodnight. She rested her head on his shoulder and waited for sleep to come.

He breathed in the aroma of her hair as he stroked it and caressed her body, subtle and beautiful curves in the gathering blanket of moonlight through the blinds, listening to the dog win races and fight off monstrous attackers with dreamed growls and impossibly sharp teeth as it slept curled at their feet.

He whispered to her as she slept, words that would change his future and hers and entwine their destinies; words that he knew would bring him children and expectations and tears and laughter; words he longed to be ready to say to her in the light of the day. That was his wish as he smiled upon seeing a searing streak of light make a graceful arc in the sky countless miles above their house outside the window; a shooting star, sent to grant him his heart's true desire.

He was rehearsing the words to her, whispering in her ear as he did so often that summer, asking his enchanting and sleeping beauty if she would wear his ring and be his wife, when he was interrupted by a polite but persistent beeping, a song from everyone's youth digitized to virtual meaninglessness.

As he surfaced to reality like a buoyant ship released from the ocean floor, he passed through an area where the temperature of the water told him that the whistle of a train wasn't a train at all but rather a car horn on the road, the highway, far below. Further up past sinking jetsam and barracudas he realized that the coyotes were silent, and when he was awake enough to see light he was hit with the awful discovery that the fountain in his little pond wasn't a fountain at all but rather the sound of the tropical surf below his window carried by the gentle breeze past the fluttering curtains; a surf which left gifts of beautiful and wondrous things on the soft sand beach and then took them back to the depths from which they came, to be washed up on another shore in a different place and reflect the sun just a little bit differently than they would in the world he knew.

His deck broke the surface and scattered sea birds bobbing on the waves. The precious seconds between the dream at the bottom and the daylight's truth made him sick with dread, and then he no longer had sleep to anesthetize him.

He turned off the alarm and pushed away the pillow he'd been clutching like a teddy bear in his sleep, a habit he'd developed after Sara had left. He stared up at the ceiling.

The pain in his heart was worse. He sat up and looked around. As he did so he heard Grant closing the front door behind him. Grant liked to be at work earlier than anyone else so he could chat with Adrian.

Passing by the window on the way to his bathroom Roland noticed an unfamiliar Mexican man slowly dragging a net back and forth in the pool. From Roland's bedroom window he could jump almost straight down into it. Another was carefully watering the plants scattered around Roxane's patio.

Roland grabbed a towel from where Maxine had left a small stack of them on a nearby rattan chair; or at least, that's what Roland had assumed it was, but the stack was in fact one bath sheet roughly half an acre in size folded over several times. He struggled to unfold it and wrap it around himself before he was noticed. The man cleaning the pool caught Roland's movement and looked up just as he finished tucking the corner in on itself.

"*Buenos dias, señor*," the pool man called out, waving cheerfully.

"Good morning, sir," echoed the gardener as he tried out his English.

"Do you always sleep naked?" asked Roxane loudly, first cigarette of the day already almost done. She was wearing a bright, thin robe and hove into view as she followed Yoda across the terracotta patio. "You know, there's lots of tarantulas and scorpions in this neighborhood."

"I didn't see you there," Roland said feebly. It was an effort to get her to hear him.

"Lucky me." Roxane threw her cigarette butt over the railing. Below their house was an area of jungle leading down to the highway. The mountain was steep here, and anything dropped over the side took a second to hit the trees. There were creatures in the greenery already making their noises in the young day.

"You should wave now, like the Pope at the Vatican."

Roland adjusted his towel to drape like a toga and did so. As he brought his arm back down it started to tingle.

"Roxane, could you please take me to a doctor this morning?" he asked. "This pain isn't going away and now my arm's getting numb."

"You hopeless chump," Roxane called. "You're having a heart attack. Get dressed and come downstairs. Meet me at my car in two minutes."

On the way down the hill Roland kept massaging his chest over his heart. He was really worried now. Even so, he was grateful that he had something to take his mind off the dream he'd had.

He knew that he romanticized his relationship with Sara too much and in that respect was responsible for a lot of his own grief, but something in him told him that it was necessary. He had exposed something that had been festering below it all and something else in him, something healthy, wanted it gone. Nonetheless, he still missed Sara. He made no excuses for that. He had loved her so fiercely that this thing inside him had wanted to protect him from his feelings but had overcompensated, numbing him so much that Roland himself hadn't known how much he loved her until the pain of her leaving brought it into the light. That haunted him.

He didn't notice that he'd been crying until Roxane put her hand on his shoulder. Assuming that he was in pain, she said reassuringly, "You'll be all right. This doctor is the best in the city, and she's just down the hill."

Roland was glad to have Roxane there. Despite their conversation of two nights ago he sensed that she wanted to trust him.

They parked outside the Medisys and she escorted him upstairs, instructing him to sit in a chair while they waited for the doctor. They didn't have to wait very long.

Dr. Letitia Lowry was a tall, commanding Mexican woman with high cheekbones and a breezy demeanor. She sat the two gringos down in her office and said to Roland in perfect English, "Well, obviously you're the sick one."

"Yes," Roland said. "My heart is giving me a lot of pain and I can't breathe properly. I think it's heartburn, lots of acid or something."

Dr. Lowry led him to a small examining room adjoining her office. Roxane watched as he took off his shirt to allow her to take his blood pressure and listen to his heart with a stethoscope.

"Nothing wrong," she said, and summoned an intern to wheel in a machine on a cart. It had a variety of cables sticking out of it like tentacles, with suction cups at the end of each one. These she placed at various points around his chest, and as Roland breathed as deeply as he could she watched it printing out information.

"Here," she said, handing the printout to Roland. It looked like a stock market graph. He didn't even know if he was looking at it right side up, but when he turned it around it looked the same. "Your heart is beautiful," she said. "Very strong, very healthy. Your heart is not the problem."

"But it's my heart that hurts," Roland protested.

"Just because it hurts does not always mean there is something wrong with it." She smiled at him. "Sometimes your heart hurts because it is a messenger and there is something else wrong." Roland wondered if she was a bit psychic. She handed him his shirt and said something in Spanish to her intern, who departed rather reluctantly. She had been watching Roland with deep clinical interest since her arrival.

"You have pleurisy," Dr. Lowry informed him. "Your heart is doing a wonderful job, but it hurts because your lungs have swollen." She produced a pad of paper and a pen, and sketched a picture of a heart and the adjoining lung. "The outside lining of your lungs is inflamed, so big it's pressing against your heart. Your heart can feel pain but the outside of your lungs cannot. So your heart is the one to tell you there is something wrong." She drew an arrow to illustrate this. "Things like pollution, smoking, they all can cause it," she said, "and now that you have it, you are susceptible to get it again."

"Icky," Roxane observed. "Is it easy to cure?"

"Yes," said Dr. Lowry, as the intern appeared tapping a needle. She turned to Roland. "Take your pants down, please."

Roland said, "Um, can I just have it in my arm?"

"No," said Roxane, leaning forward in her chair. Dr. Lowry laughed. "This is a strong antibiotic," she said. "This is the best place for it."

"A pain in the heart turns out to be a pain in the ass," Roland said. "How appropriate." He turned around and unzipped his shorts. "Roxane, could you not look please?"

"Sure, sure," she said. "Only if we're ever stuck in the jungle and I have to give you a needle it's best if I know what to do."

"Well, there is always that possibility," Roland said sarcastically.

As the intern jabbed Roland with the needle, Roxane said to Dr. Lowry, "Men. They're so vain."

"How about now, Roxane?"

"How about now what?"

"You looking at my ass?"

Roxane giggled. "Nice birthmark."

"Women," said Roland. "Can't trust any of 'em."

On their way out, Dr. Lowry presented Roland with nine pills. "Take three a day for the next three days," she said. "Also when you visit the doctor you always get a treat. Here is yours." She held out a lollipop to Roland, sealed in plastic with writing on it. As Roland took it he laughed. It said, "VIAGRA."

Not long after Roland returned to work, a slim, dark-haired woman passed by his desk and dropped a leather cell phone case in front of him. "I'm Maxine," she said, "and you must be Roland. I saw you a few weeks ago but didn't have a chance to talk."

She was very tall; probably five-foot-eleven, over six feet maybe. It was hard to tell while sitting in his chair and had been equally hard to judge when she had been standing on the stairs chatting with Amy about the yacht on Roland's first day of work. Either way, it would be interesting to see her standing next to her husband. Adrian barely cleared five feet. Roland introduced himself and thanked her for furnishing the house. She laughed as he related his and Grant's reaction upon seeing the transformation. "Glad I could help out," she said. Roland asked her how San Diego had been.

"Good," she replied. "The yacht should be here in a couple of weeks."

"Nice one?" Roland asked, though he knew he didn't need to. If Adrian bought it, it was probably a cherry, although Maxine became reflective.

"Personally, I would have spent the same money on a bigger one and done with a few less spinny things on the top; you know, it's got radar and fish finders and iceberg finders and finder finders, all kinds of shit. I was under the impression that navigating these days meant you didn't need all that stuff." She was holding two more of the leather phone cases and handed one to Grant as he passed by on his way to his office clutching two bottles of Pacifico. He drank from one as he placed the other on Roland's desk. After a quick hello and thank-you to Maxine, he continued on his way.

She turned back to Roland. "Anyway it's pretty damn big. It has three decks, comfy bunks, and a few decent-sized areas where you can get a tan, so that'll keep me happy for a while at least."

"I wonder if it has a gold detector," Roland said. "We could spend some time in the Caribbean and come back zillionaires from all that sunken pirate treasure."

Maxine rolled her eyes. "That's just what we need. More money cluttering up the place and another finder thingy on the yacht. I'm surprised that I like it, actually, seeing as how I'm not the one who chose it. Same with this goddamn house."

"Don't you like it?"

Maxine frowned. "It's too white," she said. "No color on any wall, anywhere. It's like an asylum. Adrian bought the damn place while I was away. Can you handle white walls everywhere?"

Roland couldn't help smiling. He imagined what Sara, a woman with a true eye for color, could do with the house.

Maxine looked at the floor across from his desk as if noticing for the first time that it was littered with computer boxes and packaging. Garrett was wedged under the desk that had been Roland's when he had first arrived. The huge scanner now shared space with a new computer and he was busy hooking them together.

"What's all this for?" she asked him as he uttered muffled curses from behind the desk. When he didn't respond she tapped his exposed bare foot with a jeweled sandal. "Hey, Computer Guy, what's all this?"

Garrett emerged from behind the desk holding one end of a colored cable, and pointed to the window wall.

"See all those files there? Three weeks ago, round about when Roland started, they all fitted into Liza's office. Now we have to send Tatiana to get a new file caddy every four days and it won't be long before they're going to spill all the way over into Adrian's office. If we keep growing at this rate, we are literally going to have nowhere to put them. All the membership applications, the banking documents for each member, all that crap, it's just too much. So," he said, patting the scanner, "we're going to use this. All the paperwork is going to get scanned in and saved on the server and we can start throwing all that stuff away." He rubbed the back of his neck. "Hopefully it won't be long before members can just enter their own information into the website and we won't have to do data entry at all."

Maxine looked at the files. As she watched, Shelly came into view carrying one which she struggled to stuff into one of the caddys.

"I see." Maxine turned her attention back to the scanner. "So who's going to operate this paragon of technological virtue?"

"We hired somebody," Garrett replied. "She starts tomorrow." Garrett looked at Roland as he said, "She's tall, blond, and blue-eyed. You won't mind sitting next to her, will you?"

"I think I'll manage," Roland said. The antibiotics were beginning to take effect; that or the beer Grant had given him, most of which was already gone. Either way, he was feeling pretty good.

"Fantastic," Maxine said. "Natural blonde? If her drapes match her carpet, she won't know how to turn the damn thing on."

Roland nodded and smiled as he said, "Sounds to me like she shouldn't have much trouble turning things on. Don't you worry; she'll be safe with me."

"I'm so glad she'll be in good hands." Maxine eyed Roland dubiously. Then she turned to Garrett again. "When I came down the stairs I couldn't help but notice that you have a desk there as well." She pointed to the tiny area beside the stairs and behind the wet bar. "Is that the detention desk?" Without waiting for an answer or turning around she said, "Roland, maybe you should just move there right now."

Garrett laughed. "Actually, no. Speaking of expansion, I guess Adrian didn't mention it but we have a couple of computer people coming down from Houston tomorrow to look at the database. The one we have just can't handle the growth and we're starting to notice some glitches so they're writing us a new program. Anyway, we'll put one of the guys back here and the other one—" he looked around the main office. There was absolutely nowhere left for a desk to fit. "In one of the bathrooms? Hell, I don't know. Maybe we'll set him up on the balcony."

"Well, buy him some sunscreen," was all Maxine said before she retreated up the stairs.

Roland had fitted his tiny cell phone into the case and he waved it at her. "Thanks, Maxine."

"*De nada.*"

Garrett stuck his head behind the desk and resumed cursing. Kevin materialized long enough to drop a small stack of files on one of the caddys. Ken yawned and scratched his belly. Amy cursed at the infinite stupidity of a member's question, Slogan stopped by and chatted with Roland about pleurisy, and Eric bobbed his head in time with the music through his headphones as he typed. Secret Agent Man rested his chin on his hand as he idly clicked the mouse with the other, and they could all hear Roxane warning Yoda not to cock his leg on the marble floor.

Slogan, whose shirt today said *"You're a bad girl. Go to my room.,"* finished his beer and Pinguino, sat down at his desk, and belched loudly.

Roland turned his attention back to his computer. The background image he had first applied was that of a skier enveloped in a cloud of powdery snow. After a few minutes of hunting around on the internet he chose a new one; a white sand beach with a yacht moored offshore and a couple holding hands as they lay in the sun. He stared at the image for a little while and then resumed his work.

There was hardly any breeze that day and the sliding doors to the balcony were open, allowing the subtle smell of palm trees and tropical flowers to mix with the sound of tapping keyboards and the occasional vehicle on the street below.

8
The Stranger Within

Tuesday, March 13

Roland's schedule had become very much the same from one day to the next. He was usually at work by nine and didn't leave until around seven or so. This gave him enough time to watch the sun set from his own house instead of his desk, but only just. If he happened to still be at work when it set he could watch it four times; once from his desk, again from the living room one minute later, again from the upstairs balcony a minute after that, and one last time from the roof. It became almost a ritual among those who usually worked late, meaning himself, Mick, Liza, and Eric.

Now and then he would see Mick at the Pagina en el Sol in the mornings as well, because he had resolved to walk down to Olas Altas and back at least once a day in lieu of "real" exercise. He thought that the 45 minutes' worth of walking per round trip should be enough, especially in the growing heat of the changing season, plus another trip if he elected to go back for dinner. He also liked it because he passed by so many interesting things in that short time.

There were the parrots in the cage at the Hotel Meza del Mar he'd first seen the night he'd been questioned by Roxane about his past. In the daylight they were awake, squawking madly at each other and doing their best to attract attention from passersby. The Calle Santa Barbara, as the street was called, had a multitude of walled mansions with beautiful flowers and vines draping over them, filling the air with their perfume and brightening the scenery. There were always a few Mexicans out doing whatever it was they did in the morning; washing the few sidewalks

155

there were on that street, watering the plants, or exercising by running up and down the iron stairs that led a considerable distance to the beach, and all of them greeted Roland as he passed. At night he would walk by the occasional couple holding hands and talking softly to each other, sitting on the low wall beside the steps to the beach or snuggling in cars with license plates from all over; ones that read JAL from Jalisco, of course, as that was the state Puerto Vallarta was in, but others as well including MICH from Michoacan, NAY from Nayarit just to the north, and of course D F from Guadalupe's old hangout, Mexico City. In addition there were a considerable number of North American ones. People from British Columbia usually drove down in vans, Californians in Jeeps like Mick's, and people from the east, whether Canadian or American, invariably drove small sedans.

In fact Roland himself was considering buying a car. A couple from Montreal who went to the Pagina every morning owned a Volkswagen Beetle convertible that they were selling. Beetles were still made in Mexico and this one was only a few years old. It was blue and only dented in two places.

Roland was thinking about how much he should offer for it as he made his way down the street for dinner. He passed in front of Tatiana's car rental office opposite the Tropicana hotel, where he and Mick had dropped off the visitors they had picked up from the airport on the day after his conversation with Roxane about Sara at the Pagina. Mick had been true to his word and had shown Roland all around the city that next day, and it had been no small occasion for Roland when he found himself at the airport waiting to greet others as Mick and Slogan had greeted him.

There were many moments like that now. The cowboys had started asking Roland a lot of questions about Vallarta, and Roland knew the answer to every one. He knew to roll up the windows before they passed through the tunnel on the highway, because it was long and always completely choked with exhaust fumes made even worse in the heat. He knew where the speed bumps were; not as many as in Guadalajara, where store owners would place one in front of their shops to slow people down and thereby increase the chances of their signs being seen, but still enough to be annoying. He knew what to say to timeshare vendors and chiclets girls and he was even starting to relax and return the smiles of pretty Mexican girls when they noticed him. He felt comfortable pouring himself a drink from Adrian's gigantic liquor cabinet and could order a pizza in Spanish; no small feat considering Grant hated shrimp and Roland had to figure out a way to communicate this before he knew how to say 'shrimp' in Spanish.

So in light of all this, his impromptu conversation at dinner that night with an unlikely passerby served not one, but two very important purposes – it informed him about Cyberia from a source that could provide some objectivity, and it reminded him that very often it was true that the more one knew, the less one knew.

Seated at a table on the sidewalk outside Papaya 3, Roland busied himself with a huge salad and a bottle of water. It was a slow night and there weren't many tourists around. Even the normally aggressive timeshare vendors were leaning against their arched white booths or sitting on the edges of wide brick planters as they chatted with each other. The Texans, whom everybody referred to as "the cowboys", were out for dinner with Mick, Adrian and Garrett, and Grant and Liza had gone somewhere with a few other staff members. Roland thought this was pretty amazing because Liza didn't care for Grant much, but Roland had chosen to dine alone.

He saw the chair across from him move, accompanied by a cloud of smoke. Milo smiled at him, cigar clamped between his teeth. He was wearing a striped white and black shirt that made him look like a referee, and his greying hair was smoothed back.

"Mind if I can sit down?" he asked, already seated.

"Not at all," Roland replied. "Want a beer?"

Milo eyed the table in front of Roland as he nodded. "You don't drink or something?"

"I don't like most beer but I drink Pacifico, which they don't serve here," Roland explained. Actually he drank Pacifico too much but whenever he thought of pushing one away a little voice inside him would say, 'Come on, you deserve it,' as though slowing himself with alcohol and killing off brain cells was some kind of reward for a job well done.

"I will have Sol," Milo instructed the waiter. His cigar was half-finished. He studied the ash airily as he said, "So how you like working for the Adrian?"

Roland didn't know what to say. He respected people who got straight to the point, but this had caught him off guard. He didn't want to insult the man's intelligence by denying that he worked for the Adrian, but he had made a promise too, so he decided to make it obvious that he was playing dumb.

"Who said I worked for him?"

Milo laughed. "You all work for him. The Mick, he is one cracks me up the most. I think he watches too much spy shows on TV." He pointed his cigar at Roland. "I don't think he knows that everyone knows more than he thinks they know."

Roland wasn't sure if this was Milo's imperfect English talking or if he really meant what he said. "How's that?" he asked innocently. The waiter set Milo's beer in front of him and added more nacho chips to the little bowl in the middle of the table.

Milo laughed again. He talked very loudly. "I been down to the basement, I seen those computers, all that stuff, I look at my file. I got more right than you to look at it. I was one of the Adrian's first members. Me and Duck Bill, we were there at the first."

Roland raised his eyebrows. Milo had told him that he was a member, but Roland didn't know that he had seen the computer room. The time for secrets, if there had been one when it came to Milo, was over.

"I'm listening."

"I come here every winter," said Milo. "I met the Adrian when he first came to here. Living in that apartment down there—" he thrust the neck of his beer bottle in the direction of Vista del Sol – "driving a Trans Am or something with no fucking brakes!" He laughed even harder. "You think this is secret?"

Not with you around, thought Roland, but he didn't say so.

Milo leaned across the table. "I tell you one thing, the Adrian is genius." He tapped his head, and then held a finger up in front of his face. "But for genius he can be very fucking stupid sometimes. He is kind of person where he is in science lab looking everywhere for his glasses and they are on his forehead."

Roland didn't respond. Milo took a long drink from his bottle and continued, "I remember the Adrian trying to get his very first people in to Cyberia. Anybody with one million dollars or more, he tells them no. But he has to have one million dollars at first or else these people in Panama, they won't let him in to their investment. The Adrian, he wants to let smaller investors in to it." Milo looked at Roland as he pulled on his beer. "I give to him one hundred thousand dollars. At first, he invests only for people in blocks of ten thousand dollars, but after a time he brings it down to a thousand. So when I give to him my money it is enough for a hundred people. Me and the Duck Bill, we helped start this thing. Now you live in that Playboy mansion." Milo pointed to himself as he raised an eyebrow and smiled. "Thank you to me and Duck."

Roland had forgotten all about his salad. Milo had finished his beer already and motioned to the waiter for another one.

"If this bunch in Panama won't let anyone in unless they have a million or more, that means Adrian has to wait until he has a million to invest each time," Roland observed. Milo nodded. "So what Cyberia does is submit blocks of a million dollars to this outfit in Panama on behalf of smaller investors."

"You didn't know this?" Milo asked. "I think I am telling you history and I find out it is current events. Normally that is the backwards way around."

"I knew some of it," Roland said. "But the history really is new to me." He wondered if he should add that now it made even less sense than it had before.

"You don't like the people here, I think," said Milo, relaxing. "The Adrian tells me lots. I know. I don't blame you. You know the Adrian's son, that Sidney, he doesn't talk to his dad for years and then the Adrian is rich. Next thing, Sidney comes to here. And that wife of his? Who knows how long she would stay if his dad has no money."

Interesting, Roland thought. He wondered if Sidney's estrangement from his father was in some way connected with the fact that he didn't work for Cyberia.

"It's not that I don't like them," he said. "That's not it at all. It's just annoying because they act as though they know more than they do. And I think smoking pot at work is just plain stupid. Just asking for trouble."

Now it was Milo's turn to be surprised. "This happens at the work too?"

"Yes. What do you mean, 'too'?" Roland started picking at his salad again. "I would think it's safer there than outside Hooter's, at least."

Milo laughed. "This is true, but I didn't know they do it at the Adrian's house."

"Ah, they're all okay," Roland conceded. "Nobody died and left me king."

"But none of them know how to handle being so close to so much money," Milo pointed out. "So they get jealous and strange. The Adrian, he wants people who don't ask questions, who are afraid by his money. Then guys like you and the Mick come along, not afraid, so it makes the others upset. The Adrian doesn't want people like you but he has to have, he can't grow without it."

"They aren't all intimidated by his money," Roland argued mildly, thinking of Slogan. He had never been impressed by how much money people amassed, but Milo seemed to hear this as nitpicking.

"Of course, to varying degrees, all that I mean," he said impatiently. "But overall, in the big picture there, I see what is going on."

Roland finished his water. Milo was almost finished his second beer. They each ordered another of their respective drinks and then Roland said, "Does all this sound legitimate to you?"

Milo didn't say anything. Perhaps he didn't recognize the word 'legitimate'. "I mean, does this all sound like it works the way Adrian says it does?"

Finally Milo said, "Why wouldn't it?"

Roland was thinking about a conversation he'd had with Grant two days ago. In it Grant had explained that he had regularly flown a group of government lawyers from Canada to Bermuda. They would go down to meet with some Americans and play golf for a week and then Grant would fly them back. During this time he had learned how they made their money, partly because they were all doing their banking on the island between rounds of golf, and partly because he appreciated their many suggestions about how to protect himself during his divorce. Every one of those conversations included recommendations that he move his assets offshore. Grant told Adrian about the lawyers' investments, Adrian decided to copy them, and that was how Cyberia had been born. It all sounded tantalizingly believable.

"So, three years ago Adrian is living here after coming from the Bahamas and he's driving a car with no brakes. Now he owns property all over the place and Cyberia pulls in well over half a million dollars a day and growing."

"That much?" Milo asked.

"That's what I hear," said Roland, narrowly avoiding the disclosure of his unauthorized forays into the accounting software. He wondered why Garrett didn't have it all password protected. "You're telling me this group in Panama refuses investments of less than a million dollars." Roland tried to keep the sarcasm out of his voice. Whatever Adrian was really doing, it was obvious that he had a sense of humor.

"Yes," said Milo.

"Milo, do you know any millionaires?"

Nobody wanted to admit that they didn't, and Milo was no different. "I know lots of rich people," he said, waving his beer bottle around.

"Okay, but have you ever met one who had even heard of the killing they could make if they sent their money to Panama?"

"It's a secret for rich people," said Milo. "Millionaires only."

"You put in a hundred thousand dollars," Roland pointed out. "That's doing pretty well for yourself."

"And I have more besides," Milo said proudly, looking at the forlorn remains of his cigar. "But I made that on stock market, and I sold a house that I fixed it up."

Roland was going to point out that what Milo had done was very close to how a lot of people became millionaires, but he didn't think Milo would believe him. In his mind, millionaires were a breed apart. Roland sighed inwardly. What amazed him was not that a fool and his money were soon parted, but that they ever got together in the first place. It bothered him that he couldn't get a straight answer out of anybody especially when it came to Hammer Investments, the group Cyberia purportedly invested with, and so far he hadn't had the confidence to come straight out and ask Adrian about it. There was an unwritten rule that it was nobody's business how Adrian made his money. Liza had said, 'You do your job and let Adrian do his.'

Roland decided to change tack. "What do you know about Mick?" he asked.

Milo lit up. "Good man, that Mick," he said. "One of the only people at the Cyberia who knows what is fuck is going on. But he wasn't there at the beginning, like me and the Duck Bill."

"No?"

"No," Milo said emphatically. "The Adrian gives to him job one day we are sitting outside at this computer café down this street." The dot-com café, Roland thought, still Adrian's favorite haunt. "Same way he gives the jobs to these other girls and even to your bodyguards too. This Amy, also this, what is fuck is her name, Shelly? They are working bars, wandering around the streets like dogs until the Adrian says to come working for Cyberia. That Shelly, she had airline ticket to go home the day after she met the Adrian. No hot water, Mick had only cold water and big fucking spiders in his apartment." Milo conceded that his cigar was truly finished and reluctantly dropped it into the ashtray. Roland watched it smoldering, still hot enough to burn.

"So does Mick know these guys in Panama?" he asked.

"I don't think so," Milo said, shaking his head slowly. "I think he only knows what has to keep Cyberia running, not about the investments. Liza either. She works numbers with those computers but the Adrian is the one handles all other shit. He never sleeps, he is up because he talk to those fucking idiots in Latvia at four in the morning, here time. God knows what time over there."

"Shit, that's right!" Roland exclaimed. "Isn't he going to Latvia this week?"

If Milo noticed how animated Roland had become, he didn't show it. He just said, "No, whatever he had to do he is doing from here. Now he doesn't need to go."

"Good," said Roland, letting out a deep breath. "Thank God for that."

"You don't like those places? Beautiful women, you know. All of them tall, blond, they like rich guys." Milo pointed at Roland.

"Show me a woman who doesn't."

"You should go with him if he goes," said Milo. The waiter approached and asked him if he wanted another beer, but he said no, he was going to a bar and would have more there where it was cheaper. Roland said that you didn't need to be Latvian to be a banker who charged outrageous fees for simple things and they weren't necessarily idiots.

"You ever bank at the Lloyd's here?" Milo asked. Roland admitted that he didn't, but some of his coworkers did.

"Good bank. They are fair. They are not fucking idiots."

"Okay," Roland said distantly.

Milo regarded Roland for a while and asked, "You are thinking something doesn't make sense?"

Something? Roland thought. "Yeah, a lot of somethings."

"The Adrian, he is man who does lots and says little," said Milo. "He takes a little something, makes it big something. He thinks big, is difference."

Roland looked at Milo, who was smiling at him genially. Well, that certainly would be the difference between a scam artist hiding cards up his sleeve at a game of poker and a man who ran an international banking fraud.

Milo pointed at Roland and said, "Now you know. In one hour conversation you know more than what you learn since coming here." He laughed, pleased that he'd been such a fount of knowledge. Then he became reflective. "Too bad the Adrian doesn't tell everybody what secret to say and what secret to keep."

Roland agreed. He had decided that he liked not living in the real world, but he was beginning to wonder what world his new one really was.

The girl hired to scan in the files was indeed as Garrett had described her. Her name was Lee, short for Annalee, and she was not only tall, blond, blue-eyed and in possession of a formidable body, but she was approachable and friendly to boot. She was also English and had the habit of ending every other sentence with, 'd'y'know that?' or adding 'yeah' in the middle of it. One of her eyes was lazy, so that when speaking with her straight on it was difficult to tell which one to address. But she was chipper and seemed oblivious to the office politics around her. As Roland learned later, it wasn't that she was unaware of it but rather that she just didn't care, mostly because none of it centered around her. She and Roland got along well.

Garrett had instructed Roland on how the scan program worked, just in case he himself wasn't around when Lee needed help. Given that Garrett was now spending every available moment with the two Texan software developers, that proved to be a good idea, as Lee seemed to be running into trouble every five minutes. One of the software people had indeed been given a desk out on the balcony, tapping away at his laptop and occasionally nodding his head vigorously as he talked on his cell phone, oblivious to the sunburn he was getting on the right side of his face. His name was Ricky. The other, Greg, sat behind the bar and ran his fingers through short tousled hair. He wore thin-rimmed glasses and chatted with Lee about parties and drinking. He didn't have much choice in the matter, as that was almost all Lee wanted to talk about. That and her Mexican boyfriend, a zealous Catholic who was always trying to get her to go to church and locking her out of their apartment if she came home one minute past her curfew.

Adrian and CIA Mick returned from Costa Rica that Thursday, the 15th of March. After pouring himself some coffee and greeting the housekeeping staff, Roland made his way downstairs. He found Adrian hunched over his computer, tapping his cigarette ash into a colorful ashtray. He was still in his bathrobe.

"Morning, chief," Roland said cheerily. "How was Costa Rica?"

Adrian leaned back in his chair and rubbed his eyes. "I got a lot done, I suppose," he said, "but it was a typical trip for me. Meaning it's good to travel, but it's good to be home." Adrian really liked Puerto Vallarta, and Mexico in general. "Everything go smoothly while I was gone?"

"Like silk," Roland lied. Adrian would have to find out from the Texans what a mess the system was turning out to be, and until then there was no reason to worry him. "I got pleurisy in Guadalajara, though."

"No kidding." Adrian stubbed out his cigarette and paused long enough to bring his ashtray closer before lighting another. "That's disappointing. I would've thought you'd bring back gonorrhea or something instead. How did you find this out?"

"Roxane took me to the Medisys. There's an excellent doctor there."

"That could be any one of them," Adrian said. "Who did you see?"

"Lowry," said Roland. "Letitia Lowry. She gave me a needle and some pills and I'm fine."

Adrian nodded. "She's the one who told me I had bladder cancer."

Roland was taken aback. He had thought Adrian suffered from stomach cancer, but Adrian addressed this as though reading his mind.

"I went in there for an exam after I had that operation for my stomach cancer in Europe," he said. "She held a stethoscope to my back and pushed on one of my ribs. I said, 'Fuck, that hurt,' and she said, 'That's because you have bladder cancer.' I said, 'Can you push on a different rib to make my dick bigger?' but she didn't laugh."

"She must have thought that wasn't necessary."

"Must have," Adrian agreed. "She sent me for some tests to make it official, but she got it right the first time."

"Hmm," said Roland. "I've always thought that when it comes to trauma and surgery Western medicine is great, but for the rest of it, they're out of their league."

"You got that right." Adrian watched the smoke from his cigarette as it hung in the humid air. Already it was warm downstairs and the sun wouldn't even touch the west side of the house for another few hours. "Fuckin' drug companies have a hold on the whole thing." Then, changing the subject, he said, "You'll have to come with me next time

I go down to Costa Rica. You're going to be spending a lot of time there, so read up on it."

Roland raised an eyebrow. "Will do," he said.

Adrian blew more smoke into the air. "You got a date for the wedding next weekend?"

"I thought I'd find one there."

"What about your Spanish teacher? I hear she likes you. Or did I hear that you like her?" Adrian asked, and then he frowned. "Hey, did that English girl start yet?"

Shelly breezed in holding a coffee just in time to hear the question. She put on her best English accent and said, "Oh, yes, she did rather. Quite taken with Roland here, it seems to me."

Roland snorted. "She's got a boyfriend."

"Oh, like *that* makes a difference," Shelly said, dropping a stack of folders on her desk. She turned to Adrian. Kevin had appeared and pushed past the little group on his way into the room. "She only ever talks about getting hammered," Shelly continued, "and then she tells stories about waking up with no knickers on. What the hell are knickers, anyway? Obviously they're something you have to take off in order to have sex."

"Maybe they're just something you have to pull down a little ways," Kevin said from his desk around the corner.

"I wouldn't know," said Adrian. "I don't wear them." He got up to leave.

"But that's just the thing," Kevin said, his flushed face reappearing. "Maybe you do, but you know them by a different name."

"I'm outta here," Adrian said. "I've done the real work, now you clowns can take over."

Roland stepped back to let him pass. Ken came down the stairs; rather surprisingly, as he didn't usually appear until breakfast at the earliest. Roland chatted with him about the people he talked to overseas. When CIA Mick showed up they talked about Costa Rica, and when Lee came downstairs Roland and Slogan showed her how to change the display language on the spare cell phone Maxine had brought from Spanish to English as the office gradually filled up with people. Another day began.

Saturday, March 17th, and as usual Roland was at work.

The cowboys had done their initial analysis of Cyberia's database and jetted back to Houston to digest their findings, giving Garrett some much-needed time off. He wasn't at work that day and strangely enough, neither was CIA Mick. In fact not even the inexhaustible Liza was anywhere to be found, and because meals weren't provided on weekends the house staff was a skeleton crew of Castanza and Guadalupe. Eric, however, sat tapping away at his computer, finishing up incomplete financial reports from the previous week.

Roland went upstairs to fetch beer for the two of them and got caught in a conversation with Guadalupe as he tried out his Spanish. He returned to the main office to find Eric on the balcony, relaxing in a lounger and smoking a joint.

"Want one?" he asked as he accepted the beer Roland offered. "There's more in the Octopussy room."

"Thanks, but as hard as it is to believe, I still use my brain now and then."

Eric giggled. "This stuff's harmless, you know. It's non-addictive and there are a hell of a lot less chemicals in this than in that government-approved shit." He flicked his bottle cap into the air in front of them. Five seconds later they heard it tinkle as it hit the cobblestones below.

"That's probably true," Roland conceded.

Both men were silent for a while. Eric played with his hair, pulling it straight and measuring how long it was. If he bent his head a little it reached his solar plexus. Finally

Roland said, "Eric, has Sidney ever told you if Cyberia is a scam?"

"No, but that's an interesting question." Eric didn't appear too surprised at it. "One of my new jobs is to collect all the information I can about us on the internet and hand it over to the Secret Agent."

"What kind of information?"

"Opinions about us from people who claim to have government connections, the occasional complaints—"

"Complaints?" Roland echoed.

Eric snickered. He looked at Roland for a second and said, "Take a look at this." He got up and motioned for Roland to follow him.

Seated at his desk, Eric moved the mouse and his Formula One screen saver dissolved. "This kind of stuff here," he said, calling up the internet and pointing to a bookmarked page. After a second it loaded to reveal a discussion board with literally hundreds of messages and dozens of threads.

"These are all messages about Cyberia, posted by all kinds of people. There's no way to verify who they really are, but it's easy for us to tell if the people claiming to be members are lying. For instance, check this out." He clicked on a message entitled *Cyberia is a Government Scam*. "This guy is hilarious. He's really nuts. Read this."

Roland studied the message. It read:

> Cyberia Investment Club was formed by the Government of the United States. It exists for Two Reasons: to discover which Citizens cannot be Trusted when the Invasion comes by hiding their money offshore with NO intention of ever reporting their Income to the Government. These people will be Blacklisted and Dealt With Severely by the Government because they are tax dodgers. They are Greedy who want such

a high return on their Investments, and the Government set up Cyberia so they have a list of names of these awful people. It is a Trap, to trap the greedy people. Cyberia invests in Secret Military Research used to fund Wars in other countries where our latest Developments are sold to Puppet Governments and/or Militia. So if you invest with Cyberia you are financing these Wars, and then you will be Taken Away in the night when the Tax deadline comes. You cannot Declare your income because it's illegal to invest in Cyberia in this State, Police State, but because Cyberia is Government they Know who you are and will Get You either way.

Recommendation: Invest under a False Name and Address.

Roland sat back and offered his diagnosis. "This guy is nuttier than a shithouse hen. What's with all the capital letters?"

"I know, hey?" Eric chuckled. "A man with strong convictions. They get even weirder than that. We're a CIA front, we're a drug company – I don't mean illegal drugs, either; we've been accused of being Pfizer's propaganda arm. Also we're the Russian mafia, we're a big ponzi scheme where the money from new people who join goes to pay the dividends of the ones who joined before them, and so on down the line. Then there's the boring typical stuff like money laundering. Oh yeah, some other guy offered this gem here." He went back to the discussion board and selected a different message. This one said:

Cyberia is able to offer such high returns because they have perfected human cloning and have resurrected a new race to rule the

171

world composed strictly of ancient leaders, they got their DNA from museums and tombs and have been paid by third world governments to animate the lost leaders of the past so that they can rise up and defeat us, we are lobsters being slowly brought up to the boil, we don't notice how our rights have become eroded and are nothing now, we judge our freedom by the number of channels we get on tv and sue the hell out of each other when our pathetic McLives get interrupted by the smallest thing, we read one page a week in the newspaper about world events and think we know what it's like outside our houses, investing in Cyberia is investing in your own death but paying your taxes is investing in the government's control over you, how do we stop it all, we have everything we could ever want and still can't figure out why we're all so sedated, then we watch tv to relieve that feeling and it's boring and vampiric but we watch it anyway, we let it do the thinking for us, it doesn't require us to be involved in order to entertain so our creativity atrophies, our imagination dies, then we end up thinking it's all okay because we can't imagine anymore how else things could be, stop it stop it stop the Hammer

'Hammer' of course referred to Hammer Investments, the group in Panama responsible for investing Cyberia's members' money and the group Roland had pretended to know so little about in his earlier conversation with Milo. That had been a good thing, because Milo had indeed told him things he didn't know and might not have if it seemed to him as though Roland was already informed. Come to think of it, Roland hadn't had to pretend very much. Hammer was a mystery to everyone but Adrian.

This was the only thing Cyberia ever invested in. Hammer Investments purported to use a secret method of banking securities that were traded only between certain officials; if you weren't one of these officials, you couldn't trade. Hammer was tied to an official who could not only trade securities between international commercial banks but between federal money regulators as well, giving the company a network that amounted to a license to print money. Or so the story went.

Eric leaned back and stretched before putting his bare feet up on the desk and pointing to the monitor. "There are a lot of lonely, fucked-up paranoid wackos in this world," he said. "And you thought I was weird because I saw an alien in my room. Just for the record, people say exactly the same kind of shit about Wal-Mart and Nike. We're in good company."

Roland remembered something that the Secret Agent had told him on his first day of work during their conversation on the beach. He had said that most of the people who worked for Adrian never questioned the way he did things because they had never seen wealth of that magnitude before and accepted his business methods as normal. Par for the course, Mick had said, as far as the employees were concerned. And judged against the allegations of the people behind these messages, Cyberia looked as normal as swimsuit calendars at a truck stop.

He wondered if he should retrieve his beer from where it still sat untouched but decided against it. "Surely when it comes to these, not all messages are created equal. I mean, there have to be at least some that are a little more in line with reality," he said.

"Some," Eric replied. "A few are very well-written, but that's no guarantee of sanity." Then he looked out at the ocean and his voice became distant. "Strictly speaking, we don't know any more than these people about what Adrian really invests in, and we work here."

"I suppose," said Roland slowly.

"Those guys in suits were here this morning, talking to Adrian. You know the ones I mean?"

"Yeah, I know who you mean. They were here on my first day."

Eric toyed with his hair again. "Well, as far as I can tell only Adrian knows who they are. They could be anybody."

Roland looked at Eric. He said, "What if you discovered that we really were funding secret wars or cloning people? You don't seem too convinced that we aren't."

Eric hesitated, either trying to find the right words or trying to decide how candid to be. Eventually he said, "Cyberia is really just a club. I mean, we are just maintaining a club; that's really all we do. It never takes us close to what Adrian really does, or what Hammer really does, with the money. I mean, *we* know that we're just a bunch of beach bums lounging around a mansion on the Mexican coast, but these people don't, and that's why we think they're idiots, because they're so far off base. But as for Hammer..." his voice trailed off. "I don't know," he continued after a time. "What would I do if I discovered that we really were supporting the Russian mafia or scamming people? I'd clear out." He nodded his head. "I'd take my money and go."

"Would you feel like you should pay back the money you made?"

Again Eric took his time formulating an answer. Then he said, "You used to work for IBM, right?"

"Sort of. I worked for a company that was owned by them."

"Did you know that one of IBM's first working computers was used to keep track of the Jews in 1940s Germany? I don't mean a computer like this one, obviously," he said, pointing to the one in front of him adorned with sticky notes containing girls' cell phone numbers. "I mean a simple one, mechanical, but a computer nonetheless. It was even based in Auschwitz, for Christ's sake, and IBM knew about its purpose. Now, knowing that, do you think you should give the money you made from them to your local synagogue?"

"I see your point," Roland said.

"I guess what keeps me here is that I don't think Adrian would be involved with that kind of thing. Whatever Hammer really does, I don't believe that Adrian would be involved in it if it hurt people. It's no secret that he has some skeletons in his closet, but that's his business." He nodded a confirmation at his own words. "It would take proof to convince me, not stories from weirdos about how we force people to take prescription drugs that are supposedly for curing impotence and are really magnetizing our blood so the government can find us from a satellite."

"That was one of the messages?" Roland asked.

Eric finished toying with his hair and went back out to the balcony to flick his roach over the railing. "Naw," he said. "Just something I read."

After that and a few words about what their plans were for the rest of the weekend, neither of them felt much like working. They shut down their computers and went their separate ways.

Sunday came. Roland had cleared away his work and decided that he would take a day off and spend it at the beach.

"Finally," he said to no one in particular as he settled into a huge lounger at a beach bar. "My first day as a tourist."

He chatted up the waitress and traded phone numbers with her, but Roland knew they wouldn't call each other. When it came to women, he was very aware of all the pretty ones he met but he just wasn't interested. Still, the ritual was fun.

The sun had been searching for Roland ever since he'd arrived in Mexico, and apart from the occasional fifteen or twenty minutes when it caught him by the pool or walking down to Olas Altas its prey had been elusive. Now it enthusiastically played on his body so that by the time lunch was finished and the beer was gone, his skin was a disturbingly rich pink.

He wandered back to his home and took a cool shower. High above him were large wooden beams that ran the length of the house, giving the place an air of being even bigger than it was. As he leaned back to let the water run down his neck he opened his eyes to see Dave the gecko staring at him.

"This is kinda private, Dave," Roland said. "Though I'm glad you haven't been eaten by a tarantula or poked by a scorpion." He remembered what Roxane had said about the sinister creatures populating the vicinity, and how every time Mick took his shoes off he propped them up against something so that scorpions wouldn't be able to climb into them and curl up in the toes.

"Do you think I should adopt that habit, Dave?" Roland said. "Do you prop your shoes against tables and things when you aren't wearing them?"

For a little lizard with short legs, Dave moved amazingly fast. He shot down the length of the beam to the wall, then stopped for a moment before lowering himself to the open window and, after a glance back at Roland, disappeared through it.

The heat and sun had made Roland sleepy. He had stopped on the way home to chat with Ken outside his favorite bar on Olas Altas, Andale's, where occasionally an ancient Mexican made appearances late at night riding on a donkey who flicked his ears but was otherwise oblivious to the loud music and boisterous conversation, and he had barely been able to keep his eyes open. Now his king-sized bed crooked its finger invitingly. Roland collapsed onto it and drew the sheet up around his head.

He smiled as he listened to the surf outside the window, the cries of the birds in the small patch of jungle below his house, and Roxane splashing around in the pool with her son, whom Adrian had flown down from the States for a visit – first class, of course. A fresh afternoon breeze played with the curtains before running its fingers through Roland's hair, bringing closer the smell of the clean sheets mixed with tropical flowers and the ocean.

He didn't awaken until the next morning when he heard Grant's keys jangling as he locked the front door behind him. He didn't yawn or even move when he opened his eyes; he just marveled at the fact that with the exception of the lack of noises from the pool below, everything was exactly the same as it had been when he fell asleep. Until that moment, he hadn't known how badly he had wanted to find something in his life that he could be sure of. It was the first truly restful sleep he'd had since the trouble with Sara began.

He sat up in bed and just couldn't stop smiling. For the rest of that day and most of the next, he carried that wonderful feeling with him.

But the only constant thing in life is change, and even lives that look sedate and unchanging are merely changing more slowly than others'. Roland liked change even more than permanence, for at least change was honest. Change was real. Permanence was artificial; an illusion created to mask a fear of change, and as such was always destined to fail.

It was a good thing for Roland that he was able to remember these things in the days to come.

9

Under The Lighthouse

Things began to pick up speed at Cyberia that week.

No one noticed it at first, or if they did perhaps they attributed it to a subtle change in the weather as springtime became stronger, but the biggest changes came not in the clouds or sun but in Adrian's house, and the people in it, and the things that began to happen.

The new cook whom Mick had mentioned them hiring arrived that weekend, as did a friend of Maxine's from back home called Dolores. She was a small, tired-looking but attractive Italian woman who drank and swore just as much as everyone else – in that sense, she fitted right in, and in the same sense, the new cook did not. Like all the others at Cyberia, these two were friends of an employee or a friend of a friend.

When Monday came, Garrett returned in high spirits. Usually he was at work on weekends as well, even if just for a few hours, but after spending most of the previous week in consultation with the cowboys he had disappeared and nobody had heard from him at all. Roland suspected that he had spent some time with Liza, because no one had heard from her either. After the weekend in Guadalajara, she had invited the two men to see her condo at the BayView Grand. It was a huge and beautiful place with two-storey gardens and the smell of newness still in the air, but it hadn't been long before Roland had felt like a third wheel. Liza was a gracious host and fun to be with as always, but it took a keen eye to notice that the dynamics between her and Garrett had changed.

Garrett stayed late that night, however, and after sundown he, Mick, and Roland busied themselves sweeping up the dead carcasses of small flying insects that had appeared out of nowhere for their annual two-week mating season. These tiny termite moths would fly around light bulbs, die in mid-flight with no warning and drop to the floor. Or, as the three were dismayed to find, into their coffee, beer, water; whatever happened to be directly underneath. This happened during the daytime too, but it wasn't until the sun went down and some of the heat was carried away by the breeze that the insects came out en masse. To most people this phenomenon was an annoyance. Roland found it highly entertaining.

The dead insects attracted other, more sinister visitors. The next day found everyone trooping past Adrian's office into the Octopussy room, Shelly and Kevin's office, to have a look at a scorpion Grant had penned in between the wall and the mattress pedestal with two defunct computers. It scratched around on the floor and waved its tail menacingly. Four hours later – the blink of an eye in Mexico, though not overly surprising given that Tatiana knew all the right people and they all knew Adrian had money – an exterminator came. Despite his reassurances that the substance he was spraying was not toxic to humans, no one went barefoot that day.

Wednesday the 21st was sunny and hot. When Slogan had finished chatting with Roland over a Pinguino and a bottle of Indio (shirt for the day: *Eat Your Children's Flesh! Deuteronomy 28:53*) and returned to his emails, CIA Mick stopped by Roland's desk and said, "Let's go upstairs for a minute."

Seated at a little table beside the pool, Roland took a long drink from his beer as Adrian spoke. The lime wedge he had brought was too big to fit in the neck so he sucked on it instead. He preferred doing that anyway even though it was messier.

"We deposit members' money primarily in Latvia," Adrian was saying, "and that account has a mirror account in New York. Now the way it is at this point, that's where the checks get sent from." He waved his cigarette. "But these people are greedy. I don't just mean the Latvians; the New Yorkers are just as bad. For every single check we issue, there is a charge of twenty bucks."

Roland raised an eyebrow. "You mean members with a thousand-dollar investment, who are supposed to get a hundred bucks a month, only get eighty?"

"Not exactly," said Mick. "We eat half that cost, so they get ninety."

"Right," said Adrian. "But that still stinks. It means we're paying out thousands of dollars every month that we shouldn't have to. Now, Mick here has been working on a system to pay members that will get around that problem." He nodded at Mick to indicate that the floor was now his. Roland rested his chin in his hands; not the most attentive-looking position, he knew, but it was hot out and he had overeaten at lunch again.

Mick said, "Remember those Visa cards we got the week before last? Well, hopefully by now you've read the stuff Adrian gave you."

"And more besides," said Roland. "I made a couple of phone calls to various places that issue them to find out how they usually work."

"Good," said Adrian. He adjusted his sunglasses. Mick didn't take his eyes off Roland.

"That is good, because that's how we're going to be paying our members," Mick continued. "It solves all the problems we're currently having. We can deposit dividends straight onto the member's card, and a day or two later – as soon as it goes through the Visa system – they can use it. No waiting around for a check, no twenty-dollar hit every time, and no paper trail. The cards are completely anonymous. And because there won't be any more complaints about checks not arriving and all that, it will make Liza and Roxane much, much happier."

"A damn fine thing, I'm sure you'll agree," Adrian said. "The cards have been printed up, and all the companies necessary have been formed and our Costa Rican people are on side. But there are still a few issues, not the least of which is my million dollars."

Roland said, "Which million would that be?" and sucked on his lime.

"The million I paid to set the whole thing up. These cards aren't cheap. I bought enough for the foreseeable future, and at two hundred bucks each my arm feels a little twisted." Adrian held his arm out for emphasis, and then he crooked his finger. "I want those dollars to come back home where they belong."

"Okay," Roland said slowly, picking a piece of lime from between his teeth with his tongue, "but if you paid a million dollars for these cards, at two hundred bucks each that only gets you five thousand. I am aware that we started numbering members around six thousand, and for the first couple of thousand we assigned them every second number, but this morning the ones I entered are up in the nineteen-thousand range. So we've got around twelve thousand members, more or less." He looked at Adrian. "You're saying adopting these cards isn't mandatory, I take it. Otherwise you wouldn't have said that you have enough for the foreseeable future."

Adrian and Mick stared at Roland. Adrian said slowly, "Right. It isn't mandatory. Plus, being an experiment, a million dollars is quite enough to risk." Then he turned to Mick and said, "We picked the right guy."

Mick nodded. "So, Roland, it's now your job to figure out a way to get the million dollars back, collect and organize all the information from the cardholders, distribute the cards, liaise with the accounting department about it, work with the Costa Rican office so you can synchronize the information we have here with the information they have there, and anything else I haven't mentioned that has anything to do with the project. Basically, the whole thing's yours."

"I see," said Roland.

Adrian said, "Now, I have a couple of people who will help set up our office in Costa Rica. We'll be flying down with them on Monday. Until then, your job is pretty much the same as before except on top of it you'll be doing the cards; processing the applications and entering the info into the card database." He smiled. "Don't worry, at this stage there's not a hell of a lot that can go wrong."

Roland nodded. He wondered at what stage there was a hell of a lot that could go wrong.

"One last thing," Adrian said. "You'll be a little richer from now on because as of next week you're getting a raise, and when I get my million dollars back I'll give you some of that to play with as well. Any questions?"

Roland stared at the swimming pool, its vanishing edge a calm horizon for the sea beyond. "Not right now," he said.

"Good," said Adrian. "Then without further ado, I bid you adieu. I've got an appointment to keep." And with that he got up and left.

When the smoke from Adrian's cigarette had dissipated into the afternoon air, Roland looked at Mick and asked, "It was your idea to nominate me for this?"

"Yes, right from the start," Mick replied. "I hope it's okay with you, but there's really nobody else. I would do it myself but the database project has started and I'll be working with Garrett on that. We want you there too because of your computer experience, but with Garrett and me plus the cowboys we'll be alright."

Roland sucked on his lime some more and took a long drink, finishing his beer. It was hot out and there was no wind. He toyed with the label on the bottle. He liked the Pacifico labels.

"Sure, it's okay with me," he said. "It's right up my alley. But what do you mean, there's nobody else?"

Mick shrugged. "You've been here long enough now to know how everything works but you're still new enough that you don't have a specific function yet, and it would be a waste to have you just doing data entry and gopher tasks all the time. You know the membership database, you're speaking more Spanish every day, you work hard, and Adrian trusts you. Ken would be a good choice but he's already assigned to liaise with our members and there's no way he could do both. Who else would there be?"

Roland didn't respond. He was glad that somebody had noticed the overtime he'd been putting in and was already thinking of how he was going to approach the new challenges he suddenly faced.

"Besides," Mick continued, "Liza told me that she found you nosing around in the accounting program and she showed you how it works. That might come in handy if she's not around, now that you're dealing with members' dividend payments."

Roland didn't know what to say. He was flattered that he'd been chosen for the task, but he loved Puerto Vallarta and didn't want to leave. From the way he'd interpreted things, he would be spending a lot of time in Costa Rica, if not actually moving there. Well, perhaps he would like it even more than PV.

He felt the sun on his skin and let it soak into him. Even his heart felt warm.

On Thursday, Amy and Sidney threw a party at their penthouse for the Cyberians and an impressive number of people who had come from all over the world for their wedding. Sidney showed Roland his music studio, full of all kinds of recording and effects gear, and how he and Amy had bought the adjoining penthouse as well and knocked the dividing wall down, which explained why one end of the condo exactly mirrored the other. Finally Amy stood unsteadily on the coffee table and raised a hand. "It's one a.m., people! Bachelor party at the Zoo, stagette at Christine's Disco," she announced. "Taxis are outside. Mush mush everybody, it's party time!"

Roland added his sentiments to the guest book on his way out but he didn't join the partyers, and after saying his goodbyes and making his excuses he walked back home. Tonight he would have liked having someone to talk to, but he didn't want to go to a nightclub.

The tall folding doors to the balcony off his livingroom were open, as always. Roland debated whether to light a cigar and decided not to, opting instead for a glass of water. Settling into a lounge chair, he looked up at the clear night sky.

The constellation of Orion hung motionless and majestic over the bay. Roland had spent many nights around the fire with Sara and their friends, staring up at those same stars with them and talking. He remembered every detail of Sara's pretty face illuminated by the dancing light of the fire, her dark eyes smiling at him gently, lovingly.

Being well into March now, there would be signs of life in his gardens and the roads would be slushy with melted brown ice. He wondered what his house must look like, with patches of brown grass poking through the snow and the dead silence of abandonment darkening the windows.

The next morning, Friday the twenty-third of March, Roland awoke still in the chair.

Roland, Mick, Slogan and his fiancée stood at the base of the El Faro lighthouse restaurant, admiring the boats that had come in since their last visit while waiting for the rest of the wedding crowd to assemble. One beautiful and sleek creation caught Roland's eye, a graceful forty-two foot wooden sailing yacht with its picture on the 'For Sale' notice board.

Eric had visited an Armani store in Guadalajara and had ordered a tuxedo to wear in his role as Sidney's best man, which he was adjusting and picking invisible specks of dust from after alighting from Roxane's vehicle. Despite his comments at the Camino Real about being self-conscious in ostentatious surroundings, he would have fitted in at any upper-crust party very well. He looked great and he knew it. He had even washed his sandals.

Roland chatted with some of the people from the previous night's party at a nearby restaurant until the limos arrived. By that time it seemed as though half the marina was there for the wedding, and the finely-dressed entourage that assembled on the boardwalk in the afternoon sun piled noisily into the cars amid a flurry of shutter clicks and see-you-theres.

Roland's group chose a black Rolls and settled into the L-shaped interior with a couple of loners who had been gawking at real estate ads in store windows along the causeway.

"Every limousine in Vallarta is here," Slogan said, handing out drinks from the wet bar across from him as Roland slid the sunroof back. "There aren't that many to begin with, and believe me, they're all ours today."

Sidney and Amy's wedding was a breathtaking affair, held at a rambling estate on the beach south of Punta de Mita. The wedding planner, a very gay and anxious man in a spotless white suit, had set things out perfectly. Everyone from last night's party was there, in addition to a large number of people whom Roland had seen hanging around the Shack or chatting with his fellow employees on Olas Altas or the Malecon.

The mansion had a huge covered porch a few steps up from a lawn so perfect and green that a few guests had already been inspired to practice swinging imaginary golf clubs on it. A low stone sea wall separated it from the beach, to which a cobblestone footpath led from the portico. Tables covered with white linen and set with fine china dotted the lawn, and a large bar had been set up under a colorful tent. In the swimming pool, glorious flower arrangements floated in vases anchored to painted rocks. A walkway to the site where the ceremony was to be performed was marked out by white paper bags along the beach, each containing a few handfuls of sand and a tealight candle. Already a tantalizing smell wafted from a barbecue on the beach. All in all, it was the most lavish and extravagant wedding Roland had ever been to.

Mingling and drinking under a perfectly clear sky had everyone in a wonderful mood, and finally it was time for Amy and Sidney to put on their show. Drinks and sandals in hand, everyone ambled down the beach, the sun already low. They gathered at a point in front of a high rocky outcrop which served to amplify everyone's voices, a necessity over the roar of the surf. A latticed archway decorated with flowers sheltered the couple and was flanked by Adrian, Eric, Amy's father and her impossibly beautiful maids of honor.

The woman performing the service bowed to the couple and then to the crowd. In both English and Spanish she had the two repeat their vows, and draped a large rosary over their necks as they held hands. The ocean flung itself onto the beach and rocks, blessing them all with a fine dusting of water, and as sea birds screeched overhead and the sun fell gracefully into the sea, Sidney and Amy became husband and wife.

Now that everyone turned to face the way they had come, they saw the long line of softly glowing candles leading along the beach to where the sky was still red, waiting to be lit up with a fireworks display over dinner. As Amy and Sidney walked hand in hand between these gentle lanterns, everyone spread out on either side to cheer and congratulate and take pictures and throw colorful ribbons.

Roland watched the crowd recede along the beach, and in the darkening sky the first star made its nervous appearance. He decided to wish upon it, and closed his eyes.

He knew that Sara was engaged, if not married already. But he also knew that if it hadn't been for the torrent of emotion released by her leaving he might never have come to understand himself in the way he had been forced to. Despite the anguish she had caused, Roland had a lot to be thankful for when it came to her.

Standing there that evening, feeling the warm sand under his feet and listening to the occasional excited laughter from fellow stragglers playing on the sand, he wished that Sara's wedding and her subsequent marriage would bring her as much happiness and joy as she could ever want. He wished for her many wonderful children and all the love her heart could hold.

Then he walked back to the party through the flickering candles alone.

In lieu of the Friday that everyone had off due to the wedding, Sunday was a work day. Afterwards Adrian bade Roland to stay for dinner.

Like most things that happened in that house, it was an interesting affair. Milo and Duck Bill were there, as was an older couple from somewhere in Adrian's past named Brent and Janine. Janine was a very no-nonsense kind of person, calling things exactly as she saw them. This was her first trip to Mexico. She was apprehensive and found fault with many things there and, later, Costa Rica as well. She had olive skin and shoulder-length brown hair, and Roland decided that her dark green eyes could probably give her an irresistible come-hither look if she chose. She wasn't married to Brent, as she made a point of saying, but she enjoyed teasing him and was protective of him. As for Brent, he was tall and moved and talked slowly, choosing his words with great care. Roland took an instant liking to him and took to calling him Dad. He had unruly and greying dark hair and luminescent blue eyes, and he was missing his bottom dental plate. He was rather like the older expats Roland saw shuffling around the beaches who probably hid all kinds of secrets underneath their sun hats and behind their genial smiles.

Adrian had dismissed all the house staff for the evening so that he could prepare dinner himself. He was a good cook, especially when it came to his favorite dish, crab legs. These sat on an immense platter in the middle of the table, steamed to perfection, next to a huge dish of caviar ringed with plastic spoons. Dishes of dips waited nearby, covered with lace cloth to keep the occasional falling insect from adding its flavour. Janine stared apprehensively between bites of Mexican casserole at the cloud of them congregating around the chandelier. She had eschewed the crab legs, announcing that she didn't care much for 'sea spiders'. The occasional dead moth in her wine wasn't helping her mood any, and as the sun began to set the little creatures started making their appearance with gusto.

"What are these darn things?" she asked, picking one out of her salad.

"Bugs," Adrian offered helpfully.

"Thanks." She changed the subject and turned to Roland. "Why are you eating caviar with a picnic spoon?"

"That way there's no chance that the taste of the caviar will be affected by the silver from a utensil," Roland replied.

Janine said nothing but was obviously unimpressed. Adrian grinned at Roland over the table but stopped when he realized Janine was watching him.

The bottom of the sun was almost touching the ocean now, and somewhere between the two a sailing ship rode the gentle waves. Everything in the house was touched by the brilliant reddish-orange glow; everyone's faces looked painted as though by an ancient tribe; everywhere was lit as though resonating with the dying sun. Bit by bit the sea swallowed the fiery disc, and then the ship was alone.

"That's beautiful," Janine said reverently.

"I bet you never get tired of that," Brent said to Adrian, who shook his head.

"More caviar," said Milo.

Impossible as it seemed, with the mountain of victuals that the table had supported earlier in the evening, every morsel disappeared. Most of it went not to Adrian but to Milo and Duck Bill, and forever after they were known as the Caviar Brothers.

"So Roland, where are you from?" Brent asked, toying with his lime sorbet.

"Same city as everyone else here," Roland replied, "although I moved to a little town east of it a couple of years ago."

"I used to race chuckwagons with a guy who lives out there," he said. "World famous; he's won all kinds of competitions."

Roland brightened. "I know who you mean. He lives at the end of my street. My ex-girlfriend gave their kid a ride to the hospital once after he rolled his truck."

Janine laughed. "Gosh, it's a small world," she said. "Funny how you go to Mexico to meet people who live twenty minutes away from you."

"I'll say." Roland thought of how many people he'd met from back home since his arrival, and wondered how many of them had returned with Adrian's secret.

Adrian yawned and stretched, waving his cigarette in the air. "Well, Caviar Brothers, I hate to do this to you but we've all got to shove off at five-thirty tomorrow morning, so it's time to go. I'd love to sit around and shoot the shit on the patio but it's bedtime for this boy."

Roland looked around the table. "Who's going, again?" he asked.

"Didn't I introduce you guys?" Adrian said. "Sorry, I thought I had. Roland, Brent and Janine are going to be running our Costa Rican office and they're coming with us tomorrow. They'll stay down there and supervise."

"Oh, I see. Okay." Roland addressed the pair. "I just assumed that you were here for the wedding. The house has been full of strangers for the last week or so, and I haven't been keeping track." He wondered for a moment where the two mysterious men in suits might be. He had half expected to see them at the wedding.

They all helped clear the dishes, which consisted basically of cramming the dishwasher full and leaving everything else on the counter, and dispersed. Roland knew he had to be up early but he didn't want to sleep yet. He found Grant on one of the couches in the living room, watching a movie.

"Hey, how was your weekend?" Roland asked. Grant looked up and adjusted his glasses.

"Good," he replied. "Cold back home, but good. Have a seat. There's some weird tropical juice in the fridge that the maid left here, and some Coke too."

Roland opened the fridge. The carton read 'Jugo de Naranja'. "It's orange juice," he called out. "Nothing to be afraid of." He heard Grant muttering something in the living room as he poured himself a glass.

He settled onto a couch and sighed. Grant asked him how the wedding had gone. "Did you meet any nice girls?" he inquired.

"Oh, sure, they were all nice. And everything was very well planned. Went off without a hitch, pardon the pun." He didn't mention how Sidney had loudly berated the band for playing music he didn't like, or how much ecstasy and other drugs had been freely available, or how Garrett had accosted him on the beach with his video camera and played him a surreptitiously-obtained clip of Lee and Guadalupe kissing each other after the two girls had invited Roland to spend the night in bed with them.

He paid some attention to the movie Grant was watching. A woman with a briefcase full of stolen insurance money was sweating as she passed through customs. Shortly thereafter she was lying on a beach, sipping a daiquiri with a handsome younger man and laughing at the success of their deception. As the credits rolled, the waiter approached them with more drinks and the couple discussed how they were going to spend the money.

Roland remarked at the number of movies there were like this one, and how they all ended the same way. "They're fun," he said. "All that sense of possibility."

Grant laughed.

"Happens every day," he said.

10
Over The Hills and Far Away

Monday, March 26

Roland let himself into Adrian's house as silently as he could. He wasn't sure why, because even if Maxine was home she wouldn't be able to hear anything from the master bedroom half a mile away at the top of the stairs, but nevertheless he closed both the iron gate and the glass inside door soundlessly.

Brent and Janine were talking quietly in the livingroom. Roland waved a hello and deposited his bags beside the door to the garage. Upon rejoining them he saw Adrian coming down the stairs. "You guys all ready?" he asked hoarsely, and they loaded up one of the Explorers. Adrian reversed it onto the cobblestone street, but just as the hood cleared the garage door he said, "Damn. Wait here a minute," and went back inside for something he had forgotten.

"So Roland, have you ever driven with Adrian before?" Brent asked.

"No," Roland replied. "I've never even seen him drive anywhere before."

He heard Brent rustling around in the back. "Better grab your seat belt then."

Adrian returned, closed the garage door with a button on the visor next to several unmarked others, and promptly drove onto the sidewalk on the other side of the street as he backed up. He winced and said, "Damn," again, more from pain than embarrassment, but drove them uneventfully to airport's private terminal to see their Learjet waiting on the tarmac. They headed into the lounge to await the pilot.

Roland wandered around the small building gazing at pictures of celebrities who had passed through it. Arnold Schwarzenegger clutched a cigar as he beamed at the camera during a break in the making of the movie *Predator*, filmed about ten miles south of Roland's house. Carlos Santana, who had signed the guest book that January, had autographed a picture as well. And naturally there was a snapshot of the cast of *Night of the Iguana*, the filming of which was one of the things that had brought Puerto Vallarta into the limelight from its timid beginnings as a little fishing village on the shores of the second-largest bay in the world. That and the fact that Aeroméxico had managed to secure a monopoly on flights to Acapulco in the Fifties, which had forced Mexicana to find another Pacific destination. Lucky us, Roland thought, looking at the pictures.

These were just some of the faces he recognized, and after scrutinizing them all he sank down into a huge chair and joined the conversation.

"Is the pilot who took us to Guadalajara the same one we have today?" Roland asked.

"I don't know," said Adrian. "There's an easy way to find out, though." He stubbed out his cigarette and tapped the bottom of the package for another as he yelled, "Hey, Heinz!"

Dress shoes clicked on the terracotta and became louder. Finally Heinz stuck his head around the corner. "Yes, sir?" he asked.

"Nothing, sorry," said Adrian.

The man nodded and withdrew, his footsteps fading.

"Yep, that's him."

Finally it was time to go. On their way out to the plane, Roland at last confided to Adrian his misgivings about the trip to Latvia. He also hastened to add that he wouldn't be telling him this if it hadn't been for Grant's advice that he do so.

"I'm just glad you didn't have to go," he finished. "Like I said, I just had a bad feeling about it."

"I'm glad too," Adrian said. "I like it here. I like to travel, but I like to be home." He could see that Roland was relieved. "Don't worry. We took care of everything from here, for the time being at least."

Janine didn't like the little jet very much. She made much the same comment Roxane had, remarking on how small it was, but she was more at ease than Roxane had been. Roland sat at the back, took his shoes off, put his feet up on the seat in front of him, pulled out a tray table, selected a magazine and relaxed.

"It's going to be a long flight," he said to Brent. "Make yourself comfortable."

"How far away is Costa Rica, anyway?" Brent asked after a short time.

"Well, the only country in Central America that's south of Costa Rica is Panama. We'll be flying over all of them except Belize, which is on the east coast, so there's Guatemala, then El Salvador, Honduras, and Nicaragua. So, what's that…probably around three hours, maybe more."

The sun rose when they had almost reached Guatemala, filling the little plane with new light through the windows. Brent and Roland chatted about life in the small towns they were from, and Janine kept changing seats to get a better view of the lush green mountains to their left and the ocean to their right. She was especially fascinated with the occasional active volcano, lightly tossing smoke out of its cone to be carried by the wind before it fell onto the slopes as morning mist, only to blush with a deepening red before dissipating under the sun's growing strength. The jet was high enough for them to catch glimpses of the Caribbean Sea when they had travelled far enough south for the land to narrow, over Nicaragua. Roland had wanted to see it all his life and never had until that day.

He succeeded in trading a rum and Coke for a few minutes in the copilot's seat, where he talked with Heinz about flying and Mexico and their current destination. Heinz explained that they kept to the coast because if they were to go down in any of these countries they would be detained instantly and accused of drug trafficking. They would be asked what they were doing flying over land – was their destination a quick drug drop? – and being late for their appointments in San Jose would be the least of their worries. That was if an armed group of *banditos* didn't get to them first.

"Many people, they have a romantic notion of these rebels," Heinz said. "But they only get mad when companies want to make highways or lay oil pipe through their marijuana or coca fields. For these people, life is only about money now, not preserving old Indian ways or any of those things. But it makes good TV shows." He pointed a finger at Roland. "In some of these countries, you must have a bodyguard always when you have money."

Finally they could see the Costa Rican coast. Seven miles below them lay freighters and the beach at Puntarenas, and they turned inland.

The approach to the airport at the capital, San Jose, was a bumpy one. The sporadic mountain winds kicked them around but they pulled up to the private terminal and shut down without incident. A van drove out to collect them, and they cleared customs next to a sign that proclaimed 'Welcome to Costa Rica, garden of peace and democracy.'

Two men, Diego and Franco, had been scheduled to pick them up. Adrian and Mick had recruited them on a prior visit on the merits of their extensive banking experience in Costa Rica. Roland had spoken to them both on the phone but hadn't met either of them.

They had waited barely five minutes when a dark blue BMW and a grey Lexus pulled up and the drivers got out.

Again Adrian made no introductions, but as Roland shook hands with them he could finally put faces to the names.

Diego was in his mid-twenties and a classically handsome Spanish-looking man, complete with dark skin and a goatee. Roland imagined that if he were ever to do an advertising campaign for anything Central American, this is the man he would choose. In fact, with long hair he would have fitted the picture of the quintessential pirate exactly. He had a great sense of humor but was otherwise a little reserved. He was the one Adrian wanted Roland to work with on the Visa cards, and he was also going to be expected to work under Brent and Janine. Roland smelled trouble there already. Diego knew Costa Rican banking, he knew the Visa cards, he knew how things worked. He was not going to like taking orders from two gringos who knew nothing about these things.

Franco was of Oriental descent. He was excitable and smiled a lot, and snapped his fingers when searching for the right words to say. Diego's English was near perfect and Franco's wasn't far behind. It was a little humbling to Roland that no matter where he went in the world, somebody spoke English, yet he knew no one back home who spoke any other language well at all.

"I'm going in this car," Adrian announced, pointing to the Lexus. "I bought it a month ago and I might even drive it this time."

"I'll let myself be chauffered," Janine offered, and climbed into the back seat.

"Mighty white of you," Adrian said sarcastically, and eased himself into the front. "See you guys there."

The cloud and sporadic sunshine had turned to a light rain by the time Brent and Roland climbed into Diego's BMW for the ride to Escazu, a satellite city to San Jose where their accommodations awaited.

Roland's initial impression of the city was not good. It was significantly dirtier than Vallarta, not only in terms of the quality of the air but in the vast amounts of trash thrown into the ditches along the roads. In this respect Roland knew that Puerto Vallarta had spoiled him anyway, because most other Mexican cities weren't as clean. But Costa Rica had one of the highest literacy rates in the world, and its health care was so good that some European nations were beginning to copy aspects of its system. "The States and Canada never will, though," said Diego. "They think they have nothing to learn." He guided the car onto a secondary road that led past a huge, modern hospital. At first Roland wondered if he was making a point, but he was just following Franco in the Lexus.

"What's Costa Rica's economy based on?" Brent asked.

Diego was thoughtful. "In the past, very typical things. Cocoa, coffee, bananas and plantains, and these things are still important. But now we are all over the internet. You know all those sportsbook websites, when you bet on the Super Bowl? You are betting your money here, and here it is safe." He smiled broadly. "Nowhere in the western hemisphere is your money safer than in Costa Rica."

"What's a plantain?" Brent asked.

"Delicious," said Roland, and Diego nodded in agreement. "They're basically a huge and sweet banana. Fry them up with some syrup or honey, a little rum, fantastic."

Traffic in Costa Rica was more hectic and disorganized than anywhere Roland had ever seen except China. But nobody honked their horn, nobody shouted, and everything worked as though some plan had been concocted earlier that everyone was following. They passed by an abundance of fast-food restaurants and a TGI Friday's. Next to these stood carts with fresh fruits and vegetables and furniture made of bamboo, a plant he saw growing everywhere. The occasional motorcycle courier zipped past them.

From the way Diego spoke it was apparent that Costa Ricans were a patriotic bunch, and they had a lot to be proud of. By the time they had passed through the guarded gate to the apartment building, Roland's initial impression had been altered significantly. It was altered yet again when he learned that Adrian was paying three thousand dollars a month for a three-bedroom condominium. "If you end up coming down here permanently, this'll be your place," he told Roland as they leaned on the counter in the lobby. He was buying one upstairs from Roland's unit for Brent and Janine. It was a beautiful complex, complete with maid and laundry service, swimming pool, hot tub, and – to Roland's delight – a gym. Those pounds he had put on in Vallarta would be coming off as soon as possible.

They checked in and Adrian signed the lease agreements, grumbling about the amount of real estate-related paperwork he still had to do when the lawyer showed up. He had purchased a huge acreage and mentioned something about properties on the coast as well. Finally he had signed enough papers to be going on with and they took their bags to their suites. Roland locked his passport away in the electronic safe and sank onto the leather couch.

Diego and Franco had disappeared, promising to return for dinner that evening, and had been replaced by Adrian's lawyer and a driver named Gino, whose English was on a par with Roland's Spanish. The two tried to keep their conversation quiet as Adrian sat at the table signing papers.

First, Adrian secured a property on the beach at Guanacaste. Cyberia's staff would each have a house there, and once the database system was up and running and accessible from Costa Rica they would have the choice of either working there or back in Vallarta. The property was close to a large hotel called the Flamingo, famous with the jet set and in possession of a nightclub offering everything the heart could desire.

Costa Rica wasn't famous for its paparazzi but his lawyer pointed out that a good story was a good story. He turned to Roland and waved a finger the way Adrian often did. "You be careful," he said. "You start bringing girls home and word will get around fast. You never know who's watching."

"I know what you mean," said Adrian. "My Explorers have a recording device built into them. I just push a button on the visor and say, 'You guys talk about it for a second, I'll be back in five minutes'." He smiled. "I love my toys."

So that's what those other buttons next to the garage door opener on the visor are, thought Roland.

The other order of business was the opening of several bank accounts around San Jose. From what Roland could understand, Adrian intended to open several accounts at the same branches of different banks. Hoping that he was mistaken, he waited until the others had departed before he brought this up.

Adrian was staring at his laptop when Roland asked, "So how did Cyberia start? How did you get into this business?"

Adrian kept looking at the screen but his focus changed. Roland could tell he was thinking about what to say. He fed Adrian a scrap to start with by mentioning that Grant had told him about the lawyers in the Bahamas.

"Yeah, basically that was it," Adrian said. "I managed to sit in on a few of their meetings and kept my ears open, didn't say a word. I approached Hammer in Panama – took me forever to find those bastards – and I said, 'You guys are missing a huge market here. People with a thousand, ten thousand, they can't get in because you only work with a million or more.' They said, 'Anything less is too small. We don't want to bother with it'." Adrian didn't look at Roland while he spoke. He continued, "I told them that I would handle all that and bring them blocks of a million bucks each. So I started with guys like the Caviar Brothers and some other people I knew. Before long, instead of wondering how I was going to pay the rent at Vista del Sol my employees were living there."

Roland considered this. It did coincide with what Roxane and Milo had told him, more or less.

"How exactly does Hammer trade, anyway?"

Adrian frowned. "You don't need to know that," he said. "Hammer trades the debentures, and you don't work for Hammer. You work for an investment club. Trading the money is my job."

Something occurred to Roland, a thought he had had before but hadn't put into words until now. It had struck him as strange that when he logged in to his bank account over the internet, his salary showed up as payments from Hammer Investments.

"Hammer is a Panama company that only trades in the money? That's all they do?"

Adrian nodded.

"So why are they the ones who pay me?"

Adrian's eyes flickered for a fraction of a second. Then he said, "Hammer has each of us on the books as a director, and they pay their own people. That's partly why I'm able to pay so well – they kick in some too as a bonus for bringing in business."

"You mean I work *at* Cyberia but *for* Hammer?"

Adrian coughed. "For the sake of argument, yeah."

This made no sense at all, Roland mused. The simplest thing for Hammer to do would be to deposit one huge check in Cyberia's account and let Adrian worry about disbursal, but he left it alone and asked an unrelated question. "Did you open several accounts at the same bank today?"

Adrian puffed on his cigarette and nodded. "Yeah. People get suspicious if you have more than a few hundred grand in any one account. With the amount of money we're moving, we can't afford to hang ourselves up trying to reassure them."

"But if the accounts are at the same bank, under the same name, what's the difference? A teller who handles a deposit into an account in the morning might be the same one who deposits into a different one that afternoon. They'll notice."

Adrian finally looked at Roland. He took a deep draw on his cigarette and exhaled it as he said, "Who said they were all under the same name?"

Roland was taking all this in. Adrian could see the concern on his face as he said, "Listen, this is nothing strange. Companies do it all the time. Saturn is owned by GM. They have their own accounts. Saturn dealerships have their own accounts, and accounts within accounts. I thought you knew all this shit."

I do, thought Roland, and often it does work like this. But I'm not the burning bush, I don't know everything; things slip by unnoticed all the time. Just ask Sara. She knows.

He changed the subject to the property at Guanacaste. In the car on the way over, Diego had said that in all of Costa Rica, the property Adrian had chosen for them was the best. The best location, the most peaceful, the nicest houses. Roland asked how long it would be before their database in Vallarta was accessible from Costa Rica.

"It depends," Adrian replied. "None of this snail's pace dialup shit is going to cut it for us. Satellite is the best thing, no wires to worry about. But that one we use in Vallarta drops out too much; what the hell is it?"

"SatMex Five."

"Right. Well, we're buying our own satellite, from a company in Montreal. Dirt cheap, too. A million bucks and it's exclusively ours, including launch and geostationary placement. But the solutions in the meantime – and the satellite is still a couple of months away – aren't very good. I might have to hold off a bit longer." He looked at his watch. "Time to polish our fangs and powder our noses, Roland. Dinner soon."

Diego and Franco had chosen a restaurant for them called Le Monastère. Sitting at the top of a mountain with an incomparable view of San Jose, it had been a monastery for hundreds of years until the monks finally abandoned it. Forlorn and overgrown, it lay there for over twenty years until a Belgian couple bought it and turned it into a world-class restaurant. Inside were pictures of what it had been like before being renovated, with vines hanging out of the windows and chunks of plaster and stone lying on the floors where they had fallen. In keeping with the building's history, the waiters were dressed in dark brown robes with rope belts. "They look like bottles of Frangelico," Janine observed. After dinner they were escorted into a flawlessly-restored chapel where a French lady sang for them, accompanied by a gifted pianist.

Back at the condo that evening, Roland sat in his room making notes for almost an hour before he got ready for bed. He had learned, he had experienced. He had glimpsed out the window of a private jet a place he had never seen before and had always wanted to, despite all the traveling he had done in his life; the elusive Caribbean Sea, which had captured his imagination since he was a boy.

He fell asleep wondering how many people missed their ultimate destinations in life because they were preoccupied with trying to go somewhere else.

The next morning, Roland, Brent, and Janine walked down to the office.

Roland wasn't sure what he had expected, but he knew it hadn't been this. Unseen from the street, a courtyard enclosed by a two-storey building contained a small restaurant and a garden with fountains, a movie theatre accessible from the parkade below, and a language school above. An antique store on the main floor spilled its contents out onto the piazza. In the middle, on the ground floor near an exit to a street which bordered a school playground, was their office. The name of the previous tenant, a Peruvian airline, was still etched on the windows. There was a meeting table, two offices occupied by Diego and Franco, and three cubicles with computers.

Brent's official capacity was director of the Costa Rican operations. He had signing authority on the bank accounts, but he and Janine were still unsure of what exactly was expected of them and certainly knew they didn't have the confidence to start calling the shots over Franco and Diego just yet. To start the ball rolling, Roland suggested that they get some power backups for the computers. San Jose was no place to start taking chances on whether or not their files would get deleted due to an all-too-common blackout or power drop. After agreeing to 'look into it', about as much progress as Brent would have to be content with at first, Diego sat down with them and described how the banking system worked as far as it would concern them.

Diego's bank was the only one in Costa Rica licensed to print Visa cards with whatever company name and logo the client wanted. The Visas would be issued in blocks of five hundred each. Any number larger than that required outrageous licensing fees because the issuing company would be considered a bank. Five hundred cards or fewer qualified as a club membership or company perk. So Adrian had ordered that ten different companies be incorporated, each issuing its allotted complement of cards.

The company leasing the office and liaising with Cyberia was called General Investments. GI would disburse members' dividends each month according to the amount of their investment, and would be reimbursed directly by

Hammer. Cyberia was involved simply as a place to which members sent their Visa applications.

Not having the Vallarta database accessible from GI's office in San Jose made things difficult. At first Brent and Janine offered to process all the Visa applications from there, but Roland decided that doing it that way was an accounting disaster waiting to happen. For one thing, it was paramount that Liza be advised not to send any more checks or wires to a member who knew their Visa was coming. If she wasn't notified in time there was the possibility of a double payment. Secondly it was Roland's responsibility to reclaim Adrian's million dollars, something he couldn't do if there wasn't precise recordkeeping. He knew he could manage it from PV and wasn't confident it would be done in his absence. He could see where all this was heading, and it meant a lot of extra work for him.

"Members already send their Visa applications to me in Vallarta," he informed Diego. "Instead of changing that now, we'll just keep doing it. Some of the pictures on the apps don't come out very clearly and sometimes there's incomplete information. When that happens, I'll write the member back asking them to resubmit. That way you'll know that the only ones you get from me are good ones, and you can go ahead and send them their card." Also, he thought, not yet knowing how much Diego and Franco could be trusted made it smarter to keep the database in Vallarta for now.

Franco came in laden with mugs of coffee from the shop across the square. He placed one in front of each of them and said, "These beans are picked twenty miles from here. Fresh, really good Costa Rican coffee. You have to have some," and true to his word, it was incredible stuff.

Roland and Diego explained to Franco what they had been up to that morning, and Franco filled in some of the holes that Diego had left. GI was owned by the two of them, and they were contracting to provide the cards and maintain the details of those cardholders for Cyberia. Roland asked him what he thought of keeping the database in Vallarta, and to his surprise Franco agreed that it was a good idea.

"Keep it simple here at first," he said. "Brent and Janine are new, and we are still organizing the office. Only send us names, addresses, and tell us how much money to put on each card and when. That is all our involvement will be for now."

Finally they sorted out a system that was workable. Roland would sift through all the applications in Vallarta and check which of the applicants had investments with Cyberia, which did not, and which needed to resubmit due to an illegible photo or no signature on the application. Of the members who had money invested, he would notify Liza of that member's decision to receive dividends onto the card instead of a check, instruct her to deduct the card application fee if the member hadn't already sent it in, and then send the information down to Costa Rica. He would also email GI a spreadsheet with all the pertinent members' information on it so that the cards could be mailed before the paperwork even arrived. There were also members who did not have money invested with Cyberia but who wanted a Visa with which to make anonymous purchases or keep money offshore yet have it accessible instantly. These people paid the same fee and applied the same way as any other member. Roland constructed a different spreadsheet for them. After several hours of negotiations and a few more trips to the coffee shop, everyone was satisfied with how things were to be managed.

Brent yawned as he watched the photocopier spit out a sample Visa application. "Roland," he said, scratching his cheek.

"Mm?"

"How easy is it going to be for those computer guys to keep the card information separate from the rest of Cyberia's records and still link our database with theirs?"

"I don't know. Not very, I wouldn't think. But that's why Adrian pays them the big bucks."

Brent looked at Roland and shook his head.

"Better them than me."

Heinz was finishing his inspection of the Learjet just as Roland and Adrian cleared customs and were driven out to the plane. Before long they were taxiing past a couple of hollow and rusting abandoned airliners and US Air Force transport jets. Costa Rica was one of the few countries in the world with no army. Who needed one, with friends like the US? One of the previous Costa Rican presidents had been awarded the Nobel Peace Prize in the late eighties because he had simply got sick and tired of all the civil war in the countries around him. So he had rounded up the Central American leaders, as many as would listen, and had made them sign a peace accord. Since then the only real fly in the ointment had been Panama. "Nobody liked Noriega anyway," Diego had said during a break at the office. "He never signed, and now that he is gone, Panama is one of the world's best-kept secrets. It is a good place. Not as good as Costa Rica, of course," he added quickly.

As they turned onto the runway and gathered speed for takeoff, Roland noticed just how many big jets there were parked at the main terminal. San Jose airport could be a busy place.

The weather wasn't very good, and most of their climb to cruising altitude was shrouded in cloud. Roland poured strong cuba libres for himself and Adrian and stretched out on one of the side-facing seats while Adrian occupied the back two, frowning occasionally at some papers he had brought with him.

After the sun had set, Adrian called him over. His eyes were already glassy from his third drink. Roland mixed them very strong. "What did you guys do all day?" he asked.

Roland leaned over the back of the seat the way children do on school buses as he explained the system he had developed for the Visa cards. Adrian listened attentively despite the influence of the altitude and alcohol. He said, "Good. As long as it makes sense to you and it works," and he seemed impressed. But sometimes with Adrian it was hard to tell. Most likely, thought Roland, he was probably just relieved that it wasn't an issue any more.

Night had fallen and Roland had finished his magazine when Heinz beckoned him to come up front.

"We have to land in Acapulco."

"Wind?" asked Roland.

"Partly," Heinz answered. "But there are only five airports in all of Mexico that are open twenty-four hours a day to clear customs. El Deffe, Tijuana, also Guadalajara... anyway, Acapulco is another and the closest one for us. We will be there in half an hour."

Roland reported this to Adrian, who said, "Hell. We've already been up here all fuckin' night." He studied his ice cubes. "Hey, Roland. You know we're buying a plane, right?"

"A King Air, or so I hear."

Adrian pointed to Heinz in the cockpit. "This guy knows of an old Learjet in a hangar in the States. It's been sitting there for two years and we can get it for two hundred grand."

"It would probably need all the seals replaced by now," Roland said. "Airplanes are designed to be flown."

Adrian ignored him. "Heinz was flying some people around from Mexico City to somewhere in the States. One of his stupid fucking passengers rolled a joint in the back. Next thing you know there's a sniffer dog at a spot check who goes crazy 'cause he smells a seed." Adrian shook his head. "They impounded his plane, the Mexican government seized his others, boom, he's out of work."

"You mean it was his plane? His charter business?" Roland's thoughts started moving. If Heinz had been flagged for a drug offense, he'd be tracked by the American FAA and the Mexican civil aviation division for years. Which was fine, but it certainly didn't bode well for a man like Adrian who was trying to keep his business private. And worse, what if Heinz had been knowingly involved in trafficking?

"Yeah. We charter this plane exclusively and I'm trying to hire him to fly the King Air."

Roland was still thinking about Heinz.

Adrian continued, "The King Air is a lot slower than this thing. A trip from Vallarta to San Jose will take about two, three more hours." Then he smiled, and in typical Adrian fashion he found something to turn to his advantage. "But I figure, with a couple of cigars and a nice-looking girl, an extra couple of hours is just what you need."

Roland left him with a smile and went forward again to talk to Heinz. He looked at the pile of papers between the two pilot's seats. Thumbing through them as discreetly as possible he asked, "Heinz, how much fuel did we have when we landed in San Jose?"

Heinz was thoughtful for a second. "About eight hundred pounds. Enough for about half an hour. Legal reserves, but barely." He patted the instrument panel and smiled. "No problem." Heinz loved his Learjet.

Roland found what he was looking for. When he knew neither pilot would notice, he took it, and after a few more words with Heinz he returned to his seat and studied it.

If Heinz was a shoddy operator his flight plan would show it, but after flipping through pages of weather reports and airport information specs and not finding anything amiss he felt better. In fact, Heinz had even gone to the trouble to make little red marks where their flight path would take them even on the weather reports, and his planning forms were filled out in minute detail. Nonetheless, Grant would be the person to talk to in this regard. Roland returned the flight plan during their descent into Acapulco in case Heinz needed it again and resolved to take it for good at Vallarta.

All the windows in the aircraft had fogged up completely by the time they landed, including the pilot's windscreen. The only clear section of glass in the entire aircraft was the small area in front of Heinz's seat where a rectangular heater kept it free of fog and, at high and humid altitudes, frost.

When the door finally opened and they stepped out onto the tarmac, Roland was bathed in warm humidity, and it felt wonderful. Breathing in the sweet tropical air, not present in San Jose at that time of year because the city was so high up in the mountains that the air was relatively dry, Roland truly understood what Adrian meant when he said it was good to travel, but it was good to be home.

A small gathering of customs officers were standing around the desk examining passports – Adrian had only returned Roland's two days ago after requesting it for the trip to Guadalajara – and seemed to be doing nothing more than passing the documents back and forth amongst themselves. Roland produced a 200-peso note, folded it up, and knocked it over the counter onto the officer's desk as he fumbled with his Costa Rican tourist card. Within seconds their passports were stamped and they were being invited to stay in Acapulco instead of pushing on to PV.

"You're a quick study," Adrian said on the way outside. "I hate tipping anybody in a uniform, but that sure greased the wheels."

During the short hop up the coast to Puerto Vallarta, Roland secured Heinz's flight plan again and listened to one of the CDs he'd bought at the Multi Plaza shopping mall. On the flight down, somebody had put the Gipsy Kings' Greatest Hits in the aircraft's entertainment system and it had played almost five times through before had they landed. Now Gianluca Grignane serenaded them.

Easing to a stop on the tarmac, the copilot opened the door and deployed the steps, and Roland inhaled luxuriously. He was home.

Adrian was much too drunk to drive, so he threw Roland the keys to the Explorer and said, "Don't kill anybody." He had to use the washroom, but at this time of night the private terminal was locked. "Main terminal," he slurred. To save time, Roland drove in the opposite direction from the usual daytime traffic and pulled up with two wheels on the sidewalk. "This one's closed too, boss," Roland pointed out, but Adrian had already jumped out and disappeared. When he returned, he was flanked by two security guards. The taller of them nodded at Roland.

"*Como estas*," he asked flatly. Roland returned the greeting, making sure he looked at them both.

The man took a close look at Adrian as he climbed into the back seat. He was smiling at the guard in a drunken stupor.

"Your friend's eyes are very red," the guard said in Spanish.

"He's been drinking a lot," Roland answered, also in Spanish. "That's why I'm driving."

"Your eyes are red too," said the guard.

"That's because I'm wearing contact lenses and it's dry in the airplane."

The guard looked at Roland and decided he was telling the truth. "When you leave, please drive the right way out."

"Of course," said Roland. "My friend just needed the washroom and the other terminal is closed."

The guard nodded again. "Your Spanish is not so bad," he commented, and withdrew.

"Holy fuck, Roland," said Adrian. "I've lived here for three years and I have no idea what the fuck you just said."

"We were discussing how hyperbolic topology might relate to time travel."

"Fuck me," muttered Adrian.

Roland drove as slowly as he could over the speed bumps, aware that Adrian's insides were easily hurt, but he elected to take the Malecon road instead of the highway. He regretted his choice when they reached the cobblestones and the ride became rougher. The Malecon was busy that night, with lots of vehicles and many pedestrians shouting at each other and waving.

"You been practicing in this thing?" Adrian asked after a taxi passed within inches of their rear bumper when Roland pulled in front of it, still accelerating.

"No," Roland answered. "I've just missed driving. By the way, sorry we took this road. I forgot about the highway and I know this isn't easy for you."

There was a short silence from the back seat. Then Adrian said, "Don't worry about that, Roland. We've got lots of adventures planned for you."

Roland saw Adrian in the rearview mirror staring out at the amphitheatre, where a huge screen had been set up for a showing of *Night of the Iguana*. He noticed Roland looking and met his eyes in the mirror.

"Lots of adventures planned for you."

11

Upstairs at Andale's

Roland returned home to a different world.

Grant was away again somewhere, the cowboys were back, and Eric was on vacation. He had left for two weeks with approximately $25,000 worth of shopping to do on behalf of his fellow employees, as new electronics in Puerto Vallarta were hard to come by. Sam's Price Club had them, but their computers all had Spanish keyboards and some of the staff wanted new Sonys which they didn't carry. Everyone was hoping that Eric wouldn't get the red light at customs on his way back. But the most interesting change was the arrival of two more old friends of Adrian's, grey-haired brothers who had eschewed flying down in favor of a three-day drive in their pickup truck which was now parked in one of the gated stalls at Roland's house.

The taller one, Mack, wore glasses and spoke in a deep voice. He looked permanently as though he had just woken up. He was battling some kind of cancer. His brother, Nick, had in girth what he lacked in height and was extremely talkative. He had green eyes and his hair wasn't as grey as his brother's. They both smoked like trains.

They had come down to handle Cyberia's operations in Belize, and as such they were instantly known as the Belize Brothers. Things there were growing too fast, and Adrian wanted somebody he trusted to oversee that office. So many checks were coming in now that the shipping company was starting to get annoyed because they were spending too much of their time forwarding Cyberia's mail. After lunch on the terrace on their first day back from Costa Rica, Adrian told Roland that Mack didn't have long to live and it was nice to be able to offer him the option of spending his twilight days in a tropical country enjoying himself instead of living under communist rule back home. With the addition of these two and Grant, it was not difficult to see that Adrian was surrounding himself with trusted allies. It might take a while for Brent and Janine to get up to speed, but they would never pick Adrian's pocket.

The Belize Brothers were also the type who dove right in. By the time Roland returned from Costa Rica they had learned that Sidney had a speedboat, found that it needed repair, and bribed a marine shop enough to get it fixed immediately so they could spend the day chasing frigates and splashing around on Tuesday. They had even accosted Castanza to be their tour guide; not that they had met much resistance.

Before Roland had left for Costa Rica, he had succeeded in alienating to a noticeable degree almost everyone he worked with, but on his return his reception was nothing short of frosty. Even CIA Mick, whose idea it had been to send him down there in the first place, seemed distant and uncommunicative. Garrett and Slogan were notable exceptions, as always, and Lee wanted to know if he'd met any girls, but it didn't take long for Roland to resign himself to his desk and start slogging through the accumulated pile of Visa applications. Things didn't get any better when CIA Mick mentioned that some people had come to him during Roland's absence expressing discontent because Roland took an hour for Spanish lessons during the day while everyone else was working. Apparently the fact that Roland stayed later than any of them was irrelevant.

Maybe Costa Rica would be different. Roland had already decided that he certainly wasn't going to be. If all it had taken to estrange himself was ambition and hard work, he didn't think he'd be missing much.

The weekend came and with it warmer weather. Although the sun was more zealous as the season began to change, the number of tourists wouldn't diminish for some time yet.

Friday night found Roland wandering up Olas Altas on his way home when Ken hailed him from a table on the second floor at Andale's. He was surrounded by people, as usual. Roland navigated the narrow steps and approached Ken, who introduced him to the gaggle of partyers. Beer appeared and Roland was soon talking to them like old friends. They were all from Saskatchewan and had run into a lot of other people they knew from the same Canadian province; in fact, there were so many present that Ken said, "Is there anybody left up there?"

One of them, a red-faced man in his mid forties with a generous belly, slapped Ken on the back as he looked at Roland. "How do you know Kenny here?" he asked. "You guys work together?"

Ken's eyes became wide. He said, "Yeah, a long time ago." He excused himself and motioned for Roland to follow him outside. They descended the stairs to the sidewalk next to the open doorway and the glassless windows on either side.

"We don't work here," he said.

"I didn't assume anything," Roland retorted, fully aware that Ken had told his friends that he did indeed work here. One night during Roland's first week in Mexico he had accompanied Liza to dinner at La Palapa, where they met Ken and some of his relatives who had come down for a visit. All they talked about was either the days when Ken and Liza were dating, or what it was like working in Vallarta. When he had asked Liza about it afterwards she had said, "Just tell who you trust," and judging by the number of friends and relatives who had come down for a visit, everyone trusted everyone else in spite of the spy-versus-spy games. Either that or Ken shared the same tendency most of the others had, to advertise that they had a secret in order to boost their appeal but not to divulge what the secret was in order to keep their non-disclosure agreements intact.

"Just so you know," Ken said again. "I don't work here and neither do you. Remember that. We're just on vacation." Then his eyes became friendly again.

Yes, I know, thought Roland. We're all beach bum millionaires just here to hang around.

Lee stepped out of a store across the street holding hands with a Mexican man, presumably her boyfriend. This was the first time anyone had seen her elusive other half. He looked exactly like Cheech Marin. Lee waved at them with her free hand and her boyfriend pulled her down the street away from them with the other.

Kevin came ambling up the sidewalk and greeted them. He seemed a little subdued, maybe because Eric was away. Somebody in the bar was yelling through the microphone for a scantily-dressed girl to stop dancing on a table which wobbled dangerously every time she moved her hips.

"You-know-who hired somebody to teach the house staff English," Kevin told them, looking at Roland. "I think you started something."

Roland wondered what Adrian would think of being referred to as 'you-know-who' in the interests of national security.

"How do they sound?" asked Ken, obviously disinterested.

"Don't know," Kevin replied. "They haven't started yet." He bobbed his head to the music, still very loud on the sidewalk. "Did you guys know that he's getting a guard dog?"

"He's not conspicuous enough already?" Roland observed.

"Maybe it'll eat Yoda," said Ken.

"So far, that's all I've heard," Kevin continued. "I don't know what kind it is or when it's going to be here." Then, as abruptly as he had appeared, he said goodnight and left them.

"Come on," said Ken. "Let's find some girls and start dancing."

Ken had owned several bars way back when, which had lent him an obvious gift for sociability. He could walk into a bar anywhere and instantly be one of the crowd, singing along and clinking glasses together.

Roland followed him back into the bar. He might learn something.

Ken wasn't the only one with friends who came down to visit. In fact, over the time Roland was in Vallarta, practically everyone hosted at least one friend or relative at some point. On the first of April, a Sunday, Roland was at work shredding outdated files when Garrett invited him out for a day in Sidney's speedboat with a couple of friends from Vancouver, a marine biologist and his young wife.

They set off in a Jeep borrowed from Tatiana's car rental company. Along the road to the airport was the miniature lighthouse with "Puerto Iguana" painted on it that had caught Roland's attention on his first trip through the city, which was a gatehouse to a group of colorful townhouses facing a secluded part of the marina. Garrett pulled in here.

They emptied the jeep of lifejackets and snacks and carried them down the sidewalk to the boat. Some of the townhouses had tropical garden ponds in front of them, and all were shaded by tall palms and fragrant hedges. They found slip number 92 and Sidney's little speedboat waiting patiently.

"What's it cost to rent a slip here?" the young woman asked. "Or do you have to buy them?"

"All the owners get a slip with their townhouse," Garrett replied, "so Adrian bought one." He took a bottle of sunscreen out of his duffle bag and started slathering himself with it.

"A slip?" She was still a little confused.

"A townhouse." The smell of coconuts was filling the marina.

"He bought a townhouse just so he could get a slip?"

"Yep." Garrett lowered the cooler into the boat.

Garrett's friend untied the boat from the slip at the rear, leaving the front still secure. Roland jumped in and stowed his belongings under the seat.

The girl was obviously taking this in. She'd been to the Shack and, although she hadn't been allowed downstairs, had probably seen enough on the main floor to write home about for ages.

Garrett squinted at her before donning his sunglasses. "It's good to be king."

Liza was in particularly high spirits that Monday. The yacht had finally arrived, and Maxine had seen it off in San Diego after loading it full of things. She wouldn't say exactly what, but Liza was expecting greatness. Liza and Maxine had tried to outshop each other ever since they met. Adrian and Maxine had been married a long time. No wonder Adrian ran himself ragged making money.

"It's awesome," Liza said, her dark eyes even more alive than usual. "Haven't been on it yet though. We watched it come around the point this morning."

CIA Mick asked, "So when do we see it? More importantly, when do we go for a cruise?"

Amy nodded. "No kidding, hey? Me and Sidney want to go out on it." She had Yoda perched on her knee. "It's

Semana Santa coming up. Holy week. The city's going to be packed, just one big party everywhere. No better time for us all to go out."

"Any bachelors who want to go for a cruise must do so naked," Liza said loudly.

"I'm not sunburning my dick for a ride on a boat," Slogan snorted. His shirt read *'I don't have Tourette's, you're just an asshole'*.

This seemed to deflate Liza not one bit. She had a friend from the States staying with her and the yacht's timing couldn't have been better. "Fine," she said. "When you get your own yacht, you can tell all the girls to come on it naked."

She disappeared up the stairs. At the top of the curve she noticed Roland watching her.

He smiled. "Adrian's not going to set foot on that thing for a month, is he?"

Liza laughed that laugh of hers. "Not if I have anything to do with it."

Wednesday morning came. Roland woke earlier than his alarm and stretched in front of the window where the type-A dolphins were already awake and playing in the waves. He'd seen whales as well, twice, and both times fairly early. Apparently that was out of character for them. They usually slept in.

One of the reasons Roland liked his house was because it was so private. The road in front of his entrance curved toward the beach so the closest building to his left, a short row of old but elegant townhomes, was some distance down the hill. To the right was a magnificent house which was used as a rental property. Every week brought different people lounging by the pool. Like Roland's, it was built so that the entrance was on level ground but there was a dramatic drop on the ocean side where the patios were. Due to thick bougainvillea on the other property and the jungle and palm trees in between, Roland couldn't usually see much of it even standing on his own patio on the second floor. But standing at his bedroom window he could, and this morning he didn't like what he saw. A couple in their mid-forties, dressed more for a day in Nantucket than in Puerto Vallarta, was relaxing in deck chairs by the pool. Under any other circumstances they would have been completely innocuous, but they both had binoculars trained on the Shack.

Roland had taken in the view from Adrian's balconies enough times to know that there wasn't much the couple would be able to see. Nevertheless the sight unnerved him. The woman noticed him looking and said something to the man, and they both put down their binoculars and tried to look nonchalant. In that moment Roland was glad he wasn't Roxane or Kevin or Eric. There was no telling where his overcautious imagination would have taken him with this kind of fuel.

Normally most of the mist covering the bay would have burned off by the time Roland awoke, but this morning he didn't want sleep and the thin, gentle cloud still shrouded everything. He showered with Dave watching from the ceiling again, and threw on a pair of thin denim shorts. He pulled a yellow polo shirt over his head as he padded out to the livingroom where Grant sat looking at Heinz's flight plan, which Roland had left on the table.

"Morning," he said without looking up. "You're up early."

"Hey," said Roland. "How've you been?"

"Good." The coffeemaker hissed and gurgled to itself, and the smell of fresh coffee filled the room. Roland had never used the appliance. "Adrian sent me up to Cleveland to have a look at the helicopter training facility and secure some dates," Grant told him. "I leave this Saturday, the 7th, for at least a month."

"You mean I'll have the place to myself?" This was good news, but he would miss Grant. There would be one less person with whom he felt he could spend his leisure time. Liza begrudged Grant's presence because as far as she could tell he still hadn't actually done a lick of work, but Roland liked his perspicacity and sense of humor.

"Stay out of my room while I'm gone," Grant commanded. Then he held up the flight plan. "What's this doing here?"

Roland poured himself some coffee and sat down on the couch. The folding doors were open as always, and the fresh morning breeze felt wonderful.

"I borrowed it from Heinz," Roland explained, and related what Adrian had told him on the flight from San Jose. "Not exactly a smoking gun, but if he's a slipshod pilot that'll show it." He sipped his coffee. He hadn't put any cream or sugar in it the way he normally did and it tasted great this morning.

Grant seemed to know all about Heinz and the Learjet that Adrian had told Roland about the night before. "We can't touch that airplane even if we wanted to, though, which we don't," he concluded. "The investigation is still ongoing, hung up on some witness they can't find or something; some excuse to keep an investigator employed. We're going to buy the King Air. Actually we're going for a test flight today."

Roland wanted to go with them but he refrained from asking. His mind was on the new Visa card system and whether or not it would work as well in practice as it did in theory. Not many things did.

"This is okay," Grant said, holding up the flight plan. "No problems here. Heinz is no fool."

Good, thought Roland. One less variable to worry about if things go wrong.

A little while later up at the Shack, he stood with CIA Mick, Liza, Garrett and Roxane on the downstairs balcony, admiring a magnificent sight. The mist was still visible, and in the morning sunlight a majestic rainbow arched all the way across the mouth of the bay. It was unendingly tall and perfectly round, and joined the north and south halves of the peaceful city completely. Roland wished he'd brought his camcorder that morning when he saw Mick aiming his laptop and its built-in camera at it.

The phone rang and Liza went to answer it only to return a moment later. "Come on, bachelors, we've got a job to do. Nobody's unloaded the yacht yet."

"What?" asked Garrett. "I thought you did that on Monday."

Liza shook her head. "No time. Izzy had a delay, some paperwork thing. He had to spend Tuesday at sea because he wasn't cleared to dock the boat until today." Izzy was the captain, a Cuban who employed a Guatemalan deck hand named, of all things, Gonzo.

"What is it, an airport? They put him in a holding pattern?" Roland was amazed. By now everyone was headed upstairs and the Secret Agent had grabbed the keys to the Belize Brothers' truck. "See you at the marina," he called with Garrett in tow, already on their way to Roland's house to fetch the pickup. Liza and Roland climbed into Liza's Lincoln and started off down the hill.

Roland knew which entrance to use, having been there only days before, though he was having doubts that a large motoryacht would fit the slip in which Sidney's speedboat had been moored. Nevertheless, Sidney had taken the little boat to a friend's house up the coast so that the yacht would have a home. They pulled in and parked, awaiting the two others.

Liza said gently, "You're having trouble here."

Roland didn't look at her. He knew that she was referring to his relationship with his coworkers.

"It's not them, it's me," he said at last. "I'm still pretty touchy because of some things that happened over the last year. Makes me hard to work with, I would think."

"I've seen that in you; everybody has," she said. "But you don't have to make excuses for them. I know what they can be like. Why don't you get more involved with things outside work? There's lots to do around here, you know."

"I know. Actually I'd like to take diving lessons, but I don't want to get really into something and then have to drop it when I get sent to Costa Rica."

Liza brushed her hair back. It was hot, even with the air conditioning on. "Did you like it down there?"

The truck pulled in and they could see Mick pointing to Liza's Navigator and the guard waving them through.

"I like it here more," Roland said. "I don't know. I like them both."

"What will you do?"

"I'll go where I'm sent," Roland answered, but he envied the Belize Brothers a little. He would have liked to be as independent as they and still play a necessary part in the business.

Mick parked the truck as close as he could to the gate Liza was pointing to, and the four of them started down to the yacht.

Izzy and Gonzo saw them approaching and waved. Izzy had indeed squeezed the vessel into the slip, making the thirty-foot sailing yacht next to it seem like a lifeboat in comparison. He had backed it in to make it easy to unload, showing the boat's name, *Pier Pressure*. It was sleek and white and had tinted, raked windows to the cabin and, just as Maxine had described, an abundance of radar and radio gear sticking out the top which combined to give it the appearance of something out of a space movie.

"Morneen'," Izzy called out as they approached. "Come see. Lots of stuff for you." He motioned them aboard.

He had slicked back the black hair on his round head and wore Aviator sunglasses. The two of them would have been a welcome male decoration in any bar. Gonzo was thin and very Indian, but his clothes were expensive and he wore a lot of rings. They both resembled carefree pimps. Roland wondered what a full-time captain and deckhand were going to add to Adrian's payroll expenses.

The yacht's interior was lavish, to say the least. The cabinets in the full galley were genuine oak and the spiral stairs led down to an equally ostentatious collection of small bedrooms. The bridge contained all manner of navigation equipment, and the flying bridge upstairs boasted a commanding view from high above the water.

Everywhere Roland looked he saw boxes of electronics, artwork, bags of clothes and other paraphernalia strewn about. A plastic placemat with two bowls sat on the floor near the sliding door to the sun deck.

Izzy saw him looking. "I'm glad to be reed of that fuckeen' dog," he said. "Puked on my deck twice." He held up two fingers in case Roland missed it. "Here, grab one end of this." They stood beside one of two massive plasma TVs.

"The guard dog came down on the yacht?" Roland asked. "Where is he?"

"Don' know," Izzy said, lifting one end of the box. "Don' care. Adrian came an' got him las' night. Maybe he's relaxeeng in the townhouse here." They carried the television to the Belize Brothers' truck, muscling it over the tailgate as Izzy asked rhetorically, "Why do dogs eat their own fuckeen' puke, anyway?"

Roland ignored this question. "I heard you had to spend yesterday at sea, just hanging around."

"Yeah." Izzy stepped up onto a townhouse lawn to allow Mick and Garrett to pass with their identical TV. "Fuckeen' damn near starved to death, man." He pronounced it 'maing'. "Where can I get laid aroun' here?"

"Pretty much anywhere, from what I've heard," Roland responded as they walked back to the yacht. "Go to Christine's Disco in the Krystal for your more high-maintenance girls, local or otherwise, and anywhere for tourist girls. Actually all the bars here are good for meeting up with somebody." He looked at Izzy. "Of course, if you'd rather cut out the small talk you can head over to Junior's or Cadillac behind the bullring." He pointed over Izzy's shoulder. "Don't walk there at night though; get yourself a cab."

Izzy nodded and smoothed his hair, bracelets jangling faintly in the hot and humid air. "Jhou know, they kep' me at sea because of fuckeen' Customs?" he said as they boarded the ship for a second load. Roland shouldered two sets of titanium golf clubs and gingerly lifted a painting in a crate frame that said 'Field Museum, Chicago' on it. Izzy adjusted his rings and selected a bag of ladies' clothing, making a good act of it being heavy. Even Liza was carrying more than he. Gonzo was making himself look busy with something on the flying bridge.

"Is that why? How much did all this stuff cost to clear?" Roland asked.

"Never cleared," Izzy said in disgust. "We spen' all fuckeen' day out there, then they tell us to come in and dock, they'll clear us tomorrow."

"No wonder I'm taking the morning off work," Roland said. "We could be unloading five million bucks' worth of cocaine off this thing."

"Fi' meellion bucks' worth?" Izzy said. "I don' theenk so." He smiled at Roland. "You wouldn't need this many boxes. Plus you *load* them in Mexico, not *un*load."

"How do you know all that, Izzy?" Roland asked innocently, though he knew he didn't need to.

Izzy spat on the sidewalk near a slip where a Mexican was painting his sailboat, earning himself a dirty look.

"I seen Miami Vice," he said, and Roland knew that behind his Aviators Izzy had winked at him.

By the time they arrived back at the Shack it was lunchtime and the rainbow across the bay was gone. Everyone was seated around the table talking loudly about another new arrival, Franz.

Franz was a German Shepherd guard dog, and he resembled a small grizzly bear. He was making the rounds of each employee, sniffing their hands and cataloguing the scent in order to discriminate attacker from victim later on. But when he came over to investigate the house staff, he was regarded in the same way as one might regard a circus lion – interesting, cute perhaps, but hardly something to which you offered your hand. Guadalupe reluctantly did so and Franz sniffed it, then licked it. She drew it back a little. Franz growled. She hid behind Castanza.

It was sufficiently crowded that the four who had unloaded the yacht were forced to take seats at the counter. The Belize Brothers were there, as were Grant and the cowboys. Roland tapped Adrian on the shoulder and pointed at the dog.

"Is he a good boy?" he asked.

"So far," said Adrian. "I don't know where he's going to shit, though. But at least Castanza won't have to water the plants anymore 'cause Franz will do it for him."

Slogan was wearing a plain white t-shirt with no writing on it. That's what it said on the front, anyway. He was patting Franz on the head and scratching him behind the ear. Franz's head was almost level with the table. He asked, "Can I borrow him on weekends to ride him downtown? I'm spending too much on taxi fare."

Franz came over and sat in front of Roland who, tall as he was, didn't have to bend down to let him sniff his hand.

"If he starts humping your leg, offer him a cigarette afterwards," Kevin advised.

Roland asked, "If I want to tell him to go away, what do I say?"

Adrian frowned. "I don't know yet. He only speaks German."

"You mean he didn't come with a manual?"

"Try 'Heil Hitler'," offered Kevin. "Or 'bratwurst'."

Adrian said, "He spent the first three years of his life being trained in Germany. He came over to the States just a few weeks ago; then Izzy brought him down. The trainers will be here tomorrow to show us where all the buttons are."

"Good thing I'm not the first one in to work," Ken observed. "I don't want to be the one who wakes him up."

Franz panted in the heat.

Over the past week the Shack had become much more crowded and busy than usual, and by now everyone knew that if they wanted a seat at the table at mealtimes they had to be one of the first eight upstairs. Today, though, there wasn't even room at the counter. Roland had arrived just in time for breakfast – for him, very late – and took his plate of eggs out to the patio dining table with Ken.

The first person he had seen when he had let himself into the Shack that morning was a girl with a blue shirt that said 'Harrison K-9' on it. She looked a little overwhelmed. Roland had seen Harrison's advertisements in the *Robb*

Report since he was fourteen, so this was somewhat of a novelty for him.

She was one of three people dispatched via the Learjet to show Adrian how to communicate with Franz. Aside from basic German commands (Adrian's favorite was 'Platz', meaning 'lie down', mostly because Franz was almost half Adrian's height and made him look even smaller than usual when standing beside him) he was also learning how to tell Franz to attack people. Adrian told everyone that when that phase of the activities was reached they could all take a break to watch.

Seated at his desk with a coffee that Guadalupe had brought for him, Roland waited for his computer to boot up as he thumbed through the Visa applications. Their number had begun growing exponentially as all the members who had applied told all the members they knew who hadn't to do so, and it wouldn't be long before there were more than Roland could handle by himself. Which was okay, because apparently somebody who'd had too much to drink at the wedding had told a friend what Cyberia was all about, and in typical Adrian fashion instead of chastising the employee responsible he had agreed to hire the newly-informed associate. Maybe Roland wouldn't need to work so much when the newbie came on board in another two weeks.

Slogan pushed his chair away from his desk and looked around. "This guy is certifiably insane," he said. Roland looked up. Slogan pointed to his computer screen. "He just wrote me an email asking if we were a legitimate investment."

CIA Mick laughed. "Is that his idea of due diligence?" he said. "Write him back and say no. I wonder how he'd respond."

Slogan looked at the monitor. "He goes on to ask if he should take out a second mortgage to invest with us." He shook his head. "I don't understand this."

Amy agreed. "Some people are just so stupid it hurts," she said. Of course with Amy that was roughly every third person who wrote to her.

Slogan started tapping on his keyboard. "'Dear Sir,'" he intoned, "Due diligence consists of checking objective references and you should never invest all your money in one thing." He looked around the room. "I don't think he knows that. Would you ask a pathological liar if he was telling the truth? I mean, what kind of answer does he expect from us?"

This made Roland laugh. He remembered asking Sara if she was telling the truth when she promised to stop seeing her other man. The answer had been yes, but what else could he have expected her to say?

CIA Mick thought Roland was laughing at the member's question. He said, "This blonde moment has been brought to you by Cyberia."

"Yeah, we've all had them," said Roland, still smiling.

Lee wasn't too pleased with this exchange. She pointed to her head and said, "I'll have you know I'm a natural blonde, yeah."

"Trust me, we know," said the Secret Agent. He and Roland had worked out that at the rate Lee was scanning documents, she wouldn't be caught up for six months. Thankfully she was going on vacation this weekend, something she'd had planned before Adrian hired her, and she would probably be told not to bother returning to work when she came back. She was to spend the latter half of the day training Maxine's friend Dolores in how to fill her shoes while she was away. Roland felt a little sad for her, but he knew that being let go wouldn't bother her for long and she'd find a new job in no time. Lee was like that.

Roland's computer was now awake and he was looking through his emails. Everyone in the office had been instructed to tell members to send Visa inquiries to General

Investments – in other words, to Roland – and when some of the members wrote, they included the relevant message from the Cyberian employee. He drank his coffee greedily even though it was already hot in the office. Upstairs Franz barked twice.

Roland clicked on a message. A member had written to Cyberia asking about the Visa program and Slogan – or rather, James Nicholson – had directed him to write to General Investments, all the way across the room. Lee stuffed a page into the scanner, jamming it for the first of another umpteen times that morning. At least she was consistent, Roland thought as he scanned the message. It was the first time he'd read anything sent by his coworkers to Cyberia members.

Roland wasn't sure what he'd expected Slogan's communication style to be, but it was very concise without being curt. Hardly what one would expect from someone who wore shirts encouraging women to '*Love. Honor. Obey. And we'll get along just fine*'. His fiancée laughed at him if he wore that one in the house. He gave the member the standard information – please provide us with your name, address, and a current passport photocopy and make sure the photo is clear and the signature legible. He clicked on the next message. Lee slammed the top of the scanner down after yanking out another piece of jammed paper.

This member had included the message sent to him from Cyberia as well, only this one wasn't from Slogan. It was from Clara Jackson. That would be Amy.

Roland skimmed over the message – another standard inquiry for information about how to correctly submit a Visa application and could members use it for cash withdrawals and most importantly, how anonymous was it? Good question, Roland thought. GI was the same as any other card issuer. It wasn't going to bother checking every single applicant to see if the names submitted were false. Not even a credit bureau always knew that. In that sense, GI's pledge of anonymity coupled with an applicant's potential deviousness meant that no one would ever know whose money was being spent. That was a refreshing thought. Roland had feared that respect for privacy was dead. Too many places in the world considered it antisocial and suspect rather than a healthy indication that one was living one's own life instead of sticking their nose into others'.

He began to read the message Amy had sent. This should be interesting, thought Roland. If Amy was even half as critical in the messages as she was in the office, this member had endured an absolute roasting. Beside him, Lee patted herself on the back. She had finally finished scanning the file.

Roland leaned back with his coffee to his lips. He had to read the message twice before he smiled broadly. It read:

> Dear Sir:
>
> I am pleased to be able to help you in your request for information re: the Visa cards. They are being offered through General Investments. You can reach them at gicards@generalinves tments.com. As per your question regarding deposits, to the best of my understanding you can deposit money any time you like towards your Visa balance, meaning that you don't have to rely solely on Cyberia dividends to fund your card. When you contact them, make sure you provide your Cyberia membership number as that will make it easier for them to coordinate their recordkeeping with ours. As always, I encourage you to keep careful records of your transactions with us and with them, and make sure you declare your Cyberia dividends on your tax return this year.

If there is anything else I can do to help in this or any other Cyberia matter, please don't hesitate to let me know.

Yours truly,

Clara Jackson

So, thought Roland, looking at Amy across the room where she sat next to Eric's empty desk, her headphones on, scratching one foot with the other. All that caustic talk of how stupid her members are, even when they submit perfectly ordinary questions, and all this time she's been nothing short of an absolute teddy bear. Just when you think you know someone.

He logged out of the General Investments website after sending his emails and updating one of the pages, then filled out his spreadsheets and sent them to the office in Costa Rica. He wondered what everyone there was doing today and how Brent and Janine were adjusting to their new surroundings. Probably they were washing down a late breakfast from the Burger King across the street from the office with smooth Costa Rican lattes. They hadn't returned any of the spreadsheets with the confirmations that the cards had been sent, which annoyed Roland because he was the one who kept getting mail from members saying 'I submitted my application; where's my card?'

Lee looked at him and sighed, fanning herself with her hand. It was stuffy downstairs even with the sliding doors open. There was no appreciable breeze. Finally the intercom beeped and the new cook said, "Lunch, everybody, get up here for lunch," and there was a mad rush for the stairs.

Roland made it in time to grab the second-last seat around the big glass table. Mack and Nick were sitting by the pool smoking and the trainers were splayed out on the couches. The trainer girl Roland had seen that morning was sweating profusely. Castanza was outside at the barbecue, tending the acres of grill space expertly as he flipped huge burger patties. "Do you wish we were having English fish and chips?" Roland asked Lee, who had parked herself beside him.

She smiled. "Wrapped in newsprint, yeah." But when her lunch came she attacked it ferociously, and when Guadalupe came around with seconds she kept pace with the rest of them.

Roxane pulled a piece off her bun and was about to offer it to Franz, but Adrian said, "No way." He held up a finger. "Nobody feeds this dog but me."

"I was just trying to placate him so he doesn't eat Yoda," she protested, putting the morsel back on her plate.

"If anybody else feeds him, there will be trouble," Adrian said loudly; or at least, as loudly as he was able. Nevertheless, everyone heard him. "If I catch any of you guys feeding this dog, you will be sorry." He scratched Franz behind the ear. "He's trained to regard the person who feeds him as his boss, and that's me."

When the dishes were cleared away he announced, "Stick around. This is the fun part. Franz here is going to try and kill one of these guys." He waved his cigarette toward the three trainers sitting on the couches. "If you want, you can go up to the third floor and watch. Take a beer with you; it'll be interesting."

Roland chose a vantage point on the balcony between Lee and Shelly. Finally there was a bit of a breeze, but it wasn't very cooling. The sun was too hot. Roland sipped his coffee.

One of the trainers was suiting up in padded Kevlar armor. Adrian went inside and emerged with two bottles of Dom Perignon and a large rock. He handed the items to the blond girl, who placed them on the patio equidistantly, stretching around the corner to the pool. She showed them to Franz and led him back to a line made by a piece of duct tape near the barbecue. Adrian sat watching nearby.

The armored trainer began hitting his arm with a riding crop and hissing. Suddenly Franz was transformed from the docile house pet he had been at the breakfast table to a one-hundred-and-fifty-pound cruise missile with fangs. As the trainer ran away, the girl yelled a command and Franz stopped dead at the first bottle of champagne.

"He has good taste," Shelly observed.

After some discussion and two more of these warmups it was Adrian's turn to command the beast. He had a little trouble separating two rather different commands – "*Fass*" meant 'Attack' and "*Fuss*" meant 'Heel'. Until Adrian mastered the subtleties, the ensuing confusion was rather amusing.

"Roland," said a voice behind them. Grant had appeared as though conjured from a hat. He beckoned Roland over.

"What's up?" Roland asked.

"Doesn't Adrian realize that all it would take to pick him off is some kid with a rifle on that hill behind the house while he's sitting by the pool one morning?"

Or from our neighbor's deck chair, Roland thought, remembering the couple by the pool.

"Just a f'rinstance," Grant said, "but it's worth considering. Frankly I think the dog is for show. Anyway, I came up to say goodbye."

"I thought you weren't leaving until tomorrow." Roland tried to conceal his disappointment.

Grant pushed back his darkened glasses. He was sweating a little in the heat. "I thought so too, but I just got off the phone with my daughter. She's going to fly down to Cleveland tonight so I can spend a couple of days with her before class starts on Monday. I wanted some time to get set up anyways, but this way I get to see her too."

"That's good then." Roland shook his hand. "Take care, Grant. Blue side up."

Grant chuckled. "Always."

Roland never saw him again.

12
Orion at a Distance

Puerto Vallarta had been filling up with tourists from all around Mexico for almost a week in preparation for Semana Santa. Bars that had only hosted American and Canadian tourists were suddenly full of Mexican faces and the streets were choked with cars displaying license plates from all over the country.

"It's only going to get worse," Roxane intoned. She was floating on a foam lounger in the pool, splashing cool water over herself while Yoda made little whining noises as he stood at the edge.

"It's a good time for you to meet girls, though." She paddled over to where Yoda quivered and raised his paw. "Whoever she is, you know she's going home at the end of the week." She drew up to the edge and the little dog jumped onto her lap. Roland's own lounger had been carried to the middle of the pool by the constant current created by the filter pump. Roxane pushed away from the edge and floated towards him while Yoda stared nervously into the water.

"Where did Lee say she went on her vacation?" Roland asked.

"Majorca, I think, or Ibiza. Somewhere in the Mediterranean. Is it Semana Santa there too?"

"I suppose so," Roland said. "Holy Week is a Catholic holiday."

Roxane was silent for a bit. Roland had his eyes closed and his sunglasses on, but he could almost feel her thinking. Yoda's tags jingled as he scratched himself.

"A friend of mine said he was stabbed during Semana Santa a few years ago," she said slowly. "Eighteen times. He said they broke into his place, stabbed him, and left him for dead."

"You don't sound too convinced."

"I'm not. That guy lies like a carpet."

Roxane's fingers made little trickling noises as she played in the water. "He owns that shop at the end of Olas Altas. The one with all the handicrafts and antique furniture you like."

"Really?" Roland knew whom she meant. He'd been in the store and chatted with the man several times. He made a mental note to look twice at the price tags on his next visit.

Roxane's phone rang and she paddled over to the edge to answer it. Yoda jumped onto the patio and seemed glad to be on terra firma for about three seconds, after which he wanted to get back onto Roxane's lap. She spoke in Spanish for a short time and then hung up. Then to Roland, who could tell it was her boyfriend on the phone by the tone of her voice, she said, "He's going to be here for a few days during the week."

"Why doesn't he just move here? I mean, if you two are an item, what's stopping you?" Roland had met the man and liked him although he spoke barely any English. He was an artisan and made decent money flogging his wares to tourists. When Roxane's son had come to visit they had all gone out to a restaurant called Timari, one of the finest in Mexico, located a couple of blocks behind the Malecon in a renovated building that used to house his studio.

Roland dipped his fingers in the water and flicked them in the air. He opened his eyes to see droplets on his sunglasses.

"Because that would require effort and commitment, which I don't think either of us are interested in at the moment." Roxane bit her lip. "It's not really that kind of relationship anyway."

"Well, as long as you know that."

Roxane unscrewed the top of her bottle of water. "Speaking of which, have you heard from your ex since you came to Mexico?"

"Actually yes," Roland answered. "She sent me an email about a week after I moved here. When she left I made an offer to buy her half of the house but she didn't want to sell it. Then when I came down here I wrote her with my address and told her that if she ever felt like closing the case she could just send down a deal that makes sense and I'd sign it and pay her."

"So she sent down a deal?"

"Not at first. She said she wanted a certified check with an offer."

"Did she say she'd accept an offer?" Roxane drank from the bottle and swirled the water around to watch the vortex it made.

"No."

"Then why certify a check?"

"Exactly." Roland pulled himself to the edge of the pool where a plate of nachos and guacamole awaited.

Roland offered a nacho to Yoda. He sniffed and rejected it. "Then a little while ago I got another email from her, and some documents arrived at the Shack. She sold me her half of the house for a dollar." Roland dipped the chip in guacamole. This time the dog accepted it and the sound of crunching echoed off the hot terracotta.

"One dollar?" Roxane echoed, and upon hearing Roland's "Mm-hmm" she was silent for a while. Eventually she said, "I think she has a lot to say to you, but she can't say it with words." She drained her bottle of water. "Do you still miss her?"

"Sometimes," Roland admitted. "She'd love it here, and I'd love to show it to her. But I'm sure she's happy where she is. Or at least, I hope so."

"Still love her?"

Roland said nothing and Roxane changed the subject. "So, are you going back to Costa Rica anytime soon?"

Roland flicked water into the air again. "I think I'll have to," he said. "I haven't heard from those guys all week, and I've got to know how well they're holding up their end of things."

Roxane wiggled her toes. She took a couple of breaths before she spoke. "Everything's pretty hectic, isn't it? I mean, it's in the air. You can't not feel it; it's everywhere. Big changes."

Roland agreed. There was so much happening and so many people coming and going that ever since the weekend of the wedding, things had taken a different turn. Even the cowboys had complained that their environment was too chaotic, so they had taken to working in the evenings when it was cooler and everyone else had left. Everyone but Garrett, of course, who had to stay behind after his regular day and put in overtime with them.

Roland stretched luxuriously and turned over onto his stomach. "At least I got my passport back."

Roxane did the same. "I didn't know you'd lost it."

"I didn't. I gave it to Adrian for the trip to Guadalajara and only got it back just before I went down south at the end of last month."

Roxane absently patted the water with a flat hand. "What did he want it for?"

Roland frowned. "For the flight. Didn't he want everyone's?"

"Of course not. Why would you need a passport on a domestic flight?" She splashed water at Yoda, who blinked and sneezed. "We didn't even leave Jalisco."

It took a few seconds for the truth of this to sink in, but Roxane was right. There was no reason at all for Adrian to have asked Roland for his passport. Liza didn't need it for payroll and not even Guillermo the security man had asked to see it. So what would Adrian want with it?

The sun was as hot as ever, but Roland could not suppress the tiny chill that ran down his spine.

Monday, April 9th.

The couple from Montreal who owned the blue Volkswagen convertible which Roland had his eye on had been away for some time. They had driven down the coast and planned to turn inland after a few days in Acapulco, making the small crowd of expat regulars at the Pagina that morning smaller still as some had already returned home after their winter in the tropics. Pandemonium reigned, however, as Semana Santa was in full swing and there were colorful people, cars, and buses everywhere. Even the Mayan Palace van, which passed by every weekday morning, was late.

Roland was glad he'd decided to walk back up to the Shack via the Calle Santa Barbara instead of the highway, because when it came time to cross the latter the traffic was so frenetic that he had to wait almost three minutes before it was clear enough. For this time of day in this part of town, that was a long time.

If the Montrealers' car wasn't available, maybe a laptop was. Roland had spent a couple of hours pricing some out and had decided that he wanted one. Nothing fancy; maybe not even something new, but something he could write and send emails on without wondering if they were being read by someone in the office. One of the cowboys had told him that the new system they were designing had a spy feature. It would report how many hours each computer spent logged on to the server, how many memberships were entered by each one, how many emails had been answered, and how much time spent tying up SatMex Five's bandwidth surfing the internet instead of taking care of business. For Roland that was unacceptable.

It wasn't that he didn't understand Adrian's need for this kind of software. Quite the contrary. As far as Roland was concerned it made perfect sense, but he was tiring of his sporadic connection to his coworkers and was becoming saturated with the secrets. His objection to the new features consisted of his mistrust of who would have and control the information they generated, not a skepticism of whether they were necessary.

In fact, he had already started planning how much longer he would need to work at Cyberia before paying off the rest of his debts and leaving. Even though Vallarta felt like home to him, he couldn't help wondering how much of that he owed to his connection with the city itself and how much simply to the fact that he had been dropped into a unique cross between a spy movie and a rerun of *Baywatch*. Regardless, at the current rate that he was paying off his debts he wouldn't be free of them until the end of June.

He checked his email. There was a message from a distributor in New Jersey who had the computer he wanted, and the rep had replied to Roland's inquiry. Call me, it said, we'll sort it out. So as Guadalupe set the table for breakfast, Roland did exactly that.

He sat at the bar in the livingroom. Next to it was a glass case with a model of the Shack as the architects had envisioned it before it was built. It had been initially designed to be bigger yet, but the neighbors up the hill had complained that even the first phase of building was obstructing their view. This wasn't Adrian's problem but he demurred anyway and, when he bought the Shack from the original owners he did not exercise the option to expand. Fifteen thousand square feet was enough for now.

"Good morning, Blake Computing."

Roland introduced himself and asked to speak to Gregory Blake.

"Speaking. Yeah, you're the guy in Mexico, right?"

"Yes."

"You know, I've been thinking about this. I can't guarantee that the unit will get to you. Mexican customs officers are notoriously corrupt."

Roland rolled his eyes. "I'll take that chance. If you send it via DHL or FedEx it'll get here for sure."

"Yeah. Hmm. What's your nationality?"

"Mind me asking why that's relevant?"

Gregory Blake dodged the question. "What's the billing address on your credit card?"

"Pavas, San Jose, Costa Rica. Why do you need to know that? Let me give you the number and send me the computer. Customs is my problem, not yours."

There was a pause. Then, "You're living in Mexico, but not a citizen, who wants to buy a computer with a credit card issued in Costa Rica."

"Correct," Roland said. Nothing gets by you, he wanted to add. Didn't this guy realize that not everyone in the world lived in the US? His website had even advertised that shipping overseas was his specialty. Perhaps he meant from the ocean on the east coast to the one on the west, the long way around.

"I don't think I want to do that."

"Okay, fine, send it to my friend in the States then. I'll give you the address."

"No, I don't think so."

Roland frowned. He could see the beach in the distance from where he stood and it was already packed. "You're telling me that if I'd called you up and said I was American and just given you my friend's address right off the bat, you wouldn't have had a problem?"

Gregory Blake sighed. "Sorry, sir."

"You'd have preferred it if I'd lied to you?"

"Well, I—"

Roland didn't dignify the man with a goodbye. He just hung up and stared out the window. He should have added to Eric's shopping list when he'd had the chance.

He listened to his coworkers' voices as the breakfast table filled up. He heard the wrought iron gate creak as more of them came in to start their day. Slogan waved to him as he entered, wearing a shirt that had black marks all over it and a bottle of laundry detergent on its front. He heard Amy chattering away, practicing her Spanish with one of the maids.

We're all doing just fine without the likes of you, Gregory Blake.

Adrian shuffled over holding a cup of coffee with his guard bear in tow. He was in his bathrobe, as was usual before breakfast. "Stormy weather," he said, seeing the expression on Roland's face.

Roland explained the situation and finished by saying, "Why did he try and use Mexican customs as an excuse?"

Franz sat down and looked at Roland. Adrian leaned his back against the bar and said, "Well, the ones at the border crossings up north aren't exactly angels."

"Hmmph."

Adrian took a deep drag from his cigarette and set his coffee mug on the green marble bar. Roland wondered how much he had paid in import duties to bring in his professionally-trained, thirty-thousand-dollar guard dog. If he'd paid at all, of course. Neither he nor Izzy were exactly sticklers for paperwork.

"Plenty out there like him," he said, extending an empty hand to Roland. "Here's a box. Think inside it."

Adrian stubbed out his cigarette in an elaborate crystal ashtray. He pulled out a bar stool, adjusted his bathrobe as he climbed onto it, and began tugging at an earlobe.

"That guy's thinking isn't very different from most people back home, whether you noticed it when you lived there or not. Wanna know why I left?"

"Probably lots of reasons. But sure, yeah, go ahead."

"You know Dolores, that friend of Maxine's who took over Lee's job? She's a single mom. But if she was a criminal, she'd end up living in conditions better than any other single parent trying to feed her kids on minimum wage. Three squares a day, cable TV, all that shit. She doesn't go out and rob ten convenience stores, knowing that if she gets caught she'll only do time for robbing one thanks to concurrent sentencing. But where's the reward for her? In higher taxes the more money she makes and seeing immigrants living off the government the second they arrive in the country, that's where." Adrian moved his thumb around the filter of a new cigarette. "Honest people busting their asses for minimum wage pay taxes to support criminals who are living a better lifestyle than they are. I mean, there are prisons out there that have golf courses. *Golf* courses, for fuck's sake. When Maxine and I were first married I couldn't afford a nine-iron, let alone green fees. Pretty hypocritical. You get probation for manslaughter but you get fined for not having your fuckin' dog registered."

Franz was still looking at Adrian. He was obviously tired of sitting. "Platz," Adrian instructed, and Franz sighed loudly as he sank onto the marble.

Several times Roland had noticed his coworkers watching him and Adrian, wondering what they were talking about; no doubt imagining discussions regarding top-secret Cyberia dealings. Some of them were already pushing their chairs back, screeching them across the floor as they took their breakfast dishes to Ava in the kitchen. The new cook had already returned to the States. Mexico had proven too different for her and there were concerns at home. One night when Roland was working late she had broken a dish upstairs and it had nearly brought her to tears. On top of that, her sister and mother both had problems with cancer and she'd left to attend to them as best she could.

Adrian raised an eyebrow as he lit the next cigarette as if he was about to say something else, but the doorbell rang and the small intercom television screen revealed a courier carrying a thick envelope. Franz immediately sat at attention, his eyes fixed on the door as CIA Mick went to sign for the envelope and take it downstairs. The little fountain was bubbling and gurgling happily and the sound made Roland remember his very first day here. It seemed a million years ago.

With the courier gone, Franz lay down again. This time Adrian hadn't said he could. Maybe Franz was hoping he wouldn't notice.

Adrian drained the coffee cup he'd been carrying when he came over to chat and began rubbing the dog's belly with his foot. Which, for a short man like Adrian sitting up on a bar stool, was a bit of a stretch. Apparently Franz's gamble had paid off.

"It doesn't stop there, though," he said. He took a long drag and stared at the huge domed ceiling where the smoke would be invisible long before it got there. "Look at Social Security. The government takes money from people who are paying into it, and gives that money to people who are retired. Or at least, in theory. In practice they use that money for other things. Anyway, they're using the money they get now to pay people who paid in before, just like if you ever draw from it you'll be paid with money coming from people who are still working."

"I don't see the hypocrisy there," said Roland.

"Not yet, because I haven't told you that you and I aren't allowed to do the same thing. They can do it, but we can't. But what if we did anyway? What if we were to get people to pay into our scheme, and use that money to pay people who joined before them? What if all we did was a simple thing where new investors paid in and we turned around and gave that money to old investors, and during the process we kept some for ourselves?"

Roland looked at Franz. The dog had his eyes closed, but his ears twitched and turned with every spoken nuance. "It sounds great, but it has to end somewhere, and the question is how? You're describing a pyramid scheme. When it comes time to wrap it up, how do you explain to the newest investors that there's nobody behind them to pay their return?"

Adrian shook his head. "No government I can think of has seen that as a problem. That's exactly what Social Security is."

"I guess," said Roland. In a general sense, Adrian's analysis was correct.

Adrian sighed. "I suppose I just got sick of people labelling themselves as victims so they could win lawsuits and get handouts from the government. One by one, the rich just leave so they don't get taxed to death. No wonder the industrialized countries are falling behind."

"Where do they go? The rich, I mean. Are there a lot of you millionaire expats here?" Roland asked. He was wondering about the two men in suits.

"A few that I know of. I don't spend any time with them. But yeah, some in Acapulco, and actually there are several that I went to university with who live in Mexico City now. But the Caribbean is still a pretty hot destination. Too much tax in Europe too, judging by the number of accents in the Bahamas. Though I don't see how much longer that can last."

At the breakfast table Guadalupe was collecting up the placemats and shaking out the shards of toast and cereal, wiping them into a handheld dustpan. Roland had once driven through the district she lived in when he gave her a ride home in one of the Explorers after their language lesson had run overtime. It was the kind of neighborhood that realtors diplomatically refer to as having "character."

"You don't see how much longer what can last?" he asked.

"The Caribbean as a tax haven."

"Why not?"

Adrian took a long draw from his cigarette and blew the smoke out his nose. It made him cough once, very slightly. He said, "Because the incentive to banking there, your anonymity and privacy, has been compromised."

Roland nodded. "I've heard that. Switzerland too."

"Bastards. I'd never bank there. If they can somehow just 'lose' all the money the Jews deposited before World War Two, they can lose mine. Of course, if the Jews had lost Swiss money and I'd said that, I'd be labeled anti-Semitic. Ever notice how white people are the only ones ever accused of racism?"

"But there must be *some* place your money can go."

Adrian pursed his lips into a moue as he thought about this. "Central America is getting the hang of it, and Monaco's not bad, though I wouldn't give a dry shit in a high wind for your privacy in the new and improved Orwellian Europe. Essentially what you're dealing with is a tiny nation that depends on bigger nations, and if it's a matter of either keeping you as a client and keeping the States as a friend, it's an easy choice."

"Only if your government knows you have an account overseas in the first place."

Adrian nodded. "True. There are lots of ways around it. It's just scary that nowadays all they have to do is accuse you of some criminal wrongdoing and they can poke around all they want in your accounts. You don't have to be *guilty* of anything, mind you, just *accused*. It's frightening. I mean, when I first started this club we opened overseas accounts for over half the people who invested with us. Do you think they're all criminals, all in the mafia, all selling drugs? Christ, that's almost eight thousand people investing through us alone who'd fit into that category, never mind however many others there are. The world could never survive like that. Ask somebody who's suspicious of private people if he'd walk around naked, and he'll realize everybody has limits on their personal space, including him."

The table was clear now. Guadalupe had separated the group of juice cartons that were empty from those still at least partly full, and she was throwing the empty ones away. She noticed Roland looking and said, "Breakfast?" It was amazing how loud she had to be in order for them to hear her, far away through the livingroom and over the noise of the fountain.

Roland shook his head. "*No, gracias,*" he called.

Adrian said, "After lunch I'm calling a meeting. I've been talking to Liza and Roxane, and there have to be some changes. Just so you know, and I'm asking you to pass it on."

"Okay, chief."

Eric came back that morning, and as Adrian and Roland were finishing their conversation he jogged down the steps and waved. "Hey, guys," he said, and gingerly placed a large knapsack onto the floor under the dining table. As the contents settled they made the unmistakable sound of very expensive things rubbing together. In his free hand he held a coconut with the top chopped off and a straw protruding from it.

"I had to take everything out of the boxes or else none of it would fit in my suitcase," he explained.

"What the hell did you buy?" Adrian asked. The contents appeared to be fighting their way out of the bag.

"A few laptops – nice ones, Sony Vaios. One of them's a really small one for Secret Agent Man, and a shortwave

247

radio for him as well. A couple of top-end digital cameras, headphones, some CD Walkmans and two mp3 Walkmans... let's see here, what else..." He took a long drink from the coconut. "Oh yeah, a Playstation and a Nintendo, and there was a sale on Ray-Bans and Oakleys so I got sunglasses for everybody. Also I finally got my mountain bike, five thousand dollars later."

"I guess you got the green light at Customs," said Roland.

"Actually it wouldn't have mattered," Eric explained. "I'm not importing for the purposes of resale, so they don't care. But yeah, I was nervous until I found that out." He drained the coconut with a loud slurping sound. "I used my Visa card, by the way. I like how when it prints a receipt it doesn't print the whole card number, so you can't get robbed if you lose that receipt. If somebody picks it up, all they see is the last four digits. But a lot of this I bought on my last day because those slackers down south didn't process my deposit soon enough."

Roland had talked with Diego about this several times already, and discovered through Brent and Janine that he was telling the truth when he said he made the deposits as soon as requested. The problem was that the bank itself that dealt with the Visas often didn't get around to completing the transaction for a day or two, and then the deposit had to make its way through the worldwide Visa database. All of that took time.

Guadalupe set a bowl of Vector and some milk in front of Eric, and Anita brought a juice carton. "Don't make a mess," she warned, whisking away his empty coconut husk.

Lunchtime seemed to come very early that day, mostly because the morning had been taken up with the springtime

Christmas that Eric had brought. Kevin disappeared upstairs to take pictures from the roof with his new camera, and Roland donned his Oakleys and headphones and listened to mp3 files stored on the server.

His imagination had a lot of fun with him at the meeting. Everyone was seated by the pool facing Adrian, who lit a cigarette much more slowly than usual. With the swimming pool to one side and the house's imposing columns on the other, the smoke from his cigarette mixed with the hot sun overhead to create an atmosphere of tribal significance. Roland half expected to be bound hand and foot and ceremoniously thrown off the tallest of Los Arcos sans clothing.

Adrian said, "Two things need to be addressed. The first thing is, there's confusion about how much members get as referral commission."

Roxane nodded vigorously and interrupted. "We need to straighten this out before the new program gets implemented, and from what the cowboys are saying, that's only another month away. Which sounds like a long time, but we all know how quickly month-end comes."

"It's the simplest thing, so simple that you're all missing it," Adrian went on after a brief and caustic glance at Roxane. "If somebody invests one unit, meaning one thousand bucks, the person who referred them gets fifteen percent of it, or a hundred and fifty bucks. Now, because that person's income increased by a hundred and fifty, the person who brought him in gets fifteen percent of that, and so on."

Slogan said, "So there's no cap on how many levels up somebody has to be before they stop getting commissions."

Adrian sighed. "Yeah. Just remember this one rule: If somebody gets an income, then whoever referred that person gets fifteen percent of it. That applies to everybody, no questions, period, end of story. Why are you people always looking for the catch?"

Force of habit, Roland thought.

Adrian continued, "Anyway, those members who have been short-changed over the last two months because of this confusion will be reimbursed immediately, plus ten percent of the shortage. This is bullshit. None of us would be here if it weren't for them so that has to get taken care of today. Nothing else is a priority." He directed this mostly towards Liza and Roxane. "Everybody on board here?" Heads nodded.

"Good. The second thing is, Liza and Roxane are wasting far too much time tracking down bank wire transfers and shit like that. It's a problem for the banks, it's a problem for us, and as a result it's a pain in the ass for the members. I know that those of you who answer emails have been encouraging people not to wire money, and that has made a difference already. We're working on a deal to collect through Western Union in a few months but as of today, right now this minute, we do not accept any form of investment other than money orders and cashier's checks. Garrett, get on your computer as soon as this meeting is over and send a mass mailing telling everybody. By this time next month, we are all going to be breathing a hell of a lot easier. Any questions?"

Nobody had any. Adrian looked disappointed.

After the meeting Roland pulled the Secret Agent aside and said, "Mick, is this kind of thing legal in Mexico?"

"What kind of thing?"

"The kind of referral structure Cyberia has. I mean, it's illegal in most places to get a commission for referring anyone into any kind of investment unless you're a licensed broker. This would never fly back home."

Mick said, "Hmm," and nodded. "Yeah. Maybe. But we're in Mexico, and we've never been hassled about it by anybody here."

Roland remembered what Adrian had said about Social Security being a legalized pyramid scheme, and he relayed the pertinent elements to Mick, including Roland's concern about how a system like that would end. "Statistically, the theoretical end is that everybody in the whole world invests and the previous people in get nothing. Sounds to me as though regardless of what Hammer does, Cyberia's referral structure is uncomfortably similar."

CIA Mick agreed. "I suppose, but you have to weigh the *possibility* against the *probability* that the whole world is sending us checks. It would just never happen. And even if we did receive six billion checks tomorrow, there are people being born every day and others dying off and leaving inheritances. I mean, this discussion is totally unnecessary. It is possible to sustain a pyramid scheme in perpetuity if you manage it right. The key is to give investors their capital and interest back within a year, then kick them out completely to make room for newbies."

"But Cyberia doesn't do that."

"Roland, this discussion is entirely academic. Nobody ever said how Cyberian investors make money from Hammer in the first place. And actually we are supposed to rotate the members like that, but that's not my department so I don't know if it happens."

"You don't know."

"Practice and theory. Two different animals." He pointed to the statue of a jaguar and her cubs displayed beside the stairs. "Theory," he offered. As they went downstairs Castanza passed them on his way up. He was wearing a baseball cap backwards and nothing else apart from a pair of shorts. "Practice," said Mick, completing his abstract analogy.

Tapping a pen on his desk and staring at the ocean, Roland thought about what the Secret Agent had said. Before he had come to Mexico, a friend of his had approached him with exactly the same scheme Mick had just described. At a meeting of seven people, one person received five thousand dollars from each of four people. The remaining two now became next in line to receive five thousand dollars from two more people that each of the four brought in to the arrangement, because the one who originally received the money was now out of the scheme altogether. In theory this could continue forever with all the participants benefiting. But it was a jealous and petty world, and where someone was making a lot of money, others wanted a cut. If none was offered, well, that just wasn't fair and the activity would have to cease. The easiest way to shut things down was to provide a theoretical model explaining how the system in question would, in fact, not work, despite the fact that it was working already.

Roland thought about the little red hen who planted and grew her wheat, asking if anyone wanted to help her. All the other animals said no. The little red hen baked her wheat into a loaf of bread and all the other animals wanted some, but as she had done all the work herself she refused.

In today's world, they wouldn't have let her.

That night, Roland tuned in to the news. He watched Spanish television to better his language skills, but the broadcasters spoke so fast that it was difficult to learn anything, and even the subtitles in ordinary sitcoms or English-language movies were sometimes simply wrong. He'd learned enough to know that. These things didn't deter him, though. He took in an hour of commentary regarding everything from how the World Bank and IMF were ordering around even more countries than last year to the despair that less developed countries feel when forced to adapt to others' standards. Then there was an examination of the popularity of shows about aliens including some video footage of a purported UFO that a Chilean search-and-rescue pilot had shot from the window of his airplane after a violent storm. Rounding it off was a raft of statistics comparing South American soccer teams interspersed with advertisements featuring shamelessly gorgeous Latina girls.

Roland shut the TV off and let the CD changer pick a song for him as he padded out onto the terrace with a glass of water. He settled into a deck chair and stared up at Orion, the inscrutable hunter. He wished he was back home, sitting around the fire with his friends, chatting and joking over hot chocolate and marvelling at the same constellation.

As the first strains of the song began, Roland wondered how old the light from the stars he was looking at might be. He knew that light from the sun was eight minutes old by the time it reached him. How old was the light from Orion? To him the collection of bright pinpoints looked the same as ever, but what had happened in the vast chasm between the time the light left it and the time it reached his eyes?

Roland reached for the stereo's remote and hit the 'random' button. Paulina Rubio was upbeat but he pressed 'Next' to hear Sting's 'Desert Rose'. Good but overplayed, he thought, and switched to the next. Gianluca Grignane. Not in the mood. Next. Carlos Vivez. Roland put down the remote. He retrieved a Cohiba from the humidor in his bedroom and savored it as he listened to the album.

As he gazed at the stars he remembered a story that Sara had told him about one of her friends. He remembered it because she had told him the same one twice, something she didn't often do. At the time he hadn't thought much of it, but in retrospect he understood that she was trying to tell him something about herself.

Her friend had a boyfriend who had told her that he loved her but couldn't be faithful to her, and they'd split up. That was it really. Not much of a story. But if Roland had been paying attention he would have understood that the friend was actually Sara, and that she loved him but she just wasn't the faithful kind. It was her way of warning Roland not to be surprised when the inevitable happened. If, of course, it hadn't already. At the time he'd thought that she was fishing for information about Roland himself. Well, he couldn't say she didn't warn him.

He reached for the phone. When he left his house he had disconnected all the utilities except the telephone, in case someone needed to reach him and didn't know his number in Mexico.

One ring. He imaged the sound echoing through the cold and empty rooms, a friendly signal for someone there to pick up.

Two rings. In the room Sara had used as her office there was a window she had painstakingly decorated with the pattern of a tulip, after sanding the paint from the frame to expose the beautiful wood below. The sound would be echoing off it.

Three rings. The furniture, all draped with cloth to keep it from becoming dusty, was mute. If there were messages, the answering machine would have come on by now.

Four rings. Of course Sara wasn't going to answer. He pressed the 'Off' button on the handset.

'The Belize Brothers had left that weekend, on Saturday the 7th. Adrian had them flown out in the Lear and arranged for them to be met at the airport by the shipping company rep, who had picked out a condo for them. Just to keep the momentum going, however, early that afternoon two friends of Ken's showed up. There had been several power outages at the Shack the previous week and by happy coincidence these two were electricians, so they had taken a break from drinking on the beach to investigate the problems. Roland and Garrett took a little time off to show them around.

Underneath the giant house was a maze of plumbing and electrical veins and arteries, and the room that contained them could be accessed from one of the maid's quarters behind the laundry and liquor room on the main floor down a narrow, dimly-lit staircase. It reminded Roland of English country mansions with hidden hallways that allowed the servants to pass through the house unseen. And, of course, for criminals in novels to abscond with jewelry and bloodstained knives.

There was a single bare bulb hanging from the low ceiling, but like any light bulb in a humid climate that hadn't been used for a while, it didn't work. As Garrett played a flashlight beam around, Roland noticed light coming from a crack near his feet. He looked up to see a doorknob. This must be the door that opened onto his street.

"Main breaker," said one of Ken's friends. "Corroded like crazy. I'm getting tetanus just looking at it."

"Yeah," said the other. "You need to replace it. This humidity is a bitch, huh?"

Roland liked it, but he didn't say so. Summertime in Vallarta might be too much even for him. Maybe he'd ask to be posted to somewhere cooler, like Miami. If, of course, San Jose wasn't to his liking. Garrett said, "I'll ask Tatiana to get us a new one if you tell me what you need."

They waited a couple of minutes for the two electricians to reach a consensus, then found themselves back upstairs in the bright and cheerful house as though let out of a dungeon.

At four o'clock the house staff had an English lesson, just as Kevin had predicted. Everyone was there except Ava.

Guillermo seemed to be trying the hardest to look as though he was paying attention but Castanza, whose English was pretty good anyway, was obviously breezing through it. All of them wanted to hit the beach and party. Holy Week was a huge deal, and Vallarta was a great place to spend it. The town was a circus and the churches were constantly packed, especially Our Lady of Guadalupe, built by the Spaniards in 1564. From Adrian's house its crowned tower was clearly visible, a beacon for the righteous and the curious alike, and it appeared on nearly every PV tourist brochure published. It had also narrowly avoided being decorated with regurgitated roast duck and innumerable glasses of champagne by a queasy and hung-over Lee when her boyfriend marched her there to repent for her overindulgence at Sidney and Amy's wedding.

Wandering down Olas Altas that night, winding his way among the throng, Roland caught sight of Adrian chatting outside his favorite café with some people Roland didn't recognize. Franz sat on the sidewalk beside him, generating considerable interest from passersby. Adrian's driver leaned against a post across the street near the red Explorer, looking at the crowd. Either Adrian had a very inflated view of himself, Roland mused, or there was a threat from somewhere.

Grant's comments about Franz being just for show notwithstanding, suddenly Costa Rica didn't seem like such a bad place to be.

13

The Shape of the Shadow

Walking down to Olas Altas the next morning for coffee, Roland was expecting to engage in his short daily conversation with the two tattooed Mexicans who sold timeshares half a block up from the Pagina. Instead, as he rounded the corner at Señor Book's he was greeted by the sight of a police truck parked across both lanes of traffic, empty except for the driver. Two officers with flak vests and dark blue baseball caps were pointing M16s at the convenience store beside the timeshare booth. A third ran around the corner and shouted something, then all of them disappeared the way the third had come. The officer in the truck stayed put with a walkie-talkie in one hand and an M16 in the other.

Roland decided to stay on his side of the street until he reached the Pagina. One of the regulars, the man whom Mick had talked to the night when Glenda had made her first appearance, was sitting inside at the counter facing the street with an unopened newspaper in front of him, staring through the large glassless window at the police. Roland walked up to him.

"Morning. What's going on here?"

The man held up a hand in greeting. "Some idiot with a knife robbed the Six." He shook his head. "His family will be lucky to see him again."

The waitress recognized Roland and brought him a coffee during the lull. Which, with machine-gun-toting police officers wandering around, was a very long lull indeed. All the tourists, both Mexican and gringo alike, were gawking at the sight. Roland wondered how many of them were hoping to see a gratuitous display of blood spatter or at least some good quality violence in the form of a takedown, but none came.

The man shook his head again. "You don't realize how seldom this kind of thing happens until you see the cops everywhere."

Roland poured a little sugar into his coffee and reached for the cream jug. It was already hot and the sun was noticeably higher in the sky than it had been on his first morning here.

"You serious about his family not seeing him again? They're going to whack him for knocking over a corner store?"

The man shrugged. "Mm, probably not," he said. "They'll shove him in with the spiders and gruel for a while and hope that does the trick, maybe take him out and beat some personality into him now and then."

Roland shook his head in mild amusement. Not that there weren't sickening cesspools that doubled as prisons in the world, but he hardly thought that Mexico would waste them on an amateur criminal when there were so many professional murderers longing to be rehabilitated.

Slogan came around the corner and spotted Roland. "Morning, my man," he said. "Nice shades."

Roland adjusted his sunglasses. "Thanks," he said. "Nice shirt." '*Drink 'til you want me*', it said.

"I agree." He looked around. "I thought I saw Kevin and Eric around here."

"Maybe it was Kevin who robbed the Six," Roland said.

"Is that what the blues are here for? Well, maybe they'll beat the hell out of him and let him go in time for work."

Mick's friend looked up from his paper. "Work?" he asked, smiling. He knew there was a secret; everybody did. "You mean the morning swim in Adrian's pool and the day on the internet?"

Slogan wasn't aware that anyone had been listening. "Yeah," he said. "We're working on one of Adrian's computers. I'm trying to design a web site for him but the software's corrupted."

The police truck started up and passed in front of them down Olas Altas. By now the crowd had thinned to its regular level of chaos as the possibility of a show diminished.

"Right. Of course." The man rustled his newspaper. "That's one corrupted software program you have up there. It's taking ages for all you guys to sort that mess out."

Roland looked at him. "Mind me asking what you do for a living?"

The man feigned puzzlement. "I thought you all knew," he said. "I design websites for a wealthy friend."

He folded his paper and offered it to a tourist who was poking through the Spanish papers. "This one has an English section," he said, and the grateful gringo took it.

"Holy Week," he said in disgust. "Christ, you can't get a parking spot anywhere." He hopped off his stool. "Ciao," he called, and disappeared.

Roland laughed. "You forgot to be paranoid," he said to Slogan.

Slogan didn't look fazed. He leaned against the counter. "A bad job of acting like you don't have a secret is the best way to make people suspect that you've got one."

"Amen to that," Roland agreed. "I never believed that you bought into this cloak-and-dagger stuff as much as everyone else."

"You know why they do?" Slogan said. "Because it's better to be safe than sorry. Plus, you have to admit it's a hell of a lot of fun."

"I suppose," said Roland. "Some people pay a lot of money to go to places where they simulate exactly this kind of thing. And I know they're loyal to Adrian and to Cyberia, which is great. It's just that guys like this one wouldn't have given us a second glance if it weren't for all the secret handshake bullshit."

Kevin and Eric came around the corner, both munching on coconut pieces from a plastic bag. "Hey," said Eric.

Kevin was looking around furtively. "What's with all the cops I saw down this way?" he asked.

"They're looking for us," Roland replied. "Adrian got busted. We're waiting for orders from HQ."

"*What?*" Kevin looked as though he'd been shot. "You fuckin' serious?"

Roland relented. "No, somebody robbed the Six."

"Don't *ever* do that again," said Kevin. Eric was silent.

Kevin regained his composure and decided to ignore Roland. He said to Slogan, "Those English lessons are going nowhere for the staff."

"How's that?"

"Their pronunciation sucks. I didn't know Dracula was Jewish. I mean, it's educational of course, but come *on*, man. I wish they'd hurry up."

"They've only had one class," Slogan replied. Eric nodded. "Take it easy," he concurred. "They'll come along. I'd like to hear your Spanish after only one lesson."

Kevin shrugged. "I'm tired of talking with my hands. I'm no frickin' Italian. It takes a lot of effort to always try to think in a different language every day, everywhere you go."

The four of them shared a taxi back up to the Shack. Breakfast had been delayed because nothing in the kitchen was working while the visiting electricians replaced the corroded breaker.

Mick informed them that the Belize Brothers were already running into trouble because there weren't enough hours in a day to photocopy the checks, record them in their database, then forward everything over to Puerto Vallarta. They'd bought a new photocopier and were already toying with the idea of leasing bigger office space. With no more wires coming in, every single check and money order had to be copied and recorded to make sure there were no errors in the banking, and with the amount of money Cyberia was taking in – roughly a million dollars a day according to the accounting software, Roland discovered – that was a lot of photocopying, especially since the majority of the money was in smaller denominations. Now and then there would be investments of fifty thousand dollars up to the occasional million or two, but the majority of their time would be taken up in logging subscriptions of a thousand dollars.

Adrian made two announcements at breakfast that morning. The atmosphere was much like that at school when the students have only a week to go before summer holidays. Even Franz understood that the late breakfast meant that everyone was using the disrupted schedule as an excuse to goof off. He kept playing nicely with Yoda until he thought nobody was looking. Then he put his massive paw on the little dog and held him to the floor. Yoda yelped and Franz let him go.

"I'm leaving for Belize this afternoon to make sure everything's going as well as it can over there," Adrian told them, "and then I'm going to Costa Rica for a while. Seeing as how I've got a house there I might as well live in it, so I won't be back here for some time." He held a hand up as everyone said how much they'd miss him. "I know, I know, but try and carry on without me." He puffed on his cigarette. "The second thing you'll find even more welcome," he said. "I want you all to take the weekend off."

"Gee, thanks," said Kevin. "We normally don't."

"Let me rephrase that," said Adrian. "I meant a long weekend. These guys –" he pointed to the house staff "— won't be around anyway because it's their holiday week, so neither will you. Take Friday and Monday off."

"Gladly," said Garrett. He was exhausted and in need of a break. The cowboys had left the previous day for some time back in Houston, after which they planned to go down to Costa Rica to work on the system there. Since the minute they'd left he had started work on the temporary database for San Jose to use until the two cities' networks were on line together through the same satellite, and no one knew when that would be. Adrian looked at him and said, "Take tomorrow off too."

Garrett nodded. "Thanks."

On his way out of his office to catch the plane that afternoon, Adrian passed by Roland, as everyone did if they wanted to use the stairs. He looked behind him at the sea of people, all with their headphones on, all listening to music and tapping away on their keyboards. Franz was so tall that he could almost rest his chin on Roland's desk. Roland scratched him behind the ear.

"Everyone's got their headphones on," Adrian observed in a faraway voice.

Roland looked up and stretched. "Same planet, different worlds."

Roland spent some time that afternoon on the phone with Cyberia's travel agent, a man named Jake, based out of Baltimore. This was the office that coordinated everything but the Learjet flights, so Jake had earned commission on Roland's own flight down to PV, among many others. Jake was efficient and knew what he was doing, but not even he could provide Roland with a way to get back home and return to Puerto Vallarta if he wanted to leave on Friday and return on the following Monday unless he wanted to spend an entire day traveling each way.

"Why don't you take the whole week?" he suggested. "You could jump on a Transat flight for a few hundred dollars, first class."

"Yeah," said Roland, "but I just have the weekend. I wanted to do some shopping and see some friends."

"Why don't you meet them halfway or something? I could get you some flights to Los Angeles that would only take one hop from you down in Mexico and your friends back home."

Roland grinned. Obviously Jake was used to Cyberia's money. The tickets for the wedding must have launched him into a new tax bracket.

"Maybe I could go to Miami for the weekend. How much would that be?"

Jake's keyboard clicked as he fiddled around with his schedules and fares. "On short notice, about nine hundred bucks return. You'd go to Mexico City and get a flight from there."

"Don't think so," Roland replied. The proposition was tempting but it still wasn't cheap. Nine hundred dollars would a long way towards paying off his debts.

Jake said, "Well, a couple of your buddies are going to Cuba, and a couple more are going to tool around Mexico City for the weekend as well. How about that? Closer to home."

Roland stood on his balcony, staring out at the beautiful blue ocean and the crowded beach and the parasailers and the sun. Ken had gone to Los Angeles not long before to catch the Long Beach Grand Prix, an experience in itself, and on the way back he'd sat next to the actor Patrick Stewart, who was on his way to Vallarta to film a movie. Somebody was always filming something in Roland's new home town, and there were streets cordoned off seemingly every other day and large tech vans all over the place. Come to think of it, maybe he could scare up a part as an extra. Duck Bill could point him to the right people, having filled in on the sets of several movies. Or, more likely, Roland would just end up going to work at the Shack.

"Thanks, Jake, but I'm going to stick around. Now that I think about it, the sun's just as hot here as in Cuba, and I'll have some vacation time coming up in a couple of months anyway."

"Okay, my friend," said Jake. "If you change your mind, you know where I am. Here, let me give you my pager number as well."

Roland copied down the number onto the back of an envelope. He thanked Jake and rang off, then entered the number into his cell phone's memory bank.

With Grant gone, maybe he could use his patio for some sunbathing. The fact that it was Semana Santa would mean that Liza would be out playing around on the yacht or salsa dancing in the clubs; probably both. Inevitably Roland would be invited along. That prospect appealed to him just as much as jump-ups on the Jamaican beach.

He laid out a towel on a lounge chair and closed his eyes as the hot sun relaxed him. Shouts from excited children at the seaside below floated up to him and the timeless tropical air tasted sweet.

Roland decided that by staying in good old Puerto Vallarta, he wouldn't be missing much.

Saturday, April 14th.

CIA Mick answered the phone at the Shack and mouthed the word 'Adrian' to Roland, who had shown up mostly because he had nowhere else to go. He had told himself that it was because he had a lot of work to do, but he didn't really. He was just a little lonely and felt left out because everyone had plans for the weekend except him – and Mick, apparently – not that that was anybody's fault other than their own.

Mick said, "Yeah…no, he's here actually…sure…what's that?…okay, I'll tell him…okay, and Guillermo too…Oh, no, what happened? Sorry to hear it…that's awful…okay, will do…goodbye," and hung up the phone.

He laughed. "It isn't funny really, but Franz drew first blood this weekend."

Roland's eyes widened. "What? Who?"

"Correct," said Mick. "On the 'what' part, that is. He killed one of the deer on Adrian's estate."

"No, really?"

"The worst part is, it was pregnant. Apparently he saw them running around the property and decided to eliminate them. Deer are pretty damn fast, but Franz cornered one of them and tore her throat out."

Roland wondered what the Harrison K-9 people would think of that. Franz had shown no interest whatsoever in Yoda apart from his entertainment value, much to Roxane's relief.

"I didn't know there were any deer at Adrian's."

Mick nodded. "The previous owner brought in eight of them. The place is walled, so they have no predators. Until today, of course. Adrian was out scouting for a good place to set up a shooting range and Franz got bored."

Roland imagined Franz's jaws sinking into the terrified animal's bloody neck and the sheer pleasure he must have felt at doing exactly what he was born to do. "What was that about Guillermo?" he asked.

"Oh yeah," said Mick. "Adrian needs you down there. Apparently the newbies are just as confused as the day they landed and you have to go straighten things out. Liza is arranging for your ticket as we speak."

"My ticket?"

"You'll be flying on Mexicana. Maybe the Lear got shot down over the jungle or something. Anyway Guillermo's going with you. You leave on Tuesday after work."

Roland nodded. They could hear the staff splashing around in the pool. Mick said, "Let's go have a beer upstairs," and they did.

The weekend wasn't quite what Roland had expected. He did spend time in the sun, and he did watch a little television, and he did tour some seedy clubs with Liza and her friends after a dinner at Bogart's. And on Monday, he ran into Shelly wandering down Olas Altas.

They got a table at the Pagina. She said, "Did you know that Señor Book's is changing its name?"

"No, I didn't know that."

"I've seen the new logo they're going to put out front. It's called Starbooks now, and the logo is a ripoff of Starbucks'. It's too bad. That place has been around since the dawn of time."

Roland imagined what life would have been like for the first Indians building their village around a combination coffee bar and used bookstore. "I thought you were going down to Manzanillo for the weekend."

"Ixtapa, actually." Shelly lit a cigarette. "But the buses were so goddamn crowded that I got off at Barra de Navidad. I thought it might be a peaceful little place, but everybody and his dog is there. I went to every hotel I could find and nobody had a room available, so I paid a cab driver two hundred bucks to bring me back here. Didn't get back until four in the morning 'cause the highways were so jammed with traffic." The air was so still and hot that she had to wave the smoke away. "I thought I'd stop off at that little place Slogan went to when he proposed to Amy but I couldn't remember what it was called."

"Majahuitas."

"Right, right. Well, that doesn't help me now." She exhaled, blowing the smoke towards the street. "I see your tan's a lot darker. Did you have a good weekend?"

"Better than yours, by the sound of it. Sorry to hear things were such a mess."

Shelly shrugged. "Next time I'll know better. As if it shouldn't have been obvious from what a zoo this place has been over the last week." She looked around, and they both noticed for the first time how much their little city had returned to normal. "Back to work tomorrow," she said. "Everybody's gone home already. The streets are deserted in comparison."

Eric wandered up to their table with a cute young Mexican girl in tow. She wore glasses, which either helped her to see better, or made her look smarter, or both. "Hey," he said, and introduced his girlfriend. She couldn't have been older than sixteen. It was no longer a mystery how Eric had spent his weekend. Kevin was in Cuba tagging along with Ken, so Eric had the place to himself and his girl. After a quick chat they resumed wandering up the street.

"Do you think she can read without moving her lips?" Shelly asked.

"I don't think she's been doing much reading," Roland replied.

Shelly squinted at him. "You know who that is?" she asked after a time.

Roland shook his head. "Don't think so. Why, have you seen her before?"

A sly smile spread across Shelly's face. "She's the girl that Eric and Sidney used to have threesomes with before Sid met Amy. She's got a friend in the FM3 office, which is how we get our Mexican resident alien papers so quickly whenever we want them."

"I see."

Shelly waited for Roland to say something else, but he didn't. "Speaking of threesomes," she continued, "I've been meaning to ask you how you made out on the night of Sid's wedding."

Roland raised his eyebrows. "How's that?"

Shelly puffed on her cigarette. Roland remembered his first real conversation with Roxane and thought how much Shelly resembled her right now, cigarette in hand and a tip-of-the-iceberg question on her lips.

"I saw you sitting at the table with Lee on one knee and Guadalupe on the other. I saw you get up and leave, and then I saw the two of them making out together like teenagers. Then they disappeared. I assumed you took them home."

Roland shook his head. "One day I'll probably wish I had, but I didn't."

Shelly laughed. "I'm sure it won't be your last opportunity."

"Thanks, I think." Roland tapped on the table. "Since we're on the subject, mind me asking why I saw you wearing a pink teddy at the hotel in Guadalajara?"

He immediately regretted asking. Shelly looked guilty and surprised at the same time. Finally she said, "I didn't know anyone saw me. I only opened the door to let him in."

"Who?" Roland asked, though he knew before he opened his mouth.

"Adrian." Shelly was smoking feverishly now, and in between puffs she said awkwardly, "It's just a show, now and then. I have a boyfriend, you know."

"I know." Roland had walked past him and Shelly on the street a month before. For one reason or another, whether because of the secrecy or to minimize retribution against Shelly for any jealousy on her boyfriend's part or a combination of all the above, he had done no more than move a few inches to the side on the Malecon as they passed each other. No hello, no eye contact. "Besides, those pills he takes sort of limit his abilities most of the time, if you get my meaning."

Roland nodded. "What does your boyfriend think of all this?" he wanted to know.

Again Shelly searched for the right words. "There are perks, and I share them with him," she said, rubbing her thumb and fingers together in the universal gesture that meant 'money'. The huge diamond ring Adrian had bought her in Guadalajara for her birthday glittered in the sunlight.

Roland told Shelly about his proposed trip to Costa Rica and related the incident at Adrian's ranch.

"That's awful about the deer," she said, and stubbed out her cigarette. "You're going down with Guillermo?"

Roland nodded. "Yes, on Mexicana."

"Lucky man," she said. "Guillermo, I mean. He'd started up a private security company with a buddy of his only four days before Adrian hired him on full-time. Not bad for a first assignment."

"Especially when there's no danger of him stopping a bullet," Roland said. Shelly tapped her finger on the table as she asked, "Are you sure?"

"Shouldn't I be?"

Roland was wearing one of the shirts he had bought from Ken's favorite beach vendor, and a monstrous flying insect found it attractive enough to bump into him twice before buzzing off into the back of the Sello Rojo milk truck, making a clicking sound like brand new cards being shuffled. Two months ago being accosted by a bug the size of his fist would have caused Roland more than a little concern, but now he just watched it disappear. Shelly didn't flinch.

"I don't know," she said, her blue eyes fixed on Roland. "But if I were him, I'd say things were getting to the point where that might be a possibility."

Roland wasn't sure if she was trying to tell him something or just playing spy, but he wondered what he would find in Costa Rica. For all he knew, there was an exact duplicate of Vallarta's Cyberia in Peru, or Vietnam, or Morocco, or who knew where else. Surely Shelly might know what Adrian was up to. But he could say the same about Sidney and consequently Slogan and probably Eric as well, and the look in Shelly's eyes was the unspoken assumption that she thought exactly the same could be true of Roland.

"It might indeed," was all he said, and after some discussion about what motivated people to seek out unusual situations like Cyberia, or for those situations to seek out people like them, they parted ways.

Tuesday morning found the Montrealers back at the Pagina, their little blue Volkswagen at the curb. Their trip had been wonderful and, they were quick to point out, the car had performed flawlessly. They were returning to Canada in two weeks. Roland was sure he'd be back in Vallarta by then, and he wrote down the number of one of their Mastercards and told them he'd apply the money for the car onto it through internet banking. That way neither of them had to worry about carting around an envelope full of pesos, although Roland thought that would have been a lot more fun.

Roland's computer was booting up as Liza descended the stairs clutching two American Express pouches with tickets inside for him and Guillermo. "I wish I was going with you, Bachelor," she said, "but maybe next time."

She disappeared into her office, and not long after came the sound of swearing, starting with a "Now, what the hell is this?" in a slightly louder-than-usual voice, and ending with a flurry of expletives worthy of all kinds of bad neighborhoods. Everyone started looking around the room and all yelled at the same time, "Garrett!"

Garrett appeared in the doorway to Adrian's office. "What?"

"Will you tell this piece of shit to just get the job done and quit fooling around?" Liza bellowed.

Garrett scratched his chest. "Um, I'll try," he said. "I assume it's the password giving you trouble. The cowboys put it there so that nobody could get into the accounting software but you and Roxane. I'm surprised it wasn't working last week."

"Not only was it not working, but they didn't tell me what the hell they were doing."

Well, there goes that, Roland thought. No more poking around in the accounts. It's about time somebody put a stop to it anyway. He wondered how much of Liza and Roxane's troubles were caused not by banks but by computer glitches. His own computer was already starting to do strange things during perfectly normal operations, no doubt due to the heat and humidity.

Kevin appeared and dumped a stack of files on top of one of the file caddies, as usual leaving them for someone else to put away. There were so many that they now stretched all the way in front of the window wall and ran four deep into Adrian's office. The last few memberships entered had been assigned numbers above the 26,000 mark, which meant that Cyberia had almost twenty thousand members around the world. At this rate, there would be literally no space for the caddies within another two months, although thankfully Dolores was much faster at scanning than Lee had been. There were two stacks of file boxes almost as tall as Roland jammed in behind the bar. Roland had assumed that once the files were scanned they could either be shredded or sent to an outside storage facility – even a rented apartment somewhere, more Adrian's style anyway – but there they stood, further cramping the desk where the cowboy Greg had sat.

Four o'clock, and his flight left at six. Roland stood up to leave. Collecting his notebook and file folders, including the Visa applications that he might as well take with him instead of having Tatiana send by courier, he said, "Anybody want anything from Costa Rica?"

"Coffee," Shelly said, standing in the doorway with a blank look on her face as she surveyed Kevin's files.

"A chicken wagon," said the Secret Agent. "Oh, sorry, that's Puerto Rico."

Nobody else said anything, much to Roland's relief, and he disappeared up the stairs to save Guillermo and the driver from their English lesson.

Roland couldn't believe how many people recognized Guillermo. Immediately upon their arrival at the airport, a porter approached them and shook his hand. He carried their luggage to the check-in desk, and once there the ticket agent gave them both memberships in the frequent flier program, upgrading them to the premium plan for free. The porter then carried their luggage upstairs and probably would have gone through the security checkpoint with them too if given half a chance. Obviously Roland was in good hands. The porter departed and didn't say a word about the tip, which normally the Vallartans complained about no matter how generous it was.

Conversation between the two was strained, however, as Guillermo spoke barely any English at all. Roland's Spanish had come a long way, but they couldn't exactly chat about the state of world affairs. By Roland's watch it took almost fifteen minutes from the time they reached the outskirts of

Mexico City to actually land at the airport. The last time he'd checked, El Deffe was the third-largest city in the world. He'd have to look into that again, because it seemed a lot bigger than Tokyo had. Of course, that was almost twenty years ago. He wondered which of the countless thousands of houses had been Guadalupe's.

The best thing about first class wasn't the meals, it was the seats. At six-foot-four, Roland appreciated the extra space. As they all got up to leave, he noticed a girl behind him much shorter and broader than he. Probably she thought the best thing about first class was the meals.

"Excuse me," she said, "but what time is it here?"

"Whatever time your watch says," Roland answered.

"But the clocks went forward an hour on the first," she said. "Plus we changed time zones. So we're an hour ahead, or behind?"

"Mexico City didn't change its clocks," Roland replied. "They move an hour ahead on the first Sunday of May instead, so until then PV time is the same as here. I don't know why. Maybe President Fox needs more sleep this month."

The girl looked more skeptical than confused, but he said, "Seriously. Look at the clock at the arrival gate."

She smiled. "It must be nice to be local."

Roland accompanied Guillermo to the departure gate. Their flight left on time, which meant that they only had to hang around Mexico City's spartan first-class lounge for half an hour.

At the airport in San Jose no one was allowed inside unless they were either arriving or departing. Those saying hellos and goodbyes had to stand around outside, and in the crowd Roland spotted Gino, the driver.

"We go to Adrian's house," he said, after being introduced to Guillermo. Then he looked at Roland and said, "Then we go to Escazu." Obviously Guillermo was to stay at Adrian's and Roland would have the condo in San Jose to himself.

Gino had been a taxi driver before being hired full-time by Adrian, but he wasn't driving a taxi now. Instead, a new cherry red four-door Chevy Blazer greeted them. "This Adrian bought for Brent and Janine," he explained, "but tonight I drive you."

Adrian's estate was in Alajuela, not far from San Jose in a community of gated and guarded residences. They pulled up at the first guardhouse and were waved through after a quick inspection of their vehicle by an officer sporting an AK-47. The government might have a friend in the States, Roland thought, but the Russian AK was nicknamed the banana gun for two reasons – one, because the ammunition clip was curved like a banana, and two, because it was the choice of every banana republic in the world as it was cheap, reliable, and available everywhere. Costa Rica was no exception.

The narrow, paved road led them over a stream where a large lizard was sunning himself on a rock, and then turned to the left to provide access to two driveways before gently curving to the right again. To the left were the mansions, all with high concrete or stone walls surrounding them, and to the right was someone's farm.

At the top of Adrian's wall was a menacing ribbon of double-sided razor wire. They followed it for a good three hundred yards before pulling up to a pair of huge iron gates which had a colorful painted sign on them. "*Rancho Mirage*", it said, and as Gino pressed a button to open the gates he pointed to it and said, "Previous owner."

There was an unoccupied guardhouse just inside the perimeter. Gino waited until the gates closed behind them and then proceeded up the drive.

The house was built on a plateaued hill and set back enough to be hidden from the road. After passing the house the servants lived in, however – one that would have looked at home in any city suburb and large enough to house the army of people necessary to maintain the estate – Adrian's new home hove into view. Gino guided the vehicle around the drive past the helipad to the portico, where he shut the engine off.

The house was low and white, and in the quickly-setting sun it contrasted against the green lawn and crushed red rock driveway beautifully. The front doors were made of massive slabs of rich dark mahogany and were adorned with intricately-designed brass hardware, and when Adrian opened them they made him look positively tiny. Having the hulking Franz beside him didn't help matters.

"*Bienvenidos*," he said, smiling. It was the first time Roland had ever heard him say anything in Spanish. He must have been drinking, though that was often a safe bet anyway. "Come on in."

Adrian's house reminded Roland of a sprawling moneyed-family ranch house one might find anywhere from Alberta to Texas. It was ostentatious and beautiful and a little pretentious, but Adrian's questionable taste in art had already begun to counter the latter quality. Adrian gave them a tour of the place, and to Roland's delight he discovered a very red Maserati Mistral Spyder in the garage in addition to a brand new Land Rover and the Lexus.

"That wop thing came with the house," Adrian explained, pointing to the Maserati. "It's a '68, I think. I can't drive a stick shift so I have to get rid of it."

"I need something to fill the space in the parkade at my condo building," Roland said. "Hang onto it until my boss gives me a raise and I'll take it off your hands."

Adrian chuckled. "Your boss thinks an old Maserati would be a nifty bonus to the employee who gets his money back from those cards." He turned out the garage light and they made their way back to the kitchen. To Roland, the most novel feature of the house was the refrigerator, the kind found in convenience stores with sliding glass doors on both sides. The only thing missing was a Coke sign along the top.

Maxine had appeared in the meantime, and was seated at the table chatting with Gino over her ubiquitous martini. Adrian and Roland joined them at the table.

"I heard about Franz's busy Saturday," Roland said.

Adrian shook his head. "Breaks my heart. Poor thing had a fawn coming." He looked at Franz. "At least I know he's capable of doing what I bought him for, which is reassuring. When I came down here I was convinced he was a big baby."

Roland decided not to ask if there was any venison in the freezer. "Why's that?"

Adrian smiled as he stubbed out his cigarette. "Because when the jet took off he jumped straight into my lap and stayed there the whole trip. I thought my bladder was going to explode."

Roland patted Franz's massive head. It was hard to imagine this beast afraid of anything.

After some small talk, Adrian announced that he was going to turn in. "You'll come back here on Thursday with Brent," he told Roland, "but tomorrow I need you in that office. I'll be there in the afternoon as well."

"Okay, chief." Roland rose and Gino followed. After bidding goodnight to Adrian and Maxine, they drove to the condo in Escazu.

It was still early, so after Gino dropped him off Roland put his passport and wallet in the safe and called upstairs to Brent and Janine's apartment. Brent answered.

"My residence, me speaking."

"Hey, dad. It's Roland. You still up, or has your daughter come home already?"

"Roland! I heard you were in town. At least, that's what all the papers said." Roland could hear Janine in the background. "Janine's here, she's saying…wait a minute." Roland could clearly hear her say 'Tell him to come on up for a drink'.

"Right, okay," said Brent. "Janine says there's no way in hell you can come up for a drink."

"Let me unpack a few things first."

"Don't be too long, son. Your mom really, *really* needs her beauty sleep."

Roland rang off and hauled his suitcase up onto the bed in the big bedroom. After digging for his toothbrush and cleaning his teeth he splashed some water on his face and tucked the key card into his pocket.

Janine opened the door with a glass of Scotch and a cigarette in one hand. "Come on in," she said. She was sporting a healthy tan, which looked great on her.

In the three weeks since Roland's prior visit, a lot had changed. Suddenly Brent and Janine's condo had gone from being a furnished hotel room to their home, with pictures of their children, relatives, and friends hung on the wall and stuck to the fridge. One of the pictures was of Brent and his friend the chuckwagon racer, taken in front of the latter's house. In the background Roland could see the silver dome of the church beside his own house. Funny, he thought, how he had to come three thousand miles to Costa Rica to see his old street.

In the same cupboard from which Janine dug out the sugar for his coffee was a jar of peanut butter.

"Guys, I haven't had peanut butter in ages. Mind if I make a sandwich?"

"Go nuts," said Brent, "no pun intended."

"So," said Roland, digging into the jar, "what's the story? How are things so far?"

"Oh, pretty good," Brent said in his usual slow manner.

"Great, actually," said Janine. "Though it's taking me a while to get used to the traffic." She seemed completely at ease with her surroundings. Obviously the challenge was doing her a world of good.

Brent became serious. "I don't think those other two appreciate having us around very much."

"Who's that, Diego and Franco?" Roland wished he'd added jam to his sandwich. Peanut butter by itself was actually kind of bland. He settled down onto the couch.

"Yeah. Now that we're here, we supervise all the banking operations and so on, but they're used to running the show themselves. They don't say anything, but they'll just refuse to do things they're supposed to sometimes."

Roland shrugged. "You're in charge of Costa Rica. It starts and ends there. If they don't like it, they can go somewhere else, though I wouldn't want to see that. They're good people."

"I wouldn't want to see that either," Janine said, "but we're getting pretty frustrated. Me doubly so, because not only are we foreigners but I'm a woman as well, and they sure don't like taking orders from a woman."

Roland laughed. "They don't take orders from Brent either by the sound of it. What do you mean exactly?"

Brent and Janine looked at each other. "Some of those accounts Adrian opened are in my name," Brent began uncomfortably, "and Diego is especially suspicious of that."

"As he damn well should be," Roland said. "Why are there accounts in your name?"

Brent held up a hand. "I know," he said. "I know what you're thinking and I thought so too, until Adrian explained it. It's a lot easier to do personal banking here than corporate banking, so we just decided to put some of them in my name, that's all."

"When you say 'we', do you mean you and Adrian, or you two and Diego and Franco?"

"I mean Adrian and I. Well, Adrian actually, but I went along with it."

Roland finished his sandwich and poured some rum into his second cup of coffee. "So the issue here really isn't that you're foreigners, and it isn't because Janine's a woman, it's because they're both concerned about why Adrian would open several different accounts at the same bank in your name, plus whoever else's. They're wondering what the hell Adrian's doing and I don't blame them. It can't be much different to do corporate banking here than personal. Hell, corporate banking is anonymous here."

"Anonymous?" Janine said.

"Sure. You don't have to reveal who the directors are because that's nobody's business but the company's. Unless they're trading on a stock exchange, of course. Then shareholders have a habit of wanting to know who's in charge of their investments."

Brent looked uncomfortable. "Really? I didn't know that."

Roland continued, "I know what you mean about not doing what's expected of them, though. I hadn't received any word on which Visa cards had been sent until a couple of days ago. That's something that should have been done the day after I sent the first spreadsheet." He pointed at Brent. "That's partly your fault, Dad. Mine too, though, because I should have called you more often to make sure those things got done. But there are so many of them coming in now that we can't afford not to work the plan."

Roland thought about Diego and Franco's role in Cyberia. He remembered that they weren't really employees, they were subcontractors.

"I think I know what the problem is, and it's pretty simple."

"We'd love to hear it," Janine urged.

"All that's happening here is that Diego and Franco don't think it's safe to take orders from two people who are – excuse me here, but it's true – new at the whole thing. I also think that they are suspicious of the accounts in your name, as I would be too if I were them."

"You think Adrian's doing something illegal?" Janine asked.

Roland took his time answering as he sipped his coffee and decided that it needed more rum. As he added it he said, "Look, I know you two are loyal to Adrian and your friendship with him is older than Aristotle's diapers, but it's not as though nobody has their suspicions."

"What does that mean?" asked Brent.

Roland didn't want to scare these two, but they hadn't been exposed to the Mickey Spillane novel he lived in up in Mexico, so he just said, "I have no idea what Hammer does with the money. Nobody except Adrian does. I'm not sure if even Liza or Mick know. I am sure, though, that Diego and Franco are worried about what they're going to look like if they go along with things like this." He drank more coffee and did a little backpedaling, wondering if he'd said too much. "I just wish Adrian would spend a little more time on the details, that's all."

He tapped his mug reflectively. Just because Adrian couldn't be bothered with the finer points of running a business didn't mean he was up to something illegal. Roland had worked for people whose lack of organizational skills made Adrian look like a drill sergeant on parade day. But he also knew that things only had meaning within a context, and now that his frames of reference were changing he was beginning to see more of the forest and less of the trees.

Adrian had told him once that small mistakes weren't worth his time. "You can't learn from a tiny little hiccup, Roland," he'd said. "Colossal, monster-sized fuckups are much better teachers." There was so much money floating around Cyberia that even the biggest of logistical mistakes could be absorbed, or so Adrian was apparently hoping.

Perhaps, thought Roland, the trees were fine. The forest itself, however, may just be a different story altogether.

14

The Gathering Storm

Wednesday, April 18th.

Roland finished his workout and entered the room next door, where four computers were lined up to provide internet access for the guests. After checking his email he took two glasses of orange juice and a danish from the continental buffet for a quick breakfast on the balcony, then headed back to the condo for a shower.

The first thing he noticed upon greeting Diego and Franco that morning after the short walk to the office was that there were no power backups.

"What happened to the backup batteries I requested last time I was here?" he asked.

Diego shrugged. "They are hard to find. There is a computer company in San Jose that has them, but when I checked they only had two."

"If they can get two, they can get five," Roland said. "Please get those people on the phone." He sat down at a computer and started typing, noticing that the keyboards were laid out for use in Spanish. As Diego reached for the phone he added, "Diego, please order up five English keyboards as well."

Within two hours the order arrived. "I'm impressed," said Janine as she plugged her new keyboard in and tested the backup.

Roland nodded. "Frankly, so am I."

He loaded the software program Garrett had designed and began importing spreadsheet files into it. He hadn't checked three files before he saw that the data was corrupted. With several hundred more to go and a cursory inspection revealing that the problem lay in the program, not in the data, he called the Shack. Guadalupe answered.

"*Bueno.*"

"*Bueno*, Guadalupe. *Es possible por yo hablar a* Garrett?"

He could almost hear her shaking her head. "Roland," she said. "You need more Spanish practice. I will page Garrett for you."

Roland had never been put on hold before by anyone at the Shack so he didn't know that the phone system played muzak. Garrett took his time answering.

"Hello?"

"Thank God. I thought I was trapped in an elevator."

"Eh? Roland, what's up?"

Franco set a latte in front of him, topped with whipped cream and chocolate shavings. Good thing I worked out this morning, Roland thought.

"This program you gave me is gibbled."

"Sorry, man, I designed it when I was half asleep."

Roland frowned. "That must be why it only half works. How do I reprogram the scripts that assign data from the entry fields?"

"Oops."

"Don't say 'oops'. It makes me nervous when you say 'oops'."

For the next hour, Garrett led Roland through what amounted to a virtual redesign of the entire program. Brent and Janine didn't seem to be doing much of anything except joking around with Diego and Franco. That might be another problem, Roland thought. They don't exactly lead by example.

Finally the program accepted the data correctly. "You realize, of course, that as soon as these two databases are linked, we will regard this phone call as not much more than a waste of an hour we'll never have back again," Garrett pointed out.

With the air conditioner on Roland was absolutely freezing, but under the noise of the unit attached to the ceiling above him he felt safe enough to say, "I'm not sure that will be a very good idea anyway."

"The linking, you mean? Why not?"

"Because, all we really need this office to do is coordinate the Visa program. Nothing more."

"Yeah, but it'll save a hell of a lot of time if you don't have to enter everything into a spreadsheet and email it down, then wait for them to email the confirmations back up whenever they feel like getting off their asses and doing it so you can update the database. Liza's already had emails from people with screwed-up deposits."

Garrett was right, of course, but there had to be a way to keep this office from having access to all the Cyberia member files without bogging down the process of administering the cards. "I just don't like the idea of anyone here having access to the member's financial records unless it has to do with the Visas, so there's no reason to link the complete database with this office. The one out on the coast at Guanacaste, sure, because we'll be working there." Roland thought about what he had just said. He still wasn't sure if San Jose was supposed to be his new home or not. "Well, you guys will anyway. But nobody knows when that will be available as an option."

Garrett laughed softly. "Hmm," he said. "Speaking of accessing financial records, the cowboys told me they'd hit upon some interesting discoveries."

Roland was about to take another sip of coffee but he set his mug down. "Oh?"

"Yeah." Garrett paused, then said, "Apparently someone at your computer, with your password, has been accessing the banking records."

Roland wasn't sure if Garrett was referring to the actual records of deposit or simply the daily totals of investment kept in the general ledger. He asked Garrett to clarify.

"No, I'm talking about the actual deposit and expense records, with the banking passwords and information. Your computer and also that one Grant was using, in the same office as Shelly and Kevin."

"I poked around in the general ledger on my first day there," Roland admitted, "and I've done it a few times since. But I didn't know I could access the other stuff from my computer as well. I thought that was stored on Liza's laptop."

"No," said Garrett. "It's all on the server."

"What's it doing on the server? That means anybody could access it."

"Not necessarily," said Garrett, a little defensively. "You stumbled onto the ledger because I set your computer up in a hurry, if you remember, and I networked Grant's so that he could access the internet to set up charter information and research the helicopter purchase. I just forgot to put the thingy that blacks out the file on those computers."

"Could you be a little less technical? I didn't quite catch that."

Garrett took a drink of something. Roland could hear him sipping. "The ledger shouldn't need password protection on the server," he said, "because it and the detailed files reside on a part of it that is invisible to other computers on the network. Your computer could see it because I didn't tell it that the sector it was looking at didn't exist."

"I never even saw the detailed files from my computer when I browsed the network, just the ledger," Roland said, and closed his eyes. "Then again, I didn't go looking for it. Would it not have been a better idea to password protect the whole sector too?"

"Yes," said Garrett, drinking something again. "Aaah," he said, and smacked his lips. Garrett wasn't one to waste time on what should have been.

"So who was it?"

"Who was what?"

Roland shook his head. "Garrett, did you get enough sleep last night? I mean, who was accessing the detailed files?"

"I don't know. I was hoping you could tell me."

"All I can tell you is that it wasn't me."

"Well, who else knows your password?"

"Nobody. I didn't tell anyone. Are they all recorded somewhere?"

"Yeah."

"In a file, on the server, in a sector of the hard drive that isn't invisible to at least two computers that we know of?"

Garrett took his time answering, but the quality of the silence told Roland all he needed to know. "Yeah."

Roland drained his mug. "This will be our little secret," he said. "Now run along and change that password."

"Don't need to," Garrett retorted. "The cowboys already did."

"Goodbye, Garrett."

"Goodbye, Roland."

Roland replaced the phone in its cradle. Not five minutes later a man entered carrying a large aluminum briefcase with a padlock on it.

Diego greeted him. "*Buenos dias.*"

"Hey," said the man. "Is Adrian around? I have some toys for him."

Roland checked his watch. It had gone lunchtime. As if cued from an invisible director, Adrian entered with Guillermo and Franz in tow. Diego pointed to him.

"You're Adrian?" the man said. "Nice dog. I have something here you wanted to look at, if there's an office or somewhere private you'd like to go."

Adrian raised a hand. "No need for the Bondspeak," he said. "We're all friends here."

"Good." The man unlocked the case to reveal two layers of handguns on each side.

Roland whistled. "Medusa," he said. "Great gun. Beretta too, and what's that? Desert Eagle? I've never seen one up close before."

Adrian coughed as he exhaled his cigarette smoke. "Hold on there, Rambo. What the hell's a Medusa?"

"That one," Roland said, pointing. "I don't know exactly how it works, but it's a pistol that can fire basically any 9mm cartridge or one that's roughly the same size. So it can handle .38, .38 Special, .357 and Magnum, and pretty much any ammunition designed for a Beretta or Luger or whatever else."

The gun man nodded. "I can explain it if you want," he said, but Adrian shook his head. "I just want something that my bodyguard here can whip out in front of the OK Corral and start shootin'."

"That doesn't rule out the Medusa, but maybe something that holds more bullets…let's see, how about your ordinary garden-variety Beretta?"

"Fine."

Guillermo was fooling around with the Desert Eagle. "Too big," Adrian said, but Guillermo shook his head and smiled. "What the hell," said Adrian, looking at the case, "I'll take 'em all." The gun man beamed. "Roland," Adrian said, "you can have the Medusa. You have to come out to my house tomorrow anyway, so you can do some shooting with Guillermo." He looked at the gun man. "Mind if I trade you this case for some ammunition tomorrow when you come out to my place? It's not far, just out in Alajuela there."

The gun man nodded enthusiastically. "No problem. Keep the case, and I'll bring you some holsters too." He looked at Roland. "You'll be surprised how accurate it is."

"Holsters and a case and he's still happy," Adrian observed once the man had gone. "Well, that's an easy way to find out how healthy his profit margin is."

He beckoned Brent to follow him outside, where they sat at the café for an hour. He was expecting the cowboys to arrive anytime, but they would first be sorting out some details with the web hosting company in downtown San Jose, so Roland wouldn't meet them to discuss the Visa database until at least the next day. Maxine had gone shopping, chauffered in the Land Rover by Gino, and it would be nothing short of miraculous if she was back before closing time.

The cowboys had indeed arrived that day, as evidenced by their suitcases in the other bedrooms, but they were nowhere to be seen. Probably gone out for dinner, Roland surmised, or maybe they were still in a meeting with the hosting service.

Brent and Janine had found a restaurant they loved which served great steaks and desserts. They took Roland out that evening and chatted over dinner for three hours. Their Spanish hadn't come along very far but their confidence had, and they were loving the challenges they faced together. Roland remembered what it had been like moving out to the country with Sara and renovating their old house. It had been hard, but they had done it and been proud of it, and he felt a pang of envy that Brent and Janine were enjoying that feeling now. Ironic, he thought, that people work so hard all their lives to eliminate any challenges they might face, only to discover that they are at their best only when those challenges are presented. Either that or they fell apart. In the face of adversity anything was possible.

After dinner Roland returned to find Ricky and Greg sitting at the dining table fussing over their laptops. The TV was on but they were paying no attention to it.

"I would return that underwear with the flowers on it in person for you," Greg offered upon seeing Roland, "but I'm married."

"Um...sorry, what's that?"

"Your last lady friend left her panties here."

Roland was still confused. He shook his head and said, "Sorry. I have no idea what you're talking about."

Ricky shrugged. "Well, somebody left a pair of panties hanging in the bathroom. They aren't mine or Greg's, that's all I know."

"I see," said Roland. "I have no idea whose they might be." He disappeared into his room and called out, "I'm going to the hot tub." Reappearing with a towel, he went to the kitchen and poured himself a glass of coffee liqueur, topping it up with milk. "Anyone care to join me?"

"No thanks," said Greg. "We're still going over the stuff for the website. We're meeting these guys again tomorrow and we want to have everything ready."

Roland took a sip of his liqueur. "I thought Mick designed the website."

"He did," Ricky answered, "but we're finding a way to get it to accept memberships from data fields online and import them directly into Cyberia's database, and reconcile that with the specs from the hosting service regarding how much traffic they can handle."

"Thank God." This was something Roland had been asking Adrian to implement since the day he took over the Visa program. It meant that new members could simply sign up over the internet without having to fax in their application form. "That'll save hours of data entry and tons of paper. One thing, though. How can you do that without having finished designing the new database?"

"Ah, this is it, you see," said Greg. "We're working on them simultaneously so they'll dovetail together perfectly."

"In theory," added Ricky.

Roland stifled a smile as he remembered what Mick had told him about practice and theory that day after the meeting at Adrian's house in Puerto Vallarta.

The pool and hot tub were deserted. Lush tropical vines grew up the lattice surrounding them, releasing a soft scent into the night air. Roland stared up at the stars until he could barely keep his eyes open.

Thursday, April 19th.

The phone rang promptly at seven. "Roland," Brent said. "Rise and shine, son. We're off to see the wizard."

"Hmm?" Roland grunted sleepily. "Adrian's? I thought we weren't going until this afternoon."

"Afternoon, morning, whatever," Brent said. "Change of plan. We have to go through a whole bunch of checks and he needs us both there. He wants all the totals done from Costa Rica before he leaves for Latvia later this morning. We're picking up today's courier shipment first, and that's more or less on the way."

Roland was sitting up in bed now and rubbing his eyes. The morning had already started off on the wrong foot.

"Did you say he's going to Latvia?"

"I did. I think the bank is in some kind of trouble."

Roland was awake now. "I wish that wasn't Adrian's problem."

"I know, but it is. Meet you at the car in half an hour?"

"I'll be there."

Roland stared at the telephone for a few seconds, and then headed for the shower.

Brent had become a very good driver since his arrival in Costa Rica. He guided the Blazer through gritty neighborhoods and over back roads to the industrial area of the airport, where they wandered in to the courier office. Four minutes later they emerged carrying a huge envelope full of checks that had been sent to Belize and then forwarded to Costa Rica.

"How does it feel to have a million bucks in your lap?" Brent asked as he started the vehicle.

"No complaints," Roland replied. "First exciting thing that's been there in ages." In addition to the self-adhesive flap, the envelope was sealed with packing tape. Roland pierced it with a pen he found in the glove compartment and pulled it off.

They reached Adrian's ten minutes later. The guard at the main gate knew Brent and let them through, waving at them by lifting four fingers while his thumb was hooked in the strap of his AK-47.

The gun man had already been and gone, and Guillermo was happily blasting away at his new shooting range. The aluminum case rested on a nearby rattan table alongside the weapons he'd already shot and sighted, with the as-yet untried ones on the other. As Roland approached the sound changed from the quick crack of a Glock to a boom that echoed in the still air.

Guillermo grinned as he took off his hearing protectors. "Dirty Harry," he said, holding up a gleaming nickel-plated .44 Magnum.

Roland laughed. "*Como esta mi* Medusa?"

Guillermo pointed to it and gave a thumbs-up. "*Bueno,*" he said, obviously impressed. Roland wanted to squeeze off a few rounds, but duty called. "I'll be back," he said to Guillermo, and retreated to the house to find Brent dumping the contents of the courier envelope onto the dining room table.

Maxine wandered past in an elegant gown, clutching her morning martini. Adrian sat at the table nursing a cup of coffee and reading a newspaper. He looked up when Roland came in and said, "I love working at home."

Roland poured himself some coffee and sat down to help Brent and Adrian verify that each check had been photocopied properly and recorded accurately on the accompanying CD. That alone took almost an hour, and then the eleven hundred checks and money orders were divided into three even stacks. Each man had an adding machine and began totaling up his pile. To make sure the totals were accurate, they rotated the pile to the person on their left for a recount. Thankfully all the balances matched, with a total count of just over $1,200,000. The Belize Brothers had been instructed to send half the checks to Costa Rica and the other half to Puerto Vallarta, which meant that the full amount for the day would be around two and a half million. As Roland stared at the stacks of checks in front of them he decided it was no wonder those two weren't getting any sleep. If Vallarta had as many checks to enter as they had just done, the brothers were busy men indeed.

Everyone at the office in Mexico, including Roland, had started spending at least an hour of overtime every day counting and entering checks into the database. In so doing, the full impact of not accepting any more wires became apparent. When even the largest courier envelopes proved insufficient, Tatiana had started bringing in cardboard moving boxes which in turn had contained hundreds of other courier envelopes with checks in them. After Adrian had instructed the Belize Brothers to start keeping accounting records there to avoid potential confusion, the boxes had stopped coming as the two men threw away the bulky envelopes before forwarding their contents. Still, the number of checks kept growing.

It came time for a break and something to eat, so they stretched and yawned and padded out to the patio. Adrian's pool and accompanying thatched pelapa bar were bigger than those at some hotels Roland had seen.

"This is a great place to throw one hell of a party," Adrian said. "That pelapa hut there has two huge coolers in it. There are five tables, a big bar, two sinks, everything you need to get a lot of people happy. I've got a Club Med right in my back yard."

He pointed with his cigarette. "Franz hates this pool. He was chasing a rabbit at full tilt one day and figured he'd cut him off and jumped right into it. He was so fixated that he wasn't looking at what was right at his feet." He looked down at the dog. "Serves you right, doesn't it?"

Franz lay there panting. He didn't need to respond. He'd got his deer.

Adrian patted the dog's head. "Still, he's a good boy most of the time. Works hard. He'd have made a great shepherd."

Roland said, "He *is* a Shepherd."

"In breed only," Adrian replied. "Besides, I think he'd probably rather eat sheep than herd them. It's not like the deer was a threat." He scratched Franz behind the ear. "Sheep," he repeated faintly.

"Come again?"

Adrian was already halfway through his second post-check-counting cigarette. He gazed out at the pool and tugged on an earlobe. "The more people become sheep the more they need a shepherd. I've never figured out if people really want to be led or not. Everybody cherishes freedom once they have it, and if you take it away they protest like crazy, but look at how readily they let themselves be told what to do." He shook his head. "I bitch a lot about governments taking freedoms away, but you know what? They can only take what people give them."

"Remember what you told me about tax havens?" Roland asked Adrian, who nodded. "I saw a segment about the OECD countries on TV last night. They want tax havens to start taxing their clients and nationals. They think there is such a thing as 'unfair tax competition'. They believe there is something wrong with governments competing for talented, educated, productive citizens by making their countries attractive places to live and work through having low or no tax, among other things. They think tax havens are stealing their people."

"They are."

"They wouldn't be if their own countries were more attractive. Obviously governments would like to tax whatever they want without fear that the more productive and richer citizens will move their assets offshore where they're out of reach. So as a result they're doing everything they can to make these countries look like nothing more than a haven for criminals. You know what they accuse jurisdictions of that don't confiscate wealth from their people? 'Harmful tax practices'. Apparently unless you steal money from your citizens, you're a crooked government."

Adrian nodded again. "I know, believe me. Those are sovereign nations they're pushing around. And it doesn't end there. The politicians who accuse these places of harboring money launderers are the same ones who tell their national banks to inflate the money supply, which devalues everyone's assets. If any corporation acted the way most governments do, they'd be slapped with antitrust lawsuits. And in a welfare state it's so easy to live without contributing anything that a lot of people don't understand what's unfair about any of it. If you don't hold the person who strays responsible for his actions, you can't credit those who don't." He shrugged. "What can you do, though?"

A subtle breeze had sprung up, and it carried the smell of a distant, tantalizing flower. Adrian was still talking.

"Don't worry, Roland. You are learning the one thing that so many people never get to learn, and the whole reason I started Cyberia in the first place."

"And that is?"

"That money isolates you if you want it to. You don't have to go back home and step off the plane and be spat on for wearing fur and have acid thrown in your face for accepting a woman's right to have an abortion or be labeled a warmonger for wanting to own a gun, all of it leaving you saying to yourself, 'What the hell? I never told these people to wear fur or have abortions or own guns. Why are they all trying to tell *me* what to do?' Thanks to me, there are a lot of people out there who can now afford to go somewhere where freedom is still appreciated. And you know what? If they want to pursue some fascist agenda with their Cyberia dividends, that's okay too, because I love freedom enough to let that happen." He pointed the remains of his cigarette at Roland. "You try and find someone in a Marxist country who will say you can be a capitalist if you want to. It won't happen and that's why Russia fell. It's why China will too, unless it changes in a hurry. Communism, Marxism, fascism; the problem with them all is one thing: They have nothing to do with human nature."

He let this sink in. Guillermo was still sitting there but he hadn't said a word. Brent had been staring out at the pelapa but Roland knew he'd been listening to everything.

"By the way," Adrian said, "the United States won't go for the OECD recommendations."

"Why do you say that?"

Adrian grinned wryly. "You think we paid the Nicaraguan *contras* from the piggybank on Reagan's dresser? No, sir. Accounts in the Caymans did that for us. There's no denying that criminals use tax havens, but the US uses them too. All that aside, there are tons of legitimate reasons for banking in one."

"I'm glad you think so."

"I do. Not everyone in this world is a pro-state, pro-tax, anti-privacy totalitarian. And tomorrow I'm going to be in a country that can benefit from being a tax haven and a free society and keep its traditions and all that great stuff if it plays its cards right. Meaning, of course, if they can figure out that capitalism shouldn't mean screwing over your best friend to make a buck."

"Brent told me you were going to Latvia," Roland said. "I thought that problem was solved."

Adrian frowned and lit another Derby. "I thought so too, but I think it just got postponed. We're one of their biggest customers, and if we have a sniffle, they catch a cold. I can't have that kind of a precarious situation."

Roland didn't say a word about his misgivings about Adrian's trip overseas, even though they were just as strong as before. He still wasn't sure why he dreaded it. He wasn't even sure if it had anything to do with Latvia itself. Maybe the plane was going to crash. Perhaps an overseas flight would aggravate Adrian's cancer to a fatal point. Nevertheless, he'd voiced his apprehension before and Adrian had humored him; it wasn't worth talking about again. Besides, Roland had tried in other ways over the years to understand and improve his intuition, and the times when he hadn't kept it to himself had brought him nothing but trouble.

When all the checks were accounted for and properly recorded in Adrian's laptop, the little group shared a few more drinks around the pool. Soon it would be time for Adrian to be going. He took his suitcases to the front door and checked his watch. Eleven o'clock. Gino wouldn't show up for an hour.

Roland spent a few minutes with Guillermo at the shooting range and took the Maserati for a spin to the airport and back, but because it wasn't insured Adrian didn't want it driven again until he had his money back from the cards.

"Speaking of which," he said after Roland guided it into the garage and shut off the engine, "have you come up with any great ideas about how to reclaim my money?"

Roland nodded as he fastened the convertible top to the attachment points on the windshield frame. He didn't want mildew forming on it, which would inevitably happen in this climate if it was left folded up.

"I think so," he said. "Probably the easiest thing to do is just have the members continue as they are now, receiving ninety dollars per hundred owed to them from dividends. If we were paying ten dollars for a check to be cut before, and the member was paying ten, it stands to reason that if we stop paying that ten bucks a month it's the same as us making ten a month. On top of that, if the member keeps paying ten dollars for the first ten months he's got a Visa, then bingo, there's our two hundred per card. That might sound disappointingly unoriginal, and you'd have to wait ten months for the money, but there it is. I've cooked up some pretty intricate ways to make it painless for everybody, but that's the easiest way."

Adrian said, "Hmm."

"Another way you could do it would be to have members without an investment in Cyberia pay three hundred dollars for their card, instead of two."

"I'm listening." Adrian seemed more interested in this.

"Well, you know that the number of members in Cyberia without an investment is much higher than those with. If we did an equally good job of promoting these cards as an anonymous way to spend money, give to charities, whatever, then we'd boot more cards out the door. This time, though, there'd be an extra hundred bucks in it from everyone who doesn't invest but just wants to use the cards anonymously.

For every two of those people, there's one more card paid for, because two cardholding non-investing members times an extra hundred dollars each, is two hundred dollars. Another benefit would be that you could use it as an incentive to invest in Cyberia, because if they do their Visa would cost them a hundred bucks less, and you can recoup the two hundred out of their dividends so they aren't out of pocket for the fee."

"I like that," said Adrian. "I hadn't thought of that." He didn't need to say he'd thought of the first method, perfectly obvious as it was, but it was Roland's job to point out the options whether Adrian had voiced them or not.

"I don't need to make a profit out of these cards, though," Adrian said. "That's not what my business is. I just want my money back."

"Okay," Roland agreed. "Then pool the profits you do make from the cards and return them to their rightful owners once you've got your million back. Actually you could pool all those profits and treat the pool as one Cyberia membership that pays its dividends to all the members who overpaid once they become investors. It's not like we won't be keeping track." If, that is, the database mess could be cleaned up properly. "Besides, people only pay what they think things are worth. If somebody wants to send you three hundred bucks for an anonymous Visa, let them. Compared to some offshore cards, it would be cheap at twice that."

Adrian had been listening with his arms folded, bending an elbow occasionally to smoke and tap his ashes on the garage floor. "I'll let you know what to do when I get back from Latvia," he said. "I like what you're saying."

"When will you be back, anyway?"

Adrian drew his thumb across his lip. "No more than a week," he said through a cloud of cigarette smoke. "I'm going to Belize first to pick up Mack and I'll drop him off in PV. I want him to spend some time with the Secret Agent working out how we can get things running more smoothly at their office."

They heard a car pull up outside and stop at the edge of the parking area, and then the engine shut off.

Roland had been leaning against the Maserati but he stood up when Brent came in and said, "Gino's here, so it's time for us to head out. You ready to go?"

Roland could do nothing but bid Adrian a reluctant farewell. He remembered what Roxane had said in the pool not long before, about big changes coming. She'd felt it too. Everyone did. The rhythm of late was not that of a fast train on a smooth track, Roland thought. It was more like the whine of an airliner with its nose pointed toward the ground, and although the sensation was exciting, he didn't like where it was headed. He wondered if Adrian felt it too.

The last time Roland ever saw Adrian, he was standing in the doorway of his house, Franz at his side, smoking a cigarette and giving a cursory wave as Gino loaded his luggage into the Lexus in the hot afternoon sun. Brent steered the Blazer past the helipad and down the crushed red rock driveway, and the house disappeared from view.

15
Icarus in Winter

Truth emerges more readily from error than from confusion.

-Sir Francis Bacon

Roland wandered down the road outside his condo to Los Antojitos with the cowboys for dinner that night. They were pleased that they'd finished all their business on schedule, and were looking forward to a river tour tomorrow. Gino the driver had mentioned over a dinner at Le Monastère that a cousin of his owned a tour boat company on the Sarapiqui River, and that he had arranged for them to have the boat to themselves.

They chose a table outside on the verandah, and Ricky stretched and yawned after sinking into his chair. "I think we finally have something here," he said. "The hosting service will allow us to upload all the memberships entered on line at four o'clock every morning. So it won't be a continuous thing, because every time the service uploads it has to establish a connection with your server and you don't want to leave that open all day long for security reasons. But it'll mean no more data entry for your people."

Technically they weren't Roland's people at all; in fact, Shelly was in charge of data administration and if anything Roland was still one of her people, but the Visa project was taking all his time now. So actually, he was in charge of his own department and it had one person on staff – himself.

The waiter brought their drinks and took their orders for dinner. He departed and Greg began to speak.

"There's something we want to discuss with you," he said.

Roland took a sip of his limeade and said, "I assume this has to do with somebody accessing the financial records from my computer."

Greg nodded. He didn't seem the least surprised that Roland already knew about it. "Sort of, yes. But there's a lot more to it than that."

Ricky said, "A hell of a lot more."

"I see." There was something Roland had meant to ask the cowboys since his conversation with Garrett. "One thing before you begin, though. Can you tell me when those files were accessed? There aren't many times when I haven't been around."

"Down to the minute," said Greg. "That's partly why we decided we could talk to you. Twice it happened while you were down here in Costa Rica last month, so obviously it couldn't have been you."

"Also, there's nobody else we can really talk to anyway," Ricky put in. "Garrett told us who has the passwords for the accounting records so that rules out Liza, Roxane, Mick and Garrett, because any or all of them could be responsible."

Roland said, "So whatever this is, Garrett doesn't know the whole story."

"Right," said Greg. "Now, Grant can be ruled out, because even though his computer was used for access, there's actually nothing correlating the accessing of the files to the problem we're describing, and he hasn't been at Cyberia long enough anyway. Neither have you. Also we can rule out Dolores, because the computer she uses to scan is connected to the network but we just don't think she's a candidate."

"Speaking of not being at Cyberia long enough, she's new too," said Roland, though it occurred to him that she'd been a friend of Maxine's for years. "Same with Kevin. He's only been around a couple of weeks longer than me. What about Eric? He's been pretty busy with accounting stuff for over a month now." He didn't ask exactly what problem the cowboys were trying to describe, preferring to let them come to that point themselves.

"Yes, that's true," said Ricky. "It's possible…"

"Also, guys, keep in mind that both my computer and Grant's were only hooked up around late February, early March."

"Hmm," said Ricky. "Did you know that you and Grant used the same password, and that it was one of the first ones Adrian ever used?"

Roland shook his head. This was interesting indeed.

There was a slight pause as the waiter reappeared with appetizers. When he had gone Greg said, "You aren't going to make this easy, are you?"

Roland dipped a breaded chili pepper in salsa and said, "No. It's pretty clear that you're gearing up to accuse one of my coworkers of something big, and I don't really want to help you along. On the other hand if there's something crooked happening, I'd like to know about it."

Ricky took a breath and looked at Roland. "Cyberia is losing almost a quarter of a million dollars a month. We don't know where it's going, but it's not going where it's supposed to, I can tell you that."

Roland held the chili pepper, now bitten in half, and swallowed. "Wow," he said. "Whoah. Are you sure?"

"Does a cabbie pick his nose waiting for the light to change?"

Roland wondered which names were on the cowboys' list. "Who?"

Greg spoke up. "Well, that's the thing. Basically, we've never seen a company as easy to rip off as this one, so it could be any number of people. The ones with the passwords are the most obvious choices."

Roland said, "I don't suppose this money is disappearing in a lump sum."

"No, no," said Ricky. "Actually we're kind of dramatizing things a bit, because we do know where some of it went."

"At least, we think we do," said Greg. "Some of the money is probably not missing as in stolen, just plain missing, because the database you're using up there is a complete disaster. It's based on Microsoft Excel, which is good but it just can't reliably handle the volume of members and transactions you're working with now."

"Also, it doesn't help that half the staff are whacked out on drugs when they're entering those transactions," Ricky added. "Some of the mistakes we've found are quite obviously clerical errors, but when you're talking about this much money, it adds up in a big hurry."

Roland finished his chili pepper and reached for another one. "So how much money is missing due to stoned employees entering incorrect data into a problematic database, and how much is being blatantly ripped off?"

Ricky finished crunching on his nacho before he answered. "It varies."

"From what to what?"

Greg took the last chili pepper as he spoke. "We're reasonably sure – not completely, mind you – that over the last four months, at least half of this money is missing due to incorrectly-entered data and glitches in your program or database. As for what happened to the other half, we don't know. Also we can't say for sure how much longer than four months this has been going on."

Roland didn't say anything. One of his coworkers was at the very least half a million dollars richer than if he'd waited around for his salary alone. Part of him was envious, but mostly he was indignant that he'd been working his ass off to be rewarded legitimately while somebody else was considering himself smart for taking the easy road to fortune. And a profitable road it had obviously been.

"Is there any evidence you guys have that might point to more than one person being involved?" he asked.

Ricky and Greg looked at each other. "Well, actually, yeah. That's another reason why we didn't really feel like we could approach anybody in PV with this. The most we could do was ask Garrett as indirectly as possible who was trustworthy, and we had to tell him a little bit to get that out of him. If the word got out that we knew, whoever was responsible would stop and we'd never find out."

"Not necessarily," Roland said. "Criminals are too stupid to figure out how to play by the rules and still win. They'd wait for the fuss to die down and start dreaming about their retirement again. Besides, doesn't everybody know that your new program has spy features?"

The waiter set their dinners in front of them. Roland had been ravenous when he sat down to eat, but suddenly he didn't feel so hungry. Greg said, "We always say that wherever we go. It's sort of an unwritten rule that management wants to scare its employees into compliance, and we help that along by making people think twice about screwing around when they're supposed to be working."

"So you're saying Cyberia isn't getting those features, but we're supposed to think it is?"

Ricky said, "Pretty much," as he reached for the hot sauce. "It will have some, of course, but there's a way around absolutely everything."

"I see," said Roland.

He toyed with his taco salad for a while, mulling the situation over. He had thought of many ways to line his pockets at Cyberia's expense, but they had been nothing more than interesting daydreams. Even while counting checks back in Vallarta, or earlier that day at Adrian's for that matter, it wouldn't have taken any trouble at all to drop a few in his lap unnoticed, open an account in the name of Hammer International somewhere, and start building a nest egg. He could go into the software afterwards and mark the member's investment as 'paid', so to the best of anyone's knowledge the check had been received and deposited and the member would be paid his dividends, all as though nothing had happened.

When he went through the motions in his mind, he kept waiting for something to stop him, but nothing did. No alarms went off, no lights flashed, no one looked at him suspiciously and asked what he'd been up to. Still, he had always reached a point in his thoughts where he was alone with his ill-gotten gains, and he just wasn't able to rationalize it enough to go through with it. Lying on a beach somewhere with a sexy señorita wouldn't taste as sweet knowing that somebody out there was gunning for him.

He thought about Sara, and how he'd given her so many chances to keep her word and be truthful, and for a myriad of reasons which must have all made sense to her, she didn't. Roland wondered for a moment if everyone was ripping off Cyberia but him.

"We're going to have to give whoever's responsible enough rope to hang themselves," Roland said. "Obviously you're going to have to build something in that tracks access to those files alone, and give every employee with that access a different password." Something occurred to him. "Did you say you could find out when all the files were opened?"

"Most," said Ricky.

"Well, Garrett told me about this yesterday. He mentioned that the file the passwords are kept in is stored on a sector of the server that's visible from my computer and Grant's, and that it was those computers that were used to access the records. All you have to do is find out when that password file was accessed, and that'll narrow down the suspects in a big hurry."

"We're way ahead of you," Greg said. "We checked into that."

"Which apparently got you nowhere."

"One step forward, two steps sort of sideways and a little back, I guess," Ricky admitted. "We never said that the files were accessed from your computer, exactly, just somebody with your password. We have nothing conclusive, nothing we could use to point the finger at any one person in particular, except that it was somebody who's been around for at least four months. Really, that only rules out you, Grant, Dolores and Kevin."

Pity, thought Roland. It would have been nice to pin this one on the lad.

"Regarding the complete package of security features, we want you to lobby Adrian for them," Greg said.

Roland shook his head. "I won't do that," he said. "Adrian only cares that the job gets done, and believe me, internal office politics is enough to deter anyone from screwing around too much when they're supposed to be working." Except Kevin, perhaps, who always seemed to be surfing the internet when Roland had to see him about something. "Tracking who accesses the banking information and when will be sufficient, as well as the member and Visa files, and the software should automatically generate a report that only Adrian gets to see. You can do that, can't you." It wasn't a question. "Also the network itself obviously has to be adequately firewalled to prevent anyone spiking us with a virus or stealing our records, because we're connected to the TelMex satellite with the same IP address all day long, and with the added risk of uploading information from here and the two networks talking to each other before we get our own satellite that risk is higher than ever. Other than that, though, it's my view that internal security makes criminals where there aren't any."

"But there are," said Greg. "That's exactly the point."

"Right," agreed Roland, "and if those records are properly tracked it's only a matter of time before we find out who it is.

If you don't let on about what you know, and advertise the fact that this new software doesn't track finances any better than the old one, whoever's responsible will be content to think that the only improvement is a less-cluttered database. Once Adrian is advised of this – and he will be, I promise – whoever's responsible will slip up and be caught."

Neither Greg nor Ricky seemed pleased with their lack of progress but Roland would not be budged, even though he entertained for a brief moment the disturbing possibility that the thief might be Adrian himself.

On the next morning – Friday, April 20th – the telephone beside Roland's bed rang at six-thirty. This time when he answered there were no chipper endearing words from Brent. He was all business.

"Come upstairs as soon as you can," he said. "Leave the cowboys and come on up."

"Can I shower first?"

Brent was silent for a few seconds before he said, "I guess that won't make a difference," and hung up.

Fifteen minutes later Roland knocked on Brent's door, his hair still wet and his eyes barely open. Brent opened it, revealing a smoke-filled livingroom behind him.

He and Janine had guests. Gino and Maxine were sitting on either end of the huge leather couch, and as Roland closed the door he saw one half of the Belize Brothers. Nick was in the kitchen pouring a coffee. He held it out to Roland and said, "You're going to need this." It smelled strongly of rum.

Roland set the coffee down on the counter and shook Nick's hand. "Good to see you," he said. He didn't ask where Mack was. It was pretty obvious that he was about to find out.

Everyone was smoking furiously, Maxine more so than anyone else, and there was a full ashtray on the table in front of her. The only ones not smoking were Roland and Gino.

Maxine said, "Adrian was arrested in Puerto Vallarta last night."

Before Roland could say anything Nick added, "So were Mack and Guillermo."

"Arrested for what?" Roland finally asked.

Maxine shook her head. "Right now, it isn't too clear. I only found it out because Mick was supposed to pick Adrian up at the airport and he saw him having a discussion with the customs inspector, and the next thing you know there's police cars and TV crews and all kinds of shit, so he bugged out and called me."

"TV crews? What the hell?"

Maxine nodded. "It's big news. I got another call from Mick fifteen minutes ago, and he said that Adrian was carrying almost five million dollars' worth of cashier's checks and money orders. He says that the story on TV is that he's a drug dealer."

Roland would have laughed at that if everyone else wasn't so serious. He leaned against the kitchen counter and took a sip of coffee. He wouldn't notice for another few minutes how much rum there was in it. "You mean he was carrying the week's total with him? He was going to deposit it in Latvia personally? What the hell for?"

Maxine shrugged.

"These people think drug dealers take checks, for Christ's sake?"

Maxine shrugged again and held up a hand. "I haven't actually talked to Adrian himself yet," she said. "It's Mexico, so who knows how many phone calls he'll get. Hopefully he'll be able to buy a few if he isn't officially allowed more than one. But until we hear from him otherwise, the status is that everything is officially shut down, stopped, kaput."

"Why?"

Maxine looked surprised at this question. "Well…what do you mean, 'why'? Cyberia can't function without him."

Roland said, "Sure it can. You're telling me you don't know *any* of these people in Panama?"

Maxine shook her head. "Not my business," she said.

"Well, doesn't Mick know them?"

"No. Everything is shut down," she repeated.

"This is unbelievable," said Roland. "What was he doing that would have got him arrested?"

"Like I said, so far it's just all speculation, and if they're grasping at straws like drug dealing they can't have much to stand on. We'll know more this evening. Up to now it looks like the Mexicans don't know what they've got, but because there's a lot of money involved they want to hang onto him until they find out."

"In the meantime," Brent said, "people are still going to be sending us money until word of this gets out to the members. So we have to keep banking as usual, keep records as usual, but obviously we can't pay dividends because Adrian isn't around to link us with Panama."

Roland looked at Maxine and asked, "Who was flying the plane?"

Maxine raised her eyebrows. "Does it matter?"

"It might. Do you know who it was?"

She shook her head. "No, I don't. I can probably find out, though."

"That might help clear up some confusion." Roland briefly narrated the concerns he'd had about Heinz. "I stole one of his flight plans and gave it to Grant. It looked fine but Grant checked up on him anyway with one of his friends at the charter brokerage, and apparently he's okay. Still, you never know."

Brent lit another cigarette and said, "Well, the good news is that we still have a river tour planned, and we might as well make the best of it. Maxine's going to stick around and wait for news from up north, so let's enjoy ourselves." He exhaled a cloud of smoke. "Eat, drink, and be merry, for tomorrow we may die."

Roland looked around the room. Whether or not he saw some Costa Rican wildlife wasn't going to affect the outcome of Adrian's situation one bit. On top of that, there was no need to alert the cowboys, who might decide to take off before their project was finished and leave a bigger mess than the one they'd found. If Adrian wasn't guilty of whatever the Mexicans ended up charging him with, panicking them would be pointless.

"I agree," he said. "Might as well."

Under any other circumstances, the day would have been nothing short of spectacular. Gino, Brent, Greg, Ricky and Roland rode the Blazer up narrow mountain highways, stopping at coffee plantations and waterfalls to take in the scenery and collect souvenirs. At their destination they were fed a huge lunch by a genial husband and wife, whose young daughter gawked at the gringos through a nearby fence. With the river to themselves the crocodiles and monkeys couldn't have cared less about them, and at one point their guide brought them so close to a group of six-foot-long iguanas that Roland managed to touch one's tail before it disappeared into the gnarled roots of a melaleuca tree. No matter how remarkable the vistas or how striking the experience, however, Brent and Roland each caught the other looking as though this might be their last day on earth.

Back at the condos at Escazu, Roland was getting ready for the motorcycle rally that night when the phone rang. Diego had warned him when he offered the invitation that it would be cold, but Roland had decided to ignore him. Somebody from as far north as Roland hailed would surely be used to that.

"More news, son, but it isn't very good," said Brent. "I just learned after I got back here that he's been moved from the jail in Vallarta" – he pronounced it 'Veeyarda' – "to the federal pen in Guadalajara."

"Why? Was there a dead body on the airplane too?"

Brent didn't laugh; not that Roland had expected him to. "No. Those checks they found on him, well, some of them were the ones we counted yesterday morning. Altogether they say he was carrying just under eleven hundred checks, but obviously he must have traded some of the smaller amounts for bigger ones or added some from Belize to make up what they say was four and a half million dollars."

"Mm-hmm."

"So they changed their minds and they don't think it's drugs."

"Well, that's good at least. Then why do they want him in a federal pen?" Roland tied a shoe as he shut the bedroom's TV off and looked at his watch.

Brent took his time answering. "Well, thing is, apparently there was some confusion on his customs form."

He didn't need to say another word. Roland could imagine Adrian taking one look at the customs form and thinking, 'it's none of their goddamn business how much money I'm carrying around,' and handing it over with zero to declare. "Confusion," he echoed.

"Well, things are still sketchy, and this comes from a variety of sources sort of put together by Mick, but the *federales* are now pretty sure he's laundering money. So they really want to grill him good. Nobody's too optimistic that he's going to get out of this one anytime soon."

"I see," said Roland. He wondered if the cowboys had somehow hit upon a discovery that would indicate who the half-million-dollar-thief was, but realized that his brain was just trying to divert attention away from the seriousness of the situation. "Nothing more than that at this point?"

"Not a word. We're all pretty much in the dark."

Roland put on his other shoe. "Let's get together first thing tomorrow morning," he said. "I'm on my way out right now."

"Sure thing, son. See you then."

The drive to the rally in Cartago took about half an hour in Gino's car, and during it Roland didn't say much. As night fell in the crowded stadium, he wished fervently that he'd listened to Diego and worn more clothing. It hadn't occurred to him that over the previous weeks he had become accustomed to the heat, and he stood there shivering in a temperature that four months ago he would have considered almost comfortable.

After the race Diego drove them to a local KFC where his girlfriend disappeared to retrieve dinner. Roland's arm hurt from where he had fallen as he tried to avoid being killed by a motorcyclist who flew over the berm at the TV cameras while he stood with Diego and his girlfriend, the only female sportscaster in Central America.

"I have to tell you something, and ask you a question as well," Roland told Diego when they were alone. He rubbed his shoulder and tried to move his arm, with some success. "You can tell Franco, but if you hear it from anyone else you must promise to act surprised. You aren't supposed to know, but it concerns you, and I think it's safest if you do."

Diego raised an eyebrow. "*Esta bien*," he said slowly. "Okay."

Roland got straight to the point. "Adrian was arrested last night in Puerto Vallarta. Nobody knows exactly why yet, but the Mexicans are holding him in a federal jail."

Diego had been leaning back in the booth, but now he looked decidedly more interested.

"So I have to ask you if what you and Franco are doing with Adrian is legal here," Roland continued. "I need to know if Cyberia is above board." Diego frowned. "Above board. I mean, is it legitimate, is it okay. Because if it isn't, we might all be in trouble."

Diego shook his head. "Everything we are doing is okay with the banks, and you know his lawyer here, you have met him, he thinks so too. Roland, I would not do anything illegal. Costa Rica is my home, and it is a small place. Everyone would know if I was caught doing something illegal and I cannot afford to have that happen." He held his hand up as he shook his head again. "I am not doing anything, *como se dice*, under the board. Neither is Franco. I know him well and he is my friend."

Roland nodded. "I didn't think so, but I had to ask." The situation had gone far beyond playing cloak and dagger, and Roland wasn't interested in maintaining a façade that could prove disastrous for him. "If you need to take care of things, maybe you should start thinking ahead now, because it doesn't look like you're going to see Adrian again for quite a while." Diego looked confused. "I am saying you might not get paid again for a while. You do what you like with that knowledge."

Diego looked thoughtful. "Thank you for trusting me," he said eventually.

Roland looked at him for a second. "You have driven on narrow roads at night, Diego?"

Diego looked puzzled. "Of course."

"With only one narrow little yellow line separating you from people coming toward you? And sometimes no line at all?"

"Yes."

"You are trusting those people not to drive into you, and they are trusting you to do the same. Without that, driving would be impossible. Not just a headache, like here, but impossible, anywhere. It is stupid not to trust. It is even worse than trusting the wrong people." Something I have become unsettlingly good at, Roland thought.

"I understand," said Diego. "You don't know what will happen to Adrian?"

"No. Nobody does but God, and he ain't talking." Roland sipped his Coke. "Either that," he said distantly, "or we're not listening."

Apart from the fact that our boss is behind bars, Roland reflected, this is just another day at the office.

He was sitting with Brent at one of the iron patio tables in the courtyard nursing a hot coffee with both hands. He still felt chilled from the night before. Brent flicked his cigarette ash into the wind. It was cloudy again. Roland watched the ash disappear as Brent spoke.

"I think we should move everybody down here," he said. "There's no sense in hanging around Veeyarda if there's nothing going on."

"Has anybody heard from Adrian yet?"

"Actually, yes. Contrary to what we thought yesterday, everything is to proceed as normal. His lawyers are expensive but they say they can get him out."

"That's what I'd say too if I was an expensive lawyer. What about facts?"

Brent was silent for a little while. Then he said, "I guess the only things we know for sure are that our boss is in the slammer and he's kicked up enough of a fuss and shown enough pesos that they have a doctor for him, he's getting his pills, and he's able to make calls on a cell phone. They've given the boys their own cell, they've got a television, a mattress each that Adrian says looks new enough, and a bottle of whisky a day. Also speaking of whisky, apparently the three of them were drinking like fish all through the trip. Hopefully that will help their case."

"How? By making them look more responsible than if they'd been high on coke instead?"

Brent managed a smile and said, "No. Remember, Adrian didn't fill out a customs form properly and that's why they got stopped and searched. If he can claim he was drunk, and would have filled out the form properly otherwise, everything will be okay."

"Mm-hmm. I see." Roland didn't say so, but if any drunken slob ever drove into him late at night and he lived to tell the tale, he would probably shoot the judge who allowed the lush to get off with an argument like that.

Roland could see Diego looking at the two of them from inside the office. "Those are the only facts we have?"

"Yep."

Roland wondered if the jail had a golf course.

"What do we tell these two?" he asked, pointing to the office.

"Diego and Franco? Nothing. We don't want to scare them off. Adrian could be released tomorrow."

Roland leaned forward. He said, "Brent, the guy landed in a Learjet late at night carrying over four million dollars, and was scheduled to fly overseas the next day. It's a bloody miracle they didn't immediately search the Shack when they thought he was involved with drugs, because if they'd found one of the stashes in the desks and the bags of cash in the safe there'd be hell to pay."

Brent held up a hand. "But that didn't happen," he said. "Now, we might not know about this bunch down south in Panama, but we do know for sure he wasn't involved with drugs. He is being held in prison for an offense that's ruffled some feathers, and when law enforcement people see a lot of checks, they get interested in a hurry. Especially cops down here."

"What about the cowboys?" Roland asked.

"They know Adrian got picked up. One of them saw it on the internet, on Yahoo."

"You're kidding. This *is* big news."

"They're flying home today," Brent continued. "You'll have that condo to yourself for a while, I guess. Personally I would go back to Mexico, get all my stuff, and come back down. If you get posted to this office anyway you'll already be here, and if you have to go back to Mexico you just pack your bags and hop on a plane."

Roland's coffee wasn't hot enough anymore and he pushed it away. "I hope he's okay," he said. "Adrian, I mean. His health isn't too great. How's Maxine taking this?"

Brent looked reflective as he scratched at the flaking paint on the wrought-iron table with a thumbnail. "As well as can be expected, I guess, with her husband getting thrown in jail." Which probably meant that she'd hit the bottle harder than usual but was otherwise fine.

"Poor Guillermo," Roland mused. "This looks really bad."

"Well," said Brent, "we've got a courier envelope to pick up. Janine's out at Adrian's house with Maxine and has been since last night. Care to drop in and see them?"

Roland stared at his coffee. Maxine had an espresso machine in the kitchen next to that funky fridge.

"Sure," he said. "Let's go."

With Brent and Janine talking by the pool, Roland found himself alone in the kitchen with Maxine and Franz. Maxine was sitting at the counter and directing Roland on how to use the espresso machine. Finally he fiddled around enough to produce a thick black liquid which was suitably hot and tasted more or less like strong coffee. He joined Maxine, who sucked on a cigarette and said, "I got a call from Grant this morning. He says the charter brokerage was asking a lot of questions about why Adrian wanted to fly to Europe without stopping in the States or Canada." Considering how drunk she was, her diction was remarkably clear.

"I hope he told them it was because of Adrian's health."

"It isn't," said Maxine curtly. "Lots of people want to talk to him."

Roland sipped his espresso, such as it was. "About what?" he asked, but he didn't really want to know, and he didn't ask why Adrian's health was suddenly irrelevant. Thankfully Maxine spared him any details. She waved a hand and said, "Nothing that concerns you. I don't even know most of it myself."

"Should I be worried?" Roland asked.

Maxine tapped her cigarette into a gold-plated ashtray as she replied, "About yourself? Couldn't hurt. About Adrian? I don't know. Personally, I'm worried about him, but that's kind of my job. I'm his wife."

Roland stared at her. "What do you mean, when it comes to me it couldn't hurt to worry?"

Maxine took a long drink from her martini. "Let's put it this way. It couldn't hurt to make it difficult for the Mexican authorities to talk to you. As far as worrying goes, I think we both understand that doing so is pointless but action isn't. The US consulate was happy to see Adrian because he's wanted for some real estate fraud."

"*What?*"

"The Canadians want him for the same thing," she added nonchalantly. "Next time you're on the internet, log on to the Guadalajara Reporter's website, or type his name into Google. There are lots of things there, none of them good."

"Fantastic," Roland observed. It was getting hard to shock him for very long about anything.

Roland spent the remainder of that trip wandering around the city with Maxine, Nick, Brent and Janine. There was no shortage of things to see and do in the impressive old capital, but the conversations always came back to Adrian. Eventually Monday came, and Brent dropped Roland off at the airport.

"Find out what you can and get back to us," he said. "It might not be a bad idea to have everyone down here, like I said before."

Roland couldn't imagine people like Slogan and Roxane moving to Costa Rica when they had made Puerto Vallarta their home for so long, but he reassured Brent that he would do what he could.

"I'll try and bring you the mountain, Mohamed."

Brent laughed. "Then I'll set up a cable car, and we can look at this thing from above."

16
Under The Wheels

It was early afternoon when Roland's plane touched down in Mexico City, and by the time he hoisted his suitcase off the carousel at Puerto Vallarta the light was just beginning to take on the qualities of its imminent twilight orange. He was pleased that the same beautiful woman who had greeted him at the airport on his first day was working that day as well. She looked at Roland blankly until he smiled at her, and then she took his arm to lead him to the button. He wouldn't have minded having her search his luggage, but the green 'Pase' light flashed and she said, "*Hasta luego, amigo.*"

Towing his suitcase behind him, he entered the terminal to be greeted by Yoda who bounced up to him looking as though he wanted to bark but knew he shouldn't. He was tethered to Roxane by an impossibly long leash. Roland bent down to let him lick his hand, and when he looked up to say hello he stopped dead.

Roxane looked absolutely haggard. Her eyes were sunken and ringed with dark, puffy circles. She was flanked by CIA Mick and Dolores, each of whom appeared equally harried. Mick in particular looked awful, and Dolores had obviously been drinking even more than usual.

"Hey guys," Roland said. "What are you doing here?"

"Getting a ticket for Dolores," Roxane answered almost inaudibly as she cast glances over her shoulder. Dolores disappeared without saying hello, headed for the Mexicana counter.

"Where's she going?"

"Costa Rica."

"We didn't know you were coming," Mick said. "We don't have our roster of who's coming in on which flight from where anymore." He was biting one of his nails angrily. Roland wondered if he had remembered to eat something in the last four days.

"Right, I see," he said slowly, studying Roxane and Mick as they watched every passing tourist suspiciously. Within a few minutes Dolores returned. She was wiping away a tear as she said, "Okay, there's a plane I can get on that leaves in twenty minutes so I gotta hurry. Hi Roland. Bye Roland. Thanks for the ride, guys." Then she spun on her heel and was gone. Roxane yanked on Yoda's leash and said, "Come on, we'll talk outside."

The heat and humidity were a welcome change from San Jose. Even in the late afternoon sun the day was still a scorcher. Mick walked with his head down, and when they reached his jeep Roland silently put his bags in the back and jumped in. He was about to say something but Roxane shushed him, holding up a trembling hand. "Not until we leave here," she said.

Mick paid the parking attendant with a twenty-peso note for a ten-peso charge and told her to keep the change as he sped away. He turned at the dolphin statue along the airport highway to follow the road leading to the marina restaurants and boardwalk where Roxane's little SUV waited at the curb. Mick pulled over beside it. Wordlessly Roxane moved the seat forward and got out so Roland could do the same.

"I can give you a ride as far as Olas Altas," Roxane offered, "but no farther. I won't take you home." She held out Yoda's leash. "I need a minute to talk to Mick."

Roland took the little dog onto the grass and watched him chase birds he had no hope of catching. Eventually Roxane returned and pointed to her vehicle. "Get in," she said, and pressed a button on her keychain to open the doors. The car was crammed full of clothes and kitchen utensils and compact discs. The windows had been closed during her excursion to the airport and it was gloriously hot inside.

They sat silent for a while, Yoda perched on the console between them. As Mick turned onto the highway and was lost from view, Roxane reached for the ignition, but she gripped her knee instead. She drew the back of her other hand across her mouth and closed her eyes.

Roland looked at her. "Roxane, what the hell is going on up here?"

He wanted to put a reassuring hand on her shoulder but she was so jumpy he wondered if she might go into cardiac arrest. Instead he waited for an answer. Yoda gnawed on one of his paws.

"It's all just gone to hell," Roxane said quietly from behind her fingers. "The Shack is being watched. Everybody's scattered. Nobody knows where Liza or Garrett are, and I'm too scared to go home so I'm living in a hotel."

"Who's watching the Shack?"

She was still speaking quietly, still with the back of her hand in front of her mouth. "Who *isn't* watching the Shack? Roland, have you been living under a rock for the past four days?"

"Not exactly," Roland answered, trying not to sound defensive. "But I called up here a million times and nobody answered. Not at the Shack, nobody's cell phone, nothing." Of course, most of them had call display but his long distance numbers might not have shown up. That would have made them nervous and unwilling to answer. "All I really know is that Adrian got arrested at the airport because he didn't declare the money he was carrying, so pardon me if your panic is a new wrinkle to me."

Roxane started the car. "I need you to do me a favor," she said. "I need you to tell me if the yacht is there." She pointed to the short street that led to the El Faro lighthouse restaurant and the marina beyond, where everyone had gathered for the limousines to take them to Sidney and Amy's wedding. Pulling out onto the road, she made a U-turn to park at the entrance.

"Isn't it moored over by the condo?" Roland asked, but Roxane shook her head.

"Just down here," she said. "Adrian rented a spot here so Sidney could park the speedboat at the condo slip. You'll be able to see it plainly if it's there."

Roland got out and closed the door. If *Pier Pressure* was in this part of the marina it certainly wouldn't be hard to spot, but after a quick look down the rows of boats he saw no sign of it. He looked back at Roxane's car. She was cuddling Yoda with a vengeance. Taking his cell phone out of his pocket, he scrolled through the stored numbers until he saw Garrett's cell phone number and hit 'Send'. Two rings later, Liza answered. He moved out of sight of the car and said, "Liza, it's Roland. So, what the hell is all this?"

"Roland. Thank God. Where have you been?"

"Costa Rica, remember? I just got back about fifteen minutes ago and ran into Mick and Roxane at the airport. They look like somebody just found out about their Gestapo history. What are *they* all strung out for? And where the hell are you?"

Liza ignored most of this. She said, "I've been wanting to talk to you for days." She didn't say why she hadn't just called him in Costa Rica. "I need you to fax me a list of everybody's Visa card numbers. I'm going to transfer five thousand dollars onto each of them."

"No problem. What's it for?"

"Getting-out-of-town money. And the sooner they have it and use it, the better."

"Any place in mind?" Roland was thinking of what Brent had said about bringing everyone to Costa Rica and wondering if it was still a good idea that they all congregate there, a brace of jittery gringos trying to look nonchalant.

"Down south, probably. Truth is, I don't care. It's just safest for everybody if you all leave."

Interesting, thought Roland, that she didn't say 'we' all leave. She must be already gone. "Are you still in Mexico?"

Liza laughed faintly. "I could tell you where I am, Bachelor, but then I'd have to kill you."

"Liza, if I'm in danger, you have to tell me." She didn't have to, of course, but it would have been basic human courtesy.

There was a slight hesitation on the end of the line, somewhere Roland could only guess at. For a brief moment he remembered discovering Guadalajara with her and then the picture was gone as she spoke.

"Roland, listen. If you *are* wanted for something – solely by association, of course – it would be best to put yourself out of reach for the moment, until it becomes clear that you aren't involved. And if you haven't done anything wrong, well, you get another free vacation and it won't make a difference either way."

"What the fuck does that mean, *if* I haven't done anything wrong? What have I really been doing for the last two months?"

"All I'm saying is, that's not up to you to decide, okay? We've got somebody in a federal hotel here, and for the landlords to build a case against this person it wouldn't be out of reach to think that they're going to want as much ammunition as they can get. If that includes working you over for something to use against him, it goes without saying that it's best for everybody if they didn't find you in the first place."

Roland stared out at the boats. The sailing yacht that had caught his attention on the day of the wedding was still there, waiting patiently for its new owner and its new adventures.

"Fine," he said. "I get it. Where can I reach you? I mean, a fax number to send you the list of people whose cards need money."

He keyed the digits into the memory of his cell phone as Liza dictated them. So that's where she is, he thought. He had entered enough data to know practically every country and area code in the world by heart. When it was done he asked, "Where's the yacht?"

"Don't worry, it's safe. I think so, anyway. But I'll make sure Izzy and Gonzo get their five grand as well."

"Okay. Do you need anything else from me?"

Liza paused, then said, "No, I think that should do it. Just take care of yourself, Roland." She chuckled. "Goodbye, Bachelor."

Roland closed his phone and made his way back to the car. Yoda sat shaking in Roxane's purse, looking at him with his bulging brown eyes.

"The yacht's safe. So is Liza. Let's go; I've got things to do."

Roxane started the vehicle. "You talked to her? I didn't think she was answering her phone."

"She isn't. She's answering Garrett's."

"Where is she?"

Roland pulled a notebook out of his duffel bag and a pencil from Roxane's glove compartment, and as they lurched onto the road he began making check marks beside certain strings of numbers. "Texas," he said.

After a brief stop at Lloyd's to clear out her account, Roxane parked the car at the north end of Olas Altas and looked down the road with trepidation. "You're serious?" Roland said. "You aren't going home with me?"

She shook her head. "No way. Forget it. From here, you take a taxi and take your chances."

Roland gently opened the door. He got out and took his bags and closed the door and watched Roxane drive away.

He withdrew to a silent spot beside a building and brought out his cell phone again. After four rings he was about to hang up before getting a voice mail message, but Brent answered. "Hello."

"Hey, dad, it's me. Can you do me a quick favor?"

"Didn't I just get rid of you?"

Roland didn't laugh. "Have the banks there closed yet?"

There was a pause as Brent spoke with Diego. An idea occurred to Roland. "Actually, Brent, don't worry about it. Can you just put Diego on the phone, please?"

"Fine, but you have bad taste in phone conversation partners." He could hear rustling sounds and what was probably a coffee mug being set down on a table. Finally Diego said, "Roland."

"Yes. Remember what we talked about the other night?"

"Of course." Diego was suddenly all business. A young girl came up to Roland offering Chiclets and he waved her away.

"I need you and Franco to do some banking for me, right away. Can we still do some Visa deposits today?"

Diego said, "Yes, but it is late. They will not show up until tomorrow there in Mexico, maybe not until the afternoon."

A man in a sombrero carrying a guitar sat down near Roland and started playing flamenco, his fingers dancing across the fretboard. Roland turned away to hear Diego better.

"That's okay," he said. "I need five thousand dollars on each of the cards issued to Cyberia employees. Just, all those cards that were in the A-list batch, put five thousand on each."

"All of them?" Diego asked.

"There are a few exceptions," Roland said. "You will probably need a few minutes to get Franco set up for a deposit, right?"

"Yes."

"Okay then." Two tourist girls passed in front of Roland as he spoke. One of them dropped a banknote in the flamenco player's guitar case as the other smiled at Roland. "In three minutes I am going to send you an email with a list of names that do *not* receive the five thousand. So check your email after you get the deposit paperwork ready."

"All right."

Roland could hear Brent in the background talking to someone else in the office, probably Janine. "Diego, it is very important that this happen quickly."

"I understand. I know why. I will not let you down."

"*Gracias, amigo.* Goodbye."

Roland closed his phone and wheeled his suitcase to a desk in the dot-com café around the corner, past the shop owned by Roxane's friend who claimed to have been almost stabbed to death. He sat down and accessed his email account and typed out a list of names including Roxane's son; the now officially-fired cook and her boyfriend; the Caviar Brothers, and a few others not involved with Cyberia's daily operations but who had been issued a card. He typed Diego's email address into the 'To' field and clicked 'Send'. Next he sent a brief email to Jake the travel agent, making sure to flag it as 'Urgent'. Finally he logged into his internet-based fax service and typed in the number Liza had given him. He wrote:

> Liza;
>
> Don't worry about the Visas; I took care of everything with Diego's and Brent's help. Wherever you are and whatever you're doing, I wish you luck. If you need me, you know my

email address and phone number. Looks like
I will be in Costa Rica soon. Hope to see you
again, but if I don't, thanks for everything.

Regards;

Bachelor Number Nine

Out in the sunshine again, Roland hailed a taxi and
drove to his house. Once there the taxi driver looked at him
suspiciously, or was he imagining it? Upstairs, he sank onto
the couch and stared out the window at the ocean. He'd
forgotten how much he had missed that sight.

As he picked up his cell phone to start dialing his now
ex-coworkers, it rang. "Roland here."

"Roland, it's Grant. How are ya?"

Roland moved out onto the balcony. "Better than most,
but I don't know how long that will last. Things have really
fallen apart here. How's Cleveland?"

"Same as ever," he said, but Roland didn't know how
Cleveland usually was. "I can't get Maxine at the ranch in
Costa Rica and she's not answering her cell phone either,
but I have some things to tell you."

"Shoot."

Grant cleared his throat. "First thing, I found out who
was flying the plane that night. It wasn't Heinz."

"So this was nothing to do with him, then."

"It's doubtful. Also, I don't know if Maxine told you,
but the whole thing was sparked because our friend didn't
fill out his customs form properly."

"She mentioned something about it, but I don't think
she knew the whole story."

Dave the gecko crawled out of Roland's bedroom onto
the window ledge to see what the fuss was about.

"Neither did anyone else until recently," Grant continued.
"He had divided the checks into two piles totaling four
point five million. One was supposed to be banked in

327

Latvia, and the other was supposed to go somewhere else, New York maybe. Anyway, he wrote four point five on the form, crossed it off, wrote three million and then one point five to indicate the two different piles, then crossed them all off and handed it over after writing zero. Kinda started the customs guy wondering."

"*That* is what caused this mess?" Roland almost laughed.

"Apparently. Adrian says they altered his customs form after he handed it over, but he was pretty hammered at the time and it's his word against theirs. Anyway, I need a favor from you. Do you have a spare suitcase?"

Roland thought about how many things he had bought since moving to Mexico. He would have to buy more luggage anyway. "Yeah, sure."

"Please pack up all my stuff and bring it down to Costa Rica. Leave it at the house in Alajuela with Maxine and I'll pick it up."

Roland took the phone into Grant's room and examined the closets. He should be able to fit it all in one suitcase. As he looked, Grant said, "There's something else."

"And that is?"

"I talked to the charter brokerage. They told me a few interesting things, and I filled Maxine in the last time I talked to her, but there's something you should know because it concerns you."

Roland sat on Grant's bed, his throat tightening. "Yes?"

"The *federales* have the passenger manifests from the Learjet trips, so they have everybody's names. You show up because you took that flight to Costa Rica. So that could mean that they are looking for you."

Roland could feel his pulse quickening. "Is that the only reason my name shows up?"

"I think so. What do you mean?" Grant asked.

"I mean, what about the trip to Guadalajara?"

"What about it? I don't even know if they keep passenger records for domestic flights. I would assume they do, but nobody mentioned it to me. My advice either way is, get the hell out of there."

Roland swallowed, but his throat was so dry it seemed to take forever. "Thanks, Grant."

"Blue side up, kid."

The line went dead.

Roland reflected on Liza's avoidance of using Adrian's name on the phone. Roxane had said the Shack was being watched, which would be an obvious way of figuring out where people lived and who had a key, and it wasn't much of a leap to assume that its phone line was tapped. Would that mean that his was too? Roland closed the curtains on the way to his bedroom. He still had some battery power left in his cell phone so he dug out a notebook beside his bed and, upon reaching the number he wanted, keyed it in. It took a long time for the phone to start ringing. A memory floated into Roland's consciousness. It was Adrian, telling him about wishing he had been thinking more clearly when he left the Bahamas. Finally a young woman answered, "Nordstrom Mackie Law Office."

"Could I speak with Don Mackie, please."

"Sorry, sir, he's left for the day. I'll put you on to his assistant."

Another young woman answered. "Don Mackie's office."

"Hi, this is Roland Halliwell. I need to ask some advice."

The lady didn't know Roland, but her firm had handled legal matters for Roland's family for years. She recognized his name and said, "Sure, Mr. Halliwell. What can I do for you?"

Roland explained what he felt were the salient points of his situation. The lady sighed and said thoughtfully, "Well, it sounds to me as though they've already got who they want. The only thing I can really tell you with any degree of surety is to absolutely stay away from the police. I don't care if they're Mexicans, FBI, or representatives from the Consulate, they are not your friends. Their assumption is that if you even *look* peripherally involved that means you must be guilty of something, but if you've been honest with me that's not the case and the best thing to do is to just stay away." She tried to reassure Roland with a little humor. "Sounds like things are hotter way down there than I thought. It's snowing back home here."

"You can have it," Roland said. "Thanks for your help."

"Sorry I couldn't tell you more."

Roland had barely hung up when his phone rang again. It was Mick.

"Did you get home okay?" he asked.

"I'm fine."

"Is there anybody watching you?"

Roland looked around. Dave was walking up the wall beside the window, so technically that would be a yes. "No," he answered.

"Okay if Roxane and I come over for a bit?"

Roland shrugged. "Fine with me, but Roxane's staying in a hotel somewhere because she's too afraid to come here so I doubt she'll agree."

Mick nodded. "So am I. In a hotel, that is. Several people are. But it would be a good idea to get together."

"Can I ask you to do me a favor? Please call up Kevin, Eric, and Slogan and tell them that there's five thousand dollars coming to them on their Visas. Same with Roxane." That should keep him busy, Roland thought, while I call up some others. Mick agreed to do this, and said he and Roxane would be over shortly. Roland hung up.

Shelly answered her phone on the first ring. "Hello?"

"Shelly, it's Roland. I—"

"Roland! What's going on?"

"I don't know any more than you do. I just called to tell you that there's five grand on your card."

"What for?" It took her a while to speak. Obviously she was pretty high. Her voice was shaky.

"To get out of town with."

"It's that bad?" she asked plaintively.

"It's not that good." Roland's throat still felt taut. "I don't know how or why everything fell apart so completely, but it did, and now there's a mess to clean up."

"It's Mick, man. He's totally sketchy. I met up with him on Insurgentes and we went for coffee and he totally sketched me out, man, he's looking around everywhere and totally nervous, he's totally lost it."

"Must have been the coffee," Roland murmured, but Shelly didn't respond except to say, "I need to see you. Can we meet somewhere?"

Roland didn't really have time for that and said so. "Shelly, just stay at home for a while and don't answer the door unless you're expecting somebody, okay? I'm going to help move whatever we can to Costa Rica, and if you're needed there we'll bring you down."

"Am I in danger?"

Roland still didn't know how to answer this one. Staying away from the police sounded like the kind of advice a lawyer would only give to people in danger, but Shelly wasn't the one on the passenger manifest from a Learjet flight back and forth to Costa Rica. "I don't think so," he said, "but I'd act pretty surprised about the whole thing if somebody mentions it while you're wandering around Olas Altas. Who's in charge up here?"

"What do you mean?" Shelly asked after a pause.

"Well, who's in charge now? If Higgins is in the big house and Mick's lost it, who's playing Magnum?"

"Um, I guess maybe Ken or Sidney, but I don't know. Nobody knows anything. It's all just a fucking mess, man."

Her voice was rising so Roland cut her off. "Settle down, Shelly. None of this is your problem, okay? Just pick somewhere you've always wanted to go and stay there until the money runs out, and just stay at home until it's time to catch your flight there. By the time you come back things here should be straightened out. Our friend has been out of commission for several days already, and I think if anybody wanted you, you'd know about it by now."

This seemed to have the desired effect. "Okay," she said. "Okay."

Roland hung up, but his phone rang yet again. It was Kevin. "Where are we supposed to go with this five grand?" he asked.

"Wherever you want," Roland said. "Doesn't matter to me. I'm going back to Costa Rica tomorrow."

"Are you staying in Adrian's condo when you get there?"

"Yes."

Kevin paused, and then he said, "Is that smart? I mean, it's in his name, isn't it?"

"I'm not going to fork out my own money for living expenses just because Adrian fucked up," Roland snapped. "I'll ask Brent to set things up for extra visitors and I think it would be a good idea to see what we can do down there, if anything. There is the small matter of twenty-odd-thousand members to think about. But you're under no obligation to go."

There was a knock at the front door. Roland saw through the stained glass that it was Mick and Roxane. He let them in as Kevin asked, "Okay, I think Eric and I have decided to go down there. How can I help?"

Help? Kevin offering to help? Roland felt like saying, 'Wait a minute, I have to find a feather to knock myself over with', but instead he said, "How about phoning Jake in Baltimore and getting some info for flights down south?"

"Okay, I can do that."

"Good, because everybody will be phoning you for information."

Roland rang off and held up his cell phone. "That was Kevin. He was pretty panicky so I had to give him something to do." Hopefully these two would take the hint. His phone rang yet again. It was Brent.

"Hey, son, what's going on up there?"

"Not entirely sure yet, but it looks like it would be a good idea to arrange for hotel reservations for at least five or six people. Some of us will be coming down there. Did the Visa transaction get taken care of?"

"Yes," Brent said, "but it was kind of late. Diego called from the bank to say that he doesn't think the money will be available in Mexico for a couple of days."

"Okay, as long as it's done. Do you need anything from me?"

"Don't think so. Just keep in touch."

"Say hi to Janine for me. Oh, and keep a lookout for Maxine's friend Dolores. She should be there at the airport in a few hours, flying in from Mexico City on Mexicana. I don't know which flight number, but it's probably the only one."

"No problem. Will do. The only evening Mexicana flight from Mexico City."

"Right."

"*Gracias*, Roland."

"*De nada, amigo*."

After he hung up Roland looked at the phone, expecting it to ring again. The battery indicator was reading low. He placed the unit in the charger by his bed and joined Mick and Roxane in the livingroom.

"So," he said slowly as he sank onto the couch, "how are you two?"

"Should we go to Costa Rica?" Roxane asked.

Roland threw his hands up. "I don't know," he said. "I really don't care either. But if you're nervous here, then yes, go somewhere else. Brent is booking accommodations for more people down there because we won't all fit in the condo."

"I'll not stay there," Mick said. "It's in Adrian's name."

"Fine, stay where you like. Why did everything fall apart like this? Wasn't there any plan?"

Mick looked even more uncomfortable. He knew the blame for the post-arrest breakdown would rest on his shoulders, but he said nothing. Roland shifted the conversation to other topics and talked about what to expect in Costa Rica. Eventually Mick said, "Let's get together for breakfast tomorrow morning. Are you staying here tonight?"

"Damn right," Roland answered. "This is my house. I live here. Tomorrow I will leave, but I've been away for a week and I just want to sleep in my own bed."

"You're leaving tomorrow?" Roxane asked. "Where are you going?"

"Costa Rica," Roland replied. And if I have my way, he thought, all the drug users will be there too. The last thing anybody needs is for the police to obtain search warrants for employees' residences and find narcotics everywhere. That would be the end of Adrian for sure. "Give Kevin a call. He'll have all the information for you, and you two get yourselves down there."

They rose to leave, slightly calmer than when they'd arrived. They hadn't been gone fifteen minutes when Kevin called again and said, "We're all leaving tomorrow afternoon.

Me, Eric, Roxane and Mick. The flight goes to Mexico City and then down. You coming?"

"No, thanks. I'm going to take care of a few things here first, then I'll join you."

"Okay, man. Your funeral." Kevin hung up.

Evening came, and Roland walked down to Olas Altas for dinner. He ran into Shelly, who didn't seem much more composed than she had on the phone. She was sitting with her boyfriend, and she pretended to not even see Roland. This was okay with him. His nerves were becoming as frayed as the people he'd been talking to all day. He'd tried to call Amy to speak to Sidney, because Sidney never carried a cell phone himself, but she wasn't answering and it was likely that the two of them weren't even in town. One last time, he decided, and as he finished dinner on the sidewalk outside Papaya 3 he dialed Amy's number. To his surprise, she answered.

"Amy, it's Roland. How are you guys doing?"

"Not bad, I guess," she said. "You've heard everything?"

"I've heard that nobody has a clue what's going on, yes. Is Sidney around?"

"Um, he's kind of tired. Hang on," she said, and presently Sidney said, "Hey?"

Tired, my ass, Roland thought. He sounded pretty happy and Roland could hear him puffing on a joint. "Sidney, it's Roland. Need help with anything?"

Sidney coughed. "Yeah, that'd be great. I have to go up to the Shack and shred all those documents, or at least get them out. Ken's already taken the server but the paper files are still there."

"Shred them all?" Roland repeated.

"That's what I said. They've got to go." Roland remembered what Adrian had said about protecting the privacy of Cyberia members, and decided not to force the issue. "I'll meet you at the Shack tonight, then. Eleven o'clock?"

"Fine." Sidney hung up, but when eleven o'clock came that night and Roland let himself into the Shack there was no sign of anyone. He was still alone at midnight when he made himself a snack and enjoyed a Cohiba and a glass of twenty-year-old Taylor Fladgate. He had looked around for the paper shredder, but mostly he went through all the desks to make sure there wasn't a hint of marijuana anywhere. During the process he found all sorts of interesting things downstairs, including a small collection of adult magazines with a bent towards the bizarre under the mattress in the Octopussy room, but Ken had been thorough and there was little to do except leave the three bottles of coffee liqueur Roland had bought in Costa Rica for the house staff. He scrawled a note in Spanish and put it with the liqueur in the laundry room.

Wearily he trudged back home. If anyone was watching the Shack they would know who he was and where he lived, and that was just fine with him. The defiant and exhausted mood he was in meant that he couldn't have cared less.

On the way to breakfast in Mick's jeep the next morning, Roland's cell phone rang. It was Sidney. Roland didn't ask where he'd been the previous night. If he didn't care enough to shred the files, neither did Roland. Besides, his dad was fighting off tarantulas and decomposing in an anonymous Latin American jail and there were probably other things on his mind.

"The computers are still at the Shack. Everyone who's going to Costa Rica has to take one," he instructed.

Roland frowned as he relayed this piece of news to Mick, who just laughed.

"Courier them down, Sid," Roland told him. "Nobody I know is even going to take a hard drive in their luggage, let alone an entire CPU. Personally, I haven't done anything illegal, and apart from sticking around to find out if he's going to be let out I want to keep it that way."

Sidney knew who 'he' was, of course, but Roland's objection didn't improve his mood. "I've been at the Shack all morning," he complained, "packing up Tatiana's van with files. They have to go to Vista del Sol, but I don't have a driver's license. Can you take it?"

Roland wanted to laugh. Worrying about having a driver's license to ferry paperwork for about five miles seemed about as important as making sure one's boots were polished before taking a guided tour of the Paris sewers. And why did the files have to go to an apartment block? However, Roland had nothing else to do and until he was officially notified otherwise, he was still on the payroll. "Sure," Roland said, "I can drive it down there."

"You can do that, huh?" Sidney's sarcasm suddenly bit through in his voice.

"Do I need to say it twice? I'll drive the fucking van."

Sidney simmered down. "There's a guy named Jim who's staying at Garrett's old place," he continued. Interesting that it was already Garrett's 'old' place, Roland noted. If he'd thought any further he would have realized that it also meant that Garrett wasn't coming back. "He's got some kind of disease and he sleeps a lot but wake him up and tell him you have the files. He'll help you carry them up. He knows what's going on."

Good thing somebody does, Roland said to himself as Mick parked the van. He closed the phone without saying goodbye and followed Mick to an upstairs restaurant on the Malecon, where neither of them spoke until Mick said he wanted to go to Sam's to buy some suitcases.

"Can I come with you?" Roland asked. "I need some too." So they paid their bill and left, and at Sam's they bought the last two sets of five-piece luggage. Once outside Mick asked if Roland would mind taking a taxi home. This was no surprise to Roland. He tapped on the door of a car waiting at the stand whose driver was engrossed in a newspaper. The man dropped him off at the house and offered to help him carry the box upstairs but Roland declined, pressing fifty pesos into his hand. Standard taxi fare anywhere in PV was thirty pesos. His cell phone beeped and he saw the 'Mail Waiting' icon illuminated.

Upstairs he retrieved the message, and then dialed Adrian's ranch in Costa Rica. Maxine answered.

"Maxine, it's Roland here. You should expect Kevin, Eric, Mick and Roxane on the evening flight from Mexico City, on Mexicana. Can you make sure someone meets them?"

Maxine had been drinking, but no matter how much she'd had she always remembered things like this. "Yeah," she said slowly. "Dolores and I will go, or maybe Gino. I'll send Gino for you."

"I won't be coming with them," he said. "Not for another couple of days."

"Why not?"

Roland didn't want to make bad things worse or give Maxine cause for worry, but he also had no time to paint a flowery picture. "Because I don't want to have anything to do with any of them if I can possibly avoid it until I'm down there. The police could be looking for any one of us, or all of us, and I see no reason to travel together. Besides, those guys are making me nervous as hell and it's hot enough here as it is. And I don't know how smart these people are when clearing customs and all of them except Mick do drugs."

"Right." Maxine sounded quite sober all of a sudden. "I agree. So where are you going to be coming from?"

Roland debated whether or not to tell her. The email from Jake he'd retrieved off his phone had spelled out the best route to take given Roland's request – a flight that left for the southern US today, and information on regular flights going from there to Costa Rica that did not land anywhere in Mexico. There weren't many. In the end he decided it would be best to have at least somebody know where he was in case things went even more wrong.

"I'm going up to Los Angeles," he said, "and then down through a layover in Guatemala City. I don't want to land in Mexico if I can avoid it. The only time I want to deal with a Mexican airport is when I'm leaving here."

"Okay. You take care, Roland. See you soon. Call if you have a problem."

Maxine hung up. Roland wondered if she was in the middle of making espresso for Dolores fifteen hundred miles away, but decided that instead she was probably pouring them both another martini.

He tore open the box the luggage had come in, strewing the packing materials all over the livingroom. After cramming Grant's belongings into one suitcase he set about packing his own things. When he was done he set the bags by the door and grabbed his keys.

He slipped in to the Shack and closed both doors behind him. Making his way to the garage, he saw Tatiana's blue minivan stuffed full of boxes of files and the keys on the driver's seat. He searched the console for the garage door opener, but it wasn't there. Glovebox? Not there either. Nor was there an Explorer parked beside it with the button in the visor.

He went back to the kitchen and sifted through the items on the sideboard where Adrian usually tossed things of daily significance. Not there. Nor was it on the counter where it could have been sharing space with some stale bread covered in tiny brown ants. He did, however, spy a set of keys to Sidney's speedboat. On an impulse he pocketed them.

He stood there, hesitating. He could press the button on the garage door opener itself, but he didn't want to leave the van on the narrow street as he got out to close it again. In fact, he didn't want to get out of the van even for a second until someone met him at Vista del Sol.

Turning his attention back to the sideboard he began rummaging through the drawers, starting on the left. It held an envelope of pictures of Adrian and Maxine on a beach with some people Roland didn't recognize, plus two rolls of tape and a pair of scissors. The next drawer along hosted paper clips, freezer bags, and an unopened Ginsu knife. Christ, Roland thought, if Adrian was less rich there would be a lot fewer drawers to waste my time on. He came to the last drawer on the right and by this time was becoming agitated and nervous. The drawer stuck halfway open – or would that be halfway closed? – and he put his hand in to rustle around between old calculators and pens given away by Swiss banks.

His hand closed around what looked to be a group of bankbooks. He rocked the drawer from side to side and succeeded in freeing it. It pulled out easily but not before he caught his finger in the runner. A drop of blood appeared. He put it to his mouth and opened one of the bankbooks.

There was only one deposit recorded, and it was for two million dollars. The next bankbook's deposit was for one million, and it was the same story with four others. All were bearer books, meaning anyone in possession of the books could claim the money in the accounts. The logos on the covers said things like 'CreditSuisse' and 'Banco Prima', and some contained a lot more than two million dollars. Roland yanked the drawer out and dumped the contents onto the marble floor. As he sifted through the holiday brochures and matchbooks his hand closed around another passbook, this one wrapped in a piece of paper and held with a rubber band. He broke the rubber band in his haste to remove it and cast the paper aside to look at the bank balance. Unlike the others, this was not a bearer book. It recorded only one deposit, for six hundred thousand dollars, at a bank in the Bahamas. Roland retrieved the paper from the floor and unfolded it.

The afternoon sun was reflecting off the patio and dancing on the water in the pool. The window walls were open, and a slight breeze wandered through the house and over the paper Roland was holding.

It took a few seconds for him to understand what he was looking at, and when he finally did, he slid down with his back to the cabinet because his knees were suddenly incapable of holding him up any longer.

It was a photocopy of a passport; one he knew well, but the picture was not his. His name was the same, as was his address, but the likeness was of someone else.

For a long time Roland sat there in the empty palace on the marble floor, watching the sun sparkling on the ocean and listening to the surf and thinking, *Where have I seen this man before?*

Eventually he dug out the pictures he'd seen in the far left drawer, but none of the faces matched. I *know* I've seen this man before, he thought. *Somewhere.* He began ransacking each drawer, this time wrenching them all out in turn and emptying them onto the floor. His dumbfounded shock turned to near panic when the doorbell rang. Startled, he knocked over a huge stained-glass vase and only caught it an inch before it hit the floor.

The intercom television monitor revealed two tall men at the door. Both were white and one was wearing a baseball cap. Roland couldn't tell from where he was what the three initials on the cap said, but he had a pretty good idea. He grabbed the bankbook and sprinted to the bedroom behind the laundry room. Throwing the door open, he vaulted down the stairs only to return to close the door behind him. He flipped the light switch but nothing happened. Ken's friends may have changed the breaker but they hadn't bothered with the light bulb.

He didn't realize how hard he was breathing until he tried to calm himself down on the stairwell by putting his hand on his chest. Then he heard a rustling sound on the step by his feet.

He sent out a sandaled foot to feel around, but it touched nothing. The doorbell rang again and now someone was reaching through the bars to knock on the inside door. The rustling became accompanied by a light scraping sound. Roland gingerly descended the steps. His eyes had adjusted enough to the darkness to see the crack of light coming from under the door at the bottom of the stairs and he used that as his guide, feeling along the clammy concrete wall. At the bottom he put his hand on the doorknob and turned it slowly. The doorbell had stopped ringing. Did those people know there was a door down here? Roland pushed but it didn't open. He pulled on it instead and blinding midday light appeared. The rustling grew louder. Quickly he closed the door as a vehicle approached, and when it was gone he waited, his heart pounding, before easing it open again.

Two scorpions stood within six inches of his foot, navigating the last step, and even as he watched the creatures tumbled over the edge. He pulled his foot away and flung the door open. The scorpions, drawn by the light, scurried for the opening.

Roland began to laugh. Mostly it was nervous laughter, but he also found it amusing that scorpions had to take the stairs like everybody else. "After you," he said, and when the creatures had scuttled outside he followed them. One of them disappeared under the house and the other stood there, waving its stinger at Roland.

Seeing no one, Roland closed the door behind him and crossed the street to approach his gate. He pretended to be fumbling with his keys as he regained his composure and decided what to do next. Sidney had mentioned someone staying at Ken and Garrett's place. Ken might still be there, even if…Jim, that was his name…wasn't. So Roland started walking down to Olas Altas and hailed the first cab that came along. Five minutes later he was waving to the doorman and leaping up the stairs at Vista del Sol.

"Jim!" He banged on the door. "You there? Wake up. Jim?"

After about a minute of this a man with white hair and a faded red shirt appeared. Roland introduced himself and said he needed Adrian's red Explorer, which he'd seen parked outside.

"Sure," said Jim, holding the door open. "Sidney told me I'd be hearing from you."

"Well, we need to take the vehicle up there and use the garage door opener in it." Roland told him about the two men at the door, but that was all. No need to mention the discovery in the junk drawer of several million dollars' worth of bankbooks and evidence of a forged passport.

As they cruised up Paseo de los Delfines Jim said, "Sounds like it's best if we take a drive by first, and circle the block to see if those guys are still around."

There was nobody in front of the Shack. Roland was about to give the all clear when he noticed the same two men he'd seen on the intercom monitor. This time they were talking through the gate to a woman at Mick's condo building. "Bad news," Roland said. "Those were the guys, and the building they're at is where Mick lives. Also Tatiana has an office there."

"Does that say what I think it says?" Jim murmured as they passed, glimpsing the initials on the man's ball cap as he turned to talk to his partner. Then louder he said, "We'll take care of this later."

"I won't be here later," said Roland. "I'm leaving today."

Jim nodded. "Don't worry about it then. Ken and Sidney are still around. Let's take some different files instead."

Roland was about to ask what he meant, but it became clear when Jim parked the Explorer on the street behind Mick's condo. "You used to live here," Jim said flatly. "You still have keys?"

Roland nodded.

"Then let's take these files at least."

"What files? And what if that woman lets the two guys into this building?"

"She won't," Jim said, though he didn't sound very sure. Roland dug out his key ring and soon he found himself at Mick's door, sweating from the few flights of stairs. Jim wheezed noisily behind him.

Roland opened the huge wooden door to see that the livingroom was just as full of file caddies as the accounting office had been. He whistled as Jim closed the door.

"When did all these walk up the street?"

Jim was leaning against the counter and coughing. "Same night everything else happened," he managed to say.

Roland looked around in distress at the mess Mick's apartment had become. He headed for the stairs, leaving Jim to catch his breath.

Upstairs he found his old bedroom untouched. He spent a precious few seconds staring out at the bay and tried to remember how it had been on his first day, holding back the curtains for the first glimpse of his new home in daylight. For a fleeting moment he felt nothing but an insatiable sadness, a melancholy at the multitude of brief and incongruous snapshots of lives he had lived over such a short time that they didn't even feel as though they were his own.

More lies, more confusion, more misplaced trust, more of what I came to get away from. I must have known it would end, he thought, but I never imagined it would end like this.

Back downstairs he found Jim still leaning over the counter. The man shook his head. "I can't do a goddamn thing today. We have to go."

He drove them back down to Olas Altas and parked the Explorer. He seemed to know Vallarta fairly well. "Do you want to stick around here for a while?" he asked. "Your place is up there by Adrian's, right?"

"Right in front of it," Roland answered. "We drove by it on the way to Mick's. Thanks but I think I'm just going to have a beer on the beach and then head out."

"Where you going?"

"Costa Rica, eventually," Roland said, and thanked Jim for his help. Leaning in the car window after he closed the door, he said, "Jim, why did you come down here?"

Jim coughed again. "Friend of Adrian's," he said, as though that explained everything, and drove away.

Roland watched him go. Actually, he thought with a wry smile, that did explain everything.

He found a table at a beach bar and guzzled two Pacíficos before his lunch arrived. Wolfing it down, he left a two-hundred-peso note on the table and jumped into a cab without waking up the driver first.

"*Paseo del Sol, por favor, amigo,*" he said. When the bleary-eyed driver woke up fully – only after moving into traffic, Roland noticed – he started saying things like, "*Una mujer es como una manzana.*" Roland tried to listen to why the man felt that a woman was like an apple, but the language was over his head and the beer and the heat were taking their toll. All he really wanted was sleep. He did manage to understand that the driver had decided women were beautiful and enticing on the outside, but at the core were really rotten and hosting all manner of worms. Funny, Roland thought. Perhaps in the taxi headed the opposite way was a woman describing how men were like apples.

Roland asked the driver to wait while he retrieved his bags. Seven suitcases later the car's suspension looked as though Maxine had been at it with a credit card. Because both the trunk and the back seat were full Roland sat up front. The driver started talking about women again.

Roland was not interested in the slightest. He was studying the Spanish newspaper he had found on the seat. He couldn't read every word of it, but what he understood was clear enough.

On the front page was a picture of Adrian and Mack being escorted somewhere by the police. The caption included the four-point-five-million-dollar figure, the word *extranjeros* – foreigners – and Guillermo's full name. Roland hadn't known his last name until then. His heart was pounding like crazy and he realized he was sweating uncontrollably. The driver babbled on, completely oblivious. As Roland skimmed the article he saw 'FBI', 'Interpol', and the US Consulate mentioned several times, as well as his home town. Then he saw the name of Adrian's house, *Castillo Paraiso*, and the name of the house Roland lived in, *Casa Constrella*. He folded the paper so that the middle page was now the front. If the driver had read the article he had forgotten the name of Roland's house, which was good, because it was on a decorative tile plaque right beside the gate, and if he hadn't; well, that was even better.

At the airport Roland went straight to the Delta counter. He had intentionally left the ticket purchase until the last minute, and was hurried through security as the friendly Mexicans told him not to cut it so close next time. "Thank you for visiting Puerto Vallarta, sir," one said. It made Roland want to cry. He already felt like enough of a Judas, slinking around and hiding from people he had come to love.

He had been only too glad to check all his luggage except one carry-on case which, as usual, contained his toothbrush and a change of clothes. That and a bearer's bankbook with a balance of over half a million dollars. He'd left the photocopy on Adrian's floor, but that was okay. If anyone found it and questioned him, one look at Roland and his genuine passport would be enough for them to see that the other was a fake.

Besides, he thought as the hostess set a glass of champagne and passionfruit juice in front of him, he didn't need the photocopy anyway. He had remembered who the man in the picture was.

At the United Airlines counter Roland booked a ticket for the eleven-thirty flight to San Jose, Costa Rica. Or at least, he tried to, but his five thousand dollars hadn't made its way to the US Visa system yet.

He debated whether or not to call Jake and ask him to dip into the Cyberia kitty at his agency, but after a quick search of his luggage he remembered that he'd thrown away the paper on which he'd written Jake's pager number. He tried to retrieve it from his cell phone's memory but the battery was completely dead. While he was at it, he collected every scrap of paper he could find that might link him to Cyberia and threw it all in a trash can outside the terminal. The thought of paying for the ticket out of his own money crossed his mind, but he was unsure when he would be paid next, if at all, and in the end it seemed too big a gamble.

He called the ranch. A drunken Dolores answered, and Roland's urgency only served to fluster her. In the end she said she would call Gino and they would go to the airport together to pay for his ticket there, and he was to phone back in forty-five minutes. By this time the sun had set.

She answered again when Roland called back, but she had no good news. The United Airlines counter in San Jose had insisted that prepaying a ticket was impossible. "He's new, obviously, and he was the only one there," she said in apologetic disgust. In the meantime Roland had called the Visa office in San Jose and had been informed that in fact no deposit had been made at all yesterday. He told Dolores about this and asked her to look into it.

"I'll get a hotel here," Roland said. "Don't worry about it. I'll call Diego tomorrow afternoon and see where I stand. As long as you remember to make sure he sets it straight I should see you within three days. I've got to go; my long distance card is running out." They both hung up.

Roland knew he was in a pretty unique situation, but what intrigued him most wasn't that he was still guided more by loyalty to Adrian or a need for adventure than by common sense, or even that it would be just as easy to go back home as it would be to continue to Costa Rica as planned but that for a multitude of reasons he didn't want to. What truly astounded him was that somehow Adrian knew the only alcoholics in the world who could remember every last detail of a phone conversation while too drunk to stand up.

Outside in the cold night air he flagged down a passing hotel shuttle. The driver raised an eyebrow upon seeing Roland's luggage but didn't comment as he helped him heave it onto the rack behind him. The bar was practically deserted apart from two men gawking at a table of stewardesses singing along to Jimmy Buffett and David Lindley songs. All the smokers were hanging around outside complying with some bylaw or other. He would have joined them with a cigar, but he'd smoked his last one at the abandoned Shack waiting for Sidney. That made him smile. Perhaps if Sidney was an alcoholic he would have remembered to show up. Roland signed the bill for his meal and disappeared upstairs to his room with a copy of the LA *Times*, but he fell asleep before even so much as glancing at the headlines.

The next evening he checked out, thoroughly unimpressed with the hotel's sullen personnel, but at least this time there was no problem with his ticket at the United desk and the staff were the same people who had been there the previous night. Not only had they set the record straight with the crew in San Jose but they gave him a certificate good for a night's stay in one of four airport hotels next time he was in Los Angeles. Roland thought that was very decent of them considering that the previous evening's debacle could hardly be considered their fault. In return he gave them some Costa Rican currency as a souvenir for their kids.

He made a purchase at a gift shop and entered the sumptuous first class lounge. After hunting through the papers there and finding Reuters and UPI articles about Adrian, both saying roughly the same things, he sank down into an inviting leather chair and turned his attention to his day-old copy of the Times.

There was a short article buried near the horoscopes (*Wednesday, April 24. Sagittarius – Be mindful of erratic people who may interfere with career or travel plans. You are coming out of a difficult but important phase. An older person figures prominently*) which relayed the facts as Roland knew them – in other words, sketchily at best. Still there was nothing to indicate that anyone had proven that Cyberia, or Hammer for that matter, was involved in anything illegal; just more speculation on the part of the police.

Well, that was to be expected, Roland thought as he tossed the paper aside and helped himself to a coffee from the bar. You didn't just let somebody land in the middle of the night with several million dollars wedged in next to his clean underwear and send him on his way with a Viagra lollipop.

17
Black Sand

The approach to Guatemala's capital was almost as interesting as the one into Hong Kong's old airport, where fifty yards off the wingtips people used to hang laundry between their apartment buildings and yell into their phones above the roar of passing 747s. Burdened by luggage that wasn't even all his and cheerless at the notion of leaving his home in Puerto Vallarta, Roland checked into a hotel for a couple of days of reflection before continuing his trip. In the dawn light as the aircraft taxied for takeoff, he saw old World War Two fighters and DC-3 transports stripped of their engines, and as the pilot pivoted the airliner on one wheel to turn it around he looked out his window to see why the taxiing had taken so long. Evidently Guatemala City had no taxiway, and if the winds favored a takeoff from the opposite end of the runway to where the airplanes were parked at the terminal, the runway doubled as a taxiway. Also the terrain sloped so erratically that from one end of the runway it was impossible to see the other. As the engines whined and the pilot released the brakes, Roland almost wished he hadn't noticed that.

Brent met him at the airport and tried his key in the wrong cherry-red SUV when they got to the parking lot. During Roland's absence he had bought a set of rain guards for the side windows, which almost every vehicle there had, and the Nissan Pathfinder looked close enough to fool him. Roland said, "What's wrong, Dad? Did you trash the Blazer?" as he waited right beside it.

"Not a word to Janine about this." Brent filled the back with Roland's suitcases.

It was relaxing to be near someone who wasn't panicking all the time, and Roland asked Brent to fill him in on what was happening at Cyberia's office in San Jose.

"Bugger-all," Brent told him. "Nick didn't return to Belize. He's been here with us, and the checks are still coming in. Slowly now, though."

"Did the others make it down okay?"

Brent nodded. "Yeah, they're here."

Roland rolled down the window and reached for some roasted nuts that were in the console. Janine bought them by the truckload. "You don't sound too impressed."

Brent handed the change from his parking fee to Roland, who dumped it in the console where the paper cone of nuts had been. After navigating onto the highway – with expert skill, Roland noticed – Brent said, "I kind of don't know why they're here."

"Same reason all the rest of us are here, isn't it? To keep Cyberia going? I mean, somebody has to run the show. I know what Maxine said about it being shut down, but we've still got thousands of members and the money's still coming in."

"Right," said Brent. "So you'd think they'd want to help out. But they don't want to go near the office, they don't want to stay at the condo, they just want to stay away. At least, that's how it looks to me."

"I find that hard to believe. If they really wanted to stay away, they would have gone to Europe or something. Give them time. They'll settle down."

"Well, I don't know." Brent took his eyes off the road for a second to glance at Roland as they drove over a speed bump. "Adrian doesn't think it's a good idea for them to be around anyway."

"You've talked to him? How is he?"

They came to an intersection where five busy roads converged. Brent sped into an opening as soon as it appeared and they were on their way again.

"Not too bad," he said. "But he wants us to just bank the checks as they come in and keep maintaining records of who's invested and so on, so that when he gets back we can pay the dividends and sort all this mess out."

"He'll be released soon?" Roland asked dubiously. He didn't like talking this way. He had known a girl whose husband was always in jail and she was always talking about when he would get out. He never did. Absently he wondered what Adrian would make of that, given his dim view of the legal system.

Brent shrugged as they passed by the US ambassador's house. "Well, the first bunch of lawyers he hired asked for a million-dollar retainer, which Adrian paid. After five days they showed up in new suits and new cars but hadn't filed a single piece of paper with the court and had barely interviewed him, so he fired them. Now he's got somebody else. Nobody knows what the situation really is." Gee, thought Roland, things sure have changed. "Adrian appointed Ken in charge of Vallarta, and he's still there," Brent continued. "Where's your buddy Slogan?"

"He's still in Veeyarda," Roland replied. "I'm not worried about him. He always kept to himself anyway and I think he's on an impromptu vacation." He was surprised that Brent knew Slogan even existed, much less that he was Roland's friend.

They passed the guard at the condo building's gate, near which a man stood with a small camera, and parked in the covered lot under their tower. They left Grant's suitcase in the Blazer for the next trip out to the ranch, and carried the rest into the main bedroom. Roland unzipped a suitcase and stared absently at its contents.

Brent looked at Roland for a minute. He said, "It really is over up there, isn't it?"

Roland didn't want to admit it, but he had to. He opened the window as far as it would go. He wasn't used to being closed off to the outside.

He wanted to tell Brent that leaving Vallarta had been a nerve-wracking experience and that he finally understood movies about people being hunted for crimes they didn't commit and having nowhere to go, and about the newspaper story in the cab and Interpol's interest in Adrian, and about his forged passport and over half a million dollars in his name. He wanted to tell him how terrified everyone had been, and how he had left several million dollars' worth of bankbooks scattered on Adrian's kitchen floor upon being disturbed by two men, one of whose cap had almost certainly read 'FBI'. In the end he said none of these things. All he said was, "The best that we can do is try and make some sense out of what's left."

Brent nodded. "There's a meeting tomorrow morning at nine. I did at least get everyone to agree to come to the office for that. I'm going out to the ranch tonight but Janine's going to stay here. Why don't you two go for dinner?"

Roland said he'd consider it and then went to the gym for a workout, after which he crawled into the hot tub and stared up at the sun. He was annoyed that lately he always seemed to be tired.

He wondered how much calmer everyone would be after settling in down here. As for himself, he still couldn't fully explain why he hadn't decided to pull a Liza and disappear. With the San Jose office crowded now, the main problem wasn't keeping Cyberia going long enough to wrap it up, it was what to do with the extraneous staff, of which Roland couldn't help feeling that he was a member. Not that he would mind. He had money and he had time, and with them as his companions he could explore Costa Rica at his leisure. Mostly, though, he hung around because he didn't want to admit that yet another endeavor in his life had crashed and burned, rather spectacularly this time. Good thing Sara wasn't around. He'd never have heard the end of it.

Well, perhaps that wasn't entirely fair. Sara had never complained when things he did had annoyed or hurt her. She wasn't a complainer – directly, anyway – she was a boiler, someone whose frustrations simmered in a miasma of emotion until finally the top blew off, scattering chaos absolutely everywhere. Roland wondered if her new husband really knew what he was getting himself into.

His line of thought was interrupted by a slender man in his late forties who nodded at him as he stepped down into the hot tub. He didn't have much of a tan and was sweating profusely. He said, "Hi."

"Hi."

"Day off?" the man asked.

"Every day is a day off lately," Roland replied. The man looked completely out of his element. "Was that you over by the guardhouse with the camera?"

"Oh, ah, yeah, that was me. Nice place, isn't it?"

Roland squinted at him. The condo hotel was nice, yes, but on the other side of the twenty-foot wall bordering it were buildings worthy of the abandoned Bronx. Hardly the kind of photogenic material people usually looked for to put in travel brochures. And why would he ask if Roland had a day off instead of assuming he was a tourist, as most did? Something about this man was just plain wrong.

"Time for me to go," Roland said. "Nice to meet you." He got out of the hot tub and dried off on his way to the condo.

At the beginning of April, on a night Roland had gone for dinner at the No Name Café with the rest of the Cyberia crew, Eric had mentioned that he used to manage an adult video store. Roland had also managed a store in the same chain many years ago, where gay men occasionally made passes at him. None of the women ever did, much to his chagrin, but Roland wondered now if that's what the man in the hot tub had been doing. Could be, he thought, as he unpacked his shirts into the vast closet. Why couldn't the man have been Miss April instead, or at least the cutie at the PV airport?

His hair dried and his clothes put away, he looked at his watch. Four o'clock. He made a quick call up to Janine to make some plans for dinner and began reading a novel he'd bought at Starbooks along with the very last Señor Book's t-shirt ever sold.

Janine's driving had improved even more than Brent's. She wanted to do some shopping so they wandered around the Multi Plaza, and after dinner they went to her place for drinks until Brent and Nick came home. They had no news of Adrian so Roland brought a peanut butter sandwich out to the hot tub where he at it very slowly, alone, before going in to bed.

At the office the next morning, Roland, Brent, and Janine wandered in to find Mick, Roxane, Eric, and Kevin already there talking to Diego and Franco. They didn't look any more relaxed than the last time Roland had seen them, although Kevin bragged that their hotel was the same one in which the King of Spain stayed when he visited.

Roland shook Mick's hand, the other behind his back. "I got something for you," he said. A package of beef jerky from the shop at LAX dangled from his fingers. "I forgot last time."

Mick's mood changed a little and Yoda became ecstatic, as he got the first nibble. When everyone was seated, Brent brought the meeting to order.

It quickly became apparent that the main concern on everyone's mind was not that Cyberia had officially dissolved on the night Adrian was arrested, or even the fact that Adrian was in jail, but that the ride was over. No more high salaries and houses with swimming pools.

Roland didn't say a word all through the meeting except when addressed, but he was secretly glad that the others had brought up concerns about their personal finances. He studied them each intently, but there was no hint that any one of them might be reassured by the presence of a nice nest egg socked away in the Caribbean. Each of the four who had come down together from Vallarta were making noise about some kind of payout that Adrian had promised everyone. This was the first Roland had heard of it. He'd never been promised anything.

Nothing got resolved that day but Brent made notes anyway, jotting down who had reluctantly agreed to perform which function in an attempt to organize the situation. When the meeting was over they all stepped out for a coffee at the little shop in the square, and when everyone but Brent, Roland and Janine had gone and the three had returned to the office, Brent approached Roland and said, "Do you know who took that piece of paper?"

"What piece of paper?"

"The one I wrote down everyone's names and duties on. It's gone."

Roland chewed on a piece of gum and stared at the blank pad as he sat down. "Probably Mick, is my guess."

"Why would he do that?"

Roland bit his lip. "Brent, pulling out of Vallarta was like getting out of a city falling to the enemy. In the cab on the way to the airport the driver had a newspaper opened to a page that mentioned my house, mine and Roxane's. Somebody really *is* watching the Shack, that's no exaggeration, and nobody's in control because Liza took off and Mick fell apart. So there's nowhere to go and nobody has any answers. Maybe he figures it's safest not to have his name written down or something. I don't know. But they've all been abandoned, their boss is in jail and they're just plain scared."

Brent studied Roland for a little while and asked, "How come you're not?"

Roland laughed. "I am, I guess, but I'm more curious than scared. But that's just me."

"Are you saying these people have done something illegal? And why do you call them 'they' instead of 'we'?"

Roland thought about this. "I never identified with any of them, except Mick and Roxane. I'm worried about Mick, but there's nothing we can do about him. Sooner or later he'll wake up. And if they've done anything illegal then it's possible that so have I. So have you." He leaned back in his chair. "I suppose I'm having fun playing at being wanted, but I don't think I am."

Brent looked at the floor. Eventually he said, "You know what? I want you to hang around for a while in case I need you. I want the rest to keep to themselves. I want the office closed to everybody but me, Janine, and Diego and Franco. And Nick too."

It was the first time Roland had seen Brent make a decision. He nodded and said, "If you need me, I'll be around."

The days went by, and Roland spent many of them either in the hotel gym or wandering around San Jose with Nick, who grumbled about Maxine monopolizing Gino all the time. Eventually he hired his own driver who had a white minivan, a man named Mario. This coincided roughly with the refugee Cyberians deciding that staying at the expensive hotel wasn't that great after all. One morning when Roland was on his way out to the gym, Kevin waltzed in holding up a card key from the front desk. His other hand was folded across his chest.

"I am Nintendo from the far Atari nebula, son of Coleco and sworn enemy of Sega," he announced. "Got a spare room?"

Yoda followed with Roxane in tow, and Eric's priceless mountain bike clicked as he wheeled it around the corner. Mick looked sheepish as he dropped a suitcase by the door.

"Um, okay," Roland said. "I guess Roxane can have the big bedroom; it's got its own bathroom. I'll move into the smaller one, and there's a third one with two twin beds at the end of the hall. Plus there's a couch." He felt a pang of guilt at the fact that he resented having his domain invaded.

After his workout he ran into Nick, sitting on the balcony outside the breakfast room cradling a coffee. He pulled out a chair. "No news from Adrian or Mack, I suppose," he said.

"Nothing new. Roland, I want to ask you something."

"Shoot."

"I'm too afraid to go back to Belize by myself. It's a scary fuckin' place. Brother Mack and I were almost robbed a couple of times and I don't want to go back alone."

Roland gulped down a glass of grapefruit juice, which normally he disliked, but he had mistaken it for orange while chatting up the elderly maid as she restocked the danishes and decided to live with his error. "And?"

"And, nobody has paid the shipping company for the last two months. It's a thousand measly fuckin' dollars a month plus expenses for them to forward mail here, and nobody has paid them. They're threatening to return all the envelopes to the senders if they don't get their money. Will you come with me if I have to go back there?"

"What's stopping Brent from raiding the petty cash drawer?"

Nick snorted. "It ain't that simple. This would have to be done in person or not at all, I'd say. The Belizean police have already been all over this guy. They even came to see me when I worked there. They made me open a courier envelope right in front of them but thank God it was only a letter."

"You serious?"

"Yeah. Not only that, the courier company doesn't want anything to do with us any more anyway. I had to bribe their guy to carry the last few shipments into the plane's cargo bay himself because the baggage handlers wouldn't do it. Somebody's scared them into not dealing with us."

The maid brought Roland an orange juice. The dregs, of course, as the staff was clearing the buffet, but such was life. "So what's going on now?"

Nick shrugged and adjusted his immaculate white baseball cap. "They want more money, I guess. I don't know."

"That's not exactly what I mean. With you not around to bribe the guy, how are the checks still coming in?"

"They aren't. They did for a while afterward, but they've stopped now."

Roland drained his glass and handed it back to the maid. "Really?"

"Really."

Roland shrugged. He stared out onto the parking lot and said, "Then it doesn't matter whether you go back or not, does it?"

"I was hoping you wouldn't say that." Nick scratched his chin and sighed, leaning back into his chair. "What a fucking mess. I don't know how the hell I'm supposed to get that truck home from Mexico either."

"The one parked at my place? I'll drive it back if you like." Nick looked surprised, but Roland continued, "Not for a while, but I could use another adventure." He didn't want to admit that he wasn't ready to face going home just yet. "Beats vegetating by the pool and waiting for thirty-one."

"Years?"

Roland nodded.

"Just a kid."

Timeless melancholy seemed to color the sunlight and follow the little group everywhere. Adrian was no closer to getting out than he'd ever been, and on top of that his health was failing rapidly. Guillermo was released, much to everyone's relief, but the other two stayed behind at the Puente Grande Federal Penitentiary in Guadalajara drinking whisky and probably making license plates in their spare time. Which, Roland reflected, was one of the few things they had a lot of.

Nick and Roland continued investigating San Jose with Mario, who showed them all kinds of interesting places, and Mick began accompanying them as well. One day after a late lunch Mario said, seemingly out of nowhere, "I will take us to the highest place in Costa Rica, a volcano. I think you will like it." So off they went, and the city traffic was replaced by serene and narrow mountain roads.

With five minutes to go, they pulled up at a park gate. At first the guard waved them away, saying they were closed, but after an exchange of words with Mario and some financial incentive, they were allowed through.

A huge expanse of black volcanic rock in the form of miniscule pebbles and grains of dark sand lay in a gently sloping curve around the eastern edge of a plateau. This was a volcano named Irazu, twelve thousand feet above sea level and one of the few places where one could see both the Pacific Ocean and the Caribbean Sea. True to the claim, both oceans lay between the peaks on the horizons like pastel crayons melting into the cracks in a sidewalk.

They reached the edge of the volcano and stared down into its mouth. Around the rim lay brown and black rock, and the occasional bird hovered soundlessly above. At the bottom of the volcano was a beautiful turquoise lake, so flat and calm that it was impossible to tell if it was made of thin greenish-blue ice or was unfathomably deep. The color revealed nothing of what lay beneath it. Roland followed the railing along the plateau until he was as far away from the parking lot as he could get.

He didn't know how long he stood there on that endless black sand beach high up in the mountains. He just stared into the turquoise jewel far below him and thought of Sara and her imminent engagement.

He had spent some time lately reflecting on the nature of predestiny, and his personal experience with it was leaving him undecided. He had known that he would lose Sara since the day they met. He had even known how, because his dreams weren't like the dreams that other people had. They were scripts, stories, glimpses of the future or unknown people's pasts, as though he were a radio and he had tuned in to listen to the frequency that would one day bring him here. Years ago, before he had met Sara or even heard her name, a dream had told him what would happen to the two of them, and the frustration that had brought had been almost intolerable. It had taken a long time to completely dawn on him that what he had dreamed was a snapshot of his own future, but everything, right down to the price they had paid for their house, had been spelled out as a patient parent might to a simple child. It had even ended with him leaving for a place where there were ships, beach, and ocean air – Puerto Vallarta.

He was grateful for the time he'd been given with Sara, and for the painful but necessary changes that losing her had brought. Seen in that light, what difference did it make that it had ended?

He breathed in the sweet, cool, thin air. He could still see both seas on the horizons to either side and a volcano far to the north lazily puffing grey clouds upwards to mix with the white ones around it. The Costa Rican sun was playing its usual trick of being directly overhead, even though it was well past five o'clock. In a few hours it would simply disappear as though someone had put a bucket over it.

A park warden on an ATV buzzed up along the perimeter and offered him a ride back to the staging area. "*Cerrado,*" he said. "Closed now." Roland sat with his back against the warden's as they crossed that huge expanse of eons-old volcanic rock.

Mario guided the white van down the deserted mountain highway, and as Roland took in every sight and sound he could of the little towns and farms lost in the occasional gentle sunlit mist, he came to a beautiful realization. He finally understood that those wasted years really weren't wasted at all, and that at long, long last, the memories of Sara were more sweet than bitter.

"Poor guy's starving," Roland explained as Maxine looked on disapprovingly.

"Hardly," she said. "He eats more than I do."

"Well, Adrian can't feed him from where he is."

Franz looked as though he had been doing anything but starving as he licked the sticky syrup from Roland's cinnamon bun off his lips. The whine of the espresso machine diminished and Maxine reached for her mug. She and Roland joined Brent on the patio.

"I hired a private investigator to find out if Adrian's arrest was a sting," Maxine said. "I thought the cops might have been tipped off by somebody."

Franz lay down and sighed. Roland asked, "Why would you think that?"

Maxine tilted her head from side to side, as though weighing her reasons. Finally she said, "Mick said that those cops and TV crews showed up in very large numbers, very quickly."

Roland shrugged. "I remember you mentioning that, but the airport already has police nearby all the time, and the media just listens to scanners. Besides, if it was preplanned there wouldn't have been so much time wasted wondering what to charge him with. They would have known beforehand what they were after." Maxine didn't seem very reassured. "Is there something else on your mind?"

Brent looked at Roland over his espresso and said, "You may have heard that Adrian is wanted in a lot of countries. Even Jamaica showed up on the list of nations lining up to see him, and he's never even been there."

"No, I hadn't heard that. All I know is basically what I've read on line, on English-language papers and discussion groups. The newspapers haven't made any more progress than just getting the facts about Cyberia straight, as far as I can tell, and the discussion boards are full of the usual opinions." Roland had visited the one Eric had shown him and had read a post explaining that Cyberia's recent computer problems were the result of a virus sent to the company by the FBI in preparation for the arrest that netted Adrian. If only the cowboys could hear that one.

"I just started wondering if there was anybody out there who wanted to see Adrian done in," Maxine explained.

Roland laughed. "That rules out any of the investors," he said. "They'd all still be getting paid if this hadn't happened. Same with the staff. Who else is there?"

"Governments," said Brent, sipping his espresso.

Maxine said she didn't know and changed the subject, but Roland knew exactly what had been going through her mind. It wasn't that she had a tangible reason to assume that one of Cyberia's employees or members wished Adrian ill. Logically she was probably very aware that such an idea made no sense. She had a feeling, impossible to support through reason but no less valid than the laws of basic arithmetic, and that was good enough for her. Roland understood. It was good enough for him too. He thought about the man at the hot tub who had done nothing to earn Roland's dislike or mistrust, but he had felt those things anyway.

Dolores staggered onto the patio, rubbing her eyes. "Morning, sunshine," Roland said. "What are you doing up so early?" It was eleven-thirty.

"Lai' nigh'," she mumbled, and shuffled back into the house.

They passed the rest of the day trading conjectures about what would happen to Adrian, but Roland didn't discover much that he didn't know before. He dug out the Medusa and took Franz for a walk to the shooting range. When he noticed Brent watching him some time later he replaced the gun in the case and locked it.

"Time to go, son," said Brent.

Kevin, to his credit, hadn't complained once about having been elected the one to sleep on the couch, though Roland was pretty sure he was the one responsible for pilfering twelve of his favorite CDs. On his way through customs at the airport, the security guard had stopped Roland and asked why he had so much luggage. He had responded truthfully that it wasn't all his, evidently the wrong thing to say as the man spent the next ten minutes poking around in it. Roland remembered the guard opening the CD cases, but now one of those cases was gone.

One evening they all went to a movie. Yoda came along too, peeking out of Roxane's capacious purse at a bouncing red ball in a maxipad commercial.

As the opening credits rolled, Roland thought about Franz's trip to Latvia being cancelled due to quarantine restrictions and asked Roxane how she had managed to bring Yoda into the country. "I have a friend in PV who's a vet," she explained. "A close friend. Yoda's traveling under forged documents."

Great, thought Roland. Even the dog is on the lam.

Two days later Roland decided that he wanted to visit an archaeological site he'd seen promoted on a poster at the Avenida Central the previous week. It had said 'Cartago', but he could remember nothing else. The other four obliged him as they asked cabbie after cabbie where the site was, driving further and further away from San Jose.

Finally after visiting a beautiful, haunting old 16th-century building that dominated a square in Cartago they broke for lunch. Eric and Kevin were getting into trouble somewhere and Mick was still taking pictures of the building, tantalized by the fact that although it was closed he could see through the bars to the flowers and undergrowth inside. Roland sat with Roxane under tall trees after patronizing a nearby A&W.

"Do you suppose a chambermaid would leave a pair of her panties in the bathroom as some sort of calling card?" Roland asked. No one had claimed or moved them since the cowboys had mentioned them.

Roxane laughed. "Those ones hanging up in the main bathroom? Sorry Romeo, but I don't think so."

"Why not?" Roland toyed with his french fries. He didn't like french fries but they came with everything. What he really wanted was a stiff cold drink. It had been getting a lot hotter lately. He wondered how the weather was changing in Puerto Vallarta.

"I think they belong to that friend of Adrian's who came through with her daughter."

"Who? What are you talking about?"

Roxane put her hand to her mouth as she chewed. Yoda wolfed down Roland's french fries like a mad thing, even making little growls.

"Some friend of Adrian's. I don't know why, but she's running from some thing or someone. She has a ten-year-old daughter and they've been wandering around Central America for a couple of years now. Once Adrian got the condo he offered to let her stay there. She was only there for a week or so."

"God, that's absolutely fascinating."

Roxane looked at Roland and frowned. "That's not exactly the word I'd use."

"Well, think of the *stories* she could tell!"

"Roland, from what I've heard about you, and Mick too, she'd have none more fascinating than yours. Or mine, actually, after this episode. I mean, who would believe a story like ours? Did you ever even have the slightest notion three months ago that you'd be watching my dog eat fast food outside an abandoned Spanish colonial ruin while our ex-boss is described in the papers as a 'kingpin' and a 'ringleader'?"

"Not exactly," Roland admitted.

"Not exactly, my ass! People pay big bucks for screenwriters to dream this stuff up, and even then they get it wrong. There's always some conspiracy at work and everything is always so organized."

"I'm listening." Roland was interested in Roxane's take on the situation now that she'd had a couple of weeks to think it over.

"Well, it doesn't lend much support to any conspiracy theories that Adrian's arrest was sparked by such a tiny matter. I mean, the police are saying now how they've been investigating him for years. I say, bullshit. Where were they a year ago then? Like you said when you first came, it couldn't have been hard to find us." She licked her fingers. "You know those states that put out the cease-and-desist orders against us? They're the ones now saying that they knew all along that Cyberia was a scam, but it's just a device to use so they don't get sued when somebody starts whining. It's easy to say 'I told you so' after the fact, isn't it?" She collected the empty fast-food wrappers and went to throw them in a garbage can. When she returned she said, "I guess what I'm saying is that they thought they'd done their job when they gave those orders, but they hadn't. All it meant was that as long as nothing illegal happened in their jurisdiction, they didn't care about anyone else."

Roland stared at her. "Deep," he said, with a half-smile. "Can you back up over the part where Cyberia was a scam?"

Roxane squinted at Roland. "Ah, just something I read."

He returned the gaze and nodded. "I read that too."

"People forget that the simplest explanations take the most genius to come up with," she went on. "I suppose on the movie screens, the more complicated the plot the better." She pulled a blade of grass out from under the bench she was sitting on and studied it. "Maybe they're scared they'll look stupid if the storyline is easy."

Roland laughed. Here they were, at the tail end of a secret kept in a modestly famous resort city, now in a country that never made the news back home, baked by a merciless sun and drawing on an unlimited bankroll as they waited for the next adventure. It didn't get much simpler, and it didn't get much more interesting. Roland almost mentioned his Bahamian fortune but decided against it. Maybe Roxane had one of her own anyway.

"I think this would make a great book," he said. "I'm going to try writing it."

"How?" Roxane looked at him. "How are you going to tell this story, when every day was a story in itself? You'll have to leave out so much more than what you put in."

"It'll be a lesson in priorities," Roland replied. "Something I should learn anyway."

"Good luck with that."

Roland looked around the park. A musician wearing a beret was drawing a crowd because he was playing a hammered dulcimer, not a common instrument in this part of the world. Yoda sniffed and scratched at the dirt.

"Remember that night when you first got here and we went to the Pagina for coffee after dinner, and I grilled you about your ex?" Roxane continued. Roland nodded. "Well, speaking of things you should learn, mind if I ask where that went?"

Roland closed his eyes, feeling the sunshine and listening to the sound of the dulcimer and the voices in the square. "Trust," he said. "I have to learn how to trust myself."

Roxane looked surprised. "Not other people? Having been screwed around before we got to Cyberia was bad enough already, but this on top of it all isn't much of a help, is it?"

Roland squinted in the sun. "No. But how am I going to know who to trust, unless I trust the voice inside that tells me?"

Roxane gnawed on her straw and grinned. She said, "If you two hadn't been so dysfunctional that you couldn't see how dysfunctional the other one was, you might have really had something."

Roland laughed. "Oh, we saw, all right. We just didn't know what to do about it."

Roxane poured her ice on the ground. "I doubt you'll get fooled again."

Mick returned, scrolling through the pictures in his digital camera. Roland had remembered to bring his video camera, but he was reluctant to use it because the others didn't like being on film. They had an unspoken fear that one day a detective would obtain it. Roland held hopes that a second look at this logic would reveal how silly it was, but not enough to use the camera when the others knew they were being filmed.

One long cab ride later up through jungle-covered mountains, they came to an archaeological museum. A gaggle of schoolchildren pointed at the foreigners and tittered among themselves. "This isn't it either," Roland said, aware that the patience of his friends was running thin.

Finally the taxi driver let them out at the end of a long and bumpy gravel road. They were at a park, in the middle of which was the building Roland had seen in the poster. At first he didn't recognize it, probably because he had pictured it with Indiana Jones cracking a whip outside. Instead there were scruffy kids playing soccer. His little group spent some time reading the plaque about how the building, a mission built in the 1500s, had apparently been constructed of bricks, pitchforks, and roofing tiles, and then they walked back to a dusty cantina where half an hour later they boarded a bus and returned to San Jose.

18
Curtain Call

The feeling of imminent dissolution was everywhere. By the end of the first week in May, Roland had decided to go back to Puerto Vallarta. He hadn't thought much about what he would do after that, but Cyberia in San Jose was going nowhere, Brent hadn't needed him, and he was bored.

There was another factor that helped cement his decision, something Roxane had said one afternoon. She had cut short a swim in the pool because a man there had started asking her a lot of questions.

"Receding hairline and not much of a tan?" Roland asked.

"Yeah, why?"

"Same guy hung around me for a while when I first got down here."

Roxane threw her towel onto the couch, spread it out, and sprawled on it. "He's FBI," she declared. "I'm sure of it."

Roland perked up. "What makes you say that?"

Roxane grabbed a handful of peanuts from the bowl on the table. "Because he tried to ask where we're all from and what we're doing down here about five different ways."

"Did he ask everyone's names?"

"Yeah. I gave him fake ones though."

If this had been Roland's first day in Mexico, walking along the beach with CIA Mick and still uneducated as to the secret he was expected to carry, he would have laughed off Roxane's suspicion as so much melodramatic drivel. Sitting here in a luxury condominium populated by the remnants of an underground Centroamerican investment company, however, made the situation markedly different.

Now he knew why the man had made him so uncomfortable before. It was because there had been something about him Roland had recognized. Not something in his looks, the way Roland knew that he'd seen the man in the forged passport photocopy before, but something in his mannerisms had been unsettlingly familiar. Now that Roxane had noticed it too, he knew what it was.

He remembered how everyone had behaved when he'd first landed in Mexico, protecting their secret but flaunting the fact that they had one. This man had a secret, and he was not comfortable with it. Whatever Adrian had done, it was big, and the longer Roland stuck around the more implicated he became. At first he had come to Costa Rica half believing – but only half, now that he thought about it truthfully – that he could help ensure that Cyberia continued its function uninterrupted, but that was not an option anymore. This man was not a casual tourist. He was here for a reason.

Over dinner at Le Monastère two nights previous, Eric had confided in Roland that he and Kevin had both decided that Cyberia was some sort of scam. In gratitude for Roland's request for a performance in the chapel afterwards, Kevin had taught Roland how to walk on his hands under water in the pool, but Roland's thoughts had been preoccupied with what Eric had said. Now there was more fuel for that fire.

That night when he checked his email, a voice from far away awaited. Elizabeth Anne, whose family lived across the alley and with whom Roland and Sara had talked around the fire for so long on so many nameless summer nights, had written to say that her father had died. Roland immediately sent her flowers from an online vendor and replied to her message, but even after a thousand rewrites he still couldn't get it to say exactly what he wanted it to. In the end he just left the original as it was and hoped the flowers would speak for him.

Back in his room he tried to think of anything but her or Sara or his little house or all the dreams he'd been forced to abandon; any of a million things that had been quietly waiting their turn for his attention for so long. Then one memory came through clearer and louder than all the rest.

He remembered one day eight months ago when he was in the house alone after Sara had started packing her belongings. Most of her clothes were in boxes but a few were still in the closet, and one shirt, a simple denim one, hung unevenly on a wire hanger. Unsure why and not caring, Roland had reached for it and taken it off the hanger to hold it close to him and breathe it in, feeling the fabric and enveloping himself in the comforting and reassuring scent of the woman who had inspired him, nurtured him, made him laugh, loved him and now was fading out of sight like a ghost in the gathering dawn. He had collapsed onto the floor and been wracked with uncontrollable, voracious sobs, clutching the shirt like a child with its first teddy bear, hating Sara for forcing him to be the one to make the decision, hating himself for not finding a way out of the pain, realizing for the first time in his life how useless mere wishing really was and yet unable to stop wishing that she would come back to him and that he was a better man and that none of it had ever happened.

Four a.m. came and went, and Roland barely noticed. He began packing everything except the clothes he chose to wear that day, and before the others had woken he slipped upstairs to quietly knock on Brent's door and ask if he could take him to the airport.

They drove in silence through the rainy morning. Brent didn't ask when Roland's plane left, which was just as well because Roland didn't know. The rain stopped and the sun made a tentative and groggy appearance. Brent drew up outside the terminal and Roland shook his hand and waved goodbye, and the last he saw of him, he was leaning against the Blazer and staring at the pavement.

Roland had assumed that Mexico was safe to return to, though he was still wary because of the men who had come to the Shack door and the fact that he still had the bankbook in his possession.

The security guard at the x-ray station asked why Roland was carrying so much baggage, so Roland replied that his extended stay in Costa Rica had been cut short. This time at least he didn't have Grant's suitcase to worry about, but the flight from Mexico City had been almost vacant and the luxury of time allowed the man to examine Roland's luggage anyway.

This made him uneasy. He wasn't carrying Cyberian hard drives, although by now his name might have made its way to the Mexican customs database if he was wanted and didn't know it – an alarmingly real possibility. The only thing he was really hoping they wouldn't find was the bankbook.

After a minute of fooling around and studying the iguanas adorning various 'Pura Vida! Costa Rica' t-shirts, the guard saw two boxes of genuine Cuban cigars Roland had bought. The man pointed to them, speaking rapidly. Roland understood enough to know what he'd done wrong.

The customs form clearly stated that one was allowed to bring no more than twenty-five 'puros' – cigars – into the country. Roland had forty, and almost laughed out loud when he realized that this was exactly how Adrian must have felt after being caught for fibbing on his own customs declaration. Roland's wasn't a four-point-five-million-dollar fib, which would actually qualify as an outright lie, but it was a fib nonetheless. Soon a small crowd of curious security guards assembled as he blithely tried to explain that he thought 'cigarillos' meant cigars, of which he was allowed a hundred, and had no idea what 'puros' meant, which was bigger than a fib but not quite as big as a lie.

He wondered if any of them could detect how nervous he was. He explained that the cigars might even be fakes; good ones from the Dominican Republic but fakes even so, as though hoping that this might make him seem gullible enough and therefore harmless enough not to bother with, but they would have none of it. Things got even worse when a man in a suit and a foul mood approached, after having been radioed that an infidel had penetrated the perimeter.

Finally the pretty girl who had now welcomed Roland to Puerto Vallarta three times instructed him to close his luggage and follow her. She led him to a part of the terminal closed to law-abiding travellers and went into an office with the man in the suit. The man emerged only a few seconds later and with a brief wave he disappeared back into the main terminal. The girl poked her head around the corner, pointed to Roland's carry-on bag, and beckoned him to bring it into the office.

Now Roland became even more nervous. The fear of being accused of heinous crimes against the state were no match for the apprehension he felt when confronted with the prospect of a one-on-one conversation with this woman.

She held out the cigar boxes and motioned for him to put them back in his suitcase. At first Roland didn't understand.

He asked in his best Spanish if she was sure, and she answered yes, it was more trouble than it was worth to pursue the matter. She seemed more nervous than he was. She just held out the boxes to him, so he opened one and offered her a cigar. She shook her head, so he asked, "*Por su novio?*" but she denied that too. So she didn't have a boyfriend. Roland didn't want to insult her by offering money, so he regained his composure as best he could and said, "*Muchas gracias*." He wheeled his case out of the office, allowed her to escort him to the main lobby, and watched her disappear back to the arrivals area.

Out of all the cab drivers in Puerto Vallarta, and there were quite a few, the one who took Roland back to his house was the same one who had driven him to the airport chatting away about women and apples. He had changed tack in the meantime and was now suggesting that women were more like onions, with layer upon layer surrounding them but really nothing in the center, and once a man got close enough his eyes would start to water but he wouldn't know if it was the onion making it happen or if he was really crying. This time there was no newspaper on the seat and still no sign of recognition in the man's eyes as they pulled up outside Roland's house. The only thing the driver commented on was how abandoned it looked.

This was a disturbingly accurate observation. The flowers in the stairwell were wilted and forlorn, and once inside Roland saw that in the short space of time he had been gone a green algae had formed in the pool and there was a thick layer of dust on the furniture and patches of black mold on the faucets. He felt as though he had inherited a mansion from a long-dead relative and was only now visiting it. If he had been lonely at times before, he thought as he sat on his bed and realized that even Dave the gecko had gone, he felt utterly deserted now. A few days of this, tying up loose ends, and then he would leave.

He tried calling Sidney on Amy's cell phone but there was no answer, so he put his suitcases in Grant's old room – it had a bigger balcony than Roland's old one at the opposite end of the house – and unpacked his clothes. He grabbed a cigar and walked down to Olas Altas.

In his absence the weather had turned. It was very hot and humid, the bird sanctuary on the islands at the mouth of the bay invisible in the haze. He was sweating freely and stopped in at a small store for some sunscreen, then hailed a cab and visited a Pemex for some bottled water, a couple of burritos, and a bottle of tequila. Then he continued on to the marina gate at Puerto Iguana.

Sidney's speedboat bobbed contentedly in its berth. Fishing out the keys he'd grabbed off the counter at the Shack, Roland jumped on board. His lack of familiarity with the machine was compensated for by the things that Garrett's friend had shown him, and before long he found himself rumbling along towards the harbor exit. Once clear of the buoys he spent an hour splashing himself with salt spray over the bow as he played in the waves, racing the frigates and searching for dolphins.

The *Marigalante* was heading out for the evening cruise, and Roland came as close as he dared to the waving throng on the deck. Watching it recede, he stopped the little boat to eat his burritos and open the tequila, and as the sun began its descent into the sea through the haze, finding an occasional opening in the clouds through which to send its radiant orange beams, he lit his cigar and tried not to think about anything other than savoring the moment.

There was a man who advertised psychic readings and dream interpretations at the Pagina en el Sol, and on a whim Roland decided to send some business his way. He didn't tell the man about the nature of his dreams. He explained that he was interested in a general outlook.

"Give me two days, señor," said George. "Then come back at this same time, and I will be here and I will have this written out for you." He held out a deck of cards. "But first, you must select five of these."

What he offered to Roland were nothing like ordinary cards. Each had a scene painted in the middle, most of them tranquil, but at each of the four corners were scenes of a much darker nature. Some were almost horrifying in their casual depiction of what amounted to people's worst nightmares. Here was someone buried alive; there was someone being tortured on a rack. Roland selected five that he felt described him best, shuddering at the thought, and handed them to George. He paid for the man's coffee and departed.

On the afternoon of Sunday, May 13, he wandered down to Burro's Beach Bar for a late lunch, winding his way among the crowd gathered there for an international track and field championship. No sooner had the waiter brought his margarita than he heard somebody say, "Roland! Hey, you're alive!"

Ken waved to him from a lounge chair on the other side of the palm fronds. Roland brought his drink over and by the time the waiter delivered his *chiles rellenos* he had been brought up to speed on the goings-on in Vallarta. Which, in the grand scheme of things, didn't amount to much.

"Nick gave me a call about you driving that truck back to the States," Ken said, blowing on the top of his beer bottle to make it sound like a tiny foghorn. "I wouldn't recommend doing that, though."

"Why not?"

Ken removed the bottle from his lips and waved it around. "'Cause, his brother's in jail and his last name's all over the computers. You pull up at frickin' Laredo or wherever and the best that'll happen is they ask you politely where you got a truck belonging to a convict."

"I'll insure it in my name from Lloyd's and get Mack to sign a letter saying I can drive it. They won't be looking out for his vehicles."

This time Ken actually drank from the bottle, draining it just in time for the waiter to bring him a new one. "I guess," he said. "When Nick called he asked me to draw up a letter saying exactly that. Next time I go to Guadalajara I'll get it signed for you."

Roland switched from his lime margarita on the rocks to good old Pacifico. "So how is Adrian, really?" he asked.

Ken pursed his lips, then answered, "Not bad overall, I guess. I've stayed in worse hotel rooms than that cell. But his health isn't good at all. I mean, he looked a little sunken before, but now he looks…I dunno…kinda shrivelled, I guess."

"He appointed you in charge here?"

Ken nodded. "I have power of attorney." He sounded very satisfied with himself.

Roland couldn't blame him. He now commanded, according to the newspapers anyway, almost sixty million dollars' worth of assets and bank accounts. Roland's own arithmetic placed the total much higher, closer to two hundred million and easily more than that, but he didn't ask Ken where he thought the newspapers got that figure. Nor did he inquire about the untold amount Adrian probably had squirreled away that only he would ever know about.

Sidney and Amy had been wandering along the beach and pulled up chairs beside the two. Nobody felt like discussing Adrian so instead they watched a feeding frenzy of frigates in the bay. Hundreds of them swarmed down on an area no bigger than that of a house. Roland captured them on video and noticed how overcast the sky was. It was hot, and the setting sun was almost invisible behind a thick bank of haze. Amy went off to find a washroom and Ken got up to talk to a couple of friends from Andale's bar who had parked themselves on a towel not far away, their ghetto blaster serenading everyone with Bob Dylan. This left Roland alone with Sidney. It was exactly the opportunity he had been looking for.

"Sidney, I need to ask you something." The cries of the frigates were loud and mournful.

Sidney nodded. "Sure."

"Was Hammer a scam?"

Sidney wiggled his toes in the sand. Finally he said, "I don't know." He looked at Roland, his expressive eyes covered by mirrored blue sunglasses. "I really don't know. I know that a lot of people think I do, and they think that's why I didn't work there, but the fact is that I just didn't need to. Dad was generous and I didn't need to work. Amy did because she liked it. But if it was illegal then I'm in trouble too, because some of the things he did were done in my name." He hesitated, and Roland could tell that he wanted to say something else. Finally he continued, "I think…that it's possible to try too hard to get someone to love you."

Roland said nothing and waited. His silence reassured Sidney, who spoke again.

"It's just…I don't know if I would have become involved at all if I didn't think I could show my dad I could be useful to him somehow. Before he invited me here we hadn't talked in a long time." He regained his composure and looked at Roland. "But going to Costa Rica was futile, because nobody knows what the man knows. Without him it's over."

Roland didn't bring up the fact that when he had arrived in Costa Rica he had found a box of hard drives in the office that Sidney had removed from the computers and sent down by courier. Obviously he had found merit in the notion at some point. Roland was going to ask something else but Sidney kept talking.

"The stuff he did, only he knew about. I don't think Maxine knew, and I don't even know if Liza did. I mean, who were those guys in suits? Nobody knows. Did they have some dirt on my dad or something or were they CIA? Where did he take that Learjet besides Costa Rica and Belize? Beats me. I've been on my mountain bike with Eric and Slogan and the girls, or writing songs in my little studio." He dug into the sand with a brown foot and said, "Why, what do you think?"

Roland was silent for a while. In one sentence, Sidney had answered the question he was about to ask. The man in the forged passport photograph had been the taller of the two in suits whom Roland had seen on his first day there, and no one seemed to know who he was.

He said, "I believe you."

Sidney looked at him again. "That's all?"

"What else is there?" Roland replied. "I asked you a question, you gave me an answer, and I don't think you lied when you could have." Which wasn't entirely true, but Roland would gain nothing by saying otherwise. He was patient enough to know that time would tell him whether Sidney was sincere or not.

They both looked out to sea where between the clouds the sun was announcing its departure through a greying sky.

Amy returned and made noises about it being time to go. Sidney got up and so did Roland. They said their goodbyes and waved to Ken, and then left the bar headed in opposite directions.

Roland spent the rest of that evening wandering around the Malecon, where he ran into Slogan at the amphitheatre. The back of his shirt read, *"I cannot sleep or the clowns will eat me."* A very talented Peruvian band was playing haunting mountain music.

"Sorry I got you into this mess."

Roland laughed. "It's been one of my more interesting adventures. What's going to happen to you and the wife?"

Slogan leaned against a bench. "I don't know," he said. "Adrian promised us some pretty extravagant payouts, but we'll be fine no matter what happens. There's always something doing if you know where to look."

Roland put his hands in his pockets. "Do you have any idea why Mick fell apart so completely? I mean, how could things have just come undone like that? Wasn't there a contingency plan?"

"Sure there was," Slogan answered, "but nobody followed it. Sid knew what it was, but I don't think Mick did – or maybe it was the other way around. Anyway, they couldn't agree on what to do. I stayed out of it, and by the time you got back from down south the die had been cast and confusion reigned." He hooked his thumb into the strap of his ubiquitous backpack. Roland carried a small one too, with his sunglasses, wallet, keys, cell phone, sunscreen and other items inside. Slogan's looked empty. "Mick was the overcautious type to begin with," he continued. "I sometimes wonder if he started out totally stable anyway. Could be that he knew something all along that we didn't, which might make him a legitimate target for the cops and explain why he was the fidgety type, but honestly I couldn't tell you. Maybe he's just got too many skeletons in the closet."

Roland nodded. "I did ask him once, you know. At the condo in Costa Rica."

"What did he say?"

Roland waved dismissively. "Nothing, really. He said that by the time he found out what had happened, Maxine and Sidney had assumed command of the whole thing and had buggered it up completely so he decided to stay away."

Slogan was thoughtful. "That doesn't sound like the whole story to me."

"Me neither," Roland replied. "That's why I said he didn't really tell me anything. Not that it matters either way now, of course."

Slogan made a resigned face, then after a second he said, "What are you going to do?"

"I'm in the same boat as you," Roland replied truthfully. "I don't really know. I'm tired of wasting away in Margaritaville, but I don't know where I'll go or even how. I might drive Mack's truck home, but if I do, I'll take the long way there. The *really* long way."

Slogan smiled. "You'll come back to Vallarta. You love it here."

Roland nodded. "Yes, I do." He watched the people shouting and waving at each other across the streets, some tourists but mostly Mexicans now as the summer heat was beginning to take hold, and remembered what the limo driver had said on the way home from Sidney and Amy's wedding a lifetime ago. He had said that Puerto Vallarta was still innocent, which was why he loved it. Soon, he said, it would become like Acapulco or some other cities, but for now it was still a beautiful little gem. Roland thought so too, and he felt ashamed for playing a part in bringing it so much closer to losing that innocence. A small voice inside him whispered that he was not worthy of the city. Redeem yourself, it said, but it didn't say how.

Slogan solemnly offered his hand. "Call me before you leave," he said. "Again, I'm sorry. I never anticipated any of this."

"Don't worry," Roland replied. "Possible jail time notwithstanding, this was exactly what I needed." He hugged Slogan and patted him on the back.

"One more notch for the adventure club."

Roland wandered down to the Tropicana and crossed the street to find Tatiana's car rental office open. She looked up when he entered. The midday heat was stifling.

She regarded Roland with some suspicion. She didn't smile when she asked how he'd been.

"Not bad," he replied. "How are the staff?"

She studied him and leaned back in her chair. "They are sad to lose their jobs, and they don't understand why nobody goes to visit Adrian. Guillermo's family, they stay in Guadalajara outside the prison until he was released. Why nobody is going to see Adrian?"

Fair enough question, Roland thought, and the answer is looking more obvious all the time. The papers had switched from accusing Adrian of smuggling drugs, which had been laughable, to money laundering, almost as ridiculous, to running a huge international pyramid scheme. This was something nobody wanted to involve themselves with because of the chord of possibility it struck. Apart from Ken, of course, who would put up with a little mud slung his way in order to open a beach bar or two with Adrian's millions. He would be in Guadalajara about now, judging by the clock on the wall behind Tatiana.

Roland sat there talking with her for a while, the hot afternoon air moving now and then with an intermittent breeze and the sound of an occasional passing car on the street outside, and thanked her for everything she'd done. When he left she was just staring at her desk and mumbling something to herself.

He was passing in front of the Master Baiter's Tackle Shop on his way down to the Hidden Garden for a late lunch when Lee came up to him and grabbed his arm. "You're still around then," she said from under a big straw hat.

"No, I'm not here anymore."

Lee laughed. "I'll join you for lunch," she announced.

They parked themselves at a table as far away from the other patrons as they could, which was easy in the large outdoor restaurant. Shaded by trees and serenaded by inquisitive birds and the trickling of the Rio Cuale, Lee said, "No wonder Ken called me and told me not to bother coming back from me holiday. I'm at the airport buying a paper, yeah, and there's Adrian and that other bloke on the front cover looking like somebody canceled their favorite show on the telly."

"It's a strange situation," Roland agreed. "How were your holidays?"

"Fine," Lee responded impatiently. "You know that big Croatian man, Milo? He tried to kill me last night."

"I see."

"It's true. I'm in my apartment at Vista del Sol, yeah, packing up—"

"I didn't know you lived there."

"Yeah. Adrian gave me the place to myself until somebody else needed it. Me boyfriend didn't think too much of that, so we split not long after Amy and what's-his-name's wedding. Anyway Milo comes over and starts banging on the door and asking where his money is, like. Shouting at me and carrying on, it was a terrible racket. I didn't know what to say. I just phoned the landlady and she chased him away. Then she said it's a good thing I'm leaving because those other two left their drug things all over the place, d'you know that?"

"Other two? Drug things?"

Lee waved a hand. "Eric and Kevin. They left their bongs and roach clips and beer bottles stacked up everywhere. She says it was a frightful mess."

"Same landlady that owns your place?"

"Guess so, yeah."

"Hmm. I thought Adrian owned those condos."

"He owns two and rents another one, for guests or something." Lee sipped her mango juice. "I know the guy at the front desk there," she explained. "And how about Liza taking off like that, yeah? Doesn't look too good, does it?"

"I got roughly the same advice too, and I'm leaving in a couple of days."

Lee took her hat off and laid it on the chair beside her. Running her fingers through her blonde hair she said, "So am I. San Diego, I think. I've been here long enough. I don't like the thought of angry investors kidnapping me. Besides, there are always more adventures out there, d'you know that?"

"Yeah," Roland agreed. "I know that."

George had finished analyzing Roland's cards and pushed a piece of paper towards him. "Interesting choices, señor," he said.

The sun had set but it was still hot. They sat at the inside counter at the Pagina, sipping coffee with whipped cream and watching tourists staring at the menu board from the area covered by the awning on the corner. Roland studied George's handwriting, which covered both sides of a sheet torn from a full-size notebook.

"This first one, señor, it says to seek the center, the focus, wherever it is, not where you would like it to be. But that is the first card you chose and something you already know."

Roland saw movement on his periphery but he paid no attention to it. Lots of things were moving around. It was a busy café.

"This second one says to acknowledge losses, things dissolving. Let them dissolve into their basics, señor, and use those basics to build new things."

Whatever was moving was on the floor near Roland's feet. He looked down and saw nothing.

"This third one, señor, it is important. It says to seek challenge from the ordinary and not to identify who you are with the intensity of your experiences. Señor, always look for the intense in the ordinary."

There it was again. As George kept talking, Roland looked down to see a monstrous hairy grey wolf spider. It had been under Roland's tall chair and now sat on a tile about a foot away, tapping one hoary leg on the floor and considering what to do next. It was easily as big as Roland's outstretched hand.

"This fourth one, señor, is a question. 'Is your passion stronger than your resistance? Hope stronger than fear?' It is a question about life. This card says to commit to your life."

The spider scuttled to the middle of the floor and stopped dead, as spiders are fond of doing when intending to scare the hell out of people. The waitress spied it and, although her eyes grew wide and she gave a little cry of revulsion, she didn't drop her plates.

"This last one is about choices, señor. What we choose is what we become. You must remember, señor, nobody ever built a reputation on what they intended to do. You know, and so do I, people who criticize everything they see. Some people, señor, it is their job to criticize. But keep in mind that nobody knows their names. Only people who accomplish things are remembered. People who created things, not people who destroyed them, and sometimes people, señor, they think they are creating when really they are destroying. Your task is to understand the difference and commit fully to your choices. Do not deceive yourself by making one choice and instantly waiting for the day when you can make another."

The spider, satisfied with the small panic it had caused, headed for the safety of the stand-up cooler in the corner of the café and disappeared underneath it. The waitress retrieved a broom, and as Roland watched she began to shove the bristle end underneath the cooler. Nothing emerged, however, and after a minute or so of this she felt confident enough to get down and put her head level with the floor. After a thorough inspection she conceded that the spider had disappeared and resumed serving plantains fried in rum and brown sugar.

Roland remembered one day at the condo in Escazu a couple of weeks ago when Eric had told him about an email he'd received from his ex-girlfriend. In it she said that she was worried about him, because she had dreamed that Eric drowned in a boat that sank in a violent storm. He related this to George, who looked at him over a pair of slightly crooked glasses. "And your friend is in trouble, isn't he?" he asked.

Roland hesitated. "I suppose you could say that," he admitted.

"Prophetic dreams and feelings are not unusual, señor," said George. "As I think you know." He looked invitingly at Roland. "You understand these things, yes?"

"Sometimes," Roland muttered. "But I don't understand how it works, and I don't understand why I see some things and not others. I don't know why I can see a tree now and then but I'm blind to the forest."

George looked thoughtful. "Señor," he said slowly, "I think sometimes you have seen the forest before. The whole story, all at once. But lately it is hard for you because you are clouded." He leaned forward and smiled genially. "Don't worry. You will return, señor. To yourself. You will be back."

He pointed to Roland's heart, and then to his own. "And you will find God where he always was."

Before going home that night Roland stopped in at the dot-com café. Seated in the back room he logged in to the

Cyberia internet discussion board that Eric had shown him, and read the thoughts of some now ex-investors.

None of them were happy. That was to be expected. One had written:

> Somebody named Kotch in Washington State is being prosecuted for promoting Cyberia. This wouldn't have happened if Winter hadn't been arrested. I know that a lot of people on this board have had trouble believing that Adrian Winter and Alexander Holt of Hammer are the same person but who are we kidding. Anyway if Winter hadn't been detained in Mexico the investors would still be getting paid, nobody would have complained, and Kotch and his ilk wouldn't be in trouble right now. Do you all realize that every single person in your upline is a criminal, by definition? I also know that there are a lot of people on this board who are assuming that their uplines all knew that Cyberia was a scam. Well the people they know might be like that but I think that 15% commission by itself was enough of an incentive to get people in. I don't know anybody who knew that Cyberia was a ponzi. I didn't know, and I recruited my whole family into it. Now my brother-in-law is threatening to sue me. Why? Because he didn't do due diligence before he invested? Of course I feel bad for recruiting him, who wouldn't, but it's a little frightening how much personal responsibility has been drowned in an attempt to pin the blame on the SEC donkey. I wonder if they're willing to accept it to make us think we really need them.
>
> The only difference between the scammed

and the scammers is whether or not there was anybody below them in the pyramid when Adrian was nabbed.

There were a lot of people revelling in saying "I told you so." One such example read:

> Winter and people like him prey on the weak-minded and greedy, that's all there is to say about it. Shame on all of you who brought in people just thinking about your referral commissions. How could you do such a thing? Greed is the worst thing in the world. I said when this thing first started that it was a scam and I'll say it again. How stupid do you feel now? Cyberia never filed papers in any of the US States or Canada with any of the securities commissions and was therefore not playing fair at all.

Somebody had written a rebuttal to that one. It read:

> Just because some people associated with Cyberia have been charged with securities violations means nothing. Berkshire Hathaway, Exxon and pretty much any major company you can think of have all run afoul of the Securities and Exchange Commission at some time or another. And where were all of you when Bre-X took a tumble? They jumped through all the hoops and did everything legally and in the end that proved meaningless. Who's more of a criminal, a scrappy and ambitious rural upstart like Winter with a beautifully simple and effective plan, or a slick operator who cooks his books to pump up the

price of his stock with the aid of crooked brokers and dumps it at its height so that only suckers buy behind the curve? At least Winter never pretended to have made the SEC happy and hid behind federal legitimacy the way so many 'legal' cons have. You people are government lackeys who can't think for yourselves. Eighty years ago smoking was promoted by governments as good for your health. Did that make it true? Cyberia was only a scam because people like you and your government friends said so. Has it occurred to you that Winter's company paid its dividends on time, every time since its inception? Can you say the same about your SEC-cleared companies? The next time a big company goes bankrupt and you look around for who to blame, don't look any farther than the mirror. And if you think greed is bad, think of how you chose the jobs you have, the schools your children go to, the lives you lead. I'll bet you made those choices entirely based on what was best for you, and why wouldn't you? Is that not greed?

Of course there was the usual contingent of postings by the fringe, one of which caught Roland's attention:

Winter and his cronies were stopped for one reason: They became a threat to national security. We need better control over people's bank accounts and money so we can track them, and eliminate the people who consort with alien intelligence. Go ahead and think that Cyberia was a pyramid scheme, but the truth is something the government can only cover up for so long. Cyberia marketed extraterrestrial technologies and was based in Latin American countries because they used missing people as food to placate the aliens. In the future we must learn from our mistakes and track the movement of every dollar in the world system.

Naturally enough this earned a few replies too:

Track money even more? Are you out of your mind? Every dollar Winter made went through banks in New York City, so it was right under their noses all the time. Have you been reading the news? We already know all this information but nobody used the information we have. How much good is it going to be when everybody lies on their census statements and cheats on their taxes anyway? It's no wonder the rich get richer, because they are under so much constant assault they are always on the lookout for ways to get ahead. You may not have noticed, but Cyberia was shut down because too many ordinary people were becoming wealthy. It wasn't because of aliens, it wasn't because of cloning people, it was because lots of people made lots of money and the government never got to see a dime of it because Cyberia never so much as paid for a business license, and all those millions of American dollars were being siphoned offshore. Plus, investors probably didn't declare their earnings from it, frustrating the tax man even more. Remind you of any place? It's called RUSSIA, where the only thing that worked was freedom – capitalism, the black market – where you could get blue jeans and bread and not have to stand in line thanks to of good old self-interest.

Weak-minded slobs like you are not the best argument for globalization, just so you know. Not that there is one to begin with.

Roland felt like posting a message of his own, saying that no, in fact there were no missing people used as alien food and that he found it revolting to assume that any of the investors recruited their families knowing what Adrian had been up to and that his arrest in Puerto Vallarta had been entirely an incident of chance. He wanted to say that there was no conspiracy theory needed to explain that Cyberia had been brought to its knees because its drunken director had incorrectly filled out his customs declaration form. In the end, though, he decided that it would do no good at all. People believed what felt comfortable to them, and that was about the extent of it.

Instead he wrote a letter to Elizabeth Anne. She had written him to say that her husband had seen an article about a cancer-stricken con man arrested in Puerto Vallarta and was wondering if Roland knew him and if so, was everything okay? He replied:

Yes, I know the man in the article very well actually. I used to work for him. I don't know much more than what you read in the papers, apart from the fact that the current opinion seems to be that our group is some sort of organized crime syndicate when the truth is that the majority of us are pot-smoking beach rats and/or wandering misfits who fell into their jobs through chance, but since when has the truth sold newspapers?

At first we all were sure that whatever he had done that got him arrested was separate from what we were doing in Vallarta but none of us believe that any more. We all feel betrayed to some degree or other. I am undecided about whether or not I respect his decision not to tell us what we were really involved in. On the one hand, he probably knew that none of us would have done it if we'd known that what we were involved in was illegal, but on the other hand, at least we would have had a choice. We all liked him and this isn't easy for any of us. In the papers here they reported that he took full responsibility for Cyberia's actions which was good of him. It would have been easy to say he was the victim of foul play on his employees' part.

One of the guys in Costa Rica has a brother who's sharing a cell with Adrian and is also very sick. For some reason a lot of the people involved are dying of some kind of terminal disease. Perhaps there's a lesson in there about living your life like each day was your last, because one of them eventually will be, but those aren't the lessons I would have learned. I'd rather live each day as though it was my first.

I am coming home. I don't know exactly when, and it will not be for a while yet, but there are a few things to sort out and then I am returning. I am exhausted from so many dead ends and I miss my little old house. Life is tough, but I am tougher, and thankfully that doesn't have to mean that I am coldly so, even though in the last year I have become almost constantly embarrassed by how thoroughly and how often I've been duped. I knew I was naïve but I didn't think I was stupid too. That's how I feel, anyway. I don't want to have to get an apartment somewhere for a job, I don't want to leave home for weeks at a time, and I don't want to get involved with multimillion-dollar international frauds in faraway tropical cities. I want something that at least looks like a normal life. Is that so much to ask?

Take care, see you all soon.

Roland

Sitting at a table outside Andale's the next night, Ken handed the letter he'd promised to Roland with Mack's signature on it. Roxane's sort-of boyfriend was with them, and he had apparently been invaluable in assisting Ken in moving all the furniture out of the Shack and dismantling Cyberia. Roland had offered to help as well, but only halfheartedly. It was too much of a reminder that everything had ended, and he was tired of endings. What he wanted was a beginning.

Ken looked at him suspiciously. "Where you going with the truck?" he asked.

"Home."

"What route are you taking?"

"Don't know yet. I'm making this up as I go along. If I keep the setting sun to my left it'll be hard to get lost."

Ken ignored this sarcasm and scratched his cheek. "When are you leaving?"

"Soon."

Ken stared at the sidewalk for a minute. The music in the bar was always a mix of dance music, country, hip-hop; all kinds. A song started, and Ken nodded towards the window behind Roland.

"They're playing our song," he said. "I've heard this one before."

As Roland listened, he began to smile. How appropriate, he thought. The lyrics went:

Too much of heaven/Can bring you underground/Heaven/ Can always turn around/Too much of heaven/A life and soul hell bound/Heaven/The killer makes no sound

"That's us," Ken said, pointing his cigarette at Roland. "Thanks for the letter."

"Good luck." Ken raised his bottle to Roland in a wry cheer. "Nice not working with you."

Shelly sat at the Pagina en el Sol in the afternoon heat with Roland, listening intently to his account of the goings-on in Costa Rica. Her eyes were clear and she was more lucid than Roland had ever seen her. She was smoking a cigarette and sipping a coffee.

"So that's it, basically," Roland said as he finished his narrative. "I decided to come back here because things seemed to have slowed down enough, but I see they've actually come to a complete stop."

"It was pretty wild for a while, though," Shelly said. "Lots of people ringing my doorbell all the time. I felt like a vampire; I was scared to go out during the day. I even hired a cab driver to go to Rizo's and get my groceries for me 'cause I didn't want to go alone. Finally I did, though, and you know what I saw?" Roland shook his head. "You know that blind man who begs outside?"

"The one the kids always throw rocks at and make fun of?"

"I gave him a hundred bucks. He swung out with his cane because he got mad at those little bastards but he hit some old biddy instead. He felt terrible and she was really mean to him."

Roland sipped his limeade. "There were a few people at my house too, thanks to that article in the Reporter. Did you notice that they printed two editions for last week?"

Shelly raised her eyebrows. "No kidding. No, I didn't know that. Why?"

"The first one's cover story was that Adrian and Mack made declarations about being involved with Hammer, but they published a revised edition as soon as Guillermo was released."

"Front cover as well, I guess."

"Of course. It's been on the cover of every issue since it happened." Roland drained his limeade and brought the straw out of the glass, playing with it by covering one end with his finger and sucking on the other.

Shelly stubbed out her cigarette and rested her chin on her hand. "Well, I haven't been buying newspapers lately." She paused, then said, "You know, Roland, I feel like a total moron."

"Why's that?"

Nobody, Roland noticed, ever wanted to say anything derogatory about Adrian, and Shelly was no different, but she felt wronged and said so. "I just feel like, you know, I read articles about the whole thing and I think, how could we not have known what we were really doing? Did we really believe that we were just maintaining those memberships?" She was angry and embarrassed. Everyone was. She looked at Roland and said, "You know what I feel like?"

Roland shook his head. He'd stopped playing with his straw.

"I feel like I was in a house when a murder had been committed, but I was asleep at the time. There'd be no way for anyone to prove that I wasn't, but it doesn't look very good. I just feel like an idiot. Adrian wants me to go visit him and I don't know what to say. I feel terrible for him but I'm mad at him too."

"I know, Shelly. I think we all feel that," Roland said. "We all knew there was something not right about this, but every single thing that looked wrong could have been explained away by even the worst lawyer."

"Maybe," Shelly replied, "but why did none of us think to approach this from the point of view of an investor?"

Roland laughed. "The point of view of an investor is, 'What's my return and how safe is it?'. In that respect, Adrian's scheme was rock solid. Nobody had to worry about the company's oil reserves drying up, or a negative report published on its use of child labor, or sagging fourth-quarter earnings."

"Sounds ideal, I guess," Shelly said. She toyed with her coffee mug, twirling it around slowly. Roland was silent.

She put her hand to her forehead. "That still doesn't really answer my question, though, Roland. The bottom line is, what am I supposed to say when people ask me 'How could you not have known this was a scam?'"

Roland had wondered the same thing many times, and still didn't quite have an answer. He felt as though he had to say something, though, so he just started talking.

"I think we forgot to include the knowers in the known."

Shelly frowned. "What does that mean?"

Roland chewed on his straw. "I mean, every single one of us had hushed conversations with the others about the strange contradiction between the secrecy and the extravagance," he began. "We all had our reasons for wanting to accept that it was something it wasn't, and it took the responsibility off us to make a judgment call about it when we decided to believe Adrian."

"You mean we didn't take into account who we were when we did this, and what our flaws were? What we were blind to? I don't know, Roland. For me it was just a chance to make some great money."

"You're saying that you thought it was normal all this time?"

Shelly stared at the table. "No, of course not. But as our employer he was entitled to a degree of loyalty, don't you think?"

"Sure he was. Personally, I thought he was a really rich man just playing with his money. And as smart as he was, I wondered if he had more money than brains."

Shelly snickered. "I can see that. Especially if you go by his taste in art."

Roland grinned and then was silent for a while. "There are twenty thousand people in the same boat as us," he continued eventually. "Everyone is now out there saying that they knew it all along. The ship is sinking and there aren't enough lifeboats, right? So everybody's scrambling to point the finger at everybody else. Ultimately if Adrian hadn't been arrested, this club might have continued for literally years and we'd never have to make that kind of choice. That wouldn't have made Cyberia legal, mind you."

"I suppose not."

"Besides, Shelly, all the investors are going to be asking each other the same thing. We were scammed just as much as they."

Just then Shelly's cell phone rang. She answered it with "Bueno," and followed it with "Yeah, he's right here actually. Do you want to talk to h…"

She looked at Roland, her eyes widening, and then pushed her chair back and took a short walk down the side street towards the Los Arcos Suites hotel.

Roland was still chewing on his straw when she returned. She squinted at him. "Why did you go to Los Angeles and Guatemala?" she asked.

Roland told her the truth; that he didn't want to share a plane with any other Cyberia employees. He saw no reason to tell her why, but this seemed sufficient. She relaxed but kept looking at him suspiciously. "Why do you want to know?"

She looked at her cell phone, now lying innocently on the table in front of her. "That was Ken," she said. "He asked if I had seen you around and when I said I was sitting with you he said, 'Red flags! Red flags! Get away from him!'. So I was curious to know why, from you."

"You're kidding me, right?"

"No."

"Well, did he tell you why he said that?"

"Apparently somehow you knew that Adrian would run into trouble on his way to Latvia."

Roland almost laughed. He remembered separate conversations with Adrian and Grant, when he had told them that he had reservations about Adrian's trip. Yet again he should have just held his tongue when his intuition spoke to him.

"And he told me not to tell you that either," Shelly finished.

Roland found it amusing that no matter how well you thought you knew people, they could always surprise you. Shelly hadn't seemed to be the kind of person who would second-guess the new man in charge, even if there was really nothing left for Ken to be in charge of anymore.

He folded his arms. "I went precisely because I wanted to get away from these suspicions and spy games. Some of the things people said about how serious the situation was turned out to be true, but most of them didn't. If Ken wants to think I'm a covert government operative, well, he can have his little fantasy. Not that it doesn't piss me off."

Shelly lit another cigarette and smiled at Roland. The smile turned to a giggle, and the giggle to a laugh. Despite his annoyance with Ken, Roland joined her. It felt good to release all the nervous tension they'd felt, to laugh at their own blindness, at the closure of a unique chapter in their lives and at the possibilities that lay ahead. When they parted Roland gave her a big hug and said, "See you around, blondie."

She nodded. "One day years from now we'll be wandering through a city far away, and we'll both get that 'Don't I know you?' look, and we'll sit down at a little café just like this one and swap stories."

"We'll have to pick somewhere open all night, 'cause there'll be a lot of them."

Shelly picked up her cell phone and tucked it into her jean shorts as she said, "Then I'll say *hasta luego*, and not goodbye."

Roland opened the truck to make sure that the keys were in the glove compartment as Nick had said they were. Even though they hadn't been in direct sunlight they were hot to the touch, and next to them was a road map of Mexico and the United States. Roland left them there and went up to spend the rest of the afternoon sunning himself and packing his belongings. He had been to the DHL office earlier that week and sent all his unnecessary things home including the candelabras he'd bought at Tlaquepaque, a stack of Puerto Vallarta t-shirts, and four house numbers on decorative hand-painted tiles in a metal frame.

As evening came he crept into the Shack with a cigar and the bankbook. The mess he'd left on the floor had been cleaned up, probably by Ken. No wonder he suspected Roland to be a threat. He had found out who had discovered the passbooks and was probably wondering when the blackmail letter would arrive.

In the room behind the kitchen where Adrian kept his wines, almost all the shelves were empty. Ken had been thorough indeed, no doubt hoarding all the Grand Krug and Rothschild for himself. Behind a case of dark Indio beer, however, Roland's hand closed around an elegant bottle. Carefully he withdrew it from the cabinet.

Chateau Petrus, 1946. Worth several thousand dollars at the cheapest of liquor stores, if they could even get it. Roland wasted no time dusting off a glass, opened the bottle to breathe, and set it on a table beside one of the large lounge chairs on the patio.

Back in the kitchen he withdrew the bankbook from his shirt pocket and found his cigar lighter in another, and as the sun slipped beneath the waves he brought the two together over the sink. Far in the distance, the outline of the bird sanctuary was visible through the occasional patch of heat haze.

Resting his chin on his hand, Roland toyed with the bankbook, prodding it with a fork and turning it over to make sure it was completely burnt. He had known that he would do this since the moment he had found it, but the possibilities it had fed in his mind had been too much fun to ignore. In the end, though, his children were going to have to live in the world he made, and what would he tell them when they asked what he was like before they were born? What would he say to his friends when they asked where he got the money? He'd been paid well and had enjoyed an adventure worthy of any he'd seen in the movies. He had no regrets. The last 77 days with Winter in this summer city had made his life before arriving in Mexico seem about as distant in time as the invention of the printing press. Besides, between Puerto Vallarta and his old home lay thousands of miles of countless roads begging to be explored and adventures waiting to be lived, each one both a mirror into himself and a lens through which to see the world more clearly.

He washed the ashes down the sink and ran the garburetor for a few seconds, squinting down the drain to make sure they had all disappeared. When that was done he went back out to the patio, poured himself a glass of wine and lit his cigar. By the time the *Marigalante's* fireworks boomed across the bay and lit up the Malecon with flashes of colored light, the house was dark and the bottle was empty.

He eased the chair back as far as it would go and turned on his side, resting his head on a cushion taken from the sofa, and fell into a deep sleep with a gentle smile on his face. Beneath him the sea threw itself onto the beach in an ancient, joyful rhythm that echoed throughout the deserted palace.

Far, far away, so far away that no one would think to look for it in their own heart, in the land known by dreamers dreaming and lovers loving, two figures swayed and danced where an endless prairie began. They had faded slowly to ghostly silhouettes, faint outlines of their former brilliance, but there they would stay even after the last star flickered and fell from the incorruptible heavens. Above them a circling hawk screeched and swung on the eternal breeze, diving through the timeless sunlight with joy and newfound strength, for at long last it could see through the phantoms to its prey beneath.

Epilogue
Afterimage

Adrian Winter was released from the Puente Grande Federal Penitentiary in Guadalajara, Mexico, on August 13, 2001. His bail was set at two million dollars because the judge decided that he qualified as a flight risk. He promptly fled to Costa Rica, where on September 7 of the same year the Costa Rican authorities, acting on a tip from the FBI, arrested him in a raid on Rancho Mirage carried out by over 50 agents in coordination with five public prosecutors acting on the authority of seven judges. In the process they seized, among other assets, a large house in Alajuela, a luxury condominium in Escazu, ten vehicles including a classic Maserati, a luxury yacht, a Bell helicopter, approximately one million dollars' worth of jewels, a property on the Pacific coast and ten million dollars in various bank accounts in addition to two million dollars in cash. He was extradited from Costa Rica to Sacramento in December 2002. He pled guilty to one count each of mail fraud, wire fraud, and conspiracy to commit money laundering on May 5, 2003, and was finally sentenced to ten years imprisonment on March 11, 2005.

The man known as Secret Agent Mick was arrested at a private aircraft hangar on the Pacific coast of Costa Rica during the September 7 operation. He was extradited with Adrian Winter in December 2002 and pled guilty to one count each of mail fraud, wire fraud, and conspiracy to commit money laundering. He was sentenced to 59 months in prison on February 18, 2005.

Ken operated a beach bar in Puerto Vallarta until he was expelled from Mexico and subsequently arrested in Los Angeles on May 13, 2004. He pled guilty that November to one count each of mail fraud, wire fraud and conspiracy to commit money laundering. He was sentenced to 65 months in prison on February 25, 2005.

Sidney was arrested in Dallas in December 2001 on his way to visit Adrian in Costa Rica and entered a guilty plea on April 29, 2002 to one count each of mail fraud, wire fraud, and conspiracy to commit money laundering. On July 9, 2004 he was sentenced to 50 months in prison.

Brent and Janine stayed in Costa Rica until November 2001; they spent just over three peaceful years in Canada before Brent was indicted on fraud, conspiracy and money laundering charges in December 2003. Advancing age and the stress of being labeled a 'point man' for Cyberia's dealings in Costa Rica proved too much for him, and he died of stomach cancer on August 1, 2004, while awaiting his extradition hearing.

Mack, the imprisoned half of the Belize Brothers, was released on modest bail in July 2001 on compassionate grounds because of recurring problems with cancer and heart disease; he died in April 2003. His brother Nick returned home and resumed his business as a paving contractor.

Eric remained in Costa Rica until February 2002; he is currently a fugitive whose present whereabouts are unknown. Maxine and Dolores remained in Costa Rica until December 2001 when Dolores returned home; Maxine is a fugitive whose present whereabouts are unknown. Liza is a fugitive; her present whereabouts are unknown.

Roxane lives aboard a sailing yacht moored in Belize and operates a mail forwarding service from which she coordinates charity work throughout Central America. Slogan married his fiancée in March 2002 and moved to a beautiful corner of coastal Canada where he is a computer consultant. Kevin settled in Vancouver. Shelly remained in Puerto Vallarta before joining Lee in San Diego for a short time; she now lives in Montreal. Lee married an employee of the San Diego Zoo and moved to Africa with him to operate a game reserve, but eventually divorced and returned to Puerto Vallarta. Grant escaped arrest in Costa Rica by discovering and throwing out a bag of narcotics planted in the helicopter. He is now a pilot for a research facility in the South Pacific. Garrett became a network specialist for a chain of European resorts. Sidney and Amy moved to British Columbia upon Sidney's early release for exemplary behavior in June 2005.

Roland Halliwell returned home and became a bestselling author. His first book chronicled the demise of a clandestine financial syndicate.

About the Author

Roger Harrison has won awards for his writing since he was ten years old. He has written and/or edited magazine and newspaper articles, tech manuals and poetry, and has a column in an Alberta newspaper. He comes by his writing talent honestly — his mother is world-famous author Pauline Gedge — and his unquenchable sense of adventure has led him into unique situations that many never experience. It is on one of these that this novel is based. He lives in rural Alberta.

Printed in the United States
40210LVS00001B/70-108